PEYTON AMBERG

PEYTON AMBERG

TAMA JANOWITZ

BLOOMSBURY

*The following is a work of fiction. The author
is neither fifty years old nor has lice.*

All papers used by Bloomsbury Publishing are natural,
recyclable products made from wood products grown
in sustainable, well-managed forests. The manufacturing
processes conform to the environmental regulations
of the company of origin.

First published in Great Britain in 2003

Copyright © 2003 by Tama Janowitz

The moral right of the author has been asserted

Bloomsbury Publishing Plc, 38 Soho Square, London W1D 3HB

A CIP catalogue record for this book
is available from the British Library

ISBN 0 7475 6138 9

10 9 8 7 6 5 4 3 2 1

Typeset by Hewer Text Ltd, Edinburgh
Printed in Great Britain by Clays Ltd, St Ives plc

To
Betsy Lerner

The Soul Has No Morality

We do not hear the hooves,
Although they grow louder, hourly,
And the horses are magnificent,
Snooty and vain!
And the carriage is black and stately.

The soul has no morality.
It is waiting, fidgety with hope.
It is too abstract to escape,
And not clever at all.
It is no Houdini.

The train takes its time.
At each stop there are mourners
Weeping and waving.
The soul does not weep,
It has no sense of what is proper.

The soul is not even near the train!
On another galaxy it listens to horns.
It whirls on pins. It is clapping
Restless hands. It is singing
'Blue Moon' off key.

– Phyllis Janowitz

1

There were a few hotels near Central Station but the first one she went to was more than three hundred dollars a night and she was aware she could no longer afford it. 'I'm going to look at one other place, near here,' she said. 'If I don't like it, I'll be back. You do have a room available?'

She wished she had not chosen Antwerp. The only place worse might have been Stockholm, full of forthright, good people, without nonsense. If this city contained only the wholesome, she wouldn't last a day. She had crossed an invisible line. She had become the sort of person who looked likely to skip out without paying.

'Yes, very good, we do have several rooms available if you would return,' said the receptionist with a smirk, as if he knew Peyton would not be back. 'But they will be ready only after eleven o'clock. So you can have a look around.'

Her expensive suitcase was heavy, the handles dug into her palm. Her handbag was dirty, the tan suede fraying at the seam – not the sort of thing any stylish or wealthy woman would carry. Her head throbbed, she was shaky on her feet. As soon as she found somewhere to stay she would go out to get a cup of coffee and something to eat.

By the time Peyton had re-traced her steps to the cheap-looking hotel she had first passed she thought she had better check in, no matter what the place was like. Her left arm was numb, partly from the suitcase, but mostly from too much vodka. Her face was covered in perspiration that was chilly and hot at the same time. She had been told she had 'low blood sugar', which made her think of a sugar bowl with only a few granules down somewhere near her feet. She wondered if she should even stop now to grab a glass of orange juice. But she couldn't deal with making herself understood in a foreign language.

This hotel was bleak. The lobby smelled of roach spray and wet carpet. A wheezing Pekinese with an underbite tottered out from behind the reception desk and snuffled Peyton's beige leather suitcase. The old lady behind the reception had a bristled chin – an eighty-year-old sack of boiled meats covered with talcum powder, with the same pop-eyed glare as the dog. Once, somebody must have fucked her senseless: how was such a thing even possible? Now she was melted into a shapeless blob of tallow. She managed to convey the room rate, to be paid ahead of time in cash, around fifty dollars; probably as cheap as Peyton was going to find.

She handed over her money and was given a heavy nickel key with a clumsy mace ball at one end. Obviously this was not the sort of place where she would receive a sleek plastic key-card.

The elevator was out of order. She trudged up the three winding flights; her room had a narrow single bed, a stained sink, a mirror and an armoire. A window faced a small side street onto a fifties building with boarded-up windows. Scaffolding like the bones of a dinosaur covered the wall outside and blocked almost all light coming into her room. The toilet and bath must have been down the hall.

Gone was her dream of a long, scalding soak from which she would emerge skinned and pickled. By now she was too tired to deal with one in any event. The sheets were scratchy, cold to the touch, and the blanket was stiff, but at least they appeared to be clean. She crawled under the covers and slept.

When she woke she was starving and the throbbing in her head still had not gone away.

She had the sense there was something walking on her scalp, just by her ear. Tiny feet scudding in a whispery pattern. She scratched and the idea – something on her that was not her – went away, but she was still uneasy. But if it was the DT's, why would imaginary bugs

2

crawling on her skin be confined to her scalp or have such tiny, geisha steps?

If she had not been so hungry she might have been able to face trying to find out how to get a bath in this place. As it was she could not bear to move and it was now almost noon. She might have gone back to sleep, but stealthy footsteps near her ear – and now her neck – commenced again.

In her bag she found a brush and standing in front of the sink began to roughly tug her hair over the bowl. The itching momentarily abated. She looked down, about to wipe out the hairs that had come loose, when she saw the basin was full of flecks, red crusty bits, black specks. She peered more closely, surprised at the quantities of filth.

Something feebly waved tiny legs, attached to a fat brown body. A louse. The sink was full of minute insects of varying sizes. The old hairs were covered with minuscule, clear pearls. They must have been eggs, attached to the hair with a translucent, gluten product. Some of the lice were so infinitesimal she had to peer intently.

She put her whole face in the sink. There were many of the bugs. Some, though still barely larger than the head of a pin, had plump bellies. Maybe they were about to lay eggs. Their legs waved angrily. She squished one with the back of her thumbnail. It made a satisfying crack.

She was simultaneously repulsed and pleased. The horror at first outweighed the pleasure. She would kill them all. Then it seemed hideously rewarding to brush them off her, a whole living forest of entities that she alone was responsible for, terrible alien beings that thrived because of her and would be violently uprooted by the descending brush. The black-pepper flecks must be louse feces. Louse shit.

She was going have to go out and buy louse medication; what a trashy and humiliating thing to have to purchase, especially in a foreign country where she would not be able to identify the product simply by reading the label of a bottle on a shelf.

Then she realized she would also have to find a Laundromat and wash her clothes. What if eggs or lice had fallen off onto her sweater and were only waiting until she got dressed to climb back into her hair. She pulled her hair in a tight ponytail. When she lifted her arms they hurt. She hurt everywhere: her ribs, her stomach. Her breasts. She had no soap to wash her face. This wasn't the sort of place that provided little bars.

She slapped on new make-up over the old and pulled on her black jeans. They were a little cleaner than the ones she had been wearing and she threw all the dirty things in her suitcase to take along. Still, no one would have guessed her age, nor that she had been up all night on a train, scratching her lice. Her eyes were a bit puffy, but she still looked innocent.

It was a strange time of day, the air was artificially gray, and the buildings too; the land, the sky were washed with gray; probably they were always this color, not influenced or altered by sun, clouds, weather condition, but a permanent scrim of atmosphere, possibly industrial pollution, or simply Belgian-ness.

A few streets on she found a small workman's café, the equivalent, she supposed, of an American diner. Through the large window she could see a man – a derelict, really – slumped over a table and here and there other men drinking coffee or beer, though the plate glass was so dirty it was hard to determine much.

Nevertheless, it would do. She went in. The air smelled rancid, harsh tobacco. There was an empty table near the slumped-over derelict and she sat on the banquette. It was covered with faded plush velvet. Perhaps this had once been quite a nice place.

The beaky waitress had a beaten-up, no-nonsense attractiveness, a wrecked crane, a stork with crooked wings. 'Cup of coffee, please,' Peyton said. 'And a menu.' There were two men sitting opposite, in front of the window and the waitress returned in a moment with a beer and an unnaturally colored orange juice for them, and the coffee, which she left with Peyton. 'Could I have an orange juice too, please?' she said, pointing. There was an omelet listed on the menu. 'And the omelet.'

The derelict two tables away was still slumped, face down. There was a large glass container of mustard without a lid, a crusty brown at the top edge – if he leaned over any farther his hair would be in it.

A woman passed the café window and then came in. She was dressed in her finest: a shapeless tweed suit, laddered black stockings. Her face was utterly sunken, by age, alcohol. The woman looked quite pleased with herself, an ancient chicken's lunatic pride. Her hair was piled in a remembrance of a lady's hairstyle, a monument of bluebottle black with greenish tinge. A synthetic chiffon scarf, pink and lavender, was tied around her jowls – perhaps shortly a ladies' luncheon was to commence; white gloves, a dead Christmas tree of an umbrella – a parody, a crumpled postcard in faded tints of some *jolie fille de nuit.*

It had probably taken every bit of the woman's strength to dress. It was after one o'clock. This was the woman's first journey of the day out into the world. Yet she was unaware of her debauched appearance. She was ready to strike up a conversation and go home with some new male friend.

A sort of gingery cookie came with the coffee. Peyton wolfed it down, the fragrant sandy flakes cracking between her teeth, which ached – one of her front teeth might have come a bit loose, she didn't want to think about that. A basket of bread and wrapped cubes of butter arrived; the butter was that European stuff, greasy and pungent, but by now she was used to it and had even grown fond of it. American butter was insipid by comparison. The omelet-with-chips tasted delicious. The ketchup was strong and vinegary, the lardy crisp fries had hot new skins created in the boil of the fat-fryer. If her hair was washed, and she hadn't hurt all over, she would have felt almost functional.

She noticed the derelict was now sitting up. She had taken him – in his knit cap, baggy clothes, face down – to be an old man, but now she saw that he was twenty-three or so at most. His hat had fallen off. He was the most stunning man she had ever seen. She couldn't believe it; for a second she actually forgot to breathe. It was impossible. An example of pre-war Aryan youth, hiking in the Bavarian mountains, had suddenly come to life – far better looking than any actor, he made a movie star or male fashion model look like a weak imitation of what was obviously a real god.

He stood up. He was tall, beautifully proportioned. He tidied the thick blond hair and his hat went back on his head. It was extraordinary, that a slumped-over old man would arise and turn out to be a Nordic god; she knew she was staring but could not help herself. All the horrors of the past month were skimmed away, now she would have done anything to have checked into the grander of the two hotels, to be able to invite him up to use the phone or have a decent shower – but he was obviously quite capable of rejuvenating himself. He had the total freshness of the young, invigorated simply by dozing face down on a table. Who was he? Where was he going?

From under the table he removed a knapsack of khaki canvas. She didn't see how she could go on living her life without him. She imagined that he was going now to a job interview – in a telegraph office. Or would find his way to the seaside and a freighter headed for the Orient. If he had been a con-artist, or hustler of some sort, it was unlikely that with that countenance he would have had to work at all; a million rich women – or men – would have instantly fought to buy him. Was he unaware that he had fallen from some limbo into the twenty-first century?

She stood, put money on the table. It seemed to her that as he passed he looked at her lingeringly. She was nearly as good-looking as he; always she was the one who was better looking, usually it was impossible to find a man who, physically, was her equal – with her soft, sooty-black hair, her baby eyes sparkling under thick lashes, her figure slim-hipped, full-breasted.

A bath, clean clothes, freshly washed hair, might have made her more confident, but those things were not at her disposal now. In a minute he would turn the corner and disappear forever. She had to have him, that was all there was to it. She would set up a date with him for later. This would give her time for the shaving and dressing and fresh make-up, maybe a miniskirt with slinky stockings, high heels. It was going to be fun.

She would offer to buy him dinner and then he could take her to a

6

crummy bar, a rough bar, she would drink Belgian beer until the room was bright and blurry, until the moment when she couldn't keep her hands off him, then she would start to paw him and bring him back to her room. As long as she drank too much the whole thing would be fun and she would always have the memory of spending the night with him. If things worked out she might even hang on; he looked to be a sporty boy from whom she could procure a week's worth of amusement. She knew it didn't have to be love. She had learned this lesson, finally.

It made sense to her now, the way gay men might cruise each other in a hot steam bath or shove a dick through some gloryhole; it made sense, not that that was what she wanted, exactly, but it was easier: the swooning anonymity of the experience. Not knowing whether or not the other person was a nitwit, or had no sense of humor, simply a body to grab in the dark.

She promised herself that if she could just have this one, he'd be the last. She would have this one last treat and then she would go home.

She began to follow him down the street. He walked at a moderate pace but his legs were so long she had to hurry to keep up; at the lights he waited, patiently, for them to change, this gave her a bit of a breather. The suitcase full of dirty clothes was heavy. How could he have passed out, probably for hours, in that dive restaurant, and then wake up and put himself back together? She wouldn't have been surprised if at some point he turned the corner and vanished through some science-fiction door to 1937. The streets – his route – made no sense to her, a right and then a left, across wide avenues, she wished she had bought a map of the city. She had no idea of the layout.

Perhaps he realized she was following him; he speeded up and slowed down, he glanced in her direction once or twice with an alarmed, agitated expression.

Finally he stopped at a corner that marked a bus or trolley stop. She was relieved. The pause would give her a chance to strike up a conversation. But before she could think of what to say he took a pouch from his pocket and, removing cigarette papers and a pinch of tobacco, deftly began to roll a cigarette between two thick thumbs and forefingers, looking at her awkwardly. 'Excuse me, I don't have much English,' he said. 'But . . .'

'That's okay.' She waited, smiling expectantly.

'I think you follow me?' He glared at her with vague ferocity or unease.

'I know, I'm sorry.' Her voice was a confidential murmur. 'I couldn't help myself. I just got to this city, I don't know anyone, some rather disastrous things have happened to me and when I saw you I thought – you looked . . .'

For a moment he strained to follow what she was saying. Fifty, sixty years ago, so few in this country – or anywhere in Europe – would have spoken any English at all. Now, nearly everybody did, at least the younger ones. The fact that he was struggling meant that he was a throwback to an earlier time or a genuine, authentic member of the working class.

'You . . . are looking for . . .' He sounded puzzled.

'Actually, I started out looking for a Laundromat. But . . . when I saw you . . .'

He shook his head and she saw he wasn't getting the point. 'What is it you want?'

She took a deep breath. When had it begun, that women had taken over the man's part? 'I have a feeling that the two of us could have a lot of fun. You know what I'm talking about?' She smiled with a silky lewdness. Inside she was embarrassed, but on the other hand it was like being an actress in an old black and white film, on a shadowy set, draped in tipped ermine.

He didn't seem to hear her words, but he seemed to understand exactly who she was. His nostrils curled slightly and a ribbon of smoke snaked from his mouth. Then he flung his cigarette on the ground and stamped its head with his foot.

'Lady, why you bothering me?' he said. He looked her up and down before he made the bullish sound of a man inhaling his own snot. Spitting out a lump of phlegm, he adjusted his knapsack straps and gave her a dismissive stare. 'You must be as old as my mother.' He ambled off into the gray Antwerp afternoon. A half-block away he glanced back with a sneering grin. 'You are older than my mother,' he called, one hand shifting his cock in his trousers. 'Lady, you must be fifty!'

2

The first time *it* happened – *the monster got loose*, was how she later thought of it – she had been married for two years. She was twenty-six and on her way to Brazil. The flight was packed, each passenger a snail carrying its own shell, to be removed and jammed into the compartment overhead. When she arrived in the back of the plane a man was already occupying the seat next to hers.

His arms were hirsute, his face a lunar landscape, pocked by meteorites. She felt a twinge of sympathy; his expression was impassive, his shirt was nylon, pale blue with short sleeves – a different look from an American, who would have been in a T-shirt – and she had the sense he was trying to look nice and didn't know, really, how destitute he appeared. She squeezed into her place. The seat was too small. It might have been a joke, a hidden-camera television show. Or a cell in a Bangkok prison. Across the aisle was an obese old woman, spilling out of her seat into the surrounding area, huge and yeasty. Her small raisin eyes, embedded in flesh, glittered skillfully, a puffy loaf who found it necessary to shelter such canny intelligence.

Though the announcement had asked passengers to take their seats, various family members kept getting up and going to the old lady's side; there was a boy who must have been her grandson, no older than twelve, who had a bad case of gynecomastia. To be male and also have breasts must be extremely distressing. His sister, several years younger, perhaps ten, also appeared preternaturally sexually mature. The kids kept kicking the back of Peyton's seat, the man next to her kept turning to pass them things, and leaned over her to talk to the woman. 'My mother –' he said to Peyton, his breath a mist of garlic. 'She sick.' She imagined them returning to some poor hovel in a slum, creatures bred for eons to serve as peasant-workers, inhabiting the banks of petrochemical wastelands, fed on the rotting carcasses of chickens who in turn had been fed on too many hormones. If she hadn't married Barry, that would definitely have been the route she was on.

She got up to go to the lavatory. There was a line. Once inside, the floor was sticky with urine, wet tissues. Things were no better when she was trapped once again in her chair. From time to time a gaseous odor wafted in her direction.

At last the dinner was served; really it wasn't so terrible, a chicken breast, tomato sauce, pasta, a small dish of pineapple cubes – but afterwards, with this ballast in her abdomen, she was transformed into one of those bloated clown dolls which, when knocked over, pop up again. She scrambled out from under her tray-table and went back to the toilet, leaving her handbag.

She wanted her travel toothbrush but it was too difficult to reach her bag under the seat and there was no point at all in trying to find her powder and lipstick now, in the dead of night. When she returned she dozed, and almost at once she began to dream that a slug or snail had somehow found its way into her vagina, because the snail was dried out and looking for a damp spot.

But it wasn't a dream: the man sitting next to her was actually fondling her, or trying to. She let out a yell. 'Get your fucking hands off me, you creep!' Almost everyone was asleep; the lights had been dimmed. She pressed the button for the attendant, who took ages, and when at last the woman arrived, Peyton shouted (though she was trying to keep her voice down but was shaking with rage), 'That man tried to molest me!'

'I'm sorry? What is the meaning of this, molest?'

The man's family had woken, if they had ever been asleep, and were peeping over the backs of their chairs and leaning forward from behind, all shrieking. 'He put his hand between my legs, while I was asleep!' she said. And the man shook his head and said, 'No, no,' in

Portuguese, shaking his head and yelling what must have been something along the lines of 'She's crazy.'

The attendant said, 'Listen, I don't know what is happening here but we cannot move you up to first class, if that is what you want –'

'That's not what I was trying to do –'

'First and business class are completely full. But I will see if this man is willing to move to a row in the back we have usually reserved for the attendants, if that is what you like, but the plane will be landing soon in São Paulo and he and his family will be getting off there. Is it possible, perhaps, you were having a dream, or you have taken some medication? He says nothing has happened, his wife is only two rows away, she says he was asleep.'

'I'm not making this up.' Now the family had got up, a weird nest of larvae, and they were all grinning at her and mocking her with their garlic breath and pupae faces. A small hand, yet another of the kids', wormed its way under the bottom of the seat in front of her, toward where she sat . . .

Around six in the morning the family got off in São Paulo, still chattering indignantly, dementedly. She glared at them. Perhaps three-quarters of the passengers were disembarking. A team of Americans removed ugly nylon backpacks; the women were fat-legged, dressed in khaki shorts, the men in hideous sandals, all probably her age, but alien to her. Workers came on and half-heartedly cleaned. At least now she had two seats to herself.

She was too excited and nervous, really, to do more than shut her eyes. She had imagined that, if she ever went on a trip, Barry would be with her. Now she thought of him with shame. His round bulb face was so American; his loud voice – though she was scared, she was half-relieved he hadn't been able to come with her. Her clothes might have been doltish too – she saw that now – but at least with her exotic appearance she did not look quite so ordinary. Even the Brazilian family, despite their smelliness, had vibrated with a quieter, subtler presence; worker ants, the global disenfranchised.

It was forty minutes or an hour before the plane took-off again. She should have bought a guidebook, she had no clue about Rio, the history, the size. The politics. Anyway it didn't matter, she was at the resort – whatever it was called, the name was in her handbag – for just a couple of days and there would only be time to look around the property, and swim in the pool and the sea. She was supposed to buy a voucher inside the airport for a reputable taxi service to take her there.

In the line for foreign passport-holders she began to rummage in her handbag when she realized her wallet with her cash, credit card and bank card were missing. Her passport and her airline ticket were in the side pocket but no matter how much she searched there was no sign of her wallet. The wallet had contained the address of the bungalow resort. It had to be a dream. Maybe she was still on the plane, sleeping. She put everything on the floor and tipped out all the contents of her bag. The wallet was gone.

The line ahead of her for Customs moved and the people behind her grew impatient. She had no idea what to do. Maybe it had fallen out under her seat. Had she left it in the seat pocket in front of her? Maybe at some point she had put it into her other bag. But that too had nothing in it.

She was desperate, unable, even, to think. There was no one around who looked friendly, helpful; it must have been the family surrounding her who had done this. She was being punished for her bad thoughts, against her husband, Americans, foreigners. She had conjured this situation with her bad thoughts.

Could she already have been so bored, so restless, only two years into the marriage? She must have been: she had gone back to work six months previously – the first six months of marriage she had been thrilled simply to be married, to live in a real home for the first time in her life – there was the furnishing of the co-op apartment, new wiring, papering and painting, writing thank-you notes for the wedding presents – she thought of herself with great fondness as 'the newly-wed'. The kind of person who had matching tableware that wasn't purchased at the Salvation Army; sets of fancy plates and everyday ones; a food processor. A microwave, a toaster that accepted over-sized slices. Toys for real people, grown-ups. And they screwed a lot, at first – it wasn't exactly what she had imagined, they didn't dress up, or watch porn, or buy sex toys. Now that it was all legal and above board and they had their own privacy, a lot of the thrill was over.

A cautious side to Barry emerged that hadn't been there before, or that she hadn't noticed. She helped him set up his offices – he had purchased the practice of a dentist who was going into retirement, which cost a lot of money – something she didn't understand: apart from a client list there was little benefit in buying out someone's practice, couldn't he simply open an office and hang up a sign, put an ad in the paper?

The practice was out on Long Island, which in a sense was okay because it meant that Barry was commuting against the rush hour; but why, she wondered, did they have to pay nearly three hundred thousand dollars? The old man's offices were so antiquated and shabby that Barry decided, ultimately, to redo them – and though he was supposed to have local hospital affiliation as part of the deal, something went wrong with that, and so he was in a constant state of crisis and irritation.

Finally, when everything was relatively settled, her old restlessness re-emerged. Maybe that was why she went back to work: a distraction. They were short on money, in debt with the new office equipment, rental on the space, mortgage, furniture payments and so forth – one of them had to bring in a regular pay check.

Barry thought it would be three years before his practice would show a decent profit and in fact he was relieved that she was looking for work. There was a local travel agency in mid-town who said they had no opening for her, travel was down, no one was going anywhere, a lot of agents were out of work or agencies were actually laying off. She applied anyway and, to her surprise, months later they called her – in the meantime she had done some occasional temping.

She had only been at the new job for three weeks when a trip came in for a travel agent's junket, not a junket exactly but one of those special deals that cost only 10 percent of what it would have cost, to go to Rio for three days and stay in a new beach-front resort outside the city. The resorts often invited agents, hoping they'd recommend it to clients. 'Would you mind if I went?' she said.

'You're going to go on a trip without me?' Barry said, blinking. He was a good-looking young man, on the short side – well, he wasn't bad-looking. Perhaps he lacked . . . charisma, a certain dynamic force. He had curly hair, a round face – slightly soft, too heavy on the carbohydrates and other rich feeds. His eyes were small, soft brown with fine toast-colored lashes. Behind his metal glasses he always looked worried and now he sounded hurt.

'Well, it's only three days . . . I've never been outside of the United States before, I mean, apart from Jamaica, and . . . it's really a deal, I was always hoping when I went to work in the travel business I would get to go somewhere!'

'Sure, I guess so – it's only three days, right? I'd love to come with you, but it would be impossible for me to take time off now.'

She was almost sick with anxiety, not only at traveling abroad but at going somewhere without him – they hadn't been apart before. She spent a few evenings preparing meals for him. A hamburger-macaroni-and-cheese dish which he loved. Chicken breasts in a cream of mushroom sauce for Monday night, put in the freezer to be reheated in the microwave; Tuesday, she decided he could just grab a burger at a diner near his office and Wednesday night he could do spaghetti, by himself, with sauce from a jar. She would be back on Thursday morning. She knew it was silly, that her role was that of a 1950s housewife, but she couldn't imagine Barry surviving by himself for four nights.

His mother constantly telephoned Peyton at work to make some inquiry or other: had Peyton written all the thank-you notes, could Peyton and Barry join them for brunch? She also usually telephoned them just as they sat down to dinner. And now, when she found out what Peyton was up to, she was horrified.

'You're going to take a trip without Barry? I see. Well. If you think that's appropriate. I guess you do things differently than I would – after all these years of marriage, the only time Leonard and I have been apart was when I had the kids or my mother was dying – do you want me to have Barry stay with us those nights, or make meals for him?'

'Thanks, Grace,' she said. 'I've already cooked the meals, they're in the freezer, he can just put them in the microwave, except for one night I thought he could eat out –'

'Oh, he'll come to us that night.'

'But now he's putting in such long hours, he's got all the paperwork to do – he's not even out of the office until nine o'clock.'

'I think he should get an office manager. I've told him.'

'Right now, though, there's not enough business to warrant it –'

'Anyway, we can always come into the city, maybe he can get off early one night. He's working so hard, it's nice that one of you, at least, is getting to have a holiday!'

'I'm very lucky.' She tried to sound placating.

She had acquired a passport when they went to Jamaica for their honeymoon. Now she had to take a morning off to go to the Brazilian consulate to apply for a visa and return there the following afternoon to pick it up.

She compensated for the upcoming trip by working Saturdays, which was fine, because Barry usually went into the office on Saturdays for at least half the day. Sundays, if he didn't go upstate to fly-fish, he golfed with his father. Though he always said he would be back by two, inevitably around that time he telephoned to say they weren't going to finish until much later. The courses – public, or his parents' country club – were always crowded. His mother wanted to meet at the club pool on Sundays but Peyton usually had an excuse. Instead she joined them afterwards at a diner they were enamored with, where the menu listed a thousand items – tuna salad platter, moussaka, fried chicken, pot roast, turkey – everything tasted alike and everything had to be sampled, discussed; an absurd family of food critics.

She was not unhappy, but often restless: she was a failure. Barry's mother would never approve of her. Grace tried to give her her old clothes that were very prissy, long paisley skirts, tidy suits with gold buttons in beige or gray, things she could not fathom wearing since her own taste was for things with pizazz – glittery blue jeans, tube-tops and at work, where suits were requested, shiny numbers in pink, with miniskirts.

She didn't know what to bring to Brazil. It was winter there, which meant it was cool. At night you would need a sweater. She would be doing a lot of walking to see the sights – she wanted to pack lightly. In the end she settled on fat sports sneakers, one of Grace's old long skirts patterned with flowers – Grace had pointed out that in a strange city it would be better for her to be dressed in subdued clothing: Latin men could be very aggressive – and baggy jeans she hadn't worn since college, when for a time she had attempted to fit in with the other students by wearing clogs, cargo pants, sweatshirts and thick cable-knit sweaters. Back then she still had hopes of becoming a veterinarian, before her mother reminded her she didn't have the brains for it. For the plane Peyton had an entire outfit that had belonged to Grace: a teal-blue silk shirt over blue silk pants. Grace had taken a lot of trips and felt that this was right for the airplane trip, an outfit she would have worn. 'Comfortable, yet elegant.'

Grace was tall: the pants had to be shortened. Barry's sister Belinda was tall as well; maybe Belinda or Grace would have looked fine in the baggy costume but Peyton felt short and clownish. Grace often bought things and then decided she didn't want them and gave them to her; they were perfectly new and Peyton couldn't help but think Grace had never intended to wear them in the first place, that this was her method of redoing Peyton in her own image.

Grace insisted she wear sneakers for traveling in – but Peyton balked at this and instead wore baby-blue high-heeled pumps. Barry wanted to take her to the airport.

'Just forget it, I'm going to get a car service!' she said. 'You should at least have some rest and that way you can watch football or whatever.' If she was honest with herself, on this trip she didn't want to be accompanied by Husband.

Barry looked frightened. Finally he agreed. She would go alone, but he would pick her up when her plane got in at six on Thursday morning.

'Are you sure?' she said, in a softer tone. 'I mean, I'll be fine. After all, there are taxis . . .'

'No, I'm definitely going to pick you up. We have a car – why pay all that extra money?' At last she agreed. She went over the meals with him, showing him the things in the freezer, and the eggs and cheese in the refrigerator. If he wanted a snack, there was fruit as well as pretzels and chips.

When she got up to the Customs officer words began to pour out. Her voice was loud, almost bellowing. 'Could you please help me? My wallet with my credit cards and cash and my bank card – somebody stole it on the plane! I don't know what to do!'

The officer did not seem to register what she was saying. 'Passport and ticket.'

She handed them over. 'Do you speak English?' He was unresponsive. 'I don't know what I should do now, is there some place I could go for travelers' assistance? Please tell me, I don't even know where I'm going.' She was crying, more sounds blobbing out of her mouth. 'Do you understand me? Is there somebody who can help me? Is there any way to get the name of the people sitting next to me who –'

The Customs officer shrugged. Shaking his head he stamped her passport, then waved her off. When she didn't move he began to look around, over his shoulder, as if hoping to see a security officer or policeman who might take this nutcase away.

There was a tug at her elbow. A man of average height, with dark hair, beautifully dressed in an elegant suit, carrying an expensive black valise; he had slightly coarse features, full lips, heavy black eyebrows over very kind brown-black eyes. 'Excuse me, I couldn't help but overhear you – why don't you go through Customs and I will meet you on the other side?'

'But why? What am I supposed to do?'

He spoke English with a lisping Spanish accent and she saw for a fraction of a second the tip of a thick tongue. 'Just calm yourself now, I will help.'

18

'You will? Oh God, thank you. I don't know what to do.' She snatched her passport and ticket off the counter, rummaging frantically for a tissue, trying to collect the things that were toppling from her bag and pocketbook. She was an idiot, how could she be so stupid?

She saw the man chatting to the Customs officer, though she couldn't hear what he said; they both laughed, the agent waved the man through and he caught her up. The man wore expensive cologne. Barry never wore cologne, they both agreed it was tacky. The man smelled glamorous, like an expensive hotel lobby. Sophisticated. He took her by her elbow. 'Take a deep breath, my dear, that may help. I will assist you but do not go on making a scene; if you spend the day with the Customs agents I don't think anything will be accomplished – what, exactly is missing?'

'It's not missing, it was stolen –'

'Your passport?'

'No, I still have that, and my ticket, but my cash, my credit card –'

'That's not so serious, then. Did you have a lot of money?' He looked at her with a certain kind of amusement and then decisiveness. He might have been fifty, maybe he had a daughter nearly her age – anyway he didn't appear to be a lunatic rapist.

'No, but I don't know the name of where I was supposed to stay . . . it was some new place, outside the city, I can't remember! . . .'

'Okay, if you like you will stay with me – I have a suite, you don't have to worry, you will have your own room.'

'But I – shouldn't I report this to – I mean, I know the people sitting near me must have – when I got up to go to the –'

'Did they get off the plane in Rio?'

'No, in São Paulo – I was so stupid, to leave my pocketbook under –'

'You left your handbag?'

'I still have my *bag* but my wallet is gone, I left my bag at my seat, when I went to the toilet. I never thought –'

'How much money was stolen?'

'I don't know. I had two hundred dollars but my bank card – I

19

mean, you need to know the secret number, so they can't use it, but now neither can I!'

'Two hundred dollars. Not so much . . . You can call from my suite and cancel the cards; you don't even have to stay if you wish, but from there you can decide. I will give you some spending money for your stay.'

'Oh, I can't accept that!'

'Don't be ridiculous. Are you a college student? Or is this just the silly way of American girls, told they will be sold into a ring of prostitution? Of course I would want someone to help my daughter, if she was in this situation.'

'Your daughter . . . Are you sure? Why are you being so nice, my gosh, you don't even know me –'

She was being a dope. All her life she had been waiting for something to happen to her. She took a deep breath and decided to pretend she was the kind of sophisticate who was able – who was accustomed – to living this way. Her breasts were sore, itchy from rubbing against her lace bra all night; she was acutely aware of her body.

'You have only this small suitcase? You did not bring with you other luggage?'

'No, no, it's just this.'

'Good. For me as well. My name, by the way, is Germano. Let's go. Now you must place yourself in my hands.'

3

She thought her period wasn't due yet but she began to hemorrhage profusely, large liverish clumps landing with a thud in her panties, where they quickly grew cold. She had to get back to Hotel Station Antwerp right away before everything was soaked and visibly bloody.

Before Antwerp she had been in Milan. Was that where everything had started to go wrong? And before that, Hong Kong. She got to Hong Kong on a Thursday. That had been . . . almost six weeks ago. The trip had been interminable, six hours to Vancouver, twelve more to Hong Kong. How useless it all was, a lifetime spent on airplanes or arranging trips for others, when ultimately each destination was in some way – in many ways – no different than the place she had left. If there was a way to travel without taking oneself along, that would have been the answer.

Usually as soon as she got on the airplane she forgot her home, her husband, her son, her dogs in the kennel. She was transformed into her real self when the plane took off. This time the expected had not happened. Only the grim incineration of the plane, a dull roaring in her head; escorted on a slow journey to hell by torturers specializing in ear, nose, and throat who represented an extremist political group, aspirations and politics unknown.

Even going through her mail, which she had brought along, gave her no clue as to her identity. The bills, requests for money, invitations (mostly to fund-raising events, or venues where she might be expected to buy things) – for whom might they have been intended? There was only one personal thing in the bunch, a fat envelope, heavy cream paper, fountain-pen ink. *Dear Peyton*, she read, *How are you? It's*

been a long time, no? I wonder if you will even remember me and the
enjoyable time we spent together in Rio. I will be in New York on –
and he gave the dates and a telephone number – *and would love to see*
you. Affectionately, Germano.

My God, he would be an old man by now, wouldn't he? It had to
have been more than twenty years ago; amazing that he had kept her
address, let alone that she and Barry hadn't changed apartments in all
that time. And when she thought of the suffering she had been
through, idiotic, trying to track him down, wondering why he hadn't
called – now he was old, and he was thinking of her, but she hadn't
thought of him in years. It was slightly depressing. He could keep his
tissue-lined envelopes, his thick stationery. She folded up the letter
and stuffed it into the seat pocket in front of her.

This time things would be different. A few days away, like a palate-
cleansing course of sorbet. Then home, to deal with her life. Nevertheless she was filled with excitement. She had never been to Hong
Kong before. As soon as she got through Customs and collected her
bag she set off to look for a taxi or train that would take her to her
hotel, when she saw the most amazing man outside the airport – Xian
Rong – though of course she didn't know his name then. He was
wearing tight, mint-green corduroy pants, his hair long and messy; his
hips were tiny, he had no rear end to speak of, his chin was tucked
down to one side. There was something about him so foxy, so
slouchingly insolent, that she smiled to herself, involuntarily, in
appreciation of his honeyed, Hong Kong, boy-gangster cuteness.

He noticed her staring at him and gave her a grin so personal she
felt they had bonded over some private joke. His whole face lit up in
that wicked foxy way and she thought she must be reading too much
into it. For a second she grinned back and then looked away,
embarrassed – or shy. It was just one of those things – images
constantly embedded themselves in her brain – but also the sort that
she would, by the next day, completely forget.

There was that moment, on arriving in a new city, a new country,
when it all appeared too difficult to figure out. That was the most

exciting moment, when you could pretend or believe that the people here were aliens, that they didn't use telephones, or that taxis, buses, trains, subways, were radically different modes of transportation; when in fact, after one or two rides, figuring out the basic system, route and method of payment, you quickly comprehended the place, and knew that it was, essentially, no different from anywhere else.

She took a bus over a series of bridges that were strung up high in the sky with all sorts of wires, resembling piano strings, or harps, and the city looked extraordinary, a jangle of buildings from every era, skyscrapers, some filthy and ancient – dangling laundry against sooty walls – others modern, high-tech glass, it was exhausting and stimulating, overlaid with her jet lag and the first, unrepeatable, shock of being in a brand new city.

She was exhausted by the time she arrived at the hotel, but there was a computer problem with her room reservation. When it was finally straightened out and she got to her room, she pulled down the comforter to take a nap and saw the sheets were dappled with blood. Someone – not her, for a change – had got her period and the maid hadn't bothered to change the sheets, just made up the bed. She was so appalled and disgusted she immediately called housekeeping and then asked for the manager. She went into the bathroom, which was luxurious, but that wasn't the point; the towels were also full of dried blood only they had simply been folded back into place.

The manager was horrified, he said he must make an unprecedented announcement: he would be happy to comp her for the whole weekend or, if she wished, she could stay more than a week at the highly reduced rate, virtually a freebie. She said she didn't know, she would think about it – really, she had no intention of staying for more than a long weekend though it had taken two days to get here.

In retrospect she should have known it was a sign; ominous. But Barry hated all that New Age stuff and had convinced her, over the years, that astrology, acupuncture, dream interpretation, homeopathy, coffee enemas, apricot pits – it ran the gamut – was primitive superstition. A hundred years ago women sipped minute quantities of arsenic as a beauty treatment.

Anyway, apart from this one yucky moment, the hotel was perfect. She had never stayed in such a mausoleum of perfection: the sleek black granite and mirrors, water gushing from heavy nickel taps, controlled air from a respirator circulating ion-charged air. The entire building was a Frankensteinian jumble of body parts, lungs, heart, plasma, running hot and cold. A life-support system for people so rich they had never lifted anything except in a gym. It was so soothing that the battle normally raging inside her was, at least for the moment, quelled.

In her room was a bowl of fruit – astonishing, peculiar things with long curly hairs or huge, purple, warty lumps (she had not known such fruit existed) alongside out-of-season cherries, curiously flat white peaches, tiny cinnamon-pink bananas – and the complimentary drinks that arrived on a platter of chilled ice – watermelon, honeydew, orange, coconut – shockingly pale, beautiful colors from things she had never imagined could or would be turned into juice. Cashew-fruits resembling mutant apples atop which had grown nuts. Rambutans, lichees, kumquats, a fist-sized striped melon, two swollen strawberries and a handful of minute grapes, like tiny purple pearls. It was worth having come this far. Her childhood had been bananas, apples, oranges.

The view looked over the bay to the Kowloon side, a million pointed buildings beyond the choppy gray water filled with toy boats. Once she was settled and the parade of apologetic staff halted, she took off her clothes and padded around naked in the artificial air. If only she had come here to meet some cologne-scented businessman who would give her an evening gown in a box and wait until she had put on black lace stockings and an old-fashioned garter belt before telling her to lie down and spread her legs.

What was the use of living life in a porn film now, at her age? The time to have had such fantasies was when she was twenty, when there might have been men available, willing or able. But at twenty she'd had no sex drive at all. Then she had wanted love, commitment. It was all backwards for women; meanwhile the twenty-year-old boy was looking for quick sex.

24

There was a 'Welcome Cocktail Reception' at the bar for the visiting travel agents and a buffet dinner in the hotel's Chinese restaurant but she was totally wiped out from the journey and couldn't face the thought of a couple of hundred travel agents from the US.

Ninety percent of them would be women and of those, 90 percent would have that dried-out, tinny dyed blonde hair cut in a flip style that seemed to say 'I'm a real nice gal!' They would all look at her with those eyes encircled with alarmed spiders of mascara; all of them would be talking of other trips – to Namibia, to India, to Morocco – where, traveling in packs of three or thirty they would have been escorted as carefully as a group of senior citizens on a day's outing to Niagara Falls.

At least, in comparison to the few men, the women would have a semblance, an imitation, of life. The men . . . it was a miracle how this gender, in this industry, could look so gray, so nebulous, and yet . . . women would still flock to them, pursue. One of them would ask her to accompany him to a restaurant selected from a recommended guidebook. But no matter how off the tourist-track their destination, they still seemed to be in Minneapolis or Scottsdale.

She knew she was obliged to attend at least some of the hotel's organized events. Anyway it was only afternoon. She would take a nap and decide. She couldn't sleep. She was overtired so she fished a small battery vibrator out of her toiletry bag and pulled a sheet over her as she lay back on the bed. Then a quick series of images: the slinky man from the airport lying next to her, one hand matter-of-factly prying open her legs and roughly forcing in two fingers; a group of men, looking at her naked body, hungry for her but brutish, climbing on her one after the other. It took approximately two minutes to have an orgasm and the sensation – higher and higher until, when she could go no further, she suddenly tumbled down the hill – put her to sleep almost immediately.

The act of masturbating for Peyton had no more significance than eating a meal, or brushing her teeth; an activity that had physical

pleasure but was, essentially, an enterprise to be carried out industriously, efficiently – what meaning could it possibly have? The only
difference was that, while eating, one did not require visual imagery
other than the food itself. One could eat food alone and enjoy it; to
masturbate, one had to have pictures of the act in one's brain. But the
feeling in the end wasn't that different from squeezing water from a
saturated sponge.

Most of the time sex alone was vastly preferable to having sex with
another and far less messy. Where was the sexiness in sex? A person,
single or with someone else, rubbing, oozing, struggling, then twitching –
a gasping fish on a hook, shedding thumbnail scales, had as much appeal.

It was a known fact that men masturbated all the time. What else
did they do with those magazines? Even in movies, there were guys
jerking off. It was a nothing thing. Women masturbating – that was
still the province of escorts, prostitutes, porn stars or dykes listed on
the back pages of a free newspaper. Nice girls didn't do it. Even now it
was something she did but didn't want to think about. Her husband
should never know. And Barry was too ethical – or uninterested – ever
to go through her drawers. And if he did, what could he say, or what
would she tell him? 'Yeah, once in a while I use a vibrator to
masturbate.' So what? That was what it came down to: she need
never be afraid as long as she kept replaying, in her head, a scratch on
an old CD disc, 'So what?'

When she woke it was late afternoon and she was woozy but didn't
want to go on sleeping. It was that peculiar jet-lag hour when you
notice the smell of a foreign city, even in a hotel room, and the sounds
– the clink of fork and knife, the hum of heater or air conditioner –
echo in a way that is different from whatever you hear at home. There
are only a few days before you forget that the lives of those here are
not lived in the rhythms of your home.

She knew she was supposed to be able to tell clients about the hotel,
the area. She headed out onto the streets. The hotel was in a business
area. Pouring from huge silica skyscrapers, workers – all dressed in
gray, men and women alike – flooded onto the sidewalks and

collected in human puddles at each corner, waiting for the lights to cross the street. Her pace was wrong, she kept getting tangled in the crowds, which moved with a timing that was not the speed – or motion – of New York City.

She found herself on a ramp that led to an escalator. It was the most mysterious thing she had ever seen: a gigantic escalator. Flight after flight moving up, apparently forever, an ascension into oblivion, while the horde of workers in gray somnolence filled the moving steps both ahead and behind; it was as if some catastrophe had occurred and millions of souls, all infinitely similar, were attempting simultaneously to make the trek to heaven or limbo on foot.

In the crush ahead she saw a hand, pale and slippery – a surprising shimmer, an eyeless fish emerging from darkness – glide forward and re-emerge clutching a shiny wallet; then the wallet again disappeared. The entire escalator was a magician's trick with various events that would occur along the way, vanishing acts, bodies pierced by sharp metal points and so forth. Why else would there have been an escalator rising up outdoors, a Möbius strip to nowhere?

For a second the man to whom the marauder hand belonged turned and caught her eye with a force that was not . . . malevolent . . . but as cold as that of a reptile indifferent to its mammalian prey. She was scared. He resembled exactly the devil boy she had seen at the airport, only now dressed in a dark suit, hair tidied, transformed into virtual anonymity. Only a sly smile that seemed to say he recognized her made her think she wasn't crazy.

She was about to tap the woman whose wallet had been lifted, or shout; then it occurred to her perhaps she had been hallucinating, maybe this had never happened – if she began to yell everyone would turn. She would have to find someone to translate; she envisioned the man fleeing while she spent the rest of the weekend in some police station trying to identify a person who might or might not have been a thief. A drug trip, a vision brought on by jet lag and fatigue, maybe; and in any event at the top of this particular flight the man stepped off and disappeared into a sea of bodies.

*   *   *

At the hotel she couldn't face the travel agents' reception so instead she went out to the Tong-Tong Club – a private club, of which, if you knew to ask, you could obtain complimentary, temporary membership while a guest of the hotel. The place was located in an old precolonial ocean liner of the *Titanic* era that had long since been drydocked. It was hard to tell if it had always been this way or was a parody of oriental/colonial, with velvet settees, red lacquer, Chinese ancestor portraits on glass, teak deckchairs, sweeping staircases fringed with flaking gilt, and peeling mirrors.

There was a slightly ironic atmosphere of lime rickeys and Singapore slings, ceiling fans palming the air; the bar was a narrow room off one of the dining rooms, and – apart from the many scuttling waiters all in tight, red monkey suits with Mandarin collars – almost completely empty.

This was a shame. It was only while traveling that she felt alive, and to travel to an uninhabited destination was disastrous. It was okay to be half or three-quarters dead in an empty room, but to be half or three-quarters alive when no one else was there, to have come halfway around the world to an empty bar – it was all backwards! She ordered a drink from a blank-faced bartender in a fez, which was delivered to her seat in a glass with a miniature pagoda-shaped umbrella and a slew of gelatinous berries that – when prodded with the toothpick end of the umbrella – turned out to have the consistency of softened jelly beans.

A covey of wattled Englishmen arrived, chuckling shyly. One was a vicar – or a reverend, she never knew what the difference was – very Church of England, with a red face and a tight cleric's collar. Another with thin, disapproving lips, eyed her breasts, evaluating them like a bank account for possible future trades. They were loud and jolly and ordered gin and tonics in nasal voices, mouths laden with clinking marbles that made them speak in peculiar tones – as if it took all their strength to keep the aggies from spewing out.

Then a Chinese woman in a suit that probably cost two or three grand entered with two businessmen, one Chinese and one not; the woman was almost sickeningly elegant in a way that suggested there had been money in her family for a thousand years.

The room now quickly filled. It was Friday, people were coming in for drinks after work; this was what it was like – for a certain crowd – to live in Hong Kong in this rarefied, imaginary world.

And there he was, the guy from the airport, the escalator magician-pickpocket, seated at a small table with a Japanese businessman. The last person she had been expecting to see.

The only person she had been expecting to see.

If it had been somewhere she was more comfortable she might have given him a wave, or nodded hello. But then the waiter said, 'The gentleman over there wishes to buy you a drink,' so when it came she lifted her glass to him in a gesture of a toast, and then a moment later the waiter approached again. 'The gentleman he wonders if you would join him.'

'Do you know who he is?'

The bartender looked surprised. 'Mr Xian Rong Chen? Yes. He is here all the time. He is well known – here in Hong Kong.'

Fortunately she remembered not to carry her drink, the waiter would do that. It was hard to remember this sort of thing, she had grown up without any kind of etiquette instruction: certain rules often disappeared from her head entirely, *unfold the linen napkin on your lap, place it on your chair if you go to the toilet; on the table, folded, if the meal is finished.* It was an effort to let a waiter take her drink to the table, she would rather do it herself. And when she got to the table she had this feeling; he wanted her to pretend they already knew each other. It was something in his eyes. Even though his look communicated this, he didn't trust her; he leapt up and said, 'How are you! You don't even smile hello, I have to invite you?'

He knew who she was: not really, but who she was inside. She struggled for a second with his name. 'Xian Rong! I can't believe this! What are you doing here?' she said. 'How are you, babe? I didn't even see you, I was in such a daze. I have total, like, jet lag. I was still trying to figure out how I ended up with an extra drink!'

It wasn't relief, exactly, that crossed his face, only an almost imperceptible acknowledgment. 'I would like you to meet my good friend, Mr Hiroshi Yamamoto,' Xian Rong said. The other man stood up, bowed, and using both hands presented her with his card. She took it with both hands and peered at it intently, then figured she should do the same. She had business cards; luckily this glossed over the fact that Xian Rong didn't know her name and hadn't, couldn't, introduce her. And the Japanese businessman took her card and bowed again.

'You live in Hong Kong now or just visiting?'

'Just visiting for a few days.'

'This is your first time?'

'Yes.'

'How do you find it?'

'I just arrived, but so far it's great!' She sounded so American, so falsely cheery, even to herself. If only she had been English, with one of those superior, cool voices, a sparkling lemonade voice. Pimm's, cucumber slices. Tea in a silver pot poured into thin china cups and the sugar served with tongs. Instead there was the babyish enthusiasm, the Boston accent she had been unable to rid herself of, which replaced 'r' with 'ah' and inserted 'r' where there was meant to be an 'ah'.

'I am afraid that I will be late if I do not excuse myself,' Mr Yamamoto said. 'It was very nice to meet you. Enjoy your stay.' Rising, slim as an otter, with a sushi grin, he bowed and left.

'Phew.'

'Are all American women like you?' said Xian Rong.

'In what way?'

'Able to . . . judge a situation. And you called me babe when you saw me.'

'I called you babe? That's nothing. What do you want me to say? I'm an American. I think everyone's like me.'

'You'll never know how you helped me out. What can I get you?' he said.

'I'm still working on this one.'

A drink and a half later, jet-lagged still, hungry, whatever had been in her veins before was now replaced with a substance so soothing it might have been embalming fluid and she was happy.

Maybe this was never going to happen to her again. He was the most elegant, exotic, tough creature she had ever seen.

She had two more drinks and then a third. 'My God, you're so amazing looking,' she said. 'What are you up to – now? You want to go somewhere else?'

'Okay. Where?'

'Uh . . . we can have a drink, back at my hotel.' She had no intention of going to bed with him, though she was almost sick with excitement at his physical presence.

When she got up her panties were wet, not with urine but whatever the moisture of sexual arousal was called – was there even a name for it? It was ridiculous. On the other hand, she couldn't believe it was still possible to find a man who made her feel this way. He wore a scent – ginseng? cinnamon? violets? – alien and comforting at the same time, oriental. An opiate. Looking for a cab to go back to her hotel she found it almost painful to walk. This must be what it was like to be a man with an erection in public, supercharged with lust but forced to hide it.

The hotel bar was packed and full of smoke. 'This is awful,' she said. 'Let's go to my room and have a drink there.' Maybe it was the alcohol but she couldn't stop touching him. 'Is that okay?'

'Mmmm.'

She forced herself to keep her hands at her sides. The elevator – silver steel – could have been a wartime dictator's sleek office, moving swiftly from bunker to eagle's nest high above; it gave her a hot rush. She had barely staggered with him into the hotel room before she was all over him.

'Do you have a condom?' she said. She never carried them. She never thought this was going to happen.

'I don't have any diseases,' he said. 'You're not on the pill?'

'Whether I am or not,' she said, irritated, 'you have to use some kind of protection.'

'You want me to go get something and come back?'

'Mmmm,' she said, nuzzling him and starting to undo his buttons. 'That would be divine.'

'I prefer to wait.'

'What?'

'I do not know you well,' he said. 'Why are you so quick to rush this? I will like to see you . . . tomorrow night . . . I will have time to think about you.' He detached himself from her embrace.

She was sure she wouldn't see him again. It never occurred to her that it was possible to view sex as something other than a purely physical conquest, a release. That there were people out there – including men – who believed sex might be a spiritual communion between two people.

'Geez,' she said sourly as he walked out the door. She sounded ferocious, even to herself. 'I just wanted to get laid.'

4

At first being married was fun. Her job as a travel agent had not been. It had been boring, especially since she didn't have enough money, seniority or vacation time to take advantage of the special discounts and last minute trips that the other travel agents were able to grab. Now she didn't have to work. Having an apartment in New York City's Upper West Side, a dentist husband starting his own practice (he was going to specialize in cosmetic dentistry, porcelain veneers, caps, whitening with lasers) – it was mysterious, a fortunate accident. Winning the lottery. Things like this did happen, then.

She had come from such a slummy place, the crummy apartment – outside of Boston, a bedroom that she had to share with her mother after Donny got out of prison and she had to give up her room for him. He sat around all day smoking, watching TV and whining that he couldn't get a job, when in fact he wasn't even looking.

Then her mother, Nell, was sorry for him and ended up giving him money, which he spent on beer and more cigarettes. Nell paid for Donny to go to cooking school – at least he might have done the cooking for her and Nell since they were at work all day, but the only thing he ever made was dirty dishes. If Nell spent time looking through the classifieds he would always reject the jobs she found, saying that with his credentials he could never work as a short-order cook in a greasy spoon and no fancy restaurant would ever hire an ex-con.

Donny was definitely Nell's favorite. Peyton's two older sisters, Kathy and Brenda, had long since escaped – they would have nothing to do with Nellie, who never stopped going on and on about the furniture she had inherited which they had sold for nothing – now all that same stuff was on an antiques show on TV, selling for hundreds of thousands of dollars. But at the time, they all agreed it was just a lot of depressing, dented, old junk. Growing up with such furniture had been oppressive; stuff to crush a child, the dark old highboy, the grim chairs and *secrétaire l'abbatoir* or whatever stupid name it was her mother called it . . . Things had emotions, personalities, inhabited by penurious, bad tempered forebears.

The family – according to Nell, who was manic depressive, after all, and ended up in a mental hospital from time to time and later disappeared on the streets of Boston – had been traced to the *Mayflower*, which actually meant nothing. It only showed it was possible to trace the genetic roots of insanity back three hundred years to some religious fanatic who jumped on a boat to nowhere instead of staying put in civilized England. Stupid ancestors, fleeing in pursuit of religious freedom, but now – how many generations later? Six? – she, Peyton, had no religion and no interest in what might have sent them around the world.

It hadn't even been a question, whether or not she was in love with Barry, how the hell was she supposed to know what love meant? She liked him all right – if there was none of that swoony, gushy stuff, waiting by the telephone for him to call, sobbing when he didn't, it was because he always did call – and that other stuff was for teenagers. He was reliable, he was dependable, infatuated with her, he was finishing his residency in surgical and cosmetic dentistry, that was enough. There was no use in trying to base a relationship between two grown-ups on mad infatuation, which would surely wear off at some point.

Besides, she didn't have any other choice. She knew she was beautiful, even stunning – she might have been a fashion model had she been taller, people were always asking if she was an actress – but she would have had no clue how to be an actress, even if she had wanted to be one, and in her job, 99 percent of the time on the phone, who was she ever going to meet?

She had rented an apartment with several other girls but her share of the rent was high – even though she was sleeping in the living room – and her job as a travel agent didn't pay all that much. To spend all that money on a share – one of the roommates had over-dramatic sex, nightly (each guy disposed of after one usage but all had red hair); another stole food and replaced the empty cans and cartons.

This apartment, dark, hot in summer, cold in winter, was further from where she worked than her mother's home. Peyton thought she would move back in with Nell and save the money she would have spent on rent to buy a car. That was before Donny went into rehab; he had briefly had a rich wife, she was the one who got him started on heroin, although later, when she had no trouble giving it up, he couldn't.

Peyton hadn't dated anybody in a while. She hadn't even gone out in a while. Her girlfriend Victoria was a nurse and sometimes they met at the bar across the street from the hospital. Probably she wouldn't have gone out that night – it was a week-night – but she was depressed. It was so cold at this time of year and pitch black by five o'clock. The bar was warm, brightly lit, filled with people, sports on TV.

She spotted Victoria immediately, on the far side of the room: Victoria was so tall, with her pale-pink skin and hair, her startled eyes. She had virtually no eyebrows and always had a crowd of people gathered around her, maybe because she was so vivacious.

'The worst thing happened today,' Victoria said. 'This filthy little man, a drug addict, smoking through his tracheal hole so I had to lean over to understand him, grabbed my hand and pulled it under the sheets. He wanted me to pet his weenie, but instead I got stabbed by a hypodermic needle he was keeping down there! Oowww! This sort of thing always happens to me! At least I gave his miserable little peepee a good twist. Oow! Don't repeat any of this, Peyton: the head of nursing would fire me in a second if she heard me talking like this.'

'What are you drinking, Victoria?'

'Grasshoppers. But don't worry –' she leaned forward and whispered in Peyton's ear, 'there's a flock . . . or a herd, whatever you call it . . . I know, a *gaggle* . . . of dentists in here tonight, on some convention, and they're all buying us drinks!'

Barry Amberg – D.D.S., or about to be – had a bland, big head with smallish features; he was on the short side, not bad-looking, with a kindly, phlegmatic demeanor. In another life he might have been a hired hand on some dairy farm, vaguely embarrassed about the manure on his boots, scraping them on a bootjack as he came in the kitchen door.

'You don't look like a dentist!' Peyton said.

'No? What do I look like, then?'

'I dunno . . . something with animals. Maybe more like . . . a farmer.'

He started to sing a song she didn't know: '*And there we ran a collective farm all run by husky Jewish arms / Who says that Jews cannot be farmers lies!*' Which, for some reason, she didn't know why, made her laugh.

In the past he might not have been her type.

After she found out what he did, she told him how when she was fourteen her older brother had taken her ice-skating in an empty lot nearby that someone had flooded for the kids; Donny considered himself a hockey player, and messing around with his hockey stick he swung and knocked out her two front teeth, which were now two rather poor implants.

'Oh, gee,' he said. 'Can I look?' She smiled. The men she knew would not have used the expression 'Oh, gee'. He pushed her hair away from her face to peer into her mouth. His big hands were soft as a cow's udder. 'It's just a lousy job,' he said. 'Whoever did it –'

'I didn't have a choice, it was whoever was on the insurance plan.'

'Well, they did a lousy job, that's all. They don't match, I don't know what they were thinking. You're so beautiful, you should get them redone –'

'It would probably cost ten grand.'

'I'll do it for you, once I pass my boards and have time.'

'Really? I . . . I don't know what to say.' She was vaguely embarrassed about having a man look so closely into her mouth, inspecting those little yellowish incisors. He would certainly now only see her in

36

this light, a woman whose teeth had been knocked out. She flipped her hair back into place. It was glossy, almost blue-black, with the sheen of a healthy housefly – a color that could not easily be dyed blonde, though she had from time to time considered doing so.

Having seen her teeth he had been struck by an arrow from Cupid. He grew animated, confident. 'The rest of your teeth, though – gosh, they look great, that's a shame about the front ones. I was wondering why you didn't open your mouth when you smile. After I get through with you that'll change – you have the same curvature of teeth that fashion models have, very wide. You're lucky: I'm probably going to be specializing in cosmetic dentistry, these days that's where the money is, but I'm still hoping, once I'm successful, to be able to donate services, for kids in poor places –'

'Oh, that's great. I wish I could do something like that. To . . . benefit people, and animals. Especially animals. I love animals. If I hadn't had my dog, while I was growing up . . . I would have been a complete basket case.' She looked down shyly; her mouth drooped a bit at the corners.

'I bet it's enough that you just make people feel better with your looks!' He wasn't flirting – he was the kind who did not even know what it meant to flirt – now he was embarrassed that he had blurted this out.

She was lovely: pale skin, her eyes such a fake blue, like those of an antique bisque doll, that people always asked her if she was wearing colored contact lenses, a full mouth and her perfect figure with that big bust, tiny waist, boyish hips. But thus far none of it had got her anywhere.

She was not blonde, she was not rich, and she was not smart. There had been no advantages. She hadn't even known there were various options for college; anyway, a branch of the state university was not far away. She was not an extrovert; really she was quite shy. It was humiliating, being whistled at, or if some man was absorbed not by her but her breasts – they had no brains, made no intelligent comments. And it was particularly difficult when the breasts had first grown: she was only ten.

Why would someone like her for her appearance, which, after all, had nothing to do with her? People should be brains in bottles lined up on global shelves – then let them sort out who they were compatible with! There were too many options . . . She did not realize that men were often intimidated by her, she was too pretty, too self-contained, the flawless skin, the cotton-candy lips; women were often jealous, those round high buttocks deserved to be kicked. And the clearness of her eyes made her appear cold, but she wasn't. She didn't think of herself as cold.

He was in town for a week attending a dentistry conference, various new techniques lectures, procedures, salesmen demonstrating dentistry equipment – and by the time she was ready to go (catching the MTA to the bus, she was still in debt on her credit card and hadn't saved up nearly enough to buy a car) he had asked her to go out to dinner the following night.

An emergency-room doctor on whom Victoria had a crush came in. 'There he is,' Victoria said. 'That's the one; I know he's got a big dick. I can just tell. I used to think that big noses and big feet meant something to do with the size of the cock, but now I know that's not true.'

'Whatever. I'm going home.'

'No, no – don't go now, you got to help me to meet him.'

'You have tomorrow off,' Peyton said, 'I have to work. Call me tomorrow at the office.' The dentist, Barry, was standing nearby. She hoped he hadn't overheard Victoria.

'Are you going?'

'Yeah, I've got to.'

'Ah . . . would you like me to see you home?'

She didn't want to explain it would take an hour by trolley and bus and then a fifteen-minute walk – by the time he got to her place and walked back there might not be another bus. What was the use of his seeing where she lived? He was probably rich, he didn't have to know where she came from. It didn't even occur to her there were people who had enough money to take taxis.

The house – half a house, really – where she lived with her mother was in a peculiar area of Boston. Wortington was a depressed, rather scumbly township stuffed between two other villages that over the years had grown more and more prosperous. Old Victorian and saltbox houses whose vinyl siding had been stripped were restored to pedicured perfection, while in her town, old couches bloated from rain, fat corpses, still sagged on the front porch alongside busted washing machines. In summer, wherever there was a backyard, above-ground pools were installed on the cemented-over yards and the shrieks of children could be heard braying 'Marco!' 'Polo!' in the goosey honk of the Boston accent.

This was a world of endless eight-lane highways that fed on to four-lane highways that led to giant parking lots surrounding shopping malls that on the weekends were completely full. Here one might drive for hours under an industrial sky before arriving at a state park or beach swollen with tattooed torsos in bikinis: it wasn't until fifteen years on that the fad for pierced flesh and imprinted skin became the style of white upper-middle-class educated youth. The region was a manufactured Bermuda triangle of bleakness, a disaster site ringed and sliced by barbed-wire ribbons of road. A natural declivity or abscess, had it always been so grim, torpid, when settled by the earliest white colonists (of which, on her mother's side, her mother constantly reminded her, she was one)? Had they arrived at a place without realizing it was covered by a giant, invisible sloth, permanently crushing the land?

The few trees that survived, leafless, were no more than broken twigs sunk in tiny sidewalk pockets destined to live only a season or two before being replaced. The elms had all long since died of disease. A stale, ashen pall settled on everything: the sky black at five, the dawn breaking sodden gray, the commencement of the months of snow, again ashen-colored, then the months of muddy spring leading into desiccated summer. But it was more than an atmospheric condition; more than pollution from cars and industry; it was an aura of centerlessness. This unnatural city had no pedestrian area, it was all roadways, buttressed highways, capped by cloverleaves which led to worm castings of tunnels.

There was no Boston, there were neither suburbs nor townships; as far as Peyton was concerned its existence was a lesion on the temporal lobe of the planet.

It was almost midnight by the time she arrived home; nightly she shrank into a heap of soggy apathy. There were two front doors, the house had long ago been converted into a two-family residence, what had once been the upstairs was theirs, though with its own entrance. No one had shoveled the front steps, and the snow had turned after the evening's slush-fall into a pelt of ice ermine, glossy, dangerous, while overhead hung wounding icicles which, when the weather warmed in the day, fell with glittering shrieks. The light on the neighbor's side of the porch had burned out but the two doorbells with old-fashioned protruding nipples glowed feebly on both sides, beneath the head of Santa Claus (installed some months before by the neighbor's delinquent son, the sanctification of the alcoholic fat man, jolly pedophile cast in plastic, one of the world's most peculiar cults).

The loud-ticking battery-operated cuckoo clock at the bottom of the stairs greeted her; on the hour electronic music chips chirped a barrage, tunelessly, of only vaguely familiar American folk songs – 'She'll Be Comin' Round the Mountain'; 'Shoo-Fly Pie and Apple Pan Dowdy'; 'I Left My Heart in San Francisco' – each reduced to atonal peeps. Made in China. At midnight the demented pre-programed selection was 'Yesterday'.

From upstairs came the comforting sound of cackling television laughter.

Her mother was still awake, watching a large bird, nearly six feet tall, gobble a banana in front of a television talk-show host. 'The cassowary can run thirty-one miles an hour,' explained the bird's handler to the host. 'He's the closest living descendant of the dinosaur called the raptor. Look at his legs.' From a bowl the bird selected an orange and swallowed it whole, without waiting to remove the peel.

'I thought you'd be asleep,' said Peyton, taking off her coat and flinging it over the back of the sofa where it slid and landed on the floor in an exhausted heap.

'My tooth is bothering me,' her mother said. 'I must go to the dentist, not that he's any use. The last time I was there, I told you, he was on one side and the hygienist was on the other, and he leaned over and slapped her.'

'Why?'

'I don't want to talk about it.' Customarily her mother spoke in the artificial tone of a 1940s B-movie star, a sort of faux English accent. This, she claimed, was how the girls spoke back at her finishing school.

'Darling, would you bring me my Cartier lighter that was a gift from Paul Miles, the C.E.O. of Lorce Industry?'

'Ma, just say, "Bring me my lighter."'

'Why? Does it make you jealous that I had such important beaux when I was in finishing school?'

'No.'

'Or is it that you can't bear having a Boston accent when I don't?'

'Oh, gee. Are you taking your medication?'

'Perhaps.' Her mother sighed wistfully and tried to move one of the huge dogs – Monty – who was with her on the bed. 'So how was tonight? Did you have fun?'

'It's funny about your tooth – I met a dentist tonight, he wants to take me out to dinner. He seemed nice.'

'If you screwed him, would he fix your front teeth for free? And mine?'

'Ma!'

'A dentist, that's good. They don't kill people. Too bad it couldn't have been a plastic surgeon, though.' Her mother was saving money for a facelift and liposuction. She was sixty-five; she had given birth to Peyton, her last child, when she was forty-two. The others – Donny was out of jail (drugs, relapse) and in some kind of halfway-house program in Wisconsin; Kathy (married, two kids, living in Florida) and Brenda (a healer at a New Age health spa in Colorado) had not come back this year at Christmas, which was excusable only in Donny's case. 'Well, it'll be nice to have you married off and a dentist is a good catch. How old is he?'

41

'I don't know, Ma, maybe in his thirties?'

'Is he married? Make sure he's not already married. Where does he live?'

'I don't know – he doesn't live here, he's just here for a few days attending a conference or something.'

'That's not good – a long-distance relationship is going to be hard to maintain. Well, you'll work it out. I'd like a big wedding, though, someplace outdoors. We can do it over at the arboretum, do they let people have parties there? Maybe Donny will be out by then, or could get some kind of visitation permission, like for a funeral. Anyway, I hope you won't sleep with him tomorrow, it's too soon; and try not to let him see your real personality.'

Her mother was surrounded by papers – old magazines, catalogs, heaps of mail – there was not a single surface or drawer that was not full to the point of exploding, lottery tickets whose numbers had not been checked, dead batteries removed from appliances but not thrown out, pens out of ink, staplers without staples, tubes of ointment, hairbrushes displaying old hairs, hardball candies half-sucked and attached to bits of paper, sticky emerald jewels, canary-colored pearls.

Tips from decorating magazines gone awry: the couch had come from the goodwill store, an overstuffed rubbery cadaver covered in brown and beige polyester plaid; a lampshade covered with large black and pink polka-dotted fabric; walls hung with thrift-store frames spray-painted gold surrounding oil paintings purchased at a motel-lobby sale of 'Genuine Oil Paintings $14.99 and Up' (a wood-land scene with a fawn; a bowl of flowers; snow-covered mountains). These dated from a time before her mother had become totally indifferent to her surroundings. Here and there were a few real oil paintings, the last of the family portraits still in her mother's possession, the early-American Amos and Mehitabel Fryer, the later painting of the rich American beauty great-great-great-grandmother Clarissa, who had married a gambling English lord whose descendants were occasionally written up in lurid articles, 'Aristo Oxbridge Student ODs'.

Once a theater had shut down; in the parking lot her mother had found an old chandelier, its arms dripping with cracked crystal prisms, which Donny's electrician friend had installed above a beat-up mahogany desk. Blue ribbons from dog-show wins were pinned to one lavender-rosed floral wall (her mother had papered it herself, it was crooked) alongside unframed photographs. Against the far wall was an old Federal dresser, one eagle-footed leg broken, a relic of some ancestral habitation; next to the sofa was a cobbler's table turned coffee table, and a spinning wheel mounted with false cobwebs, left over from a bizarre attempt at Christmas decoration.

And the dogs: her own, a chihuahua, Flea, who slept with her at night, and three bloodhounds, Monty, Rufus and Henry, with mournful beleaguered eyes, endlessly trailing plumes of shimmering saliva, as well as a bitch puppy, Daisy, that her mother had received as a stud fee from a fellow bloodhound owner. Her mother's weekends were generally spent on the dog-show circuit, though her time was limited now that she had a job in a cafeteria.

The TV set, huge, always babbling, had been one of Donny's acquisitions, no doubt part of one of his scams – he would want it back, when he got out of rehab. In the meantime it and the treadmill, also Donny's, were here for them to enjoy – between the dogs and his stuff, the living room was useless.

'I don't know if I want to get married to him, Ma. I mean, he was . . . nice, but maybe sort of lumpish.'

'A lumpish type is a good husband. I mean, what are you going to do, look for another sleaze like Ernie?'

Ernie was a handsome bartender of Portuguese descent Peyton had gone out with her senior year in college but who went back to his wife after all, leaving her with one memory: '*I really like to eat your pussy, but . . . a lot of the time you taste like urine. And I don't really like the taste, you know. Do you think you could wash better, or trim your pubes or something?*' These sentences replayed hideously, unsolicited, in Peyton's head whenever her mother mentioned his name. 'Well, there was Scott . . .'

'Joined the Merchant Marines! You're almost twenty-four years old, at the height of your desirability and you know you're never going to make any money as a travel agent. Don't worry about it, you can always get a divorce later.'

'I haven't even had a date with him yet!'

'We'll invite everyone to the wedding. Of course, I don't actually know anybody. Would a fall wedding be appropriate? You'd better make sure he uses a condom – take your own, there's some in the drawer next to my bed.' Occasionally her mother picked up some guy in a bar but this hadn't happened in years. The condoms had to be too old by now to be any use. 'Oh, this is exciting. You always wanted a wedding.'

'Ma! Maybe I always wanted a wedding, but I don't think I want to get married!' She could not understand or see how she could have ended up with such a mother. Bloodlines had been relatively pure since some ancestor's arrival on the *Mayflower*; at least, until her mother had met her father and screwed up the genetics. Her father was good-looking, Estonian, new to the US; he found work as a car mechanic and since he and Nell both drank it took him years to realize that Nell was . . . off, that by marrying him she was disinherited. Before Peyton was born he went out in search of oranges – he was addicted to fresh squeezed orange juice, there had been no fruit where he grew up – and never came back. It turned out he had gone to Florida. Nell hated him but always said he'd been a great fuck.

Tears came into Peyton's eyes at being humiliated so easily, twenty-three years into her stay on the planet.

'What choice do you have? No other prospects seem to be coming along, do they? You frighten men – why don't you try to be friendlier, make the first move? Surely some of them come into your office.'

'Everything is by phone.'

'Then you'll have to try to get out there more. Take a class. Go to a lecture. Anyway, let's go to sleep. We've got to get up at the crack of dawn.'

Her mother stubbed out her last cigarette of the evening and staggered off down the hall; wearily, one by one, the three huge drooling dogs got to their feet and clumped after her.

'Remember, you're all I've got left!' her mother called back. 'I'm counting on you to restore the family name to its former pride and glory. Not that it ever did anything beside exploit the poor and enslaved. Still, what else is to become of you? I see you as the mistress of a large plantation, a mansion filled with golfing sons, vaguely Kennedyesque; you, nobly presiding, à la Rose Kennedy. Occasional write-ups regarding one triumph or another in *People* magazine. With your looks and lack of personality you can do it, I know!'

'Leave me alone, Ma. Good night!' She had nobody on the planet – was this how it was meant to be for human beings, such icy isolation, able to view people but not connect? She went to brush her teeth. In the mirror under the fluorescent light she saw the front two really were pathetic, stubs of a visibly different color.

The plumbing in the apartment was lousy. A lone turd floated in the toilet bowl, paddling an endless circle.

5

'Peyton? It's me, your father-*in*-law.'

'Leonard? What's wrong?'

'Nothing's wrong. Why, do I sound like some*thing*'s wrong?' Leonard had the oddest habit of emphasizing the wrong syllable in a word. It drove her nuts. There was never any predicting which word he might abruptly hammer – the overall effect was like a deranged preacher or foreign professor who had read English in books but never heard it spoken aloud. He didn't wait for her answer. 'I was in *the* neighborhood and I remembered – this *is* where you're working these *days*, and, *after* all you're my favorite daughter-*in*-law – got time *for* a quick bite of lunch?' He had never asked her to lunch before.

'You and Grace?'

'No, Grace didn't come into *the* city with me.'

'Sure, we could meet – say, one o'clock?'

'Oh, my, I was hoping . . . a bit ear*lier* than that, so I can catch the two-*o*'clock train –'

She was going to Hong Kong in a few days. She had other things to do.

She had wanted to do some shopping in the afternoon – she didn't know, exactly, what people were wearing in Hong Kong but the days were long past when Grace could have told her what to wear or bossed her around. Nobody dressed for an airplane trip anymore, even in first class the rich women wore jeans. Only their hideous pocketbooks, in shades of beige and black, gave away their secret, that they were rich.

Peyton was flying business class; she was planning to wear a pale orange suit, tropical-weight wool, with slightly flared trouser legs, but she wanted a white shirt with ruffles cascading down the front, a shirt that would be very low-cut so she had a lot of visible cleavage. Instead she was going to have to spend her free time with her father-in-law.

It had rained heavily and gustily that morning and now umbrellas, splayed seagulls with metal bones and flaps of multicolored skin, littered the sidewalk, an ecological mystery. A rich broth, swimming with myriad bacteria, swirled, saliva-thick, down into the gutters on every corner. A splash from a passing car spattered her with the soupy stuff but the humid air made her pink cheeks pinker; her soft mouth firmly set in a pout, she still got plenty of admiring glances.

There was an upscale Chinese place a few blocks away, upscale but old-fashioned, with an aura, a reminder that once it had been a very exotic thing in Manhattan to have a Chinese meal, especially so far away from Chinatown. The menu was old-style. American-Cantonese, with its listings of Egg Fu Yung, Chow Mein, Chop Suey. A sidebar on the menu listed cocktails – Gimlets, Rob Roys, Manhattans – and at the bottom a notation read, 'And . . . For the Gentleman . . . lamb chops/steak'. As if there were still men in New York who had a Martini before lunch and said to their associates, 'I can't eat this foreign crap, gimme the chops.' It amused her, this place, that it was possible to peel back the layers of a city. And there were times when it still amazed her to eat out in a restaurant: a realm, a world only for the very rich.

Of course at lunch-hour the place was empty – perhaps it was always empty – Leonard had not yet arrived and she knew he would look askance at her drinking in the middle of the day so she told the waiter to give her a glass of ice tea and put a shot of vodka in it. She would have preferred white wine, but the wine here was terrible and there wasn't really any way to disguise it.

She was almost ready to order another when Leonard arrived, a stout, officious little man who blended invisibly into the streets of Manhattan – his yellow cashmere V-neck sweater beneath his blue suit jacket, his crisp, striped shirt and muted tie – thousands of his kind roamed the streets: industrious, fine husbands, as asexual as drones.

With a nervous twitch he glanced over the room – she had the idea he was relieved the place was empty – and kissing her on the cheek said, 'You're looking *as* beautiful *as* ever.' Then, to the beaming waiter, 'You know, I'm going to have *a* Scotch and soda.' He sat and mopped his brow. 'Sorry I'm late. I'm a little frazzled, these subways, *I'm* telling you, I don't know why you *two* chose to live *in* the city. So, tell me, how's *my* wonderful grandson, did you hear from him at school?' His voice was a marble on a roulette wheel, landing at random on one word or another. Red, black. Black, black, red.

'Not much.' Cash was in college, off in Pennsylvania. Even when he called, they weren't really communicating – he would go into a lengthy story, about, say, trying to buy a textbook and waiting forever only to be told by the university bookstore clerk that they were out of that book and back orders would take six weeks – even though the professor had assigned that book! Or how he went to a movie screening and was turned away because it was over-sold, even though he had already purchased a ticket on-line – he was not so much an injustice collector as a specialist in excruciating detail. He was the only one to whom such things happened, and every laborious step of the disastrous event had to be explicitly recounted.

'What *a* kid!' Leonard said. 'I don't know what I'd do without him, really – Grace and I were thinking, there's a two-*week* cruise next summer, around the Me*di*terranean, maybe he'd like *to* join us –'

'Oh I'm sure he'd love that. He adores his grandparents.'

'Well, that's one thing I wanted to talk to you about – shall we order first?' She was not a big lunch-eater but she let him select a number of dishes. 'You can take the leftovers home, Barry *will* like that, for his dinner –'

'He's still on this thing of keeping kosher at home.'

'Well, that's good, you know. We went *through* that for a while, then, I don't know, it just got to be too much for Grace, and there was so much food left over from her catering business, we kind *of* gave up.'

If two people had no imagination they could have a happy marriage. He had no imagination, Grace had no imagination, they had married young and they had gone along together, seemingly contented, for – gosh, it had to be nearly fifty years? He was getting up there in age – she had never thought of Barry's parents as particularly old, but now she realized –

'What do you say; shall we have a *lob*ster Can*ton*ese and the ca*shew* duck with broc*coli*?'

'Yes, that sounds nice. You know, if you're having a drink, I think I'm going to have one too –' She asked the waiter for a vodka on the rocks.

'So how's Barry? He's o*kay*?'

'Oh yes, very good. Busy as always.' What was the point in saying things hadn't turned out for Barry exactly as he had planned; maybe Leonard knew anyway. When she and Barry had married, Barry had been so confident, full of ideas, but his new techniques had ended up in malpractice suits, it was the wrong location for cosmetic dentistry, others – the *schnorrers*, the hustlers, the guys who handed out Percocets and let patients stop by for a snoutful of laughing gas on their way home from work – had surged ahead. Dentists who had been with him at school were featured in beauty magazines; Barry was too earnest, too eager, his karma was bad.

'Well, I tell you I've been luckier *than* most. It would have *been* nicer *if* Belinda stayed with her husband. Her mother and I can't understand it.' In her forties Belinda, the practical, the sensible, had run off with an up-and-coming actor, sixteen years her junior – almost immediately the guy had become famous, ditched her, and Jonathan, her husband, hadn't wanted her back either. Not only that, he had custody of the girls and Belinda was paying child support. 'The worst part is, she still can't seem to get over her *ob*session with this fellow. If it had happened when she was still in her teens, or her twenties . . . at her age it makes no sense. We always looked upon Belinda as so rea*son*able. Grace and I have lived our lives with a sense of morals that obviously hasn't trans-ferred *to* this day and age.'

They had thought if one of their children's marriages went wrong, it would be Barry's and hers. And it would be her fault. She was the bad seed, the shiksa lunatic, unreliable. It wasn't that she was pleased about Belinda, it was just that she was somehow . . . vindicated. Hadn't she handled everything with a masculine subtlety, an ability to compartmentalize? 'You've never done anything . . . incorrect?' She flushed and looked down coyly. She didn't know how to relate to a man – even her own father-in-law – in a non-sexual way.

'I suppose you'd be *sur*prised, but Grace and I smoked pot once. It was at a party. There was no e*ffect* at all.'

At her house, growing up, Nell – or Donny – always had a joint going, it had never been any big deal; they smoked cigarettes, too. It was odd that she had never wanted to smoke cigarettes and dope made her paranoid. She had tuned out by watching old movies on TV – when the TV worked, or when they lived some-where that got reception. Actually she liked being around cigarette smokers – they were more alive, more nervous, than the rest of the world, the non-smokers, placid and mooey. Would he be shocked at that?

'And tell me – how are your little dogs?'

'Oh, gosh. Well, right now I have six.' Leonard looked sickened and delighted. He shook his head. She couldn't help herself. The chihua-huas – they were such popular city dogs, especially with Hispanics in New York, and then they always ended up at the Center for Animal Control; people moved, or couldn't take care of them – every week she was in there and usually took one or two home with her at least every month. Sometimes she found other placements for them, but with their buggy eyes, if it wasn't for her they would be euthanized. Of course Barry hated them.

'Anyway, I don't know how *to* put this, exactly. I've turned to you *because* I know, well, you won't repeat any of this. *Not* even to Barry. Especially not to Barry. I talked to Grace about this – she said, no, I shouldn't discuss it with you – but I said, look, these two are modern

kids, somebody should talk to her. This woman Barry's been seeing –
Rachel –'

She didn't know what to say. If she acted shocked he might not tell
her anything else. 'Rachel . . . the office manager . . .'

'You did know about it, didn't you? I assumed you did, it would be
impossible not to know, the way she's been carrying on –'

'Um . . . oh, yes, of course. You're saying that my *hus*band has
inserted his *penis* into a *vagina* other than *mine*.' She was trying to be
sarcastic, technical – but her words came out loudly and hung in the
air of the empty restaurant, almost as if she were mocking Leonard.

There was a silence. Leonard looked shocked. In all the years
Peyton had been married to Barry she had never spoken this way; she
had always tried to act nice, polite, respectable, even though, after all
this time, Grace still looked at her suspiciously. There was a split
second when she was tempted to tell Leonard everything. Once his
small mouth, succulent, pursed in an expression that was slightly
disapproving, must have suckled – bizarrely – at his wife's breast.
Why did grown men want to imitate nursing technique?

'Well, what's it to me? I never could understand it, why would I
care where he sticks his penis, let him put it in a food processor for all I
care as long as it doesn't give me a disease.'

'I can tell you're upset. I said to Grace, Peyton is very brave.' He
didn't seem to have heard her. 'Well. Now this woman says she's
preg*nant* and wants to have the ba*by* – she called us the other night
and said what did we think she should do. I've run into *a* bit of trouble
at work. You know, I'm retiring *this* year, and . . . they decided *to* do
a major audit, the first in ten years . . . what I'm asking you to *do*,
what I want *to* do, without going into too much de*tail* here: I want to
have a large sum *of* money transferred over *to* you and Barry, *in* trust
for Cash. If something hap*pens*, if things get messy, I don't want to be
wiped out financially – I want Cash to have the money. What *a* special
young man you two have raised. And I want that someday he'll be *a*
very rich young man. And I don't want inquiries *into* my bank
account. So it's going to be done in *an* offshore transfer. I'm going
in to see my law*yer* this afternoon – I don't want to tell Barry, I don't

want you to go *over* this with Barry, you know he's going to ask *all* kinds of questions –'

Her head pounded. It was impossible to believe. It was true there had been times when she wondered if Barry was seeing someone – he would be snappish with her, act irritated, but she had always thought, well, let him have an affair, if it will make him happy, it's to be expected; after all, I haven't exactly been . . . but really the shocking thing was that it had no resonance at all, though she knew it was supposed to. What was the big deal where he put his penis? It wasn't attached to *her* body.

'Are you okay?'

'I guess I'm not really following you. Um . . . do you think . . . could I have another drink?'

'Oh, you're upset. Sweetie, you don't have to fol*low* me. I'm just going to *have* some papers sent to you *at* the office for you to sign, mail them back *certified*, that's it. It's only in the event that something happens *that* I want the family to be covered. In my business . . . well, you can't *be* too careful, and . . . you know, I had a lifetime of stock *options* in the Burmese Python Corporation. And it's partly *from* the sale of the shares – I'm divesting this week – that the money *will* be in the Caymans, in *the* trust account. Believe me, I'm not asking you *to* be involved in any way – it's all just a business procedure, but I have to *be* careful. If this woman Rachel is pregnant – you've been married to Barry for almost twenty-five years, I know how nasty these things can get; I've told Barry, just push through this thing, what's the use of trading in one woman for another. We're not that kind of people. We are so fond of you, Peyton. My, this ca*shew* duck is tasty. Can I put some *on* your plate?'

She almost could have screamed, the way he took those little words – what were they, anyway, prepositions? – and strung them up overhead like decorative lights, in order to say: 'Notice these words and syllables that everybody neglects.' She always imagined him as a jeweler, tapping away at small stones, a loupe in his eye.

She didn't have the slightest clue what he was up to. What Barry was up to. Why did she have to be told this stuff, why couldn't things go on as they always had? Now she was mad at herself, for having spent years feeling guilty when her own husband probably had not. But she had an idea that for all these years, while she had done her best to present herself – at home, in Leonard and Grace's presence – as a nice, married housewife, he had been someone other than who he had appeared to be. 'And don't forget, tell that son of yours *to* give me *a* call the next time you speak,' Leonard said as they parted. His eyes lit up at the thought. 'We haven't heard from him in ten days.'

He thought she spoke to Cash regularly, every day even, when in fact he was the same as every other boy off at college, instantly forgetting he had ever had a home.

At least she was going away, even if it was just for a short time. When she got back she would straighten everything out. Barry was her husband, she would forgive him his mistake. Still it kept pounding in her head and when he got home late she pretended to be asleep, she couldn't face tipping all the garbage out, strewing the room, before leaving on a trip. It would wait. She had never gotten that third drink. She stopped at a bar on her way back to the office.

Then, unbelievably, the next day she got a call from Belinda, who wanted to meet for lunch as well. It wasn't that this had happened often before, but she was irritated none the less. Just because she was married to Barry – Leonard's son, Belinda's brother – did that mean she had to devote every lunch-hour to their problems?

Belinda had so little free time Peyton agreed to go downtown to meet her at work. The waiting room of Belinda's office was full of panic, despair and a group of unshaven men in leather jackets. Apparently they were casting that day for male actors to play hoodlums, or gangsters, or maybe they were trying to look like downtown art-types. Only one was black and she recognized him, he was a well-known French comedian – he didn't seem to fit in – and curiously there was an elderly Orthodox Jewish man in the mix as well, in a broad-brimmed hat and frock coat, with a wispy gray beard – though maybe he was simply dressed for a part. They were all clutching photographs of themselves and wriggling as if they needed to go to the bathroom.

At least she didn't have to wait long. It made her anxious to be in a room with men who were so needy; she was used to being around women and their desperation, it was off-putting to be around so many men who were . . . hungry, but not for food. When Belinda emerged, all the men straightened up, there was a collective sigh of eagerness as they struggled to pull themselves into an illusion of composure and confidence. Belinda, their possible rescuer from obscurity, had arrived. And it was true, when she appeared, there was a sense of the goddess arriving on winged chariot. She could make them into stars.

Belinda had grown into her looks. A big woman, not overweight but Amazonian, with a small head emphasized by close-cropped hair, powerful limbs that carried her in two steps across the room. She stopped in front of the black guy. 'Yussef! How are you! Your agent said he was sending you over. I know Henry wants to see you and James Ivory is coming in to meet you at around two o'clock if you can wait that long. Guys, did you all sign in? If you want to smoke, you can go in the hall, just tell Alice where you'll be –'

The men slumped back again when they saw she was going out. There were several partners in Belinda's firm, but her strength, her massiveness, her slightly nasal way of speaking, gave her an authority that made it seem she was the one in charge. Or maybe it was just what happened to those few, rare women who every day had people kow-towing to them, sending them flowers and gifts, sucking up.

There was a place around the corner to get a sandwich. Ever since Peyton had made that pass at Belinda – but it hadn't really been a pass, had it, and it was twenty-five years ago – Belinda had always smirked at her as if she thought Peyton still had the hots for her and she was doing Peyton a favor by seeing her. And every time Peyton wanted to shout, 'You look like you think I wanted to screw you but I was only trying to comfort you, so don't think you're so desirable!' But she didn't say it.

'So how's work?'

'Non-stop. *I'm Not Surprised* has been such a huge hit we have to start looking for celebrities for the second season; we're up for seventeen Academy Awards; three movies in the works and we're actually thinking of bringing someone in just to handle commercials –' Suddenly Belinda, who had sounded so confident, stopped. 'I think he's going to marry her, Peyton.'

'Who?'

'Damian Westerly. It was because of me he met Calliope Vaughn, and it was because of me he became such an instant success, and I still can't believe this is really happening, that he would leave me for her. And all I can think is, she's younger, she's a star, she's better looking – but she's still a fading movie actress! And there is nothing more desperate on this planet than an aging actress.'

Peyton recoiled. She should have known Belinda was going to start rehashing all of this. It was like a broken record, over and over again, and she couldn't figure out what had happened to Belinda, who had always been so normal, to cause her suddenly to get stuck on this one topic, to snap, when from her point of view none of it seemed at all real. She had been lucky, she supposed; she had escaped unscathed. When she thought about what she had done . . . but she had never had a choice, the things had just happened . . .

'Um, let's change the subject or I won't be able to eat. Are you . . . seeing anybody these days?'

'You don't understand!' Belinda was snarling now. 'Who am I going to meet? Everybody's laughing at me! . . . I did something terrible: I called him last night.'

'Who?'

'Damian! He wasn't home but I left a message, I said I really needed to talk. He still hasn't called me back. The two of them are laughing at me. My mother says, go back to Jonathan – as if that's even a possibility. As if I would ever want to.'

She wanted to say, hey lady, you're fifty years old, when you going to grow up? Instead she tried to dissemble. 'But . . . What does Grace know? I mean, surely you're grown now, her opinion doesn't count . . .'

'Hey, even when you're eighty you're probably still wondering why your parents didn't love you or how they screwed up your life . . .'

'That's true. It still bugs me that my mother always said I was stupid. If she had just been more supportive . . . I don't think, now, that I was so dumb . . .'

'Anyway, the real reason I wanted to have lunch . . . I know you're not close with Victoria –'

'I haven't seen her in years.'

'Well, we stayed friends. You know she was HIV-positive for ages and then –'

'I didn't know! Gee, that's so awful. She was always promiscuous, or whatever you want to call it, but when we were young it wasn't even an issue, nobody knew about safe sex –'

'She says it wasn't even from sex though – she thinks she got it from a needle-prick in the hospital; that there was this patient twenty-five years ago . . . Anyway, then later it turned into full-blown AIDS, now people can go on for a long time, I guess, but in her case her liver is no good anymore and they don't do liver transplants on people with AIDS –'

'What?' She was in shock. Maybe she had it too. She had slept with Victoria in that three-way before her wedding, if Victoria had it then – she had already been a nurse for a few years – it was possible. Probably not too likely, but possible – 'I can't believe it!'

'I knew you hadn't been in touch with her for a long time. I thought it was better if I told you in person.'

'It just can't be! All this time? What's the . . . prognosis?'

'I don't know, a few weeks, a few months . . . It's not just the AIDS and her liver. Whatever the thing is, the – cytomega-something-or-other – is in her brain.'

Peyton thought she would see Victoria when she got back from her trip, maybe together they would go to Mexico. Despite Barry's contempt for alternative treatments . . . maybe somewhere, some-place, there was something that could be done. She would be the one to save her. 'I can't believe this. This is so depressing.' Victoria had had everything. She came from the right side of the tracks, she had grown up with two parents who loved her. She should never have turned out the way she did. What went wrong? Peyton had always been jealous of her, maybe that was why their friendship ended. Or maybe it was just that, after they had slept together, it was never quite the same. Like a guy who screws some woman and feels pressure, even if it isn't there.

'Anyway . . .' Belinda threw some money on the table of their booth. 'I have to get back. The other thing I was going to ask you . . . You look great, by the way. You're going on a trip?'

'Yeah, I'm off to Hong Kong.'

'Good for you. You deserve a holiday. Go shopping. Run up a big bill. What I was going to ask is, when people ask you, you know, about me and Damian, can you just say I'm seeing somebody else? Something like that?'

'Oh, sure, sure.' Nobody had ever asked her about Belinda and Damian. Nobody knew about it, or if they did, who cared? If there had been anybody in the world she had thought of as normal it was Belinda. Who knew, maybe there had been too much testosterone at the crucial second of gestation, or chicken hormones or MSG from a Chinese meal: a tidal wave of tampered genes that had only now smashed into Belinda.

'How's my brother, by the way? I don't know how Barry turned out to be okay, for all I know he's not.'

'He's been great. A wonderful husband. As far as these things go. I guess . . . you've heard about his affair?'

Dying. Victoria was dying and pretty soon she would be fifty. She had never thought that one day she would wake up and be this ancient. Such nastiness couldn't happen to her. Not in a world where a fifty-year-old woman was nothing. Yet she had had a good life. She had managed to steer clear of major tragedies. Wasn't that the point, after all, on a planet where most of the population worked fourteen hour days in sweatshops, lost limbs in landmine explosions, suffered hideous, painful diseases?

She should probably have a facelift. But quite honestly she hadn't seen any signs of aging, maybe a tiny bit of crinkling under her eyes but otherwise she didn't look one bit different than she had in photographs from twenty years ago; if anything, she looked better because now she knew how to dress and apply less make-up and had a better hairstyle. She had gone with Grace, her mother-in-law, when Grace had had her face done, and the whole thing had been so ghastly she really had no desire to put herself through it. She figured she could wait at least another five years.

At the time Peyton had assumed it would be basically a week's holiday in Arizona for her, and so she said she would do the nursing – it was only an outpatient operation in the doctor's office, after all. At dawn a car had come to pick Grace up and that afternoon they brought her back covered with bandages – apparently beaten with a baseball bat. A nurse had had to help her up in the elevator and into bed and when she handed Grace a plastic bowl, she threw up into it and then passed out in one of the double beds.

The nurse left after propping up her head and instructing Peyton. 'You know, she wet herself,' the nurse said irritably. 'I had to change her in the office, I put the dirty things in a bag.' And then Grace was up for half the night moaning and when Peyton went to look at her, her face was oozing with yellow pus and a kind of clear oil – a roasted pig with black stitches crusty with blood – and the pillows and sheets were stained. For two days Grace lay there and the nurse came once or twice to change the rotting bandages, which smelled gangrenous, and since Grace didn't want maid-service the whole room turned into a hospital ward in the Civil War, rotting flesh and urine. Of course a week later Grace was all right and didn't even remember, but it really put Peyton off the whole thing.

She had to admit, it was never something that was an either/or proposition – she just assumed she'd have a facelift *some day* and in the meantime an old friend of Barry's, a dermatologist, had been giving her botox injections for years and years. She didn't have a single line on her face.

She told the office she was taking off some days to go to look at a newly refurbished hotel – they were offering special rates that week for travel agents. She didn't earn much money from the job, she had only returned to work as a show of good faith to Barry that she would try to pay off the debt she had run up on the credit cards.

Instead of a facelift she went to Hong Kong.

6

It was true, her mother had come from a wealthy family with pedigree: pedigree in the sense that criminals, industrialists, religious fanatics, slave-owners who had made a lot of cash were held in high esteem. Her great-grandfather had been some sort of shipping executive, was it a captain? And before that there had been ship builders and whaling men. There had been a private island in Maine, a mansion near Boston, a summer place in Hyannis on the Cape. There had been, once, a small inheritance, from a great-uncle who had saved every penny until his death at ninety-three; but he had died intestate and the money had been divided between twenty-three distant relatives, and hadn't lasted long.

Her mother had gone to a women's finishing school in the Boston area – a college for young women, long since out of business – but dropped out, pregnant, to marry Peyton's father who disappeared just before Peyton was born. In Florida he drove a truck for a while – long-distance; when Donny had first started to take drugs he had reappeared and taken Donny back to Estonia for a summer. Donny hated it and said the people there lived like animals, but no further details were ever forthcoming. Now, as far as she knew, her father was somewhere near St Augustine, operating a small motel with his new family – wife number four? – and her two children. That was all she knew; nobody had kept up or kept in touch with anybody else, there was no glue holding anything or anybody together.

Twenty-three and she had slept with only a couple of guys and one of these had been the ubiquitous Ernie, the married Portuguese bartender, who at the time she had not known was married. Her sexual experiences had been borderline unpleasant, a hideous red member prodding her between the legs, attached to a bulky, sweating man who jigged up and down on top of her moaning, 'I'm gonna pop! I'm gonna pop! Are you there yet?'

Where? Where should she be? The act of masturbation, commenced in high school, culminated in a frenzied twitching, a satisfaction not dissimilar to the satisfaction to be found in scratching a mosquito bite. Pleasant, yet lacking in transcendent significance. Often, before Ernie, she had felt what was missing – the penis – would produce such an effect. The clitoris was on the outside, however, the friction produced by the penis was within. She had read too many books with good-and-pure heroines, or at least impassioned ones.

She rose at six to walk the dogs (part of her rent agreement with her mother). She was not used to going out, she had consumed more than one margarita, but even when she went to bed early, mornings were an effort, rising in the cold apartment and trying to muster energy for another blank day that was only another cube of time to be got through.

She would have preferred to stay in bed. Being asleep was vastly preferable to the waking state. In sleep lay dreams, and in her dreams were interesting people and skills like being able to fly and move objects by pointing at them. In dreams there were no responsibilities.

Her eyes were full of heavy sand, sub-Saharan, lunar. But she threw on jeans, sneakers, a sweatshirt and overcoat, put the coffee on to brew, rummaged for a stale donut. The dogs, bladders full, waved their whip tails while giving her malevolent glares. She hooked leashes onto braided leather collars, dragged each dog – the big ones were afraid of stairs – down the steps. Her life would go on this way, day after day, she supposed, until it was over.

Fortunately the dogs were not eager to do anything more than pee and poop in the bitter Boston winter. Their flat, chestnut-red coats were sparse. From their backsides cascaded heaps of steaming feces, so hot as to melt snow and ice, that had to be collected in gallon-sized bags. They had to be walked two at a time, or they would drag her to the ground in their haste to race back inside to the warmth, where they would plunge once more into their own yelping dreams, dog dreams that consisted, no doubt, of ancestral memories of tracking convicts along the shores of some deep, Southern swamp. Flea, her dog, was small enough to go on newspaper. He bossed the big dogs around and used them as mattresses. But her mother was deranged: so many big dogs in such a tiny place, and both of them out all day – Peyton should have been able to see it then.

Barry had said he would call her at the office that day with plans as to where and when they would meet; perhaps he would not call, or had lost her number, but in any event she dressed ready to go out after a full day at work, there was no point in coming back here to change.

Her boss, Polly Bodakian, expected them to look professional, though why did she care? Only rarely did somebody stop by to collect a last-minute ticket; everything was sent out by mail. She didn't know where Barry planned to take her, somewhere requiring a slinky evening dress? She hoped not. It was freezing cold. 'So what are you going to wear?' her mother called. 'Put on something nice. A push-up bra, nipples protruding, should do the trick.'

'Ma!' Her voice was shrill.

'Look, you want to have this guy fall in love with you or what?'

She was sorry that her mother was so crude. The way her mother talked, she might have been peeling off her skin. She put on a baggy dress she had worn in college.

'You're not going to wear that, are you?' her mother said. 'You've got such a cute figure, you might as well show it off!'

'But . . . shouldn't I look . . . respectable?'

'He was attracted to you because you didn't look respectable! You can look respectable later, after you've landed him.'

She was not sure who she was or what she represented. In the end she settled for a tiny miniskirt in hot pink vinyl and a low-cut scoop-necked shirt of some synthetic material, shiny black, worn over a push-up bra. Gold earrings, leg-warmers over her stockings, then bright yellow high heels; over all of this went a gold lamé jacket she had found – her mother had found – for seven dollars at a store that was going out of business.

In her pocketbook (red plastic patent) she threw mascara, purple eyeshadow, mauve lipstick. Her ensemble was not the fashion choice of a shy person but it was what the people around her wore. She had no idea that the image she portrayed was the antithesis of the person she was inside. Some day she would grow into her shell. One part was the soft center; the other part, a decorated façade unrelated to the trembling wreck within: a Waring blender mix of lousy genes, too many youthful hormones, a bad environment, processed diet. But Peyton inhabited a world in which shyness, modesty, sexual innocence were weaknesses that would bring you down.

Injured zebras were singled out by waiting lions.

Weekends when her mother was not at the dog shows they drove to shop at discount outlet malls or sales. Since childhood she had owned a Lane Hope Chest, made of cedar: it all seemed a bit silly now, she used it to store her old dolls, dressed in bridal veils and dresses. When she was little, she and her friend Victoria had married them off in elaborate ceremonies that curiously always seemed to end badly. One had had her hair shorn after being raped by another doll for which she – the victim – was ostracized by the group. Not only was her hair shorn but her eyes were gouged out. Some dolls spent long periods of time tied, naked, in compromising positions. There was only one male doll and he was required to service all those hard plastic tall blondes, but as he was missing genitalia he was often obliged to have distasteful organ substitutes – a gherkin, or a third leg ripped from someone else – strapped on or inserted into a customized hole pierced with a pair of manicure scissors . . .

Somehow the chest had never been filled with the trousseau it was intended to hold, and they had grown tired of torturing dolls. Now they only met up occasionally after work.

She thought about Barry throughout the day, though she couldn't remember anything about how he looked; he called her at nine, on a coffee break after his morning's first lecture, to ask where she wanted to go that night.

She had no idea really, she had never been out to dinner anywhere apart from the pizza parlor or a diner, one of a New England chain; he said he would ask around, buy a couple of magazines with restaurant reviews, and get back to her.

It was a slow day; the agency was not doing well. A few offers – invitations for travel agents – came in the morning's mail and she spent time studying them; but Peyton had only two weeks' vacation a year and on her salary she couldn't afford, yet, even the heavily discounted trips.

Then he called back to ask if she could meet him at his hotel at six or six-thirty: there was a cocktail reception on the last night of the convention that she might enjoy, and that he felt obligated to attend. They could go out to dinner from there.

The hotel in which Barry Amberg was staying was also where the conference was being held. She had seen it before only from the outside, tinkling glass, iceberg splendor, overlooking the Charles River – it belonged to such a different, glamorous world from hers, in which people could or might fly into Boston and stay here for a night or two, or a week, as tourists or on some kind of business.

An open multi-storied atrium, dripping with artificial plants, was directly ahead; in the center, on the ground floor beside a gushing 'modern' fountain, was a harpist strumming ethereal sour plucks. There was no sign of Barry, though she waited ten minutes or so. Finally she saw an announcement, the day's events, posted on an old-fashioned letterboard – the American Dentistry Convention Farewell Cocktail Reception was being held in Reception Hall 9. Perhaps he was already there.

She took the escalator. Down the corridor was a large room, carpeted, in which stood a vast number of grayish men and some women. A bar had been set up at either end and to one side a quartet – keyboard, trumpet, guitar, drums – played, rather morosely, some sort of fifties rockabilly. She was about to go in when two women seated at a large table by the doorway stopped her. 'Can we help you?' said one.

'Well, I, uh – I'm meeting a friend here.'

'I'm sorry. Are you a dentist?'

'No.'

'The reception is only for dentists registered at the convention and their guests.'

'I am a guest.'

'Sorry, you can't come in.' There was a gleeful smugness to her voice, as if hundreds of women were tying to crash this event. It was, maybe, true: gaggles of women were now gathering over at the coat check – but who were they, they certainly did not appear to be dentists and in fact, with flickering glances of wistful interest, they headed toward some other reception taking place elsewhere on the floor.

Drab dentists, singly or with spouses or dates, hung up their coats and took name cards at the front door; the receptionist continued to glare at her. Given half the chance she would have happily disemboweled Peyton.

Perhaps Barry wasn't going to show; already her feet were cramped in the high heels she was wearing and she had nothing else in which to trudge home. The bleakness of this city always made her feel as if a giant thumb was being pressed down onto her head. She knew she was out of place among these people, but in here the weight was lifted; not everyone had to endure the heavy grime. There was a chance she could escape.

She had spent so many years waiting for her life to begin. Each time a new false start: an event for which the pistol was destined to go off but no race had been scheduled, or she was facing the wrong direction on the track, the other runners heading toward her. Ten minutes had passed, she did not dare check her coat; it would be even more embarrassing to stand in the hall with her fancy clothes and to retrieve it if he didn't turn up – on the other hand she didn't know how long she was expected to wait. Twenty minutes passed, no other people arrived; she tried to peer in the room as best she could, maybe he had been in there all along.

The room contained only sallow waxen blobs in metal aviator glasses, in navy polyester suits, brown shoes, or teal polo shirts and khakis, nerds who spent leisure time on hiking trips, or birdwatching. What was to become of her? In all the years she had hung out with Victoria in the doctors' bar no other man had ever approached her, her avenues for meeting men were limited – she could see the years going by and nothing changing. Other women, things happened to.

The summer she and Victoria had worked as waitresses, a man who was older paid Victoria quite a bit when she stayed the night with him (Victoria had always had a thing for older men) and another took her to Northampton on a shopping spree and bought her a whole bunch of clothes. Peyton would have liked to turn a trick (not that she and Victoria thought of it that way, exactly) – it was something everybody did, in high school or college, once in a while, a sort of rite of passage, the same as smoking pot, getting tanked on Long Island ice tea, or huffing aerosol. Only nobody had even made a pass at her, let alone made her think they would reimburse her – from the beginning it was she who had pursued Ernie, who really did lose interest right away, which only made her pursue him more.

She thought she would just quickly go to the women's toilet and come back to see if Barry had arrived before she went home; as she was heading down the hall, he got off the escalator. 'Sorry!' he said. 'Were you waiting long?'

If she hadn't had to wait for him – if he had been there on time – she might have lost interest entirely. But she had had to wait. She paused for a second, uncertain that it was Barry. In her head he had taken on characteristics that did not mesh with who she now saw, a smallish beige man in baggy cargo pants with a lot of zippers, hiking boots, a sheepskin bomber jacket, hair in a shaggy seventies rocker do. 'Um . . . a little while.'

'Sorry, I didn't know how late it was. You should have phoned me in my room. I brought my coat so we could just head out to dinner, but on my way down I realized, I've got a nice bottle of champagne up there. I put it in the mini-bar, we should go up and drink it before we go out. Anyway, let's see how much fun we have at this shindig. Here, give me your coat, I'll put them on the rack.'

'They wouldn't let me in.' She took off her coat and for the first time thought that perhaps her outfit, the miniskirt and bright fishnets, the high heels and low-cut top, were not exactly what the other women were wearing.

She followed him to the coat check and then into the reception hall; people momentarily fell silent – even the band playing imitation jazz faltered, the tin trumpet skipped a beat, the drum rattled, strings plinked, returning in tone to their ancestral cat-gut origin. There was a sonic sniff of disapproval from the women in the room while the men stood with drinks poised, in open-mouthed admiration.

'What do you want to drink?' said Barry. 'Do you want to have a seat and I'll get you something from the bar?'

'Um . . .' she couldn't for the life of her think of what sort of drinks grown-up people consumed. 'What about a White Russian? I'll come with you.' It would be intolerable to sit at a table, alone, feeling out of place.

He couldn't get the bartender's attention or wasn't trying. Instead she stood beside him while he chatted with a man she assumed was another dentist; he didn't introduce her. Finally the other man disappeared, and Barry got their drinks.

'Sorry about that. He was the chief of our department back when I was in Chicago – I was just catching up. He's head of oral surgery now at Hillside-Bahai in Manhattan and wants to bring me in; I'm just deciding between New York or Boston, I can pretty much pick where I want to go.'

'Why would anyone want to be in Boston if they could be in Manhattan?' she blurted.

'Oh yeah, really – you like New York?'

'I've never been – but I know I don't like Boston and New York City I've always thought would be . . . so exciting.' She sounded dumb, a bimbo stuffed with platitudes but fortunately he wasn't paying much attention.

He handed her her drink; he was having Scotch on the rocks and the pale amber liquid seemed to her the height of sophistication. 'You want to go and grab a table – or mingle?'

'I guess I'd rather just sit somewhere and talk to you – I don't know anyone here or anything – unless it's something you have to do . . .'

'Naw, we don't even really have to stay. I've done what I came to the conference for: got three job offers, saw a couple of guys I wanted to connect with. I just thought this party would be something you'd enjoy and I sort of assumed it would be a good idea to stick my nose in . . .'

She couldn't figure out much about him; where he was living or had gone to school was something of a blur. Every response to her questions was a vague bit of dissembling or a saga connected to a different story that resulted in another unanswered question. Yet she knew he wasn't lying or dishonest – he just wasn't quite able to answer, perhaps he didn't really exist. A figment of her imagination having trouble coming up with factual information.

Salesmen at the conference had presented him – or at least were going to present him, when he chose where he wanted to work – with various bits of new laser equipment, free of charge, some kind of award or prize. He was planning on doing a six-week course – or was it a lectureship? – in London, after he went skiing in Gstaad.

She assumed he was very rich. She had never been around anyone very rich and after she drank her White Russian she had another one and after the third she was able to slide her chair around to his and begin to nuzzle him.

'I can't believe you don't have a boyfriend. Or that you're not already married. You're so gorgeous, you're just like the girl I had a crush on – in high school – who would never have anything to do with me. You're sure you're really single?'

Smiling, she nodded. He pulled her onto his lap and – eyes darting nervously around the room, though whether he was afraid of being seen or not being seen she didn't know – put the tip of his tongue in her ear. A soggy piece of wet toilet paper, a melting snail, probed deafeningly, wetly, down.

He wasn't really her type. Anyway, he hadn't been, before the three drinks. Normally she would have slept with him. That was what the girls did where she grew up. But then she figured, oh, no, I better not sleep with this guy, he thinks of me as someone . . . special. He's a dentist. He knows how to ski. He must be rich and he comes from a whole different world. He was obviously crazy about her. After dinner he took her to his friend's office, where he cleaned and polished her teeth.

He didn't, as it turned out, even want to sleep with her right away. She was going to be his one act of rebellion, a Christian, even though she hardly thought of herself as one.

He worked on her mouth for a year. It turned out there was much more wrong with her than bad implants in front. She needed root canal work, bridges – there was a lot of disease and getting the two front ones knocked out had wrecked the whole system. Once a month he came to Boston, usually managing to fit in a conference or convention, or something so that he could take a tax deduction. Sometimes it was just to see her. That was always the basic reason why he came. He had a friend with a practice who let him use his office. She spent hours on her back in the chair. How could anyone be interested in someone after peering into their foul cavern, a mouth lined with stubs of teeth and metal spikes? But if anything he was wilder about her. The whole time, bent over her, he would mutter, almost unconsciously, involuntarily, 'God, you're hot . . . you look tough . . . oh, this is going to be great.'

It was maybe on the third visit that she understood that he was serious, that his behavior wasn't a ploy. So she gave him a blow job, though she still wouldn't go all the way. Usually all a man had to do was look at her for her to take off her pants. But oddly not all that many men had shown much interest. She was maybe . . . too slutty, or too voluptuously scary. If she had been blonde, things might have been different. But she was also . . . desperate, she was needy; men had always sensed that about her and panicked. With Barry it was different. He was the one who was needy. Because of that, perhaps, she couldn't really give a damn. It was nothing to her. It was a thank you, getting him into the chair and unzipping his fly, putting his penis in her mouth. Plus, her mouth was so numb from Novocain she didn't have to deal with the taste of his come. And he was so sweet afterwards, so grateful, covering her face with butterfly kisses. It was the first time she didn't feel used.

She never sat around waiting for him to call. She didn't have to: he called her once a day, from Chicago, sometimes more. If she went out at night, when she got home her mother always said, 'Barry called. He wants you to call him back, collect, he said you should call however late.' All she could think was, what is wrong with this guy? And then she would call him back and she knew he was desperate to find out where she had been, if she was seeing other men. But he also didn't want to know. And so he would talk, trying to keep her on the phone. 'See, being a dentist – a cosmetic dentist – it's like being an artist, you're basically – it's the human face. And, my father, I know he's made tons of money – I swear to God, I don't know how's he's done it, good investments at the right time – but I've watched how hard he's worked to make his way up from an accountant. It has to be the most boring thing. When I was growing up I never saw him, the guy must have put in twenty hours a day at work. I'd go visit him, his office was some hole, a dark closet, I thought, God, I'd go nuts! I'm more of a people person, and, what I do, I'm really good at. I have all kinds of ideas, stuff that hasn't been done before.'

His soft voice, late at night, earnest, slightly nasal, was convincing, soothing. When she was sure her mother was asleep she would talk dirty. 'You know what I'd like right now? If you were next to me and I had your big, stiff cock in my hands.'

'What do you want, we should get married, right?' he said when her mouth was nearly done. 'But don't answer me yet, I'm gonna do it correctly, and propose – you'll see. The only problem is my parents, they expect me to marry a nice Jewish girl, but I can't help it. I know they'll get used to the idea – they'll have to.'

Why did *she* have to be his one rebellious act? She knew she could not assuage his parents. She was not a good enough actress. They didn't know what the young American girls of today – Jewish or not – were up to: that they shot heroin; snorted coke; made bets in which the loser (or winner) gang-banged seven guys in the checkroom; had lesbian affairs. Girls today – from any background – got themselves rich old boyfriends they drugged, nightly, in Sardinia, while on holidays paid for by the old guy, so they could sneak off with German playboys.

Girls today went to live in Goa with a French philosophy student or Indian cabdriver; ran credit-card scams; bought anal plugs and sex toys to try out in pairs and groups of three.

Later in life they would pretend these things never happened – or regale their girlfriends, but never tell the kids. Nobody – rich or poor – was exempt. This had been going on since the sixties. Across the board, except, maybe, for a few Mormon girls in Utah, who wore floral, ruffled dresses and fluffy hair-dos, white leatherette shoes.

But she was the one who looked bad; she looked like a naughty, naughty girl. It took her a year to realize that even if she had been Jewish, Grace still wouldn't have approved. She knew whenever Grace looked at her she saw a tramp, lacking values, culture, morality. And no matter what the other girls were up to, it was only a temporary phase they were going through. She really was bad – whatever that meant. There still had to be bad and good, didn't there? Surely, even if standards of behavior had changed, there was still that other.

And the night before her wedding, showering in the bathroom off Belinda's bedroom, she emerged soft and steamy and, wiping away the condensation from the mirror, saw the hands of the clock reflected, ticking, jerking, backwards, only noiselessly – a place where time went the opposite way. And she thought if it were possible to enter that realm, the minutes would shed, smooth and sharp as fishscales, glittering on a pier where only the opposite could happen.

There was a bottle of perfume, expensive, a heavy pyramid of crystal beside the sink. She thought she would try it out; in her nervousness it slipped from her grasp and dropped to the floor where it shattered into three triangular, splintery pieces and a thick, oily stench of musk, bergamot, greasy flowers. The shards, the spears, gleamed perfectly on the tiled floor. Spikes of melted sand that she wished she could see in the mirror. Maybe then she would know her backward self. This was something she shouldn't have perceived; but still, it didn't make sense, she wasn't different from anyone else she knew, but Grace was right, there was something inside her that was bad, rotten. As her mother had always told her, she was a slut.

7

The next morning there was a knock on the door. 'Come back later,' she shouted, thinking it was housekeeping. But the knocking didn't stop and finally she went to the door still in her robe. Xian Rong stood in the hall.

'May I come in?' he said. 'About last night – I'm sorry.'

'No, no, I'm sorry. I had no right to try to force you. Don't worry, we can just be friends.'

Then it seemed, because she had said that, he was all over her.

Maybe it wasn't even an hour that he stayed with her. Maybe it was an hour, or two; she napped briefly. When she awoke, for a few seconds she couldn't see him and she panicked: what if he had walked off with her passport, her credit cards, her cash? But he hadn't gone, he was just looking out the window.

Her skin was sticky, a newborn with the vernix only half wiped off. It was the halfness that was confusing, she couldn't tell whether the part where the waxy coating had been worn away was the part that felt raw and new, or if it was the skin protected by the candle grease that was clogged. No one on earth remembered that infantile entry, the first time, emerging out of the gelatinous liquid of the womb into the harsh, too-thin air.

Whatever had happened had not been just sex. She had prided herself on believing sex was nothing more than two body parts rubbing together, that, when successful, caused a muscular contraction. Now she saw there was something else that could occur, something to do not with the body, or even with minds connecting, but something that could only be described as spiritual.

All along she had screwed to get laid – or, in the case of Barry, to get a husband – and now she knew she had spent a lifetime eating thin gruel. Every time it occurred, she was tearing her own web, a spider entangling itself. But every time it was something she had to do. Had to. Wanted to.

There was something else out there, between two people. But the thought was too much to endure. Surely she was just imagining it. It was ridiculous. The room was cold, too cold. She would have been less cold if she was dead. She covered herself with a sheet and turned over; the white pillowcase was smeared with grapey lipstick. She was shaking.

Once there were Ten Commandments. She knew this from the movies – she had never gone to Sunday school, had never read the Bible, but she knew that once there had been Ten Commandments, edicts that no longer made sense.

In ancient times a movie star – Ingrid Bergman? Bergmar? – had got pregnant by some man who was married – or maybe she was married and got pregnant by somebody else – and they threw her out of the country and said she was a bad, evil woman. And now movie stars and half the girls she had gone to high school with had babies out of wedlock and no one thought a thing about it.

As for not coveting thy neighbor's possessions – was that how it went? – that was absurd, otherwise they wouldn't have had television ads and department stores and magazines, so that if your neighbor went out and bought a new Lexus or Mercedes then you would want one and eventually you would get one – because otherwise there would be no peace within.

Thou shalt not steal? If you were rich enough you could get away with it. Do a fake audit, sell the junk bonds, put money in offshore banks.

Even if you weren't rich, the trick was not to get caught. Once she had had a friend – she couldn't even remember her name now, one of those terrible French names – Monique, Suzanne, Yvette – that always made her think of some small provincial town in French Canada where the women all had three kids by age twenty and by thirty, flyblown, had lost their teeth. This friend – Dominique, that was it – got a coat through a credit-card scam – she charged the coat, expensive, on her card and then called the credit card company claiming her card had been stolen and she hadn't made that purchase. She kept the coat and never paid for it. Later Dominique landed a fantastically wealthy billionaire by having his baby. He was a married guy, and was obliged to support her . . .

But Dominique never walked around brooding about her lousy credit-card scam. Now she would either deny it or be pleased that she had pulled off a con.

And it went on that way, through all ten. Silly old sayings. The only one left that even had the slightest bit of power left to it – thou shalt not kill – even for that one, if the murderer was a man, and famous, a sports figure, or rich – he would not be punished and could easily walk away. A dozen or thousand or million women would be lined up waiting for him.

The family of the victim would feel bad for a while but after they got a settlement and time passed, slowly they would forget who the deceased was. A person with some good points and a lot of bad.

The only difference between anybody else who broke a commandment and her was that she felt guilty and ashamed all the time; everyone else did not, or was able to pretend – maybe it wasn't even pretend, maybe they could just erase the tape – that it was no big deal or had never happened at all.

Celebration! From room service Peyton ordered up the kookiest drinks on the menu, things that might have been for a kid's birthday party, and by the time Xian Rong emerged from the bathroom the drinks had arrived on a wheeled cart, each a different color capped with an elaborate frilly flower or paper bird. Even the sight of these didn't keep her afloat, she felt herself sinking; after he left she knew there would be nothing, no lifesaver, to keep her bobbing on top of the waves.

Oh, the crumbs from pink *petits fours* on porcelain, ostrich feather fans, wigs, the white peruke and pale doeskin gloves lined with talcum powder. You could go down a hole, the planet was one giant slice of Swiss cheese: flat, riddled, you could be strolling along on seemingly solid ground and then suddenly – empty space. Down some holes – most – lay black depression. You could pull yourself, using all your strength, up out of one of these, only to topple immediately into the next. One hole in a hundred, or a thousand, contained chaos, madness, thrills, excitement, adventure. What the hell had happened to her? Normally once she had screwed a guy she was only too happy to get them out the door, or to get away. Now this time she was totally smitten, it was horrible.

And it wasn't even all that late in the day. Lunchtime? Afternoon? She handed Xian Rong a green drink and picked one for herself. Vodka with pineapple juice and fresh pineapple – taut yellow chunks. A miniature paper flamingo protruded on a pick, all ruffled wings and teetering legs. The last brass ring on the last carousel ride of the season; she would have been foolish not to grab it.

'So you are in Hong Kong for a week, that is a shame,' he said. 'I must leave in several days, I am mostly in Milan.'

'What, uh, what's your business?'

'Well, import-export. But I would rather hear about you.' The truth was, really, she had nothing to say; or maybe this was something she had learned, not to talk about herself. She got Xian Rong to tell her – in broken English, which now sounded so charming – about how he had been two years old when he was smuggled out of China in a boat with his grandfather, who then raised him in Hong Kong. Once his family in China had been very wealthy. They had managed to get enough money out of China before everything was gone so that for the first few years things had not been too bad. Then his grandfather had died, and the money was finished. Xian Rong lived on the streets in the roughest way imaginable. His family in China were all dead, he wouldn't have even known who or what to look for; he had had no contact with anyone since he was ten.

She could not connect with his life. A red fox, dressed in natty

76

clothes, was telling her in a soothing voice, *climb onto my shoulders, little gingerbread girl, and I'll carry you across the water*. Another fairy tale; but who could resist the fox with his laughing black lips, white ruff, that bushy ginger tail?

'I am afraid, as I mentioned, I am busy this evening so I can't stay with you,' he said. 'But I would love to see you again, while you – and I – are here. Would you be free for dinner tomorrow? I will like to take you to a very special place . . .'

'Well, sure!' she said. 'That sounds fun!' Why did she sound so teenage? How she despised herself. She hoped that to him she merely sounded American. He put on his clothes. She had thought, initially, that he was very young – maybe twenty-eight or thirty – but now she saw he was nearing his perishable date, a supermarket product with fine lines beginning to appear, a sour skin, there were bags under his eyes, maybe he was closer to her age than she had thought. She wanted to ask him his age, but she didn't dare: he might want to know hers. 'Bye-bye!' she said falsely.

'Listen, I tell you what: will you mind if I return this evening, late, after my business?'

She put her face down on the pillow. 'Okay,' she said. 'Yes. Would you. Please.'

'Good. Go back to sleep then. I will see you later.'

When she woke up again she was terrified. She knew that if she really knew who he was, he would be an ordinary human being, a person, a man, but it was impossible to believe this emotionally. Intellectually she could say she lusted after him because he was imaginary. But while he had been there it was real. She hadn't been scared. He had gone, while she was asleep; had he ever been here? Or was it some kind of stupid dream?

Before the self-hatred could take over completely she grabbed her bathing suit and found her way to the pool. It was a bit after eleven at night. The pool was open late, thank goodness. Swimming was the only time when she could forget who she was. Pulling on her sleek tanksuit she could, for a moment, revel in her smooth body, top heavy, those two breasts luminous as water balloons, her tiny feet . . . such endless miles of creamy skin; how could she not be pleased with herself? She was alive but with an animal's aliveness, an unthinking entity. Though there were only two or three others in the pool they – male or female – stopped in mid-stroke to stare at her before remembering it wasn't polite.

At the deep end she did a shallow dive. There was that physical smash, the body leaving its position in the molecules of air and entering the molecules of liquid, far denser, thicker, with the slight moment of pain; a knife yanked from a drawer that now had to cut through butter. She adjusted her goggles and began her glide – the breaststroke, the crawl, the backstroke – from one end of the pool to the other. What was the use in any of this?

To have this one period of happiness only made the other times worse. There was no way to live one's entire life in a Zen, meditative state. And in a way, small half-hour or hour one-mile stretches of peace only made things worse for her the rest of the time. Normally such a swim would have washed away any jet lag. But, as if she had to be punished for accidentally meeting – picking up, she had to be honest – some guy in a bar, she could not stop thinking about Barry.

She had been married for more than twenty years and she might as well have married an eggplant, or a root tuber. There was nothing to qualify him as a person, nothing at all. Most women her age would have been content to sit on the sidelines at some grand fête or ball, discussing the young people, assisting in making marriages. Or, if they were the workers, women her age would be grandmothers, mending clothes, shelling peas, relegated to the edges of human existence. How were they able to stand it?

Peyton still believed the right time would come along: she would meet the right man and finally be freed from her mediocre existence. Now, women were still having babies at her age, climbing Mount Everest, riding a motorcycle; there were women older than she writing essays about waiting for the knight to ride up on his white horse and carry them off to give them a spanking – essays published in reputable

78

places. Only the author left out the part that came after 'and they lived happily ever after'. The part where, after galloping off on the horse (unless she had to run along behind) he took of his clothes, revealing a stumpy red penis and she either gave the prince a blow job or else removed her chastity belt, beneath which lay a large, pink, hairy, wet vulva, and then he stuck his dick in and said, 'Listen, I've got to get back to my knight business, it's very important. While I'm gone, could you run the castle?' and she was left with the dirty chastity belt and his smelly suit of armor that needed to be cleaned. And six weeks later she would either start getting morning sickness or else cramps, bleed all over the place and where do you find sanitary napkins in a castle?

Maybe what was holding her back was that she continued to go on staying with the same man, trying to live life like other, undemanding people. And now, over and over, she found herself replaying images of Barry in her head: Barry slumped on the couch in front of the TV, drinking orange soda, his doggy face attentively focused on some sporting event; Barry, bustling in his office in a white doctor's coat, telling her he wasn't going to be able to have lunch today after all, that things had gotten 'backed up'. Barry in a restaurant, trying to act knowledgeable about some wine list when he would have been better off admitting he knew nothing and asking the sommelier. Standing with him in some elevator while he laughed – his laugh a loud, peculiar honk – while others waiting with them winced.

You could hardly say that these flashing scenes revealed someone evil, just that . . . it was pathetic, if that was all there was to represent his various character traits. How could he stand it, being so non-existent?

Finally she gave up and climbed out of the pool. Maybe it was all the drinks, or the difference in time zones, or her body still complaining about having been trapped on an airplane for eighteen hours. She grabbed a couple of towels from a stack by the wall and headed back upstairs.

At least now her body was so tired it was able to win out – punishing, conquering by superior strength – over her mind. If she hadn't seen Xian Rong again she probably would have gone down to the lobby bar, started drinking, talked to strangers – strange men – hoping to decimate any thought or memory of him. But before she could even find the blower to get her hair dry she lay down on the bed and within seconds was asleep.

The streets around her hotel were closed to traffic and filled with a hundred thousand Filipino maids, all chattering in the hushed bird sounds of Tagalog, syrupy chirruping that did not sound human. Everyone in Hong Kong had one of these maids, who were paid virtually nothing and worked nearly twenty-four hours a day, six or six and a half days a week.

They had brought with them picnic lunches and guitars and blankets, which they spread on the sidewalks; they were a million sparrows who had taken over, chirping and snuggling, dusting themselves in the sun with soft flutters. What weird fate had placed her in the hotel, married to a dentist, financially sound, a nearly grown son who was not a drug addict; and she herself slim-hipped with large breasts and silky black hair, and a career – of sorts – that provided her with freedom? Everything, on paper, was perfect.

Only, inside was a gnawing animal, the sexual beast, who mostly dozed but who, on waking, would roar into a frenzy, chewing off its own leg to get out of the trap. And the trap was she.

She walked for miles, aimless, knowing if she stayed in the hotel she would just be waiting for Xian Rong. Even though he had said he would come over later, she would still be sitting there growing more annoyed, hating herself for waiting, sure he wasn't going to turn up. Like some high-school adolescent.

She couldn't be in love, that simply wasn't possible, not after having slept with him once, a lanky street tough with languorous eyes, who was probably fifteen years younger than she. He was a good lay, that was all. There couldn't be more to it than that.

It wasn't fair: she was getting old and soon no man would ever want to sleep with her – apart, perhaps, from Barry, but he didn't count.

Meanwhile all the men her age would continue to be as desirable as ever.

If she died Barry would be captured and remarried within a week; if something happened to him, she would never find another man out there who wanted her for the long term.

The air was heavy with its own tropical, fungal weight. She had no idea where she was. Now being lost was the most pleasant sensation in the world. Finally she jumped on the subway. It was very clean, with huge tiled passageways. She waited on a platform staring at electronic advertising on a giant television screen while an automated woman's voice said in Cantonese, and then in English, that the next train was due in three minutes.

It was all so civilized that she was surprised, when the train came, that her car was so packed she didn't think she would find a seat. At the last second, however, someone got up and she half slid, half flung herself into the spot, relieved to sit down and pleased to have beaten the locals.

After a time a dismembered hand appeared near her face. The hand was huge, a man's hand, fat and white, the nails manicured and the back covered with sparse black hairs; a gold and diamond ring cut into the curd of the third finger. A voice crept into her head and the voice wondered what it would be like to sleep with that hand. It was the most obscene hand she thought she had ever seen, spoiled but powerful; it might have been the hand of a chief eunuch in the Imperial palace, or a Turkish pasha with an insatiable appetite . . .

She shut her eyes. She did not want to see the owner of that hand and all she wanted to do was to get away from the hand. She knew she was being ridiculous, but if the hand touched her tits she would be powerless to stop it. So she was unchanged; this made her happy – soon Xian Rong would disappear completely from her memory. But she was still shaking. When the train stopped she struggled to her feet and shoved her way out.

She emerged onto a street of inexpensive shops. Everything in the stores was gaudy, bright, covered with glitter, stores filled with cheap clothes embroidered with butterflies or studded with mirrors. Adolescents filled the sidewalks, sullen teens, girls with pink pigtails and frilly skirts walking in ridiculous platform shoes, circus clowns' feet, or anti-geishas – tiny dolls one might knock over and watch pop back up – boys with pompadour hair-dos, or old-fashioned Chinese queues, punk-rocker attire. Everything shockingly bright and colorful; tiny noodle shops jammed with people, and the kids drinking from futuristic bubble cups in pink and green and blue, filled with chemical glop, liquid candy. Nobody seemed rich but nobody seemed angry either. She was safe and at ease, invisible.

There was a sort of shopping mall, she got into the elevator with a group of others and, arriving at the top on the fifth floor, began to go from floor to floor, looking in the window of each shop before making her way down to the next flight. She didn't understand quite what was happening. The clothes here were not gaudy but appeared to be ordinary – American style or American blue jeans, tube-tops, long skirts with flares – and the endless hordes of young who circled here were not the same as those on the streets. They were obviously searching for very specific items that they considered the height of fashion but which, as far as she could tell, she would not have recognized as such at all.

Bewildering: she might have arrived on another planet with rules and standards that were similar to those she had known on earth, yet subtly, bafflingly different. Not one of these young guys took a second look at her.

Once sex had been available whenever she wanted it; all she would have had to do was snap her fingers. Naturally she had no use for it then. When had she stopped being the youngest, looking up at a world inhabited by ancient adults, and become one of the ancients looking out into a sea of youth?

This obsession would be over by tonight. But the pounding in her skull continued, the narrow throb of the blows from a ball-peen hammer, and if she didn't see him again she would die. She wouldn't leave Hong Kong until she found him.

Billions of people on the planet, millions swirling around her, and every single one of them woke in the morning, urinated, defecated, ate

breakfast, married, divorced, fought, raised children, were children –
infinite, complicated, sorrowful lives, rich and complex – and each
had the same idea that he or she was the center of the universe. It was
impossible, on some level, not to believe this. And here she was
staggering over the anthill, one of the crazies. Only, in her own head,
she was worse than all the rest.

The sky grew dark and it began to rain, huge sweaty drops.
Everyone apart from her was equipped with umbrellas. The street
blossomed into a field of birds that unfurled their colored wings but
did not take flight. She darted into a nearby building, another one of
those strange towers that appeared from the outside to be offices but
indoors was all shops.

The first floor was quite decrepit, peeling walls, cast-iron exposed
pipes; she followed some others into a tiny, antique elevator with a
folding accordion door and mahogany paneled walls. She got out at
the top floor. Each of the shops was astonishingly beautiful; one sold
ropes of pearls coiled in glass vitrines, astronomical prices; another
had lingerie of the most exquisite quality, with bits of real lace,
embroidered; another place made hand-crafted shoes from antique
lasts, of soft kidskin in soft colors with endless rows of buttons. It was
like a dream of how people, rich people, had once lived.

At the far back of this floor was a teashop, Japanese, displaying tiny
turreted cakes, pink and blue, and frothy confectionery drinks. Within
were Japanese women in perfect, simple robes and gowns – they could
have been Buddhist nuns – so sleek and elegant that they too appeared
to be expensive statuary or exquisite aliens who had landed on this
contaminated planet. She would be a bawling heifer in such a shop.
She was thirsty, and hungry, but she couldn't – dared not – go in.

Outside the rain still dripped but the crowds were filling the streets
and sidewalks and it was beginning to get dark. A million neon lights
went on overhead, huge shabby signs strung from one side of the
street to the other, so low a car or bus might crash into one, more
lively than anything found in Las Vegas.

She pushed her way into a sort of juice bar and managed to grab a
seat at the counter. The place was hot and open to the street, damp

steam rising up from the ground. She thought she had ordered a watermelon juice but when her drink arrived it was full of pearly gray balls, far too sweet but not undrinkable until she felt something between her teeth that was not one of the tapioca beads but a bit chewier and she plucked it off her tongue and spit it onto a napkin. A cockroach had fallen in her drink.

She told herself it was just a bug, she wasn't going to die, but she couldn't help but wonder how many times, over the years, there had been things in her drinks that she had paid no attention to, globs merely swallowed. She pushed the drink away and staggered out of the place. For the rest of her life she was going to have to remember the chewiness of the roach, the crunch of shell and the mushy contents within, and think of the taste of tapioca.

All she had left to cheer herself up was the thought that a man she had a crush on would be coming to see her tonight. If he even turned up; there was some law of the universe that dictated that, because she wanted to see him, he would sense it and not turn up at all.

There was a message waiting for her back at the hotel. He would probably be by at around eleven. It was only a bit after six but already she knew he wasn't going to show up, that she would dress and sit and wait for his call that he was downstairs in the hotel and she should meet him there, a call that would never come. Or worse, it would and she would go down knowing this meant he didn't want to sleep with her again, because if he did he would have come straight up. If he didn't call her, didn't come, she knew she would start obsessing. But on the other hand if he did show up, what then? Probably she would see him differently and wonder how she had got herself stuck with some low-life idiot and what she had seen in him that she wanted to screw would have disappeared.

At least there were a few hours left in which everything could be clear, straightforward: the one linear sensation, that of waiting for him to come. If only things might have gone backwards, starting out in old age, only with a child's mind; by the time one reached forty one's body would be that of a fifty-year-old, mentally you'd be sixty when your body was thirty, seventy with a twenty-year-old body, eighty with a ten-year-old body, by ninety you'd be an infant, about to die, senile but so cuddly and cute all the young people would want you, look after you – no fear of being dumped in some nursing home. Wouldn't that all make more sense?

The way life was set up was too cruel: at twenty who knew how fleeting the whole business was going to be? One thought one would go on forever in this fashion.

She ordered a bottle of champagne from room service and ran a hot bath. Her feet were a mess from spending the day walking. She should have found somewhere for a pedicure. She took off her clothes, not bothering to pull the curtains. On the twenty-fourth floor, the buildings on the other side were offices, mostly shut for the weekend, only a few lights on. But even if someone did see her, so what? She stretched out on the bed for a moment, touching her sore nipples, trying not to think.

8

She didn't know if she had never been interested in Barry or was losing interest in him. Anyway, the dental work was finished. Half of her expected, really, that this was the end of the episode, even though he kept calling her.

Perhaps Barry sensed she was slithering away from him. Unexpectedly he came in from Chicago. Over dinner, at a fancy Chinese restaurant in a mall, he got down on his knees. A group of waiters and busboys gathered around, grinning.

'Aaah –' he said and abruptly broke out in his sweet honk of nervous laughter. A golf-course goose, she thought.

'Peyton, you know, I . . . God, this is stupid.'

'What?'

'Peyton. Would you . . . will you marry me?'

She pictured the two of them waddling at the edge of a weedy lake. The dentist and the travel agent, wing in wing. Barry Goose nibbling the grass with orange beak. It was not going to be a swan life, then, but still a step up from duck-land. And when she said 'Yes' the other diners, the waiters, the hostess dressed in a Chinese dress, all applauded. Someone sent a bottle of champagne to their table. Barry had a ring – it had belonged to his great-grandmother – in a midnight-blue velvet box; it was too big for her but he said he would have it sized.

She couldn't help but feel relieved. He really did care for her after all. She had been certain no man would ever like her enough to want to marry her once he got to know her. What else did she have to offer apart from her looks, which wouldn't be there forever? She had no money, had accomplished nothing.

Yet at the same time she was disappointed; the familiarity of the scene, the same as those shown on TV, made it impersonal. How could she ever care for a man who wanted her for life, what kind of an idiot could he be?

'Yes, Barry,' she said. 'Yes, I will marry you.' When she got cold – or nervous – her cheeks turned pink, her mouth drooped at the corners, a ruby pout.

'Great. I'm very happy.' She could hear the relief in his voice at not having been rejected. But his voice was so dry and casual she knew it was a huge effort for him to have asked. He was finally agreeing to her demands when in fact she had never raised the issue. Or maybe he felt that none of this was happening to him, either. She was sorry for him; the poor guy, what a thing to have to go through. It would have been much better if women did the proposing. Women were better organized, had more imagination and were tough enough to handle the idiocy of the situation. Women could handle rejection if it came. Women were used to being rejected.

Besides, women knew it was never as strong an emotion to get what you wanted as it was not to get it.

After that she called her mother, who said, 'Oh, I'm so happy for you, you finally found some dope too stupid to know any better, ha ha, just kidding!' and then, for the first time in eight months, she called her father who said he had put money in a bank account years ago, for her wedding, that would now probably be about two thousand dollars. She didn't know whether to laugh or cry; she couldn't believe her father had even been aware enough of her existence to picture her getting married someday, let alone to save money for her.

'I'm going to call my folks.'

'Do you want me to leave?'

'What? No, no. Why would you leave?'

'In case they're mad that you're marrying me.'

'They won't be mad. They'll be happy for me.' He picked up the phone. Even across the room she could hear Grace's response.

'Oh Barry, are you sure you want to get married so soon after finishing your studies?' Barry flinched. 'Who is this girl anyway? What do you know about her?'

'I've told you, Mom. I'll tell you again: she's just great. She's a travel agent; she comes from a very good old Boston family; her mom's a little loopy, one of those dog-show types, but I'm not marrying her mother. I've been seeing her for quite some time, and, it's like you said: when you meet the right person, you know.'

In a matter of seconds, Peyton thought, Grace was going to start muttering about the fact that she wasn't Jewish. She knew if she were to go to Barry's side, rub his shoulders, put her hand on his, he would have more courage, would not need to sound so defensive. But this, in a way, was cheating. This was something he had to do alone. She got up and went to the bathroom.

The bathroom had a full-length mirrored door, which had been left open and as she went in it began to blow closed so that in a parallel universe an opposite self, the other Peyton, was entering a room that was rapidly receding. 'Come back!' she wanted to call. But whether her howls were addressed to her mirror-twin or the room on the other side of the mirror was uncertain.

'Can you come out to my folks', for Thanksgiving? Is that cool?' Barry said after he hung up. 'You could take a train.'

She couldn't resist asking him if his parents were pleased about the news.

'I know they'll feel . . . differently when they get to know you a bit better – that's why I want you to spend time with them over Thanksgiving . . .'

'Differently?'

'Oh, I know my dad is already crazy about you, he thinks you're great just from what I've told them, it's just that . . . my mother, well, you know, she worries – that's what mothers do, right?'

Still, she could not quite get herself to believe in Barry's existence. Somewhere a mistake had been made. It was the other Peyton whom he was meant for. How come he didn't know?

'Hey, sexy princess-bride! You want to go get a hot-fudge sundae over in Harvard Square? We have to celebrate, right?'

She would have rather gone to a bar and gotten drunk but she had already finished most of the champagne at dinner – Barry had barely touched his – and she knew he wouldn't have approved. Anyway, he hated bars.

She took the train to Penn Station and then, per the directions, the Long Island railroad, where they met her at the station. She had wanted to look nice for the first meeting and wore black spike-heeled shoes, fishnet stockings, a chubby red fake-fur coat; when she stepped onto the platform in the dreary early winter of Long Island, she knew her outfit had been a mistake. Barry was in blue jeans and a seventies-style leather jacket; he waved at her from the far end of the platform. 'Hey, sexy princess!'

Seeing him next to his parents, his mother Grace's frosty smile, she felt shy, embarrassed. They embraced nervously though Barry, almost defiantly, kissed her on the mouth, stealthily inserting the tip of his tongue. Leonard, his father, was a small man with pale fish eyes behind oversized plastic glasses; the sort of person who might have been cloned by the millions: his brethren populated the American streets, disguised as bank vice presidents, insurance agents, store managers, optometrists who owned franchises in shopping malls. Grace was tall with a sort of sheared, sprayed hairstyle frozen in place, from a period in fashion's history known only to nice ladies from Long Island.

It was a short trip from the station, which was passed in querying her about her train trip and discussing where she was to sleep – in the room with Barry's sister, Belinda, so they could become friends – and the different dishes that were to be served on Thanksgiving Day. Belinda was a vegetarian, so there would be a tofu turkey in addition to the usual mashed potatoes, sweet potatoes with marsh-mallow, Brussels sprouts, sliced string beans with white fingernails of slivered almonds – all relayed to her by Grace, who seemed to think Peyton might have come from another country, perhaps an emerging nation so obscure that none of these dishes had ever been heard of before. 'And Leonard, you'll be in charge of picking up

Mary – that's Barry's grandmother – from the home tomorrow, and Arthur is coming as well.' She turned to Peyton. 'Arthur's my mother's boyfriend – of course, they don't have sex –' Grace laughed nervously.

Peyton couldn't help herself. 'Oh? Why is that?'

'Of course it's charming that my mother has a friend; but, at their ages . . .'

The driveway was heated and though it had snowed lightly there was no ice on the asphalt. In the center a brownish lump was huddled and Leonard, Barry's father, honked the horn.

'It's that dog again,' said Grace. 'The poor thing – the neighbors don't keep him tied up half the time, one of these days he's going to get run over.' The dog awoke and bounded to the side of the car happily, clawing the door.

'Goddamn it, get down!' said Leonard. 'Every time he's scrat*ching* the paint.'

She got out of the car without waiting for Barry or Leonard to open the door, then realized, too late, with Grace sitting regally in the front, that she had already lost points. She bent to hug the big smelly dog, the neighbor's, who immediately shredded her tights; as he reared up she could see the animal was emaciated. Grace shrieked and said, 'Pluto, stop that, go home!'

'Oh no, it's fine – I love dogs! Who's a big silly baby boy?' She had left her own dog, Flea, a three-legged rescued chihuahua with her mother for the weekend, but she was worried about him; her mother was more and more absent-minded. The bloodhounds had been shipped to a breeder in Texas but Peyton knew when she got home there would be piss and dog crap everywhere from her chihuahua; she would be lucky if her mother remembered to put out fresh water, let alone feed and walk him. Her dog was all she had. Her dog never told her that she was stupid. Her dog never went on a binge, or had manic highs – except with joy at seeing her.

'Poor dog,' she said. 'How can they do that, let him run around? Not feed him?'

'This has gone on for years,' said Grace.

'Do you have any pets?'

'Pets?' said Grace. 'No, I really don't care for animals, I can't deal with the dirt, and Leonard is allergic, though I know Barry wished we had a dog when he was little, didn't you Barry? But I did let him have the iguana.'

'Yeah, Uncle Igor,' said Barry. 'He got to be three and a half feet long. Come on. I'll show you around.'

She was shocked that Barry's parents lived in such a huge house. It wasn't as huge as the one her mother had once taken her past to show her where she had grown up; this one was new, not modern, but vast, a swollen New England Victorian, turned into a Disneyland mockery of quaintness and charm. It occupied a small landscaped lot; on either side, quite close, were other huge houses.

They crossed the front porch. It was the kind of porch that was supposed to have a view – of mountains, or the sea – but this porch looked out only across the street, at another house. Peyton had always studied pictures of fancy houses in magazines, but she had never actually been inside one. What struck her was that here there were real drapes with boxy valances at the top, the kind that stuck out into the room and were covered with the same fabric as the curtains. She knew these people had a ton of money, to have drapes with those ruched matching things above.

'Oh, wow,' said Peyton. 'Your home is so beautiful.'

'Thank you!' said Grace. 'Would you like me to give you a little tour?' At home, years ago, her mother had tried to install plastic fake-bamboo blinds but neither of them had been able to screw the fittings in properly and forever after they hung neither up nor down, crooked. It was the small details, she saw now, that showed whether or not people were rich. There were no wires sticking out of the walls, no peeling paint. There were Persian rugs, not badly fitted remnants of wall-to-wall carpeting. The chair and loveseat in chintz, the sofa in contrasting complementary stripes of rich burgundy and blue, gray and yellow. That six-foot-tall porcelain palm tree – how did that occur? How did rich people get these things? She had never seen a white and gold palm tree in a store. What was the dividing line between a rich person's house and a real one where normal people lived with dirty handprints on kitchen cabinet doors and bleak, dumpy rooms, bald windows, crooked blinds?

'I took a training course as a decorator,' Grace said. 'Of course, when we built this house, years ago, I hadn't completed my studies, so I worked with a decorator – now, I have my own business and there are things I'd do differently –'

'It's beautiful,' Peyton sighed. 'It's so . . . clean.'

'Over here we have the family room, I wanted that area to be a bit more masculine and I found these club chairs in a showroom –'

'Wow. Look at the TV, it's huge! Oo, and everything's so organized, and you have a pool table –'

'A cover turns it into a ping-pong table. Now, over here we have the gym and if you want to take a sauna, it takes about a half-hour to get the room heated up. The jacuzzi isn't working just now, and the repairman said he can't make it until next week, so –'

'You could really get lost here! What a great house!'

'I'm actually thinking of redoing the place, it needs freshening up and I have new ideas –'

'But . . . it's so perfect! And besides, where would you put the old things?'

She had no idea that people got rid of old furniture and got new things. In her own family, Donny or Nell drunkenly smashed up stuff and it was no good and had to be dragged to the curb for the garbage. Or some dealer came in to give them a couple of bucks for junk when it was time to move; or once again bills couldn't be met and the TV set and the sofa got repossessed.

'Come on, Ma, you'll show her later. Let me show you upstairs, Peyton. Let's go.' Barry took her by the arm, away from his mother.

They went up by elevator to his bedroom on the third floor. His mother had left it unchanged since he went to college. Bunk beds covered with spreads of red and blue baseball caps and colored balls; there was a slide and climbing ropes, a computer station, a television area with seats – leather, in the shape of catchers' mitts. A rich boy's merchandise, too much, taken for granted.

She had spent a lifetime hiking around the base of a mountain and had arrived, quite without warning, at the top. To her it represented the epitome of wealth, class, taste, style; there was no way she could have known the Ambergs were just another American family spending vast quantities of money they did not necessarily have.

They had been in his room less than half a minute when Barry unzipped his fly to show her his erection; thirty seconds later there was a knock on the door.

'What are you two doing in there?' said Grace in an alarmed tone.

'I was showing her my room.'

'Do you mind if I come in?' The door was not even fully shut but Grace apparently assumed they were having hot sex. My God, they were both in their twenties, did she really think they had to be supervised? 'Peyton, I have a lot of clothes that I was going to give to a charity shop, and I was thinking . . . maybe you would like to go through them and see if there's anything you want, before I give them away? Some things I barely wore and . . .'

'Sure!' she said eagerly.

'Oh, good. I hoped my question wouldn't offend you. Let me borrow Peyton then, Barry.'

'You didn't offend me! I shop in thrift stores all the time –'

'Well, you know what I mean, I didn't want to make you feel that . . .' She looked at Peyton with a pinched expression. 'You have your own ideas, I can see, about style, but maybe you could take some of my pieces for times when you want to look a bit more . . . fashionable . . .'

She thought at that moment that Grace was the fussiest, dreariest person she had ever met. What was it to her, that her future daughter-in-law wore spike high heels and fishnet tights? The bags of clothes contained drab, demure outfits, Long Island lady outfits, tailored suits in periwinkle, long flowered skirts, chubby sweaters appliquéd with roses, everything a nice person would wear.

'Doesn't your daughter Belinda want these things?' she said. The items were scarcely worn and obviously expensive; she had never owned this kind of clothing. It was clothing for people who were good and kind and honest. You could look at the clothes and know the person wearing them was wholesome.

'Oh, I buy Belinda so many things she never wears. It will be nice for Barry to see you in nice things, don't you think?'

But if Barry had wanted a nice girl, surely he wouldn't have chosen her, in her seedy fox-fur piece that she had once been so proud to have found in a thrift store and her pointy-toed boots, a Viva Las Vegas minx.

A sporting event blared from the TV set in the family room; Leonard and Barry were propped in front with a plate of carrot sticks, soft drinks, pretzel sticks.

'Yaaaay!' Barry shouted. 'Did you see that? Did you see that?'

'Holy moly,' said Leonard. 'Quiet, quiet – we gotta watch the replay.'

Belinda was out with some of her friends. The housekeeper had gone shopping. Peyton now possessed a chenille sweater, decorated with two felt frogs. She rubbed it against her face. She was not the sort of person to wear a sweater with appliquéd frogs – but maybe she could become one. 'Can I help in the kitchen?' she asked. Grace had taken cooking classes and considered herself a gourmet cook; she was preparing some complicated dish involving chicken breasts that had to be pounded flat and then breaded and fried before being stuffed with cream cheese.

'If you want to wash the lettuce, you can dry it in the spinner and then do the salad.' They were a perfectly lovely, happy family. Peyton could tell she was making the salad all wrong. 'Do you think maybe it would be better if you cut the cherry tomatoes into quarters?' Grace smiled a strained smile from the other side of the room. 'And there's a jar of artichoke hearts, in the cupboard to your left.' She wasn't going to be able to go through with this. Peyton knew, understood, that there was something flawed in her, that she would never be able to conform to the world that made up Grace's existence.

She went to Belinda's room to freshen up.

She couldn't believe there were girls who had grown up in such splendor. Mostly she had slept on a piece of foam, on the floor – they had lived in one place with beds, real ones, but they turned out to be infested with bugs. Here there were twin beds, canopied, white with gold, mounded with velvet pillows in shimmering hues; a glass vanity with mirrored drawers, a make-up light, a private bathroom.

There was a bookshelf with a few coffee-table-sized photo books on their sides – evidently Barry's sister was not much of a reader – and stuffed animals of every kind, bear, walrus, kangaroo, giraffe, tidy and desirable as the contents of a toy store. Her own television, and video, stacks of videos nearby; a computer and stereo system – Belinda must have had a magical childhood. Clean sheets, unfrayed towels, breakfasts of bright, crisp rolls. Tennis lessons, sleep-away camps. All the things that piled up so that when one reached adulthood one would always feel at ease.

Attempting to leave, by accident Peyton opened the door to the closet, which was full to the brim with frocks, gowns, shoes jammed into cubbyholes, hats, tennis rackets, riding equipment – perhaps when Belinda arrived she would teach her how to play tennis, how to ride, to play golf. How to be a cheerleader, how to do well in school exams. How to do all the normal things that normal people did who didn't grow up in a house filled with dog shit and stumbling smokers who left beer cans stacked in pyramid piles.

Photographs in silver frames – she imagined Belinda to be poised, serious, elegant, though it was a bit difficult to grasp what sort of personality she had – showed a large, somewhat bulky girl in khaki pants and a blue polo shirt. There she was in front of St Peter's Basilica, there she was with a group in front of a façade that might have been Angkor Wat, and again at the Wailing Wall. Belinda, age twelve, and her buddies at camp, under the banner that read 'Kamp Ko-Ko-Ko-Shire Summer 1964'.

His mother thought it would be good for the two girls – 'young women' – to get to know each other. That way Peyton wouldn't feel so alone, either. She and Barry would not be allowed to sleep together in Grace's house until they were married – and maybe not even then.

Peyton wanted more than anything to go back home. But she knew Barry would have been hurt; he had just arrived from Chicago, his parents wanted him to stay with them, and he wanted to show her where he had grown up. In the morning they would go to the house of one of his friends – his friend's parents' – also home for Thanksgiving. That afternoon there would be the family dinner; maybe they would meet other friends of his at a restaurant on Friday. Then, brunch in New York City before she took the train back home.

She wasn't going to be able to endure it. Barry was standing in the doorway. 'I don't think I can deal with this,' she said. 'What about . . . why don't I go home and come back tomorrow afternoon in time for dinner?' she said.

'But that's just crazy. You can't do that. You won't get home until late and then you'd have to get up at dawn to come all the way back out here, silly princess. Are you feeling a bit lost? But my parents love you! I can tell!'

After dinner Barry asked his father to lend him his car. 'Where are you going to go?' Grace asked. 'I don't know,' he said. 'Maybe to the movies, maybe just drive around, go to a bar and see if any of my old high-school buddies are there.'

'Be careful, don't drink and drive – don't you want to take Belinda?'

'Ma! I haven't seen Peyton in weeks, I want some time alone with her.' His lip trembled.

Grace looked pleased at having stirred Barry into a sullen response.

As soon as they were in the car he took her hand and put it on his penis. 'I'm going crazy, Peyton. What am I going to do, are you going to come up to my room later?'

'How can I do that, with your sister in the room and everyone in the house right up there? Your mother made it totally clear she doesn't want us sleeping together in the house . . .'

Two blocks away he pulled over. 'What are we going to do? I can't stand it. Feel this.' He pulled her hand to his crotch.

'Oh my God, it's so hard,' she said by rote.

'You got to help me out, Peyton. I go nuts when I see you. I haven't

96

seen you for weeks. I can't sit next to you all night like this, and at home in front of my parents, with a big stiffy.'

The suburban streets were lined with houses built in mock styles so many generations removed from the original that it was impossible to tell what they were trying to represent. Each had a huge picture window in a living room that faced a similar house across the street. The trees were denuded of leaves, stalks plugged into lawns yellowed from frost. The blanched almonds of street lamps illuminated the cubits of rumpled sidewalk, the ribbon of street. Many of the houses had already installed Christmas decorations: twitching reindeer, candy canes, tremulous plastic icicles. The sad husky who lived down the block was tied to an overhead wire that ran between two trees along the side of the house; apparently he was an outdoor dog, unusual in this upscale suburb, and didn't even have a doghouse. In the gloom she could see him curled up in the roots of the tree to keep warm.

Then she felt sorry for Barry and unzipped his fly. It must be awful to have that struggling hot chunk of meat between your legs, out of control – like having to lug a bratty child around all the time who at any minute might start thrashing for treats. His penis, as if unconnected to the rest of his body, found its way through the bruising metal teeth and out the zipper hole. He moaned slightly as her hand grasped the stout capped head.

She only hoped somebody didn't come from one of the houses to inquire what they were doing there, or a cruising police car. But who could or would enjoy giving a blow job? She saw no pleasure in the activity: some guy lying there while she tried to cram a rubbery tube down her throat; sucking away, while once in a while he would twist at her nipple, miming the winding of an alarm clock.

There was nothing erotic about it: a mouthful of stray pubic hairs or the sour taste of warm ejaculate. A pathetic and hateful enterprise that one was expected – required – to do, like mid-term exams in college, or balancing a checkbook, a way to make torture take place year round, so one always had something unpleasant looming on the horizon. Probably the only people who really truly enjoyed such an endeavor were gay men; they must like it. After all they were not obliged, the way women were. For them it was a voluntary activity.

The weather had warmed and it began to drizzle. For a moment she looked up. On the windshield, mouse paw prints were appearing, one by one, followed by the larger treads of an equally invisible cat. It was raining heavily now. His penis rammed the back of her throat as he held on tightly to both sides of her head, pumping up and down.

9

Belinda was a huge girl in her late twenties, much larger – taller – than Peyton had expected. She was huge not in the sense of weight, though she might have weighed a hundred and fifty – she was huge in her manner of occupying space, her brusque, competent movements, the Henry Moore thighs, two haunches of meaty beef. There was nothing girlish about her, though she was wearing a skirt, low heels, a tailored shirt and jacket in twangy shades of pale red. Her earrings were dull gold shells, her nails dull pink shells: a scarab beetle, hardworking, industrious, could not have had a more professional demeanor.

'So, how's it going?' she said, plopping down on one of the twin beds. 'I can't believe my brother's finally getting married. He always had the hots for dark-haired shiksas with big boobs. I hope you don't mind my saying that – it's always been something of a family joke, although my mother would kill me if she heard me saying that to you.'

'They started to grow when I was ten. It was awful, having big breasts at only ten years old. Men were always leering and making remarks. And I was just a kid. I thought half the planet suddenly went insane.'

'That's horrible, I feel sorry for you, it must be so yucky . . . I've always been so happy to be flat-chested. I could never understand women who wanted big breasts to carry around drooping down to their waist by the time they're twenty-five.'

Peyton was going to say, Don't worry, I feel sorry for *you*, being flat-chested, but all she said was, 'Gee, how did we get into this? So . . . um, Barry said you're a casting agent? That must be great.'

'I've just started at this company. I love it. Every two seconds either an agent or an actor sends over a gift. I meet so many people.'

'And do you go out with movie stars?'

'Oh, guys are constantly begging me to go out on dates and some of them actually are famous. But to be honest with you, I have absolutely no use for them: it's not just that actors are basically totally self-absorbed, it's their pathological compulsion for attention and then their bitching when they get it.'

'Who's the most famous actor that's asked you out?'

Belinda named a name. Peyton couldn't believe it was true. 'Oh, I'm so jealous. So, what was he like?'

'Oh, I never went out with him. He was sending me flowers every day for weeks – months. It got to be embarrassing. I have a perfectly nice boyfriend, anyway. He's a lawyer, he works for his father's company, corporate law. But . . . you're an agent, too, right?'

'Well, a travel agent.' She was still mulling over having a famous actor send flowers on a daily basis and turning him down. 'Not quite the same thing!'

'Gosh, I wish I could take a trip someplace. I can't believe I choose to spend all day with neurotic actors. So, how did you meet Barry? Things are pretty serious between you two, right?'

'Yes . . . I mean, it looks like we're going to . . . do it.'

'I know, my mom said. It looks like you're getting married! Are you excited?'

'I always wanted a wedding, it still doesn't seem real . . . it's as close as I'll ever come to being a movie star!'

'How you're going to stand my brother, I don't know. I'm just kidding, really – my brother is great. But you two seem, like, totally different.'

'He loves me,' Peyton said simply. She didn't know, exactly, how to add that – apart from her looks, her tits – she had nothing and had come from nothing and would never be anything. She knew it was wrong to think a man was going to take care of her, but married women, at least, were not looked upon as desperate – not the way single women were.

'And do you love him?' Belinda asked.

'I love him – as much as I'm able,' she said. 'I'm not even sure I know what love is.'

They drank hot chocolate and brushed their teeth. Belinda was 'religious': being vegetarian made keeping kosher easy and though, according to Belinda her family wasn't very religious – that meant they only went to temple on Saturday mornings and unlike her friends she hadn't gone to a private Hebrew school – she had been bat mitzvah and gone on a number of Hadassah youth trips to Israel.

Peyton tossed and turned after they had turned out the lights. It was amazing to her that there were women who wore tidy suits and would choose a corporate lawyer over a movie star. Women who were calm, placid and did not believe that eons ago a vulture had settled on their heads so that they were doomed to spend a lifetime being weighed down by curved claws, about to be slashed by a beak.

Finally she drifted off to sleep. But in the middle of the night she woke to the sound of Belinda, in the other twin bed, crying softly. 'Belinda?' Peyton said. 'Are you okay?'

The sobbing continued. 'You want me to sleep in your bed?'

'Okay . . .' Belinda was so big, Peyton thought, such a competent giantess, it was odd that she cried, soon her bed would be mushy with tears. It might have been a fairy tale, the crying giantess. It was too sad even to contemplate. Almost involuntarily she crept into bed along-side her and put her arms around her. She wasn't sure she wanted to know what was wrong, only she thought just by holding her Belinda might feel better. She found herself stroking Belinda's hair and one of her hands slid around Belinda's waist and began to caress her soft stomach. Belinda's muffled sobbing had stopped but now she stiffened and, pushing Peyton's hand away, let out a shout. 'What is wrong with you? You are one sick chick!'

There was nothing to be done, she climbed back into her own bed. She didn't want to say, Belinda I was never attracted to you, I just felt sorry for you! 'Please don't tell anyone,' she said at last.

'You can bet on that,' came the bitter reply. After that it took Peyton ages to fall asleep.

'You should have borrowed something of Belinda's to wear!' said Grace in the morning when Peyton came down dressed in an off-the-shoulder calypso outfit.

'Oh I couldn't do that, not without asking –'

'She went out jogging. I told her, when you get home, let's go through your stuff and give some of it to Peyton. She never wears the things I buy her anyway. You're shorter than Belinda but a bit slimmer; after breakfast we'll go and see what will fit you.'

'But . . . are you sure she won't mind? Shouldn't we wait to ask her?'

'She's got so much stuff – she won't even notice!'

Peyton was accustomed to preparing her own breakfast – toaster cakes with artificial strawberry filling, iced donuts out of a box, instant coffee. Here there was a maid, milking the cappuccino machine, offering fresh squeezed orange juice, displaying a cabinet full of cereals, bright hued boxes of low-calorie enriched flakes, muesli. On the table, a crock of butter, a basket of bagels and wholegrain breads – 'Or maybe you just want a poached egg, or pancakes?' Grace said.

'Oh, no, cereal will be just fine.'

'Agnes, make Peyton some pancakes. Agnes is only here for the morning, she has her own family coming for Thanksgiving dinner – and she won't be here tomorrow, either, so it'll be back to cereal for us. Eat her pancakes while you have the chance – real buttermilk.'

'No, no thank you.' Peyton looked nervously around. It was beyond terrifying, to stay in someone else's house; she could not peel off that top layer that would allow her to relax. Around Grace she never would. 'Oh, bananas!' she said feebly, as if she had never or only rarely seen one.

'You want a banana?'

'Okay, sure!'

'Well, you're going to have to just go ahead and help yourself, I don't know what you like. Well, I got all these things for Belinda, I know what she likes, and there's more than enough for you. Did you say you wanted some cereal? Which sort?'

'Um, the crunchy barley looks good?'

'Why don't you have the whole-corn puffs? Anyway, I thought you'd like to have a day or two to settle in, have a look around the city, and then . . . well, I don't know how well-off you are, pretty well, I should imagine, coming from your family . . . you'll want to do some shopping – how about a haircut? I'll see if I can get you an appointment –'

'I don't really want a haircut, but if Belinda had some clothes she was getting rid of, that would be great.'

'Well, we can take you to see the clothes, and I know you'll be happier if something is done with your hair . . . and then, what do you think your plans will be?'

'I really don't know, go back to my job.'

'But surely you don't need to work; we'll have so much to do planning the wedding – why don't you stay on here, that way we can look at houses for Barry to move to after he's finished his residency, and –'

'I do need to work!' She giggled nervously. 'And besides – my mother's not well . . . I guess maybe Barry told you, I'm kind of taking care of her.'

'Yes, he mentioned . . . isn't there some hospital you can put her in?'

Her future mother-in-law was a handsome woman, at least by Peyton's standards, with a taut, expressionless face that managed to project at the same time a vague malaise. Grace had short hair, heavily coiffed, which only emphasized her mannish features. Leonard, on the other hand, was on the more girlish side, with sympathetic, brown, vaguely froggy eyes. Perhaps this was why their marriage was such a success: on some scale of male-to-female, each had selected a position midway.

In Belinda's room Grace threw open the closet, yanked at drawers, tossed things in Peyton's direction – there were things with the price tags on them, obviously never worn, perhaps never tried on, cashmere twin sets in the softest, palest beige, floral-print skirts, plaid blouses, all good quality but . . . so collegiate. Preppy penny-loafers. Maybe Belinda had been switched at birth and now Grace was going to have a daughter-in-law who would be obedient, a lady, demure.

Imagine having the money to buy shimmery tulle skirts in brilliant candy stripes, gold lamé jackets and velvet frock coats, to own smocked shirts with tipsy lace sleeves in shades of iridescent purple and orange – and instead to purchase the most innocuous, *lady-like* things! But now she would belong to this family, a rich family: maybe it was time to change. 'Oh, ah, I don't think any of these things will fit me but, uh . . . gosh, I guess I'd look a lot different, if I wore stuff like this. I . . . could try. Though of course . . . Barry always says he likes the way I look.'

Grace blinked, displaying a snarky flicker of disapproval. 'Of course we could have them altered – but I don't know if they can adjust the bustline. Maybe you're right and we should wait to see what things Belinda doesn't want; you can do your own shopping, later in the week.'

Crestfallen and slightly ashamed of her own giddiness, she returned the clothes to their hangers. 'Such beautiful things,' she said. 'But anyway, if there's somewhere – a discount place – to get some fabric, I can sew –'

'But my dear, you must have so much money, you and your mother living so frugally for all these years, surely you're fantastically well-off –'

'No, we had no money.'

'But. Your family name . . . Cheadle . . . you're not from the Boston Cheadles?'

She shrugged. 'No . . . my dad's Estonian, he changed his name from Chedokumo, something like that – my mother's such a snob, she was the one who told him to do it! It didn't even make any sense, first she deliberately picks a guy knowing she'll be disowned, and then she makes him change his name to a rich one! Because she was a Tole, you see, like the saying goes, "The Toles own the money but the Cheadles own the banks." And that saying was only true, like, a hundred years ago. Actually I think my grandfather on my mother's side was kind of rich – once my mother showed me the house where she grew up – they turned it into a bunch of condos or something. But Barry . . . wow, he really must have given you the wrong idea.'

Grace's face had stretched into a tight smile: 'I'm going now to pick up my mother, Barry and Belinda's grandmother, at the nursing home; she and her – her boyfriend, though of course, at their age it's really just a *friendship* – are coming for Thanksgiving dinner. In the meantime I know Barry wants to show you all his old childhood haunts – just make sure you're both back by say, two o'clock.'

Barry had a friend named Neal who had grown up around the corner and worked on Wall Street. The neighborhood was quiet; it was Thanksgiving Day – bald trees, a gray sky. The houses were big enough to hold twenty residents, the people had money, but how staggeringly bland it must have been to grow up here, a realm of white people, summer camps, no real worries except trading in the old Volvo for a new one.

Neal's parents' house was much smaller than that of Barry's; this family was stouter, less ostentatious, and Neal was in a family room watching TV – his hair was shaggy, he wore aviator glasses and he corroborated her impression that the early 1970s had yet to leave Long Island. 'Hey, dude, how's it going?'

'What's happening, man? I want you to meet Peyton, man. Peyton, Neal's gonna be my best man.'

'Hey, lucky you, dude!' Neal slapped Barry on the back. 'I'm like, real happy for you, man, even happier that it's happening to you and not me. No offense intended,' he addressed Peyton, 'but, I'm, like, having too much fun playing the field. These city chicks are wild, ya know what I'm saying?'

'Ah, you're the same old dipstick. He's making up for lost time,' Barry explained. 'His zits were so bad in high school he was known as Pizza Face.'

She tried to smile sweetly but inside she was cringing: *dude, man, like, zits* – it was appalling to find people who really talked this way. Irene, Neal's plump mother, scurried in, over-attentive, placing bowls of olives, carrot sticks, potato chips, staring at Peyton too earnestly while asking, 'Can I get you something, some soda, Diet Coke? Or juice? I know you're going to be having a big meal in a while –'

'Thanks, I'm fine –' She knew that later Irene and Grace would probably discuss her – her trashy rock and roll appearance, her big boobs, too-bright lipstick – at length. But even if she hadn't been wearing these clothes, this make-up, there was something about her that caused everyone – but particularly mothers – to look at her suspiciously.

Neal and Barry reminisced by talking in bad, fake English accents. 'So, mate, how's it going? You're looking as grotty as ever!'

'You're a bit pongy yourself – as the actress said to the bishop!'

Simultaneously playing imaginary guitars, they launched into ancient rock hits, lyrics that went, '*Hello hello, I'm the submarine man, meatloaf, peppers blam blam blam,*' and '*No-no-no-no more Nostradamus!*', as they leapt around the room. She had never paid all that much attention to pop music. Their singing, their jerking motions seemed expressly showing off for her benefit, but she couldn't help but feel that what was happening between them was far more intimate than any male-with-female intercourse.

They walked home in the chilly air. 'Neal really liked you, sexy princess!' Barry said.

'How do you know?'

'Huh? I could tell.'

He might as well have said an alligator was fond of her, or a pigeon.

By the time they returned Barry's grandmother had arrived.

Mary was in her nineties and wore a pink acrylic sweater with pearl buttons, a blue flowered skirt and large white track shoes – she was in a wheelchair, smiling beatifically, absently.

'She's so lovely!' Peyton whispered to Barry. 'But I didn't know Jewish people could be named Mary.'

'Huh?' Barry looked puzzled. 'Why?'

'I don't know. I guess I just thought . . . that was a Christian name.'

'Peyton, would you put the kettle on for us, thank you,' Grace said.

'Mother's said she'll have a cup of tea.' As she left the room Grace was saying, 'All her clothes were on backwards and I had to change her. I don't know what they do at that place, but I'm going to complain next week.'

Mary's boyfriend, Arthur, wore a plaid cap and a stained blue suit-jacket and after she returned he insisted on giving Peyton a wet kiss on the cheek, although she proffered her hand. Why did they have to go and do that, and always such wet, slurpy kisses, even to complete strangers? At this age, Peyton thought, old people were no different than infants; only less lovable, more wrinkled, and it was impossible not to feel they had only themselves to blame. Arthur proudly announced he was a younger man. 'I'm eighty-six, Mary's ninety-three,' he said. 'But I've always gone for older women, isn't that right, Mary?'

'What's that?'

'You're older than me!'

'I'm sorry?'

'You're old, Mary!' Unexpectedly a shrill, high-pitched scream, an alarm, began to resound from her head. 'Mary! Fix your hearing aid!'

'Maybe you can adjust my hearing aid, Barry darling. I brought new batteries with me.'

'Granny,' Barry said. He took off his grandmother's hearing aid and fiddled with it before putting it back in her ear. 'I want you to meet my fiancée.'

'Oh yes, darling, Grace has told me.' The grandmother smiled apologetically in Peyton's direction. 'You'll have to excuse me, dear, I'm a little confused these days. I think it's wonderful. Will you marry in our temple here?'

'No, Bubby,' said Barry. 'Peyton's not Jewish.'

'What's that?'

'Mom didn't tell you?'

'I didn't think – I didn't think she needed to know, Barry!' Grace said.

Barry shook his head disgustedly. 'I said, Bubby, she's not a Jew!'

'No, dear, I don't want any juice. Thank you.'

'A Jew! A Jew! She's not a Jew!'

'Barry, that's enough,' said Leonard, calling from the other room. 'The whole neigh*bor*hood can hear.'

Sometimes Peyton had to admit that she had anti-Semitic thoughts about Barry: oh the cheap Jew. But what was she going to do about them? They hung there, unspoken, in the air; or they were the voices of her mother and brother, or even her father, from a distant childhood when she believed (though she had never received anything much in the way of religious education) that the Jews had killed Christ.

'Bubby!' Barry took his grandmother's hand and leaned over toward her ear. 'She's a Christian.'

'Oh my God,' said Mary. 'I had no idea.'

Peyton felt obliged to contribute, to aid Barry. 'I'm not much of a Christian, Mary. Anyway, wasn't Jesus Jewish?'

The family appeared uninterested, though Belinda was bent over the piano in the corner, her shoulders heaving, and emitting tiny squeaks, a giantess crammed into a baby grand. 'I'm sorry, Granny,' said Barry. 'But I love her.'

'This would kill your grandfather.'

'Well, then, thank God that's he's already dead.'

'What's that?' said Mary.

'Mom, he's upsetting Bubby,' said Belinda petulantly. 'Is it really necessary?

'That's enough, Barry!' said Grace. There was a pause and the room was silent apart from Belinda who made a triumphant wheezing sound. If she sneezed, Peyton thought, the whole place would topple over.

'You see, you always take her side,' said Barry. He was indignant. 'Granny doesn't need to be sheltered from the truth, she's tough enough to handle it.'

'You come from five thousand years of Jews marrying Jews. When I think of what Bubby has been through – no one expected you to be Orthodox, Barry, but there are other alternatives to marrying some-one not of your own faith. But obviously none of this has any value to you. And what about you, Peyton, don't you think you'd be happier with someone of your own . . . kind?'

I don't even want to get married, she wanted to say, *I just wanted to have a wedding!* But fortunately Arthur interrupted. 'So, you believe in all that stuff – about the virgin birth?' he asked her.

'The virgin birth?' For a moment she thought he was implying she was pregnant.

'Let's face it, the man comes home after how many years and Mary's pregnant.'

'What's that?' said Mary.

'I'm not talking about you, Mary. I'm talking about the other one, the one who kept telling her son he was the Messiah. What's she going to say to her husband? That Joseph believed her – this man was not so bright, right? A stupid Jew. Not a good beginning.'

For a moment they all stared at Peyton suspiciously, waiting for a response.

'Come on,' Grace said at last. 'Leonard, turn off the TV! We're going to eat!'

On Sunday Barry's parents drove them from Long Island to a restaurant in the lobby of an expensive hotel on Madison Avenue for brunch. Belinda refused to join them. Leonard was always very jolly, a soft new boiled potato with round eyes, but Grace – though Peyton knew she was trying to be kind – had the bright glittering expression of a praying mantis, a knack for producing sentences or statements that had the same effect as needles on her skin.

'So, to reiterate once again: we're very excited and happy for you both,' Grace announced grimly. She was dressed in a pinstripe suit, low heels, sheer black stockings, while Peyton, thinking it was casual, had put on blue jeans embedded with glitter and rhinestones and a tight sweater. Now in the restaurant with its muted lighting and women diners in red suits with padded shoulders, she saw she was dressed all wrong and her big breasts in her bubblegum-colored sweater made her look like a prostitute or porn star.

'You know, Grace *and* I have always been so happy. In all these years we might have spent one *night* apart. I hope the two of you should be so happy. The only advice I would *tell* you, is never go to sleep angry with one another. Is it easy? No. You will have your ups and downs. But when it *is* most down it will go up again; when initial passion fades, trust and strength –'

'Okay, Pops,' Barry said. 'You're making it sound really bleak.'

Leonard looked hurt.

'I like to hear this stuff,' Peyton said.

Grace wore a patterned scarf tied at the throat and large dangling earrings that probably contained real stones. She toyed with her scrambled eggs from which bits of pink smoked salmon protruded, fleshy fingertips in yellow fat. 'One thing, of course, we wanted to bring up, were your feelings on religion.' There was a pause. 'You may have your own strong religious beliefs, and we can respect that. But the Jewish religion . . . we wonder how you would feel about making sure our grandchildren – and I'm sure you'll be blessed – are given a Jewish education, which Leonard and I would like to pay for or at least contribute to.'

Religion. It had nothing to do with her, and, from what she had seen, had no importance for Barry either. She was speechless.

'You needn't answer now, but it's something to think about. This is such a joyous time for you both. And, Peyton, we want to know about all of your plans for the wedding and . . .' Here Grace hesitated and Peyton knew she had practiced what she was going to say, at least in her head. 'Forgive me if I keep repeating: I'd love to help, you know I've been planning a wedding for Belinda for years and this would be a wonderful trial run since your own mother . . . can't help!'

Grace looked to Leonard for approval. His eyes, gentle behind his glasses, blinked, almost about to cry. 'Whatever you kids have *in* mind, we'd love to be a part.'

'I . . . don't know,' Peyton said. She looked at Barry. His plate was blanketed with spongy brown pancakes, a mound of fluffy butter in the center edged with curly strips of bacon. All the food looked unreal. 'I mean, I've never had a wedding before!' The three of them laughed as if she had said something funny. She had the sensation of leather straps being tightened around her arms and legs.

'You've never had *a* wedding before!' said Leonard. This was a grand jury inquisition.

'But was it a childhood fantasy of yours?' said Grace. 'I remember when I was a girl . . . but of course, young women of today may not have that as a dream. Though I read recently . . .'

'I think, probably, it would just be something small,' Peyton said. 'My family . . . you know, my parents are divorced, I don't know if my sisters would come – they live so far away and we're not close – and my brother . . . I know he's not going to come . . . also isn't it the bride's family who's supposed to pay? Because . . .' They might as well learn this now, what the hell did she have to be ashamed of? 'My mother doesn't have any money, I don't have any savings and my dad said . . . he'd give me two thousand bucks.'

Grace flinched and then attempted to regain control of her emotions, or to put on a brave face now that she had heard what she must have believed to be the worst. 'Of course we know so little about you, Peyton, but I know if my son loves you, you must be a warm and intelligent person.' Her expression indicated her son had selected a highly contagious leper to be his bride. 'It's going to be wonderful to get to learn all about you and love you as our daughter. Leonard and I were talking last night, and if you want to have a small wedding we don't want to interfere, but I was saying to Leonard we would love to hold a big reception for you and I hope you kids would let us do this, even if it's not according to the norm; Barry is our only son and I always had hoped for a big celebration, something to remember!'

By the time the brunch was over Peyton had agreed the unborn children would receive a Jewish education and she herself would think, possibly, about converting to Judaism, or at least taking some lessons. Grace would go to a fancy hotel later in the week to try and get an appointment with the wedding planners on the staff. 'My friend Corinne says there's somebody good there, who did the wedding for her friend's daughter. I want to make this easy for you, though you'll have to give me your list, for your guests, not that I expect you plan to have many. Oh, I'm going to be so busy for the next six months, unless you were thinking of waiting for a year?'

'Grace – these are young *people*, they're not going to wait *a* year!' Leonard blinked his eyelids apologetically, the signal for everyone to chuckle. 'We have to con*sider* ourselves fortunate that they're even willing to have a wedding, especially *be*fore they've had children.'

Grace's smile was thin. The very idea was obviously so appalling she could scarcely pretend this was humorous. Where had Grace and Leonard been, during the 1960s and the years that followed? How was it they were able to go on pretending it was still the middle of the fifties? Had Grace only read nice books, seen nice movies, belonged to a garden club, shopped at Saks, taken resort vacations – and spent her life working hard to maintain a status-quo of blinkered blandness?

'I've always dreamed of a really fantastic wedding,' Peyton said shyly. She wondered what would happen if she had suddenly told them about her past sexual experiences – which, though not numerous, were bleak. Or the various kinds of drugs she had tried, courtesy of her brother. Or how it really was, never to have eaten in restaurants, to get beaten up in the girls' toilet in junior high because of being so hungry you stole a candy bar from someone else's locker.

Grace would have found a way of simply not registering any of it. Perhaps she too had once been wild, in some distant, five-minute youth. In any event, she probably thought Peyton would soon 'settle down' and stop wearing high-heeled shoes.

Peyton could already see, with the announcement of their engagement, a swarm of bees descending. She was not to be the queen but an ordinary drone, one of a crowd. And for the first time, she realized that no matter how successful Barry might become, he was always going to be just a dentist.

10

A room. A fancy room. Clean cold sheets, smudged with wine, lipstick, the soot of mascara. Hands two claws at her sides. Where was she? She remembered now, she was an adult, though she would never feel adult. Sometimes she looked around her own apartment and thought, this is a grown-up's place, what am I doing here? The others looked like adults, she looked like an adult, but inside her was an eighteen-year-old, incompetent, trying to balance a checkbook like some homework assignment.

She must have fallen asleep. It was the jet lag, that and the two glasses of white wine she had ordered up from room service. She shouldn't have had the wine, it had given her a colossal hangover and she was in that paralyzed state that occurred on an almost daily basis; her hands were frozen, her legs were tightly crossed, she knew she was awake but couldn't move.

It might have been some form of narcolepsy, or something akin to those patients with sleeping sickness who sat for a lifetime in wheelchairs, neither dead nor alive. It was the most peculiar condition, it made her nervous because it took longer and longer to snap out of it. On the other hand if she could have relaxed it might have been enjoyable, this sort of heavy, custardy fog of immobility. Finally she looked at the clock. It was after eight; in a panic, now motivated, the clock springs had unwound inside her, she leapt out of bed.

A printed sheet had been slipped under her door, 'Typhoon Warning'. There was no imminent danger, the notice proclaimed, but it was possible that in the next day or so there would be typhoon conditions of as much as 8 on the 1–8 scale, in which case guests were advised to remain in their hotel room, well away from the windows, and not be alarmed at any minor swaying in the building. It was best not to go out on to the streets at that time. It sounded so thrilling, Typhoon Warning. If only she had been born a century ago and been able to come here when junks still plied the harbor and a hotel was only a few stories tall, a woman then could really have had adventures. There would only have been Asian prostitutes and she, a white woman, a bad girl, could have found an opium den or a man who became obsessed with her in an era when women did not freely have sex. Now she was just one of a hundred million bored women, looking to get laid, no better than your average man of the 1950s.

Black lace. She saw herself in black lace, she put on the black lace dress with the low-cut neck, encrusted with glittering carapaces, she had patent leather stilettos with diamonds at the back and thigh-high stockings, garter belt, annoying panties, thong style, that rode between her buttocks. She wasn't dressing to screw him or get screwed, only because it made her feel attractive, erotic, a married woman alone in Hong Kong in black lace, elbow-length gloves. She couldn't help but sneer at herself, she was such a cliché.

On the other hand, she had to find her fun where she could. Was she supposed to curl up and die, just because she was married, because she was past the nubile, pursued, gazelle years? In the book the old ladies – old! forty, fifty, the thirty-two-year-old spinster! – sat in the corner, out of the sexual marketplace. They kept the old ladies – forty – out of the movies, no matter how big a star they were when young. Why should she excuse herself, knowing her age, when it was only now that she was old enough to start having some fun?

The second glass of wine, unfinished, was still on her room service tray and she threw some half-melted ice cubes from the ice bucket into it and sipped. She didn't wash her face but put on mascara, powder, pale lipstick on top of what was already there. Under her eyes the skin was swollen but she thought it gave her that debauched, sexy look. She was set, and it was still only quarter to nine.

There was part of a *China Sun* and she grabbed it but it turned out to be the business section, too difficult to read, so she just looked out the window, which faced the harbor and the Kowloon side. The water had grown choppy, bilious; a Star ferry was just pulling out and beginning to chug, illuminated with mosquito-sized lights, across to the other side.

He was waiting in the lobby, sleek suit, the thin hips of an Apache dancer. Her younger self, twenty, untraveled, uneducated, would have been scared witless and decided he was dangerous, out of her league. He might have been a trafficker in white slavery, shipping dipsy girls to a sultan, head of a heroin conglomeration, or an arms dealer. Probably in some previous incarnation he had been a warlord, with a Chinese *huang tang* full of quarreling concubines and a blond horse with furious black eyes and blood-red nostrils. How could she not grin when she saw him? He was infinitely sexy, with a slightly crooked smile, and eyes that glittered as if there was some ridiculous joke no one else knew about. His gaze slid across her with an expression that managed to combine adoration, appreciation and lust.

Since she didn't know him she could make up whatever she wanted to about him.

She extended her hand. The way he held it for a moment, a thin-skinned fruit, before pulling her forward to kiss her on both cheeks, made her nervous; she looked down.

There was no use in feeling shy, she thought, she was too old now to get mileage out of being shy. 'So where are we going?' she said, a bit loudly.

'It's a surprise I have planned,' he said. 'Where we will go, it will be a one-, one-and-a-half-hour journey.'

'Okay' she said. 'Can we just stop and have a quick drink first?'

The bar here was of gold and pink blistered glass, mirrors, wall-to-wall carpeting patterned with pink bows, a 1980s Italian chandelier – jagged stalactites of neon-blue crystal. The international pop-whine blared over loudspeakers, the same vibrato girl crooner who sung in France, Brazil, American supermarkets, words indistinguishable yet the same in any language, '*Aiiiiiieee . . . love . . . yeeeew . . .*' and the refrain, '*Broken haararart . . .*', the endless dirge that always made her want to seek out the singer, punch her in the nose and tell her to get on with it, no wonder the guy left her.

All the tables were occupied, the bar itself was two-deep in drinkers. An American girl, standing, belted khaki shorts, pink polo shirt, white track shoes making her appear clubfooted, and her three male comrades in virtually the same outfits, stuffed into numbness by dairy and cereal diets, cheesy bacon burgers. Two were wearing those rough suede sandals, nobody wanted to look at their crusty feet and horny, curling toenails. Pale hairy legs on public display. Midwesterners jammed, clinging to one another, wearing teal and cranberry sweatshirts and matching pants like figgy sacks, staying at the hotel for various conventions or on their cocooned way to places in the world where they could pretend they had never left home. Why did Americans have to dress this way? But the other global representatives weren't much better: two loud Irishmen, glittering with hypertension, marbleized with broken capillaries. A saggy French entourage permeated with the scent of Gauloises, sallow, darting weasels. A wealthy Filipina in ruffled polka-dots, hair pulled back so tightly she appeared skinned.

'Will you have a drink?' he said. He kept looking around, maybe he was worried about the cost. When the drinks came she'd put them on her room.

'I don't know – we're going to be traveling for an hour and a half? I guess I'd like a dry vodka Martini.' The bartender was also Chinese but homely, somehow disapproving. Ignoring Xian Rong, he took the orders of every Caucasian up and down the bar. Once she and Xian Rong would have been considered a 'mixed' couple, maybe not even allowed in here. Surely that wasn't why he was having trouble getting service. But at last Xian Rong obtained her drink.

It made her nervous to drink with someone who wasn't having anything. But at this stage there was no other way she was going to get through any time with him. The double whammy, jet lag and infatuation, made it too difficult without alcohol.

116

The Martini was icy cold and went down beautifully, the clear oily stuff slipping straight into her veins. Instantly the room lost its corners, gained a French polish, a waxed patina of soft, deep alcohol.

She could have had another. But they went, by taxi, to a modern pier, steel and concrete, similar to an airport, where he bought two tickets for Macao, first class. There was an empty waiting room for first-class passengers, plastic seats in military rows. She had traveled around the world to end up in what was essentially a bus station in New Jersey.

At last the announcement came to board the boat, and they found seats in front. The boat idled for a time, engines roaring, and then louder, furious. When the boat was farther from the shore it picked up speed, whirring along, a dull knife over boiled gray beef.

The seats were in long rows of five, a gap and then another five; next to her was a woman whose mobile phone kept ringing; each time she answered it with an incredibly seductive yet annoying, 'Wei . . .' that sounded almost French in its nasality, more like 'Oui . . .'

'Macao is where people go to gamble and for affairs,' he said. 'I thought we could just have dinner.'

Through the windows were visible peculiar islands, so evocative they could have been the backdrop for a bad movie, a war film with elements of James Bond and an Asian love story. The waitress brought around wilted sandwiches in plastic cartons and a brownish drink in a cup with a picture of small, artificial-looking fruits. The sea in darkness was choppy. Out of the water rose mountains the shape of sideways-toppled blimps, crashing through the charcoal blue. A deranged flea hitching a ride on a dog's back, the boat jerked through the waves.

She had thought Macao would be narrow alleys scented with sewage and incense, red lanterns, dusty shops stuffed with opium pipes and amber beads, but instead, at least by the waterfront, it was a bleak cement highway, massive modern hotels; there was nothing special about the place. The black straps of her heels cut into her feet; she had to hobble along beside him wondering how far he expected her to walk. To take her an hour and a half to some dull spot – all he had had to do was find a place near her hotel for them to eat and she would have invited him back up to fuck.

'We might eat at this hotel – it is new and reputed to be very good – before going to the casinos or the old part of town, as you wish.'

'Whatever.' It occurred to her that people with foreign accents made her tired. It put her off speaking altogether, there was always that sense that they weren't following what she was saying, maybe it was the difference of expression. Even if they understood totally she always wanted to start speaking in a fake foreign accent, as if this would help them to understand. Now she was going to have to endure this weird, formal date with some guy in a shiny suit who wanted to take her to dinner in a hotel and show her around Macao like a tourist. Her fun was smashed before she could even sniff it.

He led her past a large neon sign advertising 'Casino'; just beyond was the ferocious hotel, more glass and bricks, a granite floor, the sort of place she might have come to with her husband on one of his dentistry conference weekends, which were often in locations that sounded exotic but were in fact just another convention center. The place might have been any other place; and here she might have been simply one half of a couple, like so many others, in hotel oblivion.

But when she caught a glimpse of herself on one of the mirrored columns in the lobby she saw instead a crazed slut, hobbling on pinioned heels, shrouded in heaps of black Spanish lace, while alongside strutted a swaggering youth who at any moment might flash a knife from beneath his sleeve.

It was the weekend, crowded, apparently, with the wealthy Hong Kong citizens who wanted to get out of town – families, sleek Chinese women in the muted beiges of designer clothes, blunt-nosed bags in beige canvas, gold necklaces and mabé pearl earrings, husbands in sporting clothes, glossy children, stuffed intestines with zany red cheeks and stout legs. Xian Rong led her through the hordes to the restaurant, outside in a sort of courtyard near the pool. She could just as easily have been in Las Vegas, the grind of the air-conditioning system, the smell of grilling food, chlorine, the sewagey salt air swollen with dust. There was that peculiar imbalance of ions before a storm.

With his Chinese-inflected English she couldn't quite follow what he was saying – something about an alternative underground literary magazine in Beijing, trouble with the government, before Hong Kong was given back. How old was he, anyway? She was restless, frightened. There was no sign of the waitress. 'Will you excuse me?' she said.

In the lavatory, paper towel napkins were stacked tidily on shining granite beside the tap. It appeared there was no running water. Everything was off. For a moment she thought she would just bolt and catch a boat back to Hong Kong, let him realize she had left, but it was too cruel, needlessly cruel. She could tell him she wasn't feeling well and wanted to go home. On her way back to the table she stopped at the bar by the lobby. Only Chinese men were there, sitting on the bar stools, smoking. They stared at her. 'Let me have a vodka on the rocks.'

The stuff wasn't working. It floated on top of the white wine, Martini, the sluggish stomach which had not woken from its nap before being churned on its boat ride. The alcohol would never get through to her veins. There were three businessmen at a table; the handsome one was looking at her appreciatively. Probably his wife was upstairs with the kids. He wasn't as sexy as Xian Rong, but at least she felt slightly restored, to get an admiring glance. There were still other possibilities in the world even though there was only one she wanted.

When she returned to the table, Xian Rong was smoking, nervous, or bored. There was a beer in front of him and a vodka Martini at her place. 'I hope that is what you want,' he said. 'Please, pick what you like.' He gestured to the menu.

'What are you having?'

'I am really not hungry. But you must eat.'

Maybe he never ate. He was an entity that lived on air, or electricity; or he fed off the energy of others. Her foot tapped beneath the table. God, she was nervous. Unless the drink kicked in she couldn't speak. He was obviously no talker. She tried to remind herself she needed nothing from him. She wasn't some character in a movie, aging, broke, desperate to find some man who would give her a place to stay for the night. She had a credit card. She had a cash card. She had a husband at home, a kid who was in college, she had a life – or the approximation of one. She swallowed the vodka and ordered a salad. The menu advertised it as a spinach salad, but when it arrived it was dripping with strange fishy oil, small pine nuts, white, chewy as larvae, and the viridian leaves were topped with overpoached quails' eggs that reeked of sulfur so strong she couldn't eat it. The whole place might have been put together by aliens who had read about the United States or California, and attempted to re-create it but got it all wrong.

The first greasy drops of rain began to fall; huge, hot syrup. The wind picked up. There was no shelter from the sky here on the atrium and the fairy lights wrapped around the palm trees hissed and puffed tiny flowers of steam. The other diners screamed and ran back inside for cover. The area should have been somewhat sheltered but now the wind was so strong it began to blow over the chains, the silverware flew off the tables, the lone waiter at first attempted to scuttle to put things back but retreated. The rain blobbed across the surface of the spinach leaves; Xian Rong grabbed her by the arm and they made a dash for the lobby just as the full downpour began.

She was drenched, shivering inside the air-conditioned lobby and the wet black lace. Beyond the glass windows the sky was now totally black, water poured down. People had run in from everywhere, drenched crowds stood shaking off rain and reeking of lily perfume and cigarette smoke.

In the crush he had disappeared, maybe he had decided to leave, though she didn't really think so. She went back to the bar but the crowd there had grown and with her wet doggy hair, her sodden high heels, she couldn't attract enough attention to signal the bartender. Finally Xian Rong reappeared at her shoulder. 'I was trying to find out about the storm,' he said. 'Apparently it's supposed to go on like this all night and they've canceled the last jet-boat back.'

'What, did you plan this or something?'

'What?'

'Just kidding. What are we going to do? I'm soaking wet and freezing, I'm going to get a room here so I can have a hot bath and dry my things.'

'It . . . is very expensive, are you sure?' he said. 'There are other places . . . I have a little money.'

'No, I'll just put it on my card, I can't deal with going anywhere else!'

And so they spent the night together, floating on a bed atop a skyscraper in Macao, two phosphorescent eels in a black sea. They didn't talk, there was no need to. There was a place human beings could go, she now saw, where the body was only a vehicle for the mind to connect with another.

It was what she had always been waiting for and she would keep it this way, as long as she didn't max out her credit.

11

In the afternoon Barry flew back to Chicago and she took the train home.
It was Sunday night, end of November, in Boston, dark and bleak at five
P.M., the radiator hissed and clanked a bleary tune of old steam.
Normally Sunday afternoon and evening would have ground on endlessly, a stretch of time unrelieved by the ringing of the telephone, a
duration that would be filled by the weekly realization that others in the
city were occupied with friends, boyfriends, husbands, while her life was
permanent isolation in this cell that faced a brick wall and measured
fifteen-by-thirteen feet, with a crazy mother and convict brother.

She could not envisage spending so much money on a dress she
would only wear once. The whole concept of a wedding dress was
ludicrous: a long white gown made of some drab lace, covered with
pale beads, totally useless apart from the one act of trudging down an
aisle, white for virgin which not only was a joke but too shameful and
tawdry to advertise even if true.

She went shopping with her mother. She knew Grace would have
liked to supervise the purchase of this item but since Peyton was
paying for it, out of her own pocket, she couldn't see that it was any of
Grace's business. 'Let's go first to the Salvation Army,' her mother
said. 'Probably plenty of women whose marriages didn't work out
gave their dresses away.'

'But Ma! I want a real wedding dress, not something used, or from
the second-hand store. Why can't we just go to the wedding dress
place that everybody goes to?'

'Don't be so . . . conformist. At least we can have a look, you never
know what you may find!'

The air in the thrift store was stale and on a Saturday the place was crowded with the poorest kind of shoppers, though by their standards the prices in here weren't so cheap. Millions of sweaters hanging on racks, pulled, misshapen, stained or spotted, but some perfectly new and apparently never worn, pink fuzzy acrylic, blue polka-dots, old yellowed cashmere with sequins; hundreds of pairs of blue jeans in every style, spandex blends, bell-bottoms, acid wash, baggy legs; heavy-metal rock T-shirts and rows of dresses with puffed sleeves, padded shoulders, baggy sacks, or narrow tubes – each item had been worn or purchased by a living person.

She was visiting a cemetery of discarded souls and skin. They were supposed to clean the clothing but she knew each item was laden with the cells – saliva, hairs, mucus, dander – of the original occupant. The place filled her with despair as did her mother, who was holding up dolman-sleeved sweatshirts with gold lightning bolts or crushed velvet jackets for her to look at, pleased with her discovery which she assumed to be just Peyton's taste.

In the back was a rack of wedding dresses, wretched entities of polyester white satin, sweetheart necklines, detachable trains – surely none of them had been expensive to begin with – pearl beading made of plastic; she would look buffoonish, traipsing down the aisle, a mockery of good taste. Even these, already used, cost more than a hundred dollars. It was supposed to be a place for poor people to shop. 'This one's not so bad.'

'But it's much too long.' Her mother looked worried. 'I mean, I suppose it would be okay – if that's what you want – but it would take forever to hem it, especially the way I sew.'

'Don't people take these things in? To a tailor or dressmaker?' In the flickering greenish fluorescent light they looked at one another. Her mother's face had small blue pouches under the eyes, her hair a freakish tangle of yellow tinged with metallic copper red.

'Do you know a tailor or dressmaker?'

'No.'

'I suppose . . . there might be somebody who does that at the dry-cleaner. Are you sure, though? A chiffon shirt and a skirt? You don't want to go look at that wedding dress place that's supposed to have discounts?'

'I don't know. I guess! I don't want to wear some hideous kind of thing with idiotic sleeves and beads.' In her head she saw herself as someone sophisticated and sleek, hair pulled back simply, a church festooned with flowers. 'If this is what they cost at the thrift store, I'll never be able to afford an unused dress!'

'Isn't his mother . . . isn't Grace . . . From what you've told me, she's not going to like it. I advise you not to tell her where you purchased it.'

'I'm the one getting married, not her! It doesn't matter anymore, Ma! The one I wanted, in *Bride* magazine, the only one I really wanted, cost ten thousand dollars! Since I can't get that, I might as well wear this stupid thing!' She was having a temper tantrum.

'Don't worry, you shall look beautiful in it. I myself shall sew a train and add embroidered flowers. I took embroidery classes in Back Bay, many years ago, you know.'

'Ma, I know you didn't!'

Stapled to the waistband was a blue cardboard tag. Blue tags were half off today. The wedding gown cost fifty-nine dollars instead of the hundred and eighteen it had originally been marked at.

'I will buy it for you, my darling daughter,' her mother said, and put it on her credit card, along with a hat that appeared to have been fabricated out of rat fur. 'What do you think? Is it me?'

'I don't know. It's . . . it has some bald patches, Ma.'

'It does? Oh, why do you have to say such things? That's its style, it's meant to look that way.'

'Whatever.'

The air outside had grown colder and in the parking lot the puddles of rain and transmission fluid had turned to ice. She held her mother by the elbow as they crossed. Her mother's car was more than fifteen years old and rusted on the sides.

'Can you see if anyone's behind me?' her mother said, peering over her shoulder as she reversed. 'I'm so short, that's the problem, I can't see.'

Peyton was trying to remove the stapled tag from the waistband of her dress when she saw that in a fold of cloth near the zipper there was a huge reddish stain, as if the original bride had been deflowered while still in church. 'Damn,' she said. 'Do you think it will come out?'

'I don't know. We can tell them at the cleaners, they can try. It depends what it is. If it doesn't, maybe we can embroider something over it or, I don't know, pin some flowers. Are you hungry? Do you want to stop and get something to eat? There's a fast-food place ahead. I could use a cup of coffee.' They had given her mother a series of electroshock treatments. It was remarkable, Peyton hadn't thought they still did this, but none of the medications had been working and the doctors had been very reassuring; it did make her mother less irate, but now there was something . . . a bit blurry about her. Maybe it was an improvement, though.

'I'm on a diet.'

'You're too thin! Besides, you need to eat to keep your strength up. It'll give you energy. At least have a cup of coffee and some French fries.'

'Okay.'

Noon on Saturday; they were lucky to get the last space in the lot. Inside, McDonald's was sweltering, a steamy cage of plastic and airborne grease, with a cacophony and crowds equal to that of a monkey house in a Victorian zoo. Long lines of odd people stood in front of each cashier; the cashiers had thick, criminal, adolescent faces, surly beneath shrunken billed caps, while the people waiting were gigantic in their huge winter parkas and boots, each occupying twice as much space as he or she would have done in summer.

There was a baffling array of choices: varying kinds of meals including drinks or side orders with names that had no significance, meat sandwiches with titles that gave no clues as to the contents – 'The Big Slam', 'Deluxe', 'Slap-Happy Meal' – alongside photographs showing brightly colored layers protruding from two circles of bread. They each decided to have a salad that came in an oversized clear plastic cup from a refrigerated case.

'Ma, let me take you out to lunch. You're driving me around, let me treat.'

'I don't know why. I have money. Money, money, money. I'm rich, rich, rich!'

They found an empty table near the back next to two men who were discussing, loudly, methods of doctoring store-bought spaghetti sauce in a jar to make it taste home-made. 'What I do is, I fry a lot of garlic, slowly – you don't want to let it get burned –' one was saying.

'Oh, that sounds so delicious!' her mother announced and added, in a coy tone, 'Perhaps you are a professional chef? I would love to be invited to try that!' The man pointed angrily at her cigarette, which she was about to light.

'Ma!' Peyton hissed. 'You can't smoke in here!' She could tell her mother was entering that manic phase; she sounded even grander than ever, a deranged queen in a fast-food joint. Inside the plastic cup were cubes of iceberg lettuce and white chunks of meat that was supposed to be chicken but might have been processed wood-chips.

'How's your salad?'

'Quite foul. Maybe I should have taken the one you're having, that looks better. What did you get, the Chef's Salade?'

'Here, have some. I'm not going to be able to finish it all. It's not very good, anyway.'

'No, I'm fine, Ma. It has ham. Jews don't eat pork with cheese.'

At least, she thought so. The laws of kashrut, whatever they were, were so complicated she would never be able to figure them out. Outside Grace and Leonard's home, anybody could eat whatever they wanted but not bacon, shrimp or lobster – although Barry did when he wasn't with his parents. Inside the home, there could not be pork chops; some of the time you could have milk in coffee after a meal, or ice cream, other times not at all, even though Grace had prepared chicken breasts stuffed with cream cheese. Then too, the meat had to be obtained at a kosher butcher.

'You know, you don't have to go through with this, the wedding, if you don't want to. I wasn't planning to say anything, but . . . well, it's up to you, of course, it's your life. You have to decide how you want to live it.' Her mother was now twitching in an odd way. Her head was trembling.

'Keep your voice down, Ma! I want to get married! What else am I going to do?'

'I don't know. I don't know what choice you have. I didn't have any choice. Barry seems . . . nice, and a dentist, and he obviously adores you. But if you don't love him . . . you could go back to school, and do something else.' Nellie plucked bits of lettuce and began to flick them at the window. 'Look at these people around us!' She pointed. 'Everyone thinks it was your father who was a Boston Cheadle – but he wasn't a real Cheadle! It was my idea he change his name because nobody could pronounce that other one! I have the family name, I am a genuine Boston Tole!'

'Ma, what are you doing with the lettuce?'

Her mother didn't respond but began to sing, in a high voice, '*I'm getting married in the morning! Ding-dong the bells are going to chime!*'

'Quit it, Ma! What's wrong with you? . . .'

'*My heart goes bump-bump-di-ump-ump, bump-bu-di-ump-ump, over the sight of you! What is the meeeeeaning of all these flow-how-how-ers!*'

'Okay, okay! Are we going to go shopping for more stuff, or what?'

'*It is the stooooory, the story of love – from me to you!* The Toles came here in search of religious freedom! They were pure!'

'What kind of nutcase has to move to some primitive country in search of religious freedom? It lasted, what, a couple of generations? Their religious freedom was just another form of . . . um . . . repression, old men branding women with a, um, you know, Red A!'

She knew this because it was something she had learned in high school, the only time she had had a decent teacher turned out to be in a Remedial English class – Mr Steele. Remedial English – it wasn't called that, but there were two tracks, she was in the vocational one. He had let them see the movie based on *The Scarlet Letter* before they read the book, for which, fortunately, there had been Cliffs Notes.

'Don't you talk that way about my ancestors, they were pure! Not like these people! My God, look at this scum, eating their filthy burgers,' Nell lowered her voice to a hiss. 'Look! That one – he's a catamite!' She pointed accusingly. 'Hustler! Ponce! Jackaroo! And what about you, you filthy slut!'

'Aw, leave me alone . . . You're losing it, Ma. You gotta ask the doctor to adjust your meds. Get with the program, nobody cares any more.'

'Point taken.' Her mother was abruptly calm.

'Anyway, if I don't get married, what else would I do?'

'Anything! Accounting . . . or law, you could be a paralegal, or, I don't know, there are probably plenty of things. A nurse? I think there's a two-year course, you could live with me while you went to school . . .'

Peyton rolled her eyes. 'Come on, let's get going, if we're going to the mall and you still want to check out the wedding dress place.' She could not speak to her mother. Her mother did not understand, would never understand. There was the world of the poor people, those who frequented McDonald's and the Salvation Army and day-old bread shops. They worked at grim jobs. They never met the right people and if they did it was only because they were fawning fans who had won some mail-in sweepstake.

She could go back to school, get a degree in accounting and go to work in some gloomy office, hoping she might meet an accountant or some doctor who had brought in his tax forms, but why? She already had a dentist and her job at least wasn't so terrible, soon she would be able to travel and have something resembling a glamorous, interesting life. It was true there was something about Barry which wasn't quite right. But if she did not take this opportunity, there might not be another. Besides, he cherished her. That was worth something, wasn't it?

The Salvation Army dress really was a disaster, and she was sorry she had bought it and they weren't going to take returns. Grace was so horrified at the thought of her wearing a 'used' dress – it was bad cess.

She should start fresh, not in a dress previously owned by someone whose marriage had failed. She was forced to allow Grace – as a gift, but to whom? – to buy a dress for her at the annual one-day sale at Klinefield's.

Klinefield's was a wedding dress palace located in Queens: on this day gowns that had previously, allegedly, sold for anywhere between four and ten thousand dollars were marked down by as much as half.

On the appointed day – for which you actually needed an appointment – a kind of shark-feeding frenzy appeared to be taking place; thousands of young women, accompanied by their friends and mothers, were in line to try on the dresses inside the tiny dressing rooms and emerging to show off and examine themselves in the mirrors. Only three try-ons were allowed at a time and then you had to go back and wait in line all over again. The procedure could take a whole day but fortunately they had arrived early. Peyton didn't think she would have the strength to try on more than three dresses anyway; she emerged from the dressing room to be told by Grace who was waiting patiently outside the cubicle (unlike the mothers and friends, who crammed inside to hook and zip) that the first gown made her look too 'chesty', while the second was 'unflattering'.

She finally settled on the third, a peau-de-soie draped Grecian number.

'Perfect,' said Grace. 'Timeless, classy, elegant. You look beautiful – or you will, after we do your hair and make-up. It'll have to be altered, though, around the hips, and it's too long, but we'll take it to my dressmaker, not here. You have good taste,' she conceded before adding, 'although actually I think that's the one that I picked out.'

Three thousand dollars. Unbelievable. Nothing could cost that much. Pausing to admire the gown in the mirror one last time before going back in to take it off, she saw not herself but a host, of other girls – plump, svelte, plain, acned, beautiful, blonde – all of whom were in the process of trying on dresses of their own, destined for the same sepulchral fate . . .

*   *   *

129

'Ray really wants to do a three-way with you, Peyton,' said Victoria.

'Ray? But he's *so* old. He must be forty. How can you stand it?'

Victoria snickered. 'It's not his age that's so bad. It's his body hair. The first time we screwed I thought I was fucking a chimp. But you get used to it. It's actually kind of cute.'

'Oh, God, Victoria,' said Peyton. 'I don't want to do a three-way, it's not you personally, but –'

'I don't care, I don't want to do this either, but you have to do it. What am I supposed to do? Ray's on my case about doing a three-way, he says I can pick the other woman, since I don't want to do it. I love him, Peyton, I want to keep him, he says he'll marry me and I can have a baby – I don't want him to start saying I'm like his ex-wife.'

'But Victoria – you're cute, but I don't have any lesbian feelings!'

'It doesn't matter – just do this for me! Didn't I take you to the bar, and because of me you met Barry, so now you're all set? You have to pay me back – it's just one night; we can, I don't know, get really drunk and smoke some pot and we'll just, I don't know, get through it! Please say you'll do this, Peyton. If you don't do it then he'll find somebody I don't know and that's going to make me totally sick! At least if it's you, I know you, and you don't have any disease, and you're my friend . . .'

She didn't know what to say. She was supposed to be in love with Barry but this needn't interfere with love, this was just doing Victoria a favor. She really could not muster any lesbian inclinations. What was wrong with her? It wouldn't make any difference in the long run. And after all, once Victoria had taken her on a ski trip to Vermont where her family had a condo, and the two of them had got drunk and slept with the same guy, a ski instructor, first Victoria and then her, and that had been nothing more than a sick joke.

And even though Victoria was from the right side of the highway and Peyton was from the wrong, they had both smoked pot in high school and college, dropped acid, done all the things that every other girl their age was doing. It was only the outside world, the one on television, or on that planet inhabited by adults (a planet of which they were now allegedly members) who acted incredulous at the very thought of such goings-on, who still continued to pretend that this was not how people behaved. 'He doesn't have herpes or something?' she asked suspiciously.

'No, believe me! I've had him totally checked out. And I know he'll give you a present. Like, a bracelet or something? From Tiffany's . . . ?'

'Oh, I don't know,' Peyton said. 'Just forget that. It's too much like . . . it puts me in the position of being a prostitute.' Once, one summer while the two of them were working as waitresses on Cape Cod, Victoria had turned a trick – he wasn't a real trick, he was just an older man with glasses (Victoria had an obsession about men with glasses) whom Victoria had taken home and who, in the morning, had left two hundred dollars on her night table.

She tried to tell herself it wouldn't be so awful. Ray was attractive, though he was short, in a kind of swarthy, Italian movie-star way, broken Roman nose. She had an image of a hairy paw dipping into her twat, lifting fingers up to nostrils for a sniff. Men always did that, unconsciously. It reminded her of dogs thoughtfully mulling over piss deposited by some earlier canine. And Victoria – her pale, lanky friend, for whom she had only ever had vaguely maternal feelings – her pinky coloring, an unripe strawberry with a curly pink mouth, something so reddish and innocent; she should be dancing with other girls in an Irish jig.

'I swear, just do this for me Peyton and I'll never ask you for anything again! It'll be one last crazy thing. Later you can use it as material to turn him on or something. What is it with men wanting to be in bed with two women, anyway? I don't get it. You'd think it would make them feel left out, if the two women were into each other, and if they weren't, then the guy would just feel like he'd have to do twice as much work. And why is it always these old guys who want it? Do you get it?'

'I don't get anything. It just – it just seems yucky.' She was an average American girl. But the problem was, inside her there was still a place that was shocked and horrified.

She was twenty-four years old with a pretty face, black hair, big eyes an acid shade of cerulean. Belladonna pupils, huge, intense, two birds' eggs that had been cracked open and slipped onto half-lidded white frying pans. Her expression – the droopy, pouty mouth, the heavy-lashed, sleepy eyes – was involuntary. She was at that moment of full blossom – in a few years if she was not careful she might be overblown but at the moment the petals were dewy and the morning sheen still on the plum, so sweet and cold.

Her mother had made a hash of her life and she was determined not to do the same. When her mother was young she lived in a large Victorian house in a fancy suburb outside of Boston. She had been disinherited when she met and married Peyton's father and then when he left, there wasn't any alimony. Somehow her mother had survived, as had she, even though where they had ended up was the wrong side of town, the wrong side of the eight-lane highway where the language of the neighbors did not contain the letter 'r' unless it was the first. 'Remembah?' 'Fahget it.' A girl named Marcia would introduce herself as 'Masha' as if she were a Russian spy in a bad movie. The most commonly used words were *dufus, asshole* and *butthead*. Then there was *dipstick* and *wicked* as in 'He's kind of a dipstick, but it was wicked cool bumping into him at the packie.' Packie was short for 'package store' – the liquor store, and dated from a time, maybe, when people were so prim alcohol had to be wrapped up and hidden – a package.

Now she would marry a dentist. And get the hell out of Massachusetts. In six months Barry would have a practice; she would at last be, if not secure, at least in the position of flying over a trampoline. There would be somebody else on her team, on her side, someone with a safe job who was there to help and protect her. The only problem was, she couldn't quite remember what Barry looked like, or what sort of a personality he had, now that he was out the door. And she could not imagine being married, not to Barry, nor, really, to anyone.

So a few months before the wedding – looped on enough crank to screw a horse – she did the three-way with Victoria and Ray. In a room he had rented in an out-of-town motel for just this purpose,

Victoria and Peyton giggling nervously, they all took off their clothes. Immediately Ray came over and hefted a breast in each hand. There was something oddly sexy in being treated no differently than market produce, though maybe it was just the crank that gave her this detached sensation.

At least Victoria was kind of flat-chested, with only a wisp of pinkish-roan pubic hair, very pretty. She could almost pretend she was some screwing some young Irish boy. Ray was short, hairy, with a pair of swollen testicles the size of navel oranges. He lay on the bed with his legs parted, dick up, doggy furry balls slung one on each side.

The crank made her numb but wild. It was a bit of a loss, though. She *still* couldn't summon the interest to mess around with Victoria but she went at it with Ray while Victoria basically had to provide him with extra stimulation. Afterwards Ray kept calling her, for months, wanting to go out with her again; and even though Victoria was still crazy about him, he never asked her out again at all.

Sex with a chimp and a mermaid. She still liked Victoria but things were different now. It had been a rite of passage, no different from the way that young men had bachelor parties with a prostitute available for the prospective groom.

12

Caustic light, sun, ripples, the glass-bottomed boat. Dried fish, sand, her tongue a stiff sail flapping through a reef of algae-covered teeth. The pimpled web of the ringing telephone jingled her from sleep. She floated up through the net, fumbled for the buoy. She had told the hotel in Hong Kong to forward any calls to Macao. 'Hello?'

'You sound terrible. Were you asleep?'

'Um . . . yeah, kind of. Still have jet lag. There's a typhoon here, I got stuck overnight.' Xian Rong wasn't in the room. Maybe he had gone for good. She felt too dreamy to care.

'Oh, I didn't mean to wake you up. What time is it there? Are you having fun?'

'Yeah, I'm having a great time . . . it's quite amazing, it's sort of like being in a science fiction film.'

'What have you been doing?'

'Well, I, the trip seemed to take forever, and I went swimming in the hotel pool, the hotel is great –'

'And did you take the cable car up to the top of . . . Victoria, I think?'

'I didn't do that yet, but you can take a trip up there. How did you know about it?'

'That's supposed to be quite a sight. You should do it, really.'

'I've been busy.'

'Oh, you can't miss that, while you're there. Really, you should try to make time. Also the Star ferry.'

'Yeah, sure.' The more she said she was busy the more he would insist on her taking in some tourist site. She knew he was well

134

meaning. If she could have just had a cup of coffee and a minute to pull herself into a wakeful state. Her brain had been dipped in formaldehyde, one of those victims of encephalitis in a state that was neither awake nor asleep; it was not unpleasant, only the familiar nasal whine in her ear. 'Barry . . .'

'Yes?'

'Is everything okay there?'

'Fine, fine! Work's been quite hectic, I've been spending a lot of hours with the lawyer and on my own doing research –'

'I thought the suit had been dropped?'

'The insurance company wants to settle out of court, but I said, there's no reason you have to settle out of court with this woman, I had told her from the beginning there were certain risks associated with the implants and it was going to be her responsibility, afterwards, to make sure –'

'I know, you told me, and the things you said she was doing didn't make any sense.' She had to be loyal, how could she not be; on the other hand he was always so overconfident, certain that he knew how to operate some tricky equipment sold to him by a medical salesperson whose company, later, would declare bankruptcy, shut down, become the subject of a television magazine show's investigative report . . . 'Are you going to care if I spend a few extra days here? Because the hotel promised me a discount if I wanted to stay for the whole week, and it's this totally amazing place, normally I think it would cost –'

'Of course I *care*, it's always nice when you're at home, but I don't *mind*, you should stay, stay as long as you like, have a great time, it sounds terrific! Anyhow, I'm holding down the fort here and –'

'Barry, would you be an angel and call my office for me?'

'What? Yeah, sure. Have a great time!'

Mission accomplished, as Barry would have said. She dialed room service and asked for a pot of coffee. 'Will that be coffee for one or two?' The voice sounded almost lewd.

'A large pot for *one* person, please. And . . . do you have any toast?' Maybe she was just being paranoid. She would spend the day trying to put her pieces back together, trying to forget this guy. She was an idiot. But she couldn't believe . . . he had just left, not even a goodbye.

She knew there were all sorts of things she could do to make herself feel better: get a massage, go for a swim, have a salad and a glass of cold white wine, see when the jet-boat back to Hong Kong was running again. Or kill herself. Wearily she staggered to the bathroom to try and find where she had left the hotel robe. A heap of sour terry-cloth hunched on the floor by the toilet, fluffy white, stained with jagged lipstick and the black ashes of mascara.

There was a knock on the door and she opened it; it was Xian Rong.

'Where were you?' she said.

'I was out. Walking. Look, I don't know what's happened to me. I'm not accustomed to this feeling. You . . . we should get going, the boats are running again . . . Will you . . . are you free to be with me tonight?'

Oh, she thought, so this is what it feels like, oh. It was as much physical as anything else, hit in the stomach with a baseball bat, toes run over by a truck. He had a wispy Fu Manchu mustache, he looked tough, even dangerous but his eyes were soft, suffering and if their two skulls had been cracked together – eggs, contents scrambled, creamed into custard – she couldn't have felt closer to him. She would never want to be separated from him, not now. She could never be separated from him.

If this feeling she had never known existed, what other emotions were out there, unexperienced? Or colors, or tastes? What if a person had been stupid, a low IQ, and suddenly received a high dose of intellect?

'You have to . . . I have to see you,' he said. 'I have to have you. I feel like . . . this is our honeymoon.'

She and Barry had gone to Jamaica for their honeymoon. It was a long flight from New York and then there was a two-and-a-half-hour bus ride to Ocho Rios where there was some confusion with the room – the honeymoon suite had been taken by someone else, and they were too tired to argue about it. She wished Barry was able to be more forceful, but at the check-in desk his voice took on a particularly whiny tone. She wasn't much of a fighter, either, and finally they decided just to grab what they could get. It was afternoon by the time they unpacked and headed to the pool for their complimentary welcome cocktail. A steel band was playing dated, vaguely tropical-sounding songs.

The resort had been advertised as 'couples only' and judging by the number of people they saw – in the lobby, down below at the beach, which was surrounded by a chain-link fence, and at the pool – the place was three-quarters empty. A man and a woman – puffed, freckled, red – sat, two crustaceans on lounge chairs, reading paperback thrillers. Peyton and Barry took their coconut-rum punches in plastic cups and sat on two lounge chairs at the far end.

'The air smells great,' she said.

'So tonight, I thought we should just stay here at the hotel for the Jamaican buffet dinner and there's dancing afterwards on the patio,' Barry said. 'Then maybe the other days we'll try eating at local restaurants.'

'That sounds good.' She was already restless. What was she doing here, anyway, at this hokey place, with a man who was supposedly her husband? He ran his fingers through his hair and she realized it was already thinning and she felt terrible for him. She reached over and took his hand. 'I'd like to get some exercise, do some hiking or something while we're here.'

'I'll look at a map; I think I read in the brochure there was a mountain trail that starts up behind the hotel. And there's supposed to be a restaurant up in a cave with a waterfall, would you like to try that tomorrow?'

'Oh, great. Let's finish our drinks and go to the ocean. I've never been in the Caribbean before.' At least the rum punch had a vaguely numbing effect, like drinking kiddy punch laced with lidocaine. 'That reminds me,' she said, 'your mother said you burn really easily, we have to make sure we keep slathering suntan lotion on you.'

'You too. Your skin is very white.'

There were four or five couples on the patch of sand that was protected by a high fence with a guard at the gate. 'What do they have to fence the place off for, I wonder?' asked Barry. 'It's so ugly. You'd think at least they could make it out of bamboo, this looks like a prison.' They put down their towels. 'I'm going to go check the water, want to come?'

'In a minute.'

Barry walked down to the water and waded in up to his waist. The water was unnaturally blue. In a minute she heard him let out a yell and he came staggering, hobbling, back onto land. 'Shit!' he shouted. 'Something bit me!'

He had stepped on a sea urchin and had to be helped by the guard up the steps to the hotel. Fortunately the nurse was still on duty and she applied some antiseptic and removed a large spine that had become embedded in the flesh. 'Why don't they put up a goddamn sign, saying to watch out for the sea urchins?' He was livid. 'You'd think, if they bother to put up a fence to protect the guests –'

By dinner his right leg was swollen up to his knee. He wasn't much of a drinker but had two more rum drinks before dinner, although they weren't complimentary and would be added to their bill. His face took on a hectic flush. 'This food is terrible!' he said.

It was true that each dish at the buffet – macaroni and cheese, chicken in some kind of a cream sauce, chunks of meat – goat? – in a mild curry, something called 'salt cod and ackee' was bland, pulpy or oversalted. The same steel band that had played at the poolside was now playing on the terrace next to the dining room. There were only twenty or thirty other diners, pink-faced, eyes shrunken with terror; everyone was under some tremendous strain, perhaps the strain of vacationing or honeymooning, she wasn't certain which.

'I think I should probably go see a doctor,' Barry said. 'Feels like septicemia.'

'It's worse?'

'Yeah. I'm going to find out if there's a clinic or hospital we can go to. I don't think that nurse knew what she was doing. It was just some kind of over-the-counter cream she put on.'

'Didn't you bring anything?'

'I brought some Vicodin – I'm going to take one of those. The pain is pretty bad, it's a good thing I thought to bring some painkillers along.'

'Do you want to wait until morning, and see how you're doing?'

'No, anything in the tropics can get serious quickly.'

They spent an hour in a taxi to get to a clinic where they waited for another hour and a half. Barry grew more and more impatient. 'You know, there's nobody else here! This is ridiculous. If I wasn't worried about it, I'd say we should go now.'

'Well, we've come this far, let's just stick around.'

Finally a doctor appeared who said that while it was no doubt painful, he didn't see any signs of infection and Barry should just observe it and come back in a day or two if the swelling hadn't gone down.

It was after midnight by the time they got back to the hotel and Barry fell asleep almost immediately. There was a hole in the screen and mosquitoes came in. Finally she pulled the sheets over her – then it was too hot but at least she wasn't getting bitten. In the morning, though, Barry was so covered in bites he was furious. 'Why didn't you put the air conditioning on, if you knew there was a hole in the screen!'

'I'm sorry. I didn't know there was an air conditioner, I thought the fresh air was nice and . . .'

'So you just let me sleep and get bitten! Thanks a lot. You know, sometimes you amaze me.'

'Want a divorce?'

'What kind of way is that to talk? You shouldn't say that, not even joking around, it just sets up an expectation –'

'I was only kidding!'

The housekeeper/cook arrived – they had decided to have breakfast in the room – and she prepared greasy eggs and tough bacon, served with a large wedge of a tasteless orange fruit that neither of them could identify. 'So you want to head to the beach this morning?' Barry said. 'I was sort of hoping to do some deep-sea fishing later, but I don't think that's such a good idea right now.'

'You were going to go fishing on our honeymoon?'

'I figured, while you were shopping or something. Would you mind? I don't think I want to go, anyway, probably it's not going to do my leg any good – it's still puffed-up. I wonder if I have a temperature?'

Although the beach was supposedly private, an endless procession of salespeople came along, very insistent – one wanted to sell them coral earrings and necklaces, another wanted to braid Peyton's hair, and another wanted them to buy a fresh coconut which he would hack open so they could drink the milk. The security guard asked if they would carry a package for him back to New York to mail to his relatives. 'God, these people!' said Barry. 'You know, we're paying all this money, it's supposed to be romantic, I'm going to register a complaint that it's non-stop harassment!'

'Barry, don't you want to put some sunblock on?'

'No, I'm fine. I'm wearing a hat – besides, we're not going to be out long. I just hate the way that stuff feels. I don't know why they can't make some sunscreen that isn't slimy and doesn't stink. I swear I'm allergic to it – every time I put it on my nose gets stuffed up. Who's smoking pot, anyway? Can't they do it someplace else? I don't want to inhale someone's marijuana.' He glared across the beach. 'Come on, Peyton, let's go. I can't take this place.'

'You go and I'll meet you back in the room. I want to go for a little dip.'

'What, and step on a sea urchin like me, or some coral? Forget it, swim in the pool.'

'No, look, I brought water shoes, these'll protect me.'

'All right, I'll meet you back in the room at noon. If I'm not there come and look for me in the lounge, I might need more coffee. That coffee at breakfast was pathetic. You sure you going to be all right? If any of these creeps bothers you –'

'I'll be fine.'

He trudged pinkly across the sand. That was her husband. She was married. Who was he, anyway? She had married a set of attributes, various personality traits, which were as random and as arbitrary as those belonging to an ant – or a bee, or a crocodile.

No doubt he was as much of a person as she, yet when she tried to remember him after he was out of sight, he had vanished mentally as well as physically. It didn't matter whether she loved him or not – after all, weren't there parts of the world where people married without even knowing each other, where it was a business arrangement that later might lead to love – or might not. Here, a grand passion might just as likely lead to its opposite. No, what perturbed her was that he didn't seem to exist.

At least not for her. He was adept at tying flies – bits of squirrel fur and feathers, things that would attract trout; was pretty good at tae kwon do; had some hypochondriac qualities. He needed only six hours' sleep, liked butter-pecan ice cream. He was adequate-looking, had bad taste in clothes. Yet these things did not make him a fully realized three-dimensional person. Would she have felt the same about anyone she'd married? Or was it that men only looked real from across the room and the closer one got, the more time one spent with a man, the less tangible he became?

Anyway, it was too late. Maybe this was what everyone went through on their honeymoon, thinking, what the hell did I do? Though if that was the case, it was not something talked about.

A young man came and sat down next to her. His skin was sleek as a seal's, he was muscular, lithe; she couldn't understand a word he said. 'Let's get together, correspond, woman.'

'What?'

'Darryl Smith and me den ya we haffi ease off the tension. Sexy lady, wanna par wit us?'

'I don't understand a word you're saying.' She should have sounded miffed, but somehow the two of them were laughing; he knew she didn't understand him and was having her on, at least a bit. 'What are you asking?'

'What cause me sit down and a watch you, cause me see say that you giving me the eye.'

'I did not! I'm here on my honeymoon.'

'Woman, do not sweat it, don't get agitate. Got free up you mind, cause nobody can dis you. A fine beauty like yourself, so young, what you have to go and marry for? He one lucky guy, but I tell you what: why not the two of you come to a par tonight: we going to have music, it's at the home of Cheryl Black, you ever hear of she?'

She shook her head. The man looked at her admiringly but wasn't overly aggressive, merely curious. 'No, but we might come – I'll have to ask my husband.'

'So, you're down here on your honeymoon, do you need to buy some ganja?'

'I guess so. Just a little.'

'I tell you what, if you only want a little, and you newly-weds, why don't you meet me at the corner by the post office, this afternoon, and I'll give you some as a present.'

'Really? That's so nice of you. Okay, that's good, because I wanted to go into town this afternoon anyway. What's your name?'

'My name is Darryl. And what about you?'

'I'm Peyton. Tell me, what do you do here?'

'Oh, I'm just home for a few days, on vacation. I'm actually an architect, I live in Trinidad.'

'You mean . . . your accent and stuff, you don't really talk that way?'

'Oh, I do – when I'm home here in Jamaica.' He grinned. 'So I'll see you later on then, Peyton, and tonight for some wining and liming, up the hill.'

'What? Wining and liming?'

'You don't know that Trinidad expression? A party, you know. Anyway, it was nice to meet you. Walk good.'

It would have been so easy, she thought abruptly, to call after him, 'Wait!' and when he turned to rise, follow him down the beach.

'So this guy said he's going to give you some marijuana?'

'As a honeymoon present.'

'Oh, great, Peyton. I bet he's a cop. If we see him in town, just act like you don't know him, or at least don't accept anything from him!'

'I don't know, he seemed perfectly legit. He's an architect, he lives in Trinidad. He was nice. Interesting. It wasn't like that security guard who wanted us to carry a "package" back to New York.'

'Yeah, right. I mean, there's a million tourists, this guy is inviting us to a party?'

'Maybe he's just a friendly guy who wants to meet new people.'

'Yeah, new people who are sitting alone on the beach with beautiful breasts and white skin.'

'Whatever. I just thought it would be something fun for us to do that wasn't a regular tourist thing.'

'Yeah, a thing where the tourists get mugged and murdered. These people hate us, Peyton! Don't you get a sense of how hostile they are?' He had already had too much sun, his face was turning pink. Maybe he was right; probably he was right. But she knew if she had been on her own she would have gone, no matter how scared she was.

After lunch they strolled through the town. There was a row of stalls off an alley, selling straw hats and baskets, carved coconuts, tie-dyed fabric and Bob Marley T-shirts and she bought some postcards from a small girl who said, politely, 'Thank you, Auntie.'

Nearby two old women with sad, wrinkled faces sat beside a pile of fruit in front of the supermarket. She had never seen the fruit before, greenish unwieldy balls the size of grapefruits but with thicker skins. 'Shall we get a couple of those, just to see what they are?'

'What are we going to do with them? You don't know if they're ripe, or have to be cooked. How would we peel them, anyway?'

'I don't know. I just thought it would be fun . . .'

They headed up the road but almost immediately the village ended; cars and trucks rushed by on the two-lane road. Off to one side there was a gap between the bushes that led to a trail. 'Come on,' she said. 'That looks like the nature trail that they said started nearby. Shall we try it?'

'I don't think this is the trail, hon. It's not marked.'

'Well, let's see, anyway.' A path wide enough for a small tractor ran between lush jungle; shortly there were floppy-leafed banana trees growing in a ravine. The forest smelled of rot, mystery. A cat-like animal, golden, with short legs, ran across the path ahead of them. 'Oh, wow! A mongoose.'

'I really think we should turn back, Peyton. This is someone's private property.'

'I want to go on.'

The path grew steeper; now it was too narrow for a tractor and beginning to look more overgrown. A small stream burbled nearby and, when they walked on, the water widened into a pool fed by a waterfall. 'Oh, this is so beautiful! Let's go for a dip!'

'Don't go in the water!'

'Why?'

'You don't know how safe it is; it could be polluted, or have some kind of parasite – I don't know anything about what's down here. There could be worms –'

She had dipped her foot in the water but now snatched it out. 'Oh.'

'Come on, Peyton, let's go back.' As they rounded the corner a man with a machete stood by a large banana tree. He had dreadlocks and stoned eyes, huge and red. He was probably in his sixties though it was impossible to say; he had the look of someone who had not seen civilization in twenty years.

'Oh, hi,' said Peyton.

'Excuse us,' Barry said. 'We're just heading back down to our hotel – sorry, we thought this was the nature path, we're not from around here and got kind of lost. Is this the right way back down to the village?' He didn't give the man a chance to answer but forged on ahead down the path. It felt like they had walked miles; actually they might have been walking less than ten or fifteen minutes; the point where the man had been standing was just a couple of hundred yards from the road. 'Geez, that was pretty spooky!' said Barry.

'What was?'

'That guy! With the machete! You have to be careful when you travel, Peyton, you're totally innocent about stuff like this.' They headed back to the pool for a rest.

At least if she had been here with a girlfriend they could have gone out to have some real fun and adventure. And Darryl, she imagined, would probably know the most interesting places to take her for a good time.

They were given directions for the nature path on which they could walk to the restaurant with the waterfall where they had a reservation for that evening, but Barry thought it would be better to take a taxi.

It was only a short drive. Barry discussed the price with the driver, who said it would be fifteen dollars US, which Barry said was highway robbery and he was going to complain to the hotel, though the man gave them his card and offered to take them home later, privately, for seven.

The grotto really was beautiful, with tables on a stone terrace facing a huge natural waterfall. The kapok trees were strung with twinkling lights, though the place was practically empty.

They each had a rum drink, hers with pineapple, his with coconut and lime. Then they decided to have lobsters – she went for the Chinese-style, he chose grilled. There were only another fifty years to get through before he died. He was a very nice person. It was a shame they didn't have much to talk about, but when she considered it, she had very little to say to anyone. He thought the apartment they had looked at just before they left would make a good first apartment. He didn't know why, really, she wanted to live in Manhattan – they could find a bigger place near his parents, but if that was what she wished –

It was better not to get in too deep financially at this point, considering how much it was going to cost to start his dental practice, although his parents were helping out quite a bit with that. The apartment was dark, but in a good neighborhood – the Upper West Side – and would probably go up in value eventually, especially if they redid the kitchen and turned the maid's room into a guest room/study.

'How many glasses of wine do you think you'll drink?'

'Maybe two,' she said.

'So I guess I should order a whole bottle, it seems like a lot, though. Are you sure you're going to drink that much?'

'We're on our honeymoon!'

The waterfall splashed ceaselessly but even above the racket she could hear, from some distance away, the pounding thud of loud Jamaican reggae, angry blows of the bass. Her lobster was quite tasty, though perhaps a bit bland, but his was very dry and tough and he expressed great disappointment in it. The wine, he said, was okay, but overpriced at forty-three dollars a bottle. 'I'm telling you, it's a ten-dollar bottle of wine, I can't believe they get away with charging that much for it!'

For dessert they had some sort of ginger pudding cake, far too sweet, though he pronounced it very good.

The driver dropped them back in the center of town. Barry did not leave him a tip. It really should have been only a three-or four-dollar cab fare. There was a bar, practically a closet in the wall, with six or eight black guys sitting on stools drinking rum and it looked fun and she wanted to go in, but Barry said he didn't like the look of the place and they should stick with the hotel bar if she wanted a nightcap. It did look rough. The moon came up over the water and it was very clear and sparkling and they went back to their room and she took off her clothes and put on a nightgown and the air conditioner and got into bed and started to read the magazines she had brought along. The covers advertised articles that would reveal the secret sex thoughts of men, and offer tips on how to make him your sex slave, but somehow after she had finished reading them she was no wiser than before.

Then Barry got into bed. Pulling up her nightgown he kissed her stomach and slid down further in bed and began licking her between the legs. She had a momentary pang of anxiety: did she smell? Also it was awkward, with his head down there it was as if she was giving birth to a grown man. What the heck was *she* supposed to be doing, while he slurped away? Then he turned around so that his dick was in her mouth while he still went down on her, but from the opposite direction, so now she knew she would never relax and be able to have an orgasm. Finally she pushed him away.

Somewhere she had once heard that women – lesbians – were experts at this because they knew what another woman wanted. That wasn't true. When she and Victoria had done it, it had been like trying out some strange Japanese cuisine, something that wriggled, still alive, in a dish. Or having to swallow the contents of a bearded mussel attached to a rock, while all the while one knew the tide was rapidly coming in. She was never going to be a lesbian. Being heterosexual was already strange enough.

Barry put a pillow under her buttocks and kept licking until finally she got excited and had an orgasm, her legs squeezing against the sides of his head as involuntarily as a jellyfish pulsing through the water. She made some small squeaky sounds when she came. Then he slid himself up and into her and her legs wrapped around his back and her arms wrapped around his neck as he pumped and she had another orgasm, this one brief. A velvet hand was squeezing her uterus spasmodically. Uttering a guttural yelp, Barry stopped. They lay together for a few minutes, his softening penis inside her. At last he pulled himself out and got up. 'Thank you, princess,' he said.

'Thank *you*,' she said.

'Now 'oos baby-waby ees happy?' he said in a fake French accent.

'I am.'

'I'm just going to clean myself off,' he called from the toilet. 'Do you want a towel or anything?'

'A glass of water, please.' She pulled up the sheets and closed her eyes.

'Here you go,' he said. 'Are you sleeping?'

'Just about.'

'I'm going to watch some TV in the other room, if it gets any reception. Is that going to bother you?'

'No, go ahead.' As she drifted off she watched herself hurtling toward some black hole in space, a sucking spot in the firmament, that she had no power to resist.

13

The air in Rio had a different smell, richer, more entangled: vegetation mixed with cheap gasoline. A driver was waiting with a car; he got out just as she opened the door to the back seat. Then she remembered she was supposed to wait for the man to open the door but it was too late. The man went around the other side and got in. He made a comment to the driver, who was glad to see him. They chatted in Portuguese. The driver left the airport. They were on a long highway that ran parallel to a canal or river. The car smelled of fresh leather and more faintly of cigar smoke. 'So,' the man said. It sounded as if he had said, 'Tho'. 'You are tired, no?'

'I didn't really sleep much on the plane. Listen, I know you told me – but would you tell me your name again? I was so upset I blanked it out!'

He smiled mildly, for some reason apparently amused. 'My name? Germano Schmitt-Nausen. And yours?'

'Oh I'm Peyton Cheadle.' She didn't know why she gave her maiden name. 'Would I have heard of you somehow?'

She supposed she could call Barry and tell him what had happened; get the name and number of where she was supposed to be staying. Borrow money from the man, take a taxi there. She was meant to call Barry later that evening, just to let him know she was okay. At least first she would go to Germano's hotel, take a shower, see how she felt. They drove through tunnels and on roadways that zigged around the edges of lagoons that lay directly beneath huge hump-shaped mountains. Along the side of the road she saw a stray dog, obviously starving, hobbling along and she said, 'Oh, my gosh, listen, do you see that dog out there? Do you mind – could you ask your driver to stop the car, and I'll – I don't know, I'll take it to a vet or something.'

'Excuse me?'

'Sir, sir, stop the car!'

'What is the matter? What do you wish?'

'Oh, God! Now we've gone too far, we'll never find him. Didn't you see? There was a stray dog back there that was hurt!'

'A dog? Yes? And what do you want to do with him?'

'Never mind. It's too difficult to explain.' It was a beautiful city. She wished now she had gone to pee before leaving the airport, she wished she wasn't so grubby and had chosen a different outfit than the dorky jogging suit or whatever it was supposed to be. Nevertheless from time to time, he glanced at her with an appreciative, admiring smile. He was older but there was something extremely sexy about him. The slightly thick lips, the sloe eyes, the hands with stubby yet elegant fingers. He was the sort of man who lived in a penthouse, where everything was pale leather and glass and there were bottles of champagne and top-shelf Scotch. 'We are staying at the Leopold-Saraband.'

'That's . . . I've heard of that, that's very fancy, isn't it?'

'I always stay there, even though for business it is not so convenient. I think you will like it. It is just on the beach. You have never been to Rio before?'

'No, no. I've never.' She was about to blurt that the only place she had been was to Jamaica on her honeymoon but something stopped her. If she mentioned that she was married it would seem she was trying to let him know there was no possibility of romance between them – but such a thing wasn't even in the air. 'Where are you from?'

'Me? I am Italian-German but born in Spain and raised in Chile and Brazil; now, however, I am living in Cologne.'

The front of the hotel was an old mansion, large and white with ornate balustrades and frosted cakework so white and frothy it might be nibbled; behind it a tall, modern glass structure had been attached. Across the highway was a beach of white frosting. She got out of the car and went to the back to collect her bag. Germano had already walked up the front steps into the hotel and nervously she followed. What if something happened to her overnight bag? Then she would really have nothing left. At least in the bag was her swimsuit and clothes – well, Grace's clothes. The lobby was cool and elegant with an ornate marble tiled floor as tinkly as musical notes; in the center was an old marble fountain and curved palace-sized stairs winding up either side. Other women in outfits of beige, their impervious faces wrapped in dark sunglasses, hair swept sleekly into ponytails, swept by regal as thoroughbreds, the sort of women who appeared torn from the pages of magazines.

Germano had gone to a discreetly placed desk. In the teal-blue outfit she felt dumpy and busty and wondered why or how Germano had deigned to be seen in her presence. She sat on a nearby couch with a high back covered in lavishly patterned fabric, shimmery pale shades of coral and mauve. Nearby sat an elderly lady in a hat with a tiny veil and white gloves. The hotel was a fishtank of liquid money, oxygenated and filtered.

'Come,' said Germano. The back of the mansion had a second area, the modern lobby with banks of elevators; they rode in silence to the twenty-fourth floor. The living room of the suite had floor-to-ceiling windows and a large planted terrace that looked out over the sea and, to the right, the mountains. The sea was ice blue, fringed with a perfect white frill where the waves crashed onto the white Brazilian beach. It was breathtaking, the beige pigskin sofas on each of which were placed one or two vivid shot-silk pillows, turquoise, tomato pink; the chocolate leather chairs; the white and ochre-yellow orchid in the center of the rosewood table. A hi-tech television could be hidden behind a glazed wall.

She saw now this was how she should have decorated their new apartment on the Upper West Side, not with the hideous cabbage-rose prints and sad mock-antique end-tables with spindly legs that Grace had given them. She wondered for a minute where she was supposed to sleep, if there really was a bedroom for her or if she had been the victim of a trick – but she wasn't sixteen after all, she was too old to be tricked, she thought, even if the whole place – and

Germano – felt totally out of her league. 'Do you mind if I remove my jacket?' he said.

She laughed, involuntarily. 'Well, no – I mean, it's your place!'

'You don't mind to take the room on the right? Or, if you wish, have a look at both and you may choose. But I think the room on the right you will find the nicer.'

'Don't you want the nicer room?'

It had a bathroom the size of her living room at home with a shower and a gigantic bathtub almost as big as a swimming pool which one entered by climbing steps; everywhere were more displays of flowers, orchids in pots. There were heaps of fluffy towels and oversized bottles – pale lavender bath salts, a deep purple shampoo, a chartreuse conditioner – with exotic-looking labels, never before touched, apparently meant for every new guest. She picked up each in turn. She wanted to stuff them into her cosmetic bag; if nothing else she would have a souvenir when she got home. It was impossible to believe people really lived such lives of gem-like perfection. He was standing behind her while she held one up to the light. 'This will do?' he said.

'Oh my gosh, yes!'

The doorbell rang and the bellman came in with their bags; his looked expensive, canvas, leather, some kind of important brand, and the sleek garment bag that zipped and folded in half. Hers was a piece of junk with wheels. She had been pleased with it, proud of it, now she saw it was all wrong, that awful green color, American. 'So, now I must shower and begin my day of meetings. You will be all right?'

'Sure, I guess so!'

'I am going to order a little breakfast for myself, some coffee – you would like some too?'

'But I don't want to inconvenience you –'

'It is a telephone call. You must make yourself at home, if you wish to order something to eat or drink in the room or at the pool – I don't know what your plans were for your stay in Rio, but if you are able I would invite you to be my guest for dinner this evening.'

'I don't really have any plans . . . now.'

'So. You will want some cash, I know that is missing, here is two hundred and fifty Brazilian reals, that is maybe one hundred US, for the beach, if you wish to have a drink, a coconut, or to buy a pareo –'

'I can't accept. My goodness, it's too much!'

'*Da nada.*'

'No, no. Really, I'll pay you back, you'll have to give me your address, and then I'll mail you a check –'

'I will be back around five-thirty, six – I am afraid I will need a nap – I must meet some associates for a drink after that – and then you will join me for dinner at ten.' He looked at her fondly. He had removed his suit jacket and his shirt, which even after traveling all night, was crisp and white, with French cuffs and discreet gold cufflinks. Her feet ached in her high heels and the hem of one of the legs of her pants had caught in the heel at some point and torn. Her face was furry with make-up and probably by now her mascara had smudged. 'You will be all right? Here, I will give you my office number, you must telephone if you have any questions or trouble during the day; or the concierge downstairs I know to be very helpful.'

If she had known this could happen she would never have married Barry. She thought of the hotel they had stayed in on their honeymoon, first near the airport and then overlooking an airshaft in Jamaica. Thousands of tourists arriving by bus and van, a buffet table of greasy oxtail and pink sliced meats. A band of men with dreadlocks playing steel drums and guitar by the side of a swimming pool around which fat Americans sat baking, pink pigs in plastic lawn chairs. But it had seemed glamorous at the time. Until she had known there was something more.

'You've been so nice!'

He was so handsome, so confident, so calm.

She was too frightened to go to the beach dressed in her swimsuit. Certainly it would be awkward to cross the lobby in a bathing suit and if she wore her clothes over it she would have to undress on the beach. But at least she thought she would go for a stroll. She was tired but there was no way she could nap. Everything she had brought was wrong, the tight spandex blue jeans, the one slightly dressier outfit of khaki polyester that Grace had said she should bring 'just in case'. She settled on a pair of Bermuda shorts that made her rear end look fat and a stupid pink striped T-shirt.

It was even frightening to cross the street, the cars here were different entities from those in the States, traveled at a different speed, rhythm. The beach was not so crowded. There was a small kiosk with a few plastic chairs and tables on the sidewalk where a couple sat drinking from coconuts with straws and staring at her, knowing she was out of place. A few steps more and she was on the beach, her bulky exercise sneakers filled up with sand. A man in a bikini, shiny, greased, approached her with a suitcase and an armload of fabric, swathes of vermilion, iridescent blue, batiked, painted – what were they possibly for? – holding them up to her and she shook her head wildly: perhaps he was going to grab her handbag or, if she wanted to buy something, it would be the wrong price, far too much, or he might rip the money from her hand. Then another came up and said, in English, 'Umbrella? Chair?'

She shook her head again and stumbled forward. She would have liked to sit for a minute on the sand, but yet another man came over with a cooler decorated with pictures of ice creams and though it was clear she didn't want an ice cream (though maybe she did, it was just too overwhelming) he was so insistent she wanted to escape. She stood for a moment looking out across the beach, trying to ignore him.

No one else acted frightened. Strollers marched along the harder sand near the water's edge – a huge woman with great folds of flesh, jiggling, in a tiny bikini that revealed the entire cheeks of both buttocks, accompanied by a slim man also in a bathing suit that scarcely served to cover his genitals. Ancient ladies, young girls, men, a parade of nude flesh. A boy stood next to a net bag holding gigantic beach balls, each larger than a watermelon, amazingly colored, clear red, blue, opaque white shimmering with ribbons of pink and splatters of yellow. Her staring into space only encouraged the man selling ices and he began to remove them, one kind at a time, from the chest and wave them in front of her face. After a while she turned and went back to the hotel.

*   *   *

153

She spent the afternoon at the hotel pool. It was fairly empty and at least she felt safe here; from time to time a waiter delivered drinks to others sitting on lounge chairs, frothy whipped drinks, pink, skewered with pineapple slices, kiwi green – she felt too overwhelmed and embarrassed to gesture to the man. She grew hungrier and hungrier. She supposed she could go back to the room and look for a room service menu but she didn't want to run up the man's bill – Germano's bill.

Under an awning was a bar and small tables and almost against her will she rose and strolled to the end. A woman and a child were eating grilled sandwiches accompanied by French fries. Normal food. 'Menu?' she asked the bartender. He handed her a printed paper. She could have cried. She couldn't make head or tail of any of the dishes, none of it made sense and there was no way to determine the prices – seven, ten, fifteen – she had never been any good at math. For a moment it occurred to her she could just point at what the woman was eating and say she wanted the same, but what if the sandwich made her sick? Grace had warned her . . . Finally she handed the menu back and went up to the room.

When he returned, about six o'clock, she was freshly bathed and made up, dressed in the pleated skirt and T-shirt. 'You have had a good day?'

'Very! I . . . I took some nuts and a diet pop from the mini-bar, I just want to tell you so when you get the bill . . . I want to make sure you keep track of what I spend, not for the room I mean, but the other stuff, to pay you back . . .'

He shook his head. 'And you are able to join me for dinner tonight?'

'I didn't really bring anything dressy – I hope –'

'You have nothing in your bag other than this?' He looked her up and down then looked at his watch.

'It's all I brought, I mean, other than jeans –'

He picked up the telephone and spoke. 'Come,' he said. 'They will keep the shop open for us. You have been to the shop downstairs?'

'No, where?'

'In the lobby; they have some very nice things. Please do not be foolish. Allow me to buy for you – as a new friend – some special dress for this evening. It will make me very happy.'

14

'I'm about to get my period.'

'You should have gone on the pill.' Peyton's sister Brenda had flown in from Colorado with a suitcase of rocks, crystals, two jadeite stone pillows – a wedding gift – on which, for health reasons, she and Barry were supposed to rest their heads at night. 'If you were on the pill you could have arranged your cycle so you didn't get your period on your honeymoon.'

'I didn't know you could do that. Anyway, at least you came, Brenda, I was disappointed Mom claimed she couldn't get a pass from the institution to come to my wedding –'

'Well, what do you expect? She's crazy.'

'I just can't help thinking that she isn't any crazier than anybody else, that's all. Anyway, I'm going for a walk. Can you distract Grace, if you see her? She'll have a nervous breakdown if she doesn't find me getting my hair done or my make-up or something; she'll think I've flown the coop. Just tell her I had to get some air but I'll be back in plenty of time.'

Having a wedding had been her one dream but Grace had carried out the wedding plans, taken over with the precision of a military strategist. The whole thing made Peyton extraordinarily nervous. She had never thought it through beyond reading the bride magazines and envisioning herself walking down the aisle.

There was a registry so guests could purchase table linens, or glassware, or china: in patterns that, ultimately, had been selected by Grace. There were dinner forks and salad forks, dessert spoons and grapefruit spoons. Sauté pans, omelet pans, and bed linens. Glassware – ice tea glasses, wine glasses, tumblers. Did Peyton want jacquard towels or flat-woven? A floral pattern china that was dishwasher safe? But any time Peyton tried to contribute ideas of her own, or at least act vaguely interested, she had the sense that she was the site that was going to be bombed. Grace was horrified by her taste. It was appalling, to Peyton, the idea of owning so much stuff, cooling racks and mixing bowls and muffin tins. She had grown up eating off paper plates – to clean up was to throw them in the garbage. Now what was she going to have to do, start entertaining on damask tablecloths? She tried to distance herself.

It only got worse. Should voluptuous fresh cattleya orchids decorate the cake or buttercream roses? One magazine showed the guests arriving to pluck their table seating number from tiny blackboards placed on a table covered with freshly sprouting wheat grass. A flower girl wore a hand-made wreath of strands of raffia painstakingly woven with stephanotis. Just flipping through the pages featuring brides in different gowns with subdued make-up and white shoulders made her want to puke. Beaded boutonnières, dusted sugar flowers, candle favors ('wedding guests will appreciate a simple, thoughtful favor of hand-made beeswax candles') – the whole concept, the wedding, seemed to be a public offering to a deranged, controlling, obsessive-compulsive god, who, in her case, was Grace.

After all, having a big wedding was not something she had ever wished for or cared about. She had dreamt of having a wedding, and while it was true she had pictured the outside of a church thronged with well-wishers, the reality was she had few friends and fewer relatives. It was so strange, the whole enterprise, so much money spent on a mock event. It was the two of them who were going to try to spend their lives together. Suddenly it seemed . . . humiliating, having a large crowd judging her.

More than three hundred people were expected, and it was finally decided it was to be held in the backyard. A tiered cake, lemon interior, marzipan-iced and decorated with cascading sugar violets;

bags of white and silver almonds; matchbooks and napkins embossed with the names of the bride and groom. Crates of fat black Bing cherries arrived from California. Pink and gray chiffon dresses for the bridesmaids. If she had been an anthropologist she would have been at a loss to explain such customs.

All morning workers were setting up a tent, white with clear plastic windows and a dance floor. A florist arranged bouquets of lilacs and tuberoses everywhere; a klezmer orchestra descended from a large van and began to practice in the basement, belching exotic sounds that honked out into the yard. There was to be a chamber music group, too, for the bit before the ceremony (a young rabbi had finally been located who was willing to marry a Jew and a non-Jew) and then later in the evening would be a DJ playing pop music, though zoning laws meant the whole thing had to be finished by midnight.

The only thing was that the septic tank was starting to overflow – maybe because of the extra guests in the house, but maybe just because it should have been emptied or something, anyway, there was a lot of arguing going on, and it was too late to do anything about the overflow, only a few hours before the wedding, on a Sunday – and so the ground became strangely very squishy and there was no denying there was an odor.

She had been staying at Barry's parents' house, along with her sister Brenda, who had come in from Aspen, and Belinda, and Belinda's boyfriend; and Victoria had arrived the night before, so they slept in Barry's room and Belinda's room and the guest bedroom, as well.

Barry was staying with his friend Neal around the corner and she hadn't seen him for four days, some kind of peculiar wedding tradition or an idea of Grace's.

She had to make an escape. In a sweat she bolted, unable to go through with this farce, a play in which she had been cast against her will. Probably no one would notice if she wasn't there; she was not important. Let Grace step in from the bullpen, let them find the first runner-up; surely Barry had an old girlfriend nearby who would happily substitute, pinch hit.

And then, when she was two blocks away, she found a dog in the street, the same husky with the two different colored eyes – which had on a collar but was running loose, obviously about to get run over, so she found a bit of rope and walked it over three blocks to a veterinary clinic. All this took a lot of time but at least it was a distraction and she resigned herself to going back to the house. She was supposed to be getting her make-up done by someone Grace had hired to come over, so the job in the end had to be rushed. Anyway, the make-up artist said she really didn't need much make-up, her skin was flawless, less was more, especially with her youth, beauty and the fact that it was – the service – being held outdoors, so the light was a bit harsh.

She couldn't believe her mother wasn't going to be there, but then in a way that was a relief – her mother wouldn't have fit in, with her great clouds of hideous hippie hair sprouting from her head in various colors, like some terrible mutant dandelion, and would have chosen no doubt to wear something eccentric. Her brother Donny wasn't invited, her sister Kathy in Florida couldn't come but that was okay; and actually she was pleased with her dress – in the end Grace was right. And the food was delicious, though she was too nervous to eat – cold poached salmon in lemon sauce or filet mignon – and the rabbi, who was known for performing mixed marriages, was really quite funny, jocular and moving. Then, thank God, it was all over, the cutting of the cake, the dancing, the champagne toasts – what had taken place had happened to someone else, all that fuss, she might just as well not have been there at all; in fact, she didn't really feel she had been. But otherwise the only thing to mar the event was when the neighbor came over, right in the middle of everything, and started shouting at Peyton, 'Did you take my dog? I heard you kidnapped my dog.'

And though the music didn't stop the guests did, and started staring at the scene. 'Well, I didn't know it was your dog,' Peyton said, lying. 'I just found a dog, I didn't know who it belonged to. I took it around the corner to the vet's –'

'You knew it was my dog! You stole my dog, now I know who did it, the next time this happens I'm going to call the police!'

'Lady, it was a stray dog about to get run over!' she said. 'If it was

159

your dog you should be thanking me!' Her face got pink and her mouth, lips swollen from biting at them, puffed out in petulant indignation. 'How could you let a dog run loose and leave it outside all winter? You're the one who should be reported to the police!'

Grace came and led her away. 'You sound hysterical,' she said. 'Take a deep breath.'

'Grace, don't tell me to take a deep breath! How can you just ignore suffering that's going on right in front of your face?'

'This day cost a hundred thousand dollars,' said Grace. 'And we're paying for all of it.'

'A hundred thousand dollars! Are you crazy! Why would it cost so much money? You got ripped off! That's just nuts!'

'Well, that is how much it cost and I'm not going to let you spoil it. Do you know how loud you sound? And all the work and trouble I went to, and how you are ruining this day not just for me but for everyone? You are so ungrateful. If you won't consider me, can't you think about Barry?'

'Yeah, well he'd be a lot better off if you'd stop smothering him!'

'Smothering him? How dare you! I can already see, you're turning out like your schizophrenic mother and criminal brother – bad genes, my son's married into bad genes! Belinda told me last night what you tried to do to her! I didn't want to talk to Barry, it was too late to cancel everything, but he's willing to give you a chance!'

When the party was over they checked into a hotel near the airport with their travel bags. It wasn't a very nice hotel – the room smelled stale, an odor of old ashtrays and cigarettes – the walls were covered with a hideous pattern of beige and mauve vinyl wallpaper, the coverlets on the bed were a harsh, shiny fabric with a synthetic feel. But she didn't know any better.

She had never stayed in a hotel before. Maybe she had stayed in a motel, once or twice, she remembered at least being eighteen and going somewhere with Victoria, up to Vermont, they had just got their driver's licenses and Victoria's dad had lent them a car for the weekend; there was some party Victoria wanted to go to, and they somehow ended up getting some man, an older man, to buy them a bottle of tequila . . .

Now their sixth-floor room looked out over the pool surrounded by a white metal mesh fence. Beyond was the highway, eight lanes, on which traveled an endless bumper-to-bumper procession of automobiles. In the bathroom mirror her face looked yellow; the floral dress with ruffled cap sleeves had been a mistake. It was the wrong color for her. It made her arms look fat and her neck short. 'Come on, let's go down to the bar for a nightcap,' Barry said.

'A nightcap? Didn't you have enough to drink at the party?' Her eyes felt gritty. She was going to get her period. Her sister was right, she should have gone to her gynecologist and gone on the pill so she didn't get her period on her honeymoon. She had stuffed her suitcase with boxes of tampons and sanitary napkins. Husbands, she knew, were never supposed to see tampons, or Kotex; they would never want to have sex again if they saw a used one.

When she was twelve or thirteen, her grandmother had once arrived for a visit; though an old woman, she was immensely regal and beautiful, with taut, flawless skin, so white, and she had actually arrived in a car with a chauffeur – God, somebody at sometime had certainly had a lot of money in her family. When her grandmother had come out of the bathroom (Donny was still at home then, and one of her sisters, and they all had to share the same bathroom) she had said to her, 'I have found some items that someone had mistakenly left out, and I've hidden them away.' What could she have been talking about? She had no clue, though her grandmother added, 'You know, it would be very wrong if Donny were to see them.'

And a short time later, when Brenda – or was it her mother? – screamed, 'Who took my tampons? There was a whole box on the windowsill, where are they?' it occurred to her that that was what her grandmother had been talking about. Why? This stuff was on TV, being advertised.

She had only seen her grandmother one other time, at least that she could remember. She had gone into some kind of very fancy nursing home, shortly thereafter, but it was a long drive away and mostly they didn't have a car, so when they went there she was surprised to see how much her grandmother had deteriorated. She sat in a wheelchair in a nasty-looking nightdress, pink, with brown stains, and kept saying over and over again 'Eye wash station.'

For the longest time they couldn't figure out why she kept saying this, until they realized she was reading from a sign on a doorway that read 'Eye Wash Station'. And then, in one moment of lucidity, when the others had gone down the hall, her grandmother turned to her and snapped into normalcy – had the rest just been an act? – and said, 'You must never let your husband see you when you are unclean. You must always remain a lovely mystery.' She had had three husbands – later, after her death, they found out it had actually been four – and left Peyton her pearl necklace in her will, which she had lost or eventually given to Kathy. Her grandmother – who, admittedly, she really didn't know – had come from a time so different that it might have been another planet.

'You gotta understand, when my mother was young, women didn't even have sanitary napkins, they had bits of cloth – rags or something – which had to be washed out by hand and hung up to dry,' Nell said, when Peyton asked, perplexed, what the big deal about the sanitary napkins was.

Nell herself had been around through two different eras – the first, in the early fifties, when she was in finishing school, or some college that was the equivalent to a finishing school, outside of Boston. Then if a woman slept with a man she would never get married, because she wasn't a 'nice' girl any longer, she wasn't a virgin; and if she got pregnant there would be the terrible stigma of bearing an illegitimate child.

'Stigma?' Peyton said. Impossible to believe this, when every other movie star was publicly pregnant with no sign of husband or even man. And then her mother had come into the 1960s, when all of a sudden everything was the opposite. But throughout this nothing was better or worse or even radically different for men; only the availability of sex, which, from what Peyton had seen, most of them didn't want anyway.

And now her own mother had gone into a mental hospital, three days before the wedding, to dry out (leave it to Nell to start drinking again and stop taking the lithium simultaneously) at a time when there was no way she could have gone up to Boston to see her. There was so much that she had to do to get ready.

Her mother had never even *liked* her. She had always told Peyton, 'You know, you're not very smart.' To be the center of attention – it was obvious that was what her mother wanted; she didn't want Peyton to be the star even for the day of her own wedding. But whenever she could really have used Nell's help, Nell had always chosen that time to disappear, enter a kind of depressed torpor, stop taking the medication or start drinking, so there was no way to reach her.

It was just too bad. If things didn't go smoothly, here, now – the wedding, the relationship – she would never pull herself out of her situation: the swamp that was Boston, commuting to a fifth-rate job, ending up with somebody like Ernie, dregs, whatever was left in the dirty glasses at the end of the night.

'But don't you want to see what the bar is like here? I'm too excited to go to sleep, anyway.'

It was touching, Barry's enthusiasm. She felt only exhaustion, and depression. Everything she had looked forward to, anticipated for so many months, was over. What could she have been thinking? It would have been far pleasanter to attend someone else's party. She had a pounding headache and Barry complained of an upset stomach. 'Do you think people had a good time?' she called.

'I don't know. I've got to go to the bathroom. Are you going to be in there long?'

'No, no, I'll hurry. Just let me brush my teeth. I'm sorry, honey. Do you think it was something you ate? Or just nerves?'

'I don't know. Maybe I got bad chopped liver or something. I'm wondering if I should call my mother and see if she got any reports that anybody else is sick.'

She changed into a pink silk dress, more of a slip than a negligee, that Grace had given her at the bridal shower. It came from an expensive department store. It was stupid, to be preparing for a honeymoon night. What if she had really been a virgin, how hideous and terrible that would have been: after going through all the preparations and the hours of ceremony, reception, meals and party then to return to a room with a man who suddenly took out a penis. She still wasn't entirely used to the whole thing. Maybe she would never get used to it. Barry ran past her as she came out and slammed the bathroom door. While he was in there, there was a knock on the bedroom door; someone from the hotel was delivering a bottle of champagne and a plastic ice bucket with two plastic champagne flutes. 'We didn't order this!' she said.

'Some of your friends sent it,' the bellboy said with a grin. 'Happy honeymoon.' His smirky attitude might have been left over from another century.

A note said 'Happy honeymoon from Neal and Greg.' 'Honey, Neal and Greg sent us a bottle of champagne,' she called. 'Isn't that sweet?' Probably she was supposed to tip the delivery person. 'Hang on just a second.' She lowered her voice, 'Barry, do you have any small bills for me to give the bellboy? I only have twenties.'

'Look in my pocket of my suit jacket, the inside pocket.'

She found four singles and gave them to the bellboy.

From the bathroom a terrible odor emerged.

'How much did you tip him?' Barry called weakly.

'Oh Barry, you sound really bad. I gave him four dollars, was that all right?'

'Four dollars! Geez! One or two would have done it, all he had to do was carry it upstairs. Would you call down and find out if they have any Alka-Seltzer and Pepto-Bismol?'

She was frightened. She was sure that whoever was at the front desk would act contemptuous and say of course they didn't stock medications. 'Um, excuse me,' she said. 'My husband . . . isn't feeling so well and I was wondering . . . if you – do you have anything like Pepto-Bismol or some Alka-Seltzer?'

The woman at the other end paused for a long time. 'No, we don't carry anything like that. There's a pharmacy about five blocks away, but I think it closed at eleven.' Now she was married to this man in the bathroom and she couldn't imagine ever sleeping with him again. Before, at least, there had been a certain element of – not risk, but anticipation, excitement: at any moment he might leave her, she had to do her best to win him. Now he had committed, there was obviously no need to fear rejection. After a while he emerged and sat on the farthest of the two queen-sized beds. His face looked white and exhausted. 'Sorry about that. Did they have anything in the lobby?'

'No. There's a drugstore nearby but it's already closed.'

'And you didn't bring anything?'

'No, I totally forgot. I can't believe you got sick before we've even got to Jamaica!'

'Yeah, well, if I don't feel better soon then we probably shouldn't even go. Wait a minute, I think my mother put a case of stuff in my bag, Imodium A-D and other shit.'

If only he hadn't said the world shit; it was so awful, it made a mental image of a plastic bag filled with feces. Quickly she went to scrounge through his suitcase. 'Oh, please feel better, Barry, I don't want to have to cancel our honeymoon! It's going to be my first trip out of the country, and it's going to seem so weird if we don't go.'

'I'll probably be fine. It's probably just a bit of tummy upset, nothing serious. What do you say, shall we go get a drink?'

'With your stomach already upset? I don't think that's a good idea. Anyway, we could always just open the champagne and drink it here.'

'Come on, we're only going to have one honeymoon night. We'll take the champagne with us to Jamaica. I'll get a soda or something downstairs.'

She put a thin cardigan over her silk slip – she doubted anyone would guess it wasn't a dress – and found some sandals. How could she not go along with what he wanted? They would already be off to a bad start. The bar was almost empty. They sat at the bar on tall stools. 'Let me have a sambuca,' Barry said to the bartender. 'What do you want?'

'Isn't that going to make you worse?'

'No, it's a digestif.'

'I guess I'll have a, um . . . what other sort of drink is there?'

'Why don't you have that stuff?' Barry pointed to a bottle in the shape of a beehive. 'That's, like, honey-flavored schnapps, you'll like it.' The bartender poured them the drinks. 'Righty-o, cheers, toodle-oo, down the hatch, chin-chin, here's mud in your eye and all that.' Once – was it only a few days ago? – she would have found Barry's recitation of various drinking salutations to be amusing, even charming. Now she looked at him with irritation. 'Oops, excuse me for a minute, must find the Gents.' He staggered off his bar stool.

The bartender had ginger hair and was attractive in that American-Irish way. He wasn't much older than she, and there was something about his top lip she couldn't help but find immensely appealing. He watched Barry for a moment. 'You folks aren't driving, are you?'

He had the same Boston accent that now, for the first time, sounded – at least on him – sexy, masculine, he was able to look after himself. 'No, we're staying here. An early flight tomorrow. Where are you from?'

'South Boston. How about you?'

'Wortington.'

'Oh yeah? That's not too far from where I grew up.'

'I know.' She looked into his eyes which were blue, earnest, and shifted forward a bit on her bar stool so that her cardigan slid off her shoulders a bit, pushing her breasts, which were not in a brassiere, forward. 'I noticed your accent.'

'So where are you off to in the morning?'

'Um, Jamaica.' She didn't add that it was their honeymoon, it wasn't his business anyway, she told herself.

'Oh, that's cool. Club Med?'

'No –'

Barry returned from the men's room. He didn't appear to notice that she was half naked, leaning forward, talking to the bartender, that only a thin shell of pink silk separated his new wife from another man. 'You ready to go up? This place is kind of dead, huh?' He gulped his sambuca and put some money on the bar. She saw he pocketed all the change.

'Barry,' she whispered. 'Shouldn't you leave him a tip?'

He shrugged. 'For somebody pouring a drink from a bottle into a glass and handing it over? They already overcharged for the liquor! Come on, let's go.'

There was some change in the pocket of her cardigan and she left it at her place. She looked back at the bartender on their way out. He was polishing a glass. Probably he sailed or roller-skated or had grown up playing ice hockey. By comparison Barry was pudgy, slightly soft. He would always take care of her. Now they were married. He would never know what it was like to sit at a bar in Back Bay with a bunch of cops or firemen, drinking brewski. It was totally unlike him to have come down to a bar to have a drink anyway.

'Are you okay?' she said in the elevator.

'That place just sucked! It was so depressing and now my clothes stink. I'll have to send them to the cleaners as soon as we get to our hotel – if there are any cleaners there. Otherwise everything I own's going to smell!'

'You think you'll feel well enough to go? I was surprised at you anyway, that you wanted to go to a bar. I thought you hated bars.'

'We met in one, didn't we? See, I can still surprise you. I thought you'd remember!' They were back at the door. Barry fumbled with the key-card in the door for so long she wanted to snatch it away from him and try it herself, but at last the door worked. 'Why do they make these things so difficult anyway? Oh, God, I've still got the squits.' He went into the toilet.

'Do you think it was the chopped liver? What did you drink that sambuca for?'

'You know, I figured it would coat the stomach,' he yelled. 'It's that damn duodenal stenosis, it happens sometimes. Acid reflux. Usually not this bad, though.'

She went to adjust the air conditioner. A sour smell emerged from the unit by the window, not yeasty but rancorous. Beyond the high-way one last late-night plane took off in the darkness. They would go to Jamaica. They would buy an apartment, fix it up, furnish it. They would have children, take trips, maybe to Alaska or London. A million things would happen to her; why then was it so monotone, a gray line looming ahead: an electrocardiogram in which the hills were no more interesting than the valleys? Barry had undressed and was lying beneath the sheets. 'Come here for a minute.'

She went to his side and he pulled her down over him.

Removing his glasses he kissed her gently on the mouth and then playfully pinched both her nipples through the cloth. He apparently didn't know they were attached to her body. 'Hello, my sexy princess!' he said.

'Hello, sexy prince.' She had to fight her own irritation.

'I think everybody had a great time. Everybody said you looked beautiful. Neal said he really liked your friend Victoria. Wouldn't that be cool, if two people met at our wedding?'

'Yeah.'

'And did you have an okay time?'

She tried to come up with the appropriate thing to say. 'Your cousin's kids were so adorable! I couldn't believe it, nobody cried during the ceremony, and it was really fun dancing with your dad, I didn't know what a good dancer he is –' It was over. Somehow the day that she had looked forward to hadn't been about her at all. It hadn't had anything to do with her. The only time it had been about her was when Grace took her to one side and screamed at her, even though nobody else could hear. Otherwise it had been a party with a dressed-up doll, a party at which the main focus was on how much food the guests could eat and how quickly they could get out of there. She had lines to say, a few, a pre-programed marionette, and now that it was all over she was expected to say a few more things: as long as they were platitudes, clichés.

He was stroking her body over her silky dress and when his fingers got down to where her dress ended, just below her thighs, he reached up between her legs and plunged two fingers into her vulva, and began to probe her vaginal canal, as if he was searching for lost car keys.

After a time he removed them and spread whatever lubrication he had found there across her labia. 'Good girl, good girl,' he said. 'Oo, that feels nice.'

His penis was prodding her leg and she took it in her hand like the snout of a dog.

Her life, she knew, could have been so much worse. There was only a thin, illusory wall that separated her from a Chinese woman working in a sweatshop, ten, fourteen hours a day, at less than minimum wage. That woman would have given anything to be her. She closed her eyes. Removing her hand she licked Barry's penis, then rubbed it until it was wet enough for her to mount him and slip it inside.

15

If the stupid affair with Sandy hadn't been such a disaster – what affair had that been, anyway, number two? Three? – that she lost interest in him and then realized her period was late, she might never have come home and said, 'Oh, Barry . . . let's have a baby!'

He had suggested having a baby before – talked about it a lot, in fact – but she had always objected. He looked mildly surprised but taking her by the hand led her down the hall.

She studied the men on the subway wondering what it would be like to sleep with them. A vast pyramid-shaped man, tiny head broadening into shoulders and huge belly and hips: Humpty Dumpty – what was wrong with her? – seriously envisioning herself picking him up, and by then she was almost nine months pregnant . . .

When the credit card bill for all the baby furniture came Barry was horrified. 'But my God!' Barry said, 'This is . . . do you know how much you spent this month? What were you doing? We can't afford this!'

She had been so proud of the baby's room. She had studied one of the women's magazines which told where to buy stencils for the walls – giant pigs, raccoons, bucktooth chipmunks familiar from children's cartoons; had hung curtains, striped red, yellow and blue at the one small, square window, which looked out to the building on the side; bought a large, white, wooden crib with sides that could fold down, so that eventually it would become a youth bed. 'You can't possibly expect me to let the baby sleep in some junky plastic crib from Love for Kiddies!' she snarled, surprised at her own vehemence.

'But you didn't need to get this . . . was it custom-made? Or an antique? I mean, he'll outgrow it –'

'No, it's a crib that adjusts to a junior bed. And it'll be an heirloom. Besides, there were the other things I need, the layette, and oh, you don't understand anything!'

Barry turned his pinched face back in the direction of the TV screen.

The room for the baby was plain and boxy, even with the border of lambs around the top. She had bought a bassinet, a layette, a changing table; there was a rocking chair, a rug in the shape of a large blue fish. From the ceiling, above the crib, she had hung a mobile of musical teddy bears. In the magazine the room had looked warm, friendly and inviting. But it wasn't the room in the magazine at all, not even with the fresh yellow sheets and towels stacked under the layette, the fluffy appliquéd quilt. She couldn't help but think of a display in a zoo, cement icebergs for polar bears.

Ashamed, she crept back out into the TV room. 'I'm sorry,' she said. 'I know I shouldn't have spent so much, it's just that . . . well, we'll probably have more than one kid and it was more economical to buy good quality stuff that will last than a lot of junk . . . and besides, it's our first baby.'

Barry would drive ten miles out of his way to buy cases of paper towels that were ten cents less a roll than the same product sold nearby. Rather than have a meal delivered he would go and get it himself, to save the two or three dollars he would have had to tip the delivery person. Even so, they were still in debt: the laser equipment, redoing the offices, buying the previous dentist's practice, the mortgage on the apartment, the car payments – bills came in each month for thousands and thousands of dollars.

He was staring at the TV set. Some sort of sporting event was on – tennis – the ball being whacked back and forth while the heavy drone of two men, slow as bumblebees, blared across the room. An empty liter of diet soda was in front of him, a bag of pretzels. Even this room, the den, was a mistake: the white leather and chrome sofa, the glass coffee table, the kilim rug, the framed poster of Bette Davis in *Mr Skeffington*. The room looked cheap, dated, imitative – but of what?

Now she saw how tawdry it was. Barry's white smear of a face was a blob of anxiety. She went and put her arms around him. 'Do you want me to see if I can return the stuff?' she said.

'I don't know what to do any more, Peyton,' he said wearily. 'You've got to try and understand my position. I feel like a squirrel in a wheel, I keep running and running to stay in the same place. But I'm not even staying in the same place! Every time I think I'm getting on top, I wake up and find you've spent more money and I'm farther behind.'

She took her hands from his shoulders. 'I said I'd see if they'll take the stuff back!' she said. 'We'll put the baby in a drawer or a mattress on the floor or something!'

'No, no,' he said. 'It's fine. It was just a shock to get the credit card bill, that's all. Just promise me you won't spend any more money without talking it over with me.'

'I'm sorry,' she said. 'It's just that . . . I wanted everything to be perfect for him.'

'I know.' He turned back to the TV with a dull, glazed expression. She went to the side of the lounge chair and stroked his crotch across the surface of his khaki pants. Then she unzipped his fly. His penis was curled in its nest of scratchy hair, slightly sticky. She moved around to sit between his legs. 'You're blocking my view!' he said, craning to look over her shoulder.

'You just keep watching your television show,' she said, bending over. She unbuttoned his trousers and put his penis in her mouth. The baby sloshed inside her. She could feel one angry foot kicking her side. Suddenly she saw herself, her bottom on the arm of Sandy's leather couch, her knees spread, at the height of Sandy's waist, wrapped around him while he fucked her, looking down at her with half-closed eyes.

A hair had got caught between her teeth. She held his penis in her hand and sat back, wiping her mouth with her other hand and trying to pull loose the hair. He was hard now and he pushed her head back toward him. 'Don't stop now!' he said.

If only he would call her, just once, to say he still thought of her. If only it had been his baby, not Barry's, what would he have done then? She would have just packed her things and arrived at his door; there would have been nothing he could do. Sandy would have seen, then, that they were meant to be together.

Barry pulled down his pants until they were at his ankles. His penis pushed at the back of her throat with increasing force until she almost gagged.

She might have been having the most tremendous bowel movement of her life, something inhuman, impossible – whatever was inside her had no business being there, it was far too large – bigger than she. Had her doctor let the baby get too big? Perhaps she should have been induced weeks ago; her doctor did not seem that competent. It would be just her luck that this parasite inside her had no intention of leaving its comfy womb. Maybe she had become pregnant from someone other than Barry, six months earlier, and what would now emerge would be a fully grown man, mutant, talking, with teeth and stereo headphones, and a brokerage account . . . One final push; still nothing was happening, the doctor was actually using forceps to pull out the monster . . . and this time she thought she really must have been ripped in pieces . . . 'Here he is,' said the doctor, and held up a greasy bloody object which he handed to Barry. Beneath his white hospital cap Barry's face was white and exhausted.

Her room was full of flowers, she couldn't imagine where they had all come from. Mostly they were dreadful arrangements, candy-striped carnations, fat yellow mums from a toll-free number. But one bouquet was so perfect, so sophisticated, purple violets and even tinier lavender roses with green tendril things, that for a moment she thought Germano must have found out where she was and knew what was happening . . .

'Look at those!' she said. 'Who sent them?' Her hair was stringy and greasy, soaked with dried sweat and she had on no make-up; she began sitting up to look for her compact.

'I did,' Barry said. 'You like them?' He came and sat on the edge of the bed and picked up her hand.

173

'Pretty,' she said wearily and pulled her hand away.

'Sexy mommy princess,' Barry said. 'We have a baby! How did that happen?'

'What kind of a nitwit are you?' she wanted to snarl but was too tired to make more than a whimper. A few minutes later the nurse brought in their baby. His eyes were too close together, she thought distractedly, but he smelled sweet and his round, bald head was pure and comforting. Even though he had been inside her only a brief time before, she felt awkward holding him. He was swaddled but the parts flopped, breakable armatures. She handed him to Barry, who instantly cradled him with assurance.

'Little baby boy!' he said. Irritated, she took him back. Now what was she going to do? If there was only some way, not to stuff him back inside her, but forget this entire project. What a mistake it had all been. It would be okay maybe if it were just for a day or two, but she now saw it was going to be for the rest of her life – she was saddled with this object that would stop her from having fun, this object that was permanently going to brand her as that dreary entity, MOTHER.

Then Barry's parents arrived. 'Our first grandchild!' said Grace and reached for the baby. The new grandparents made cooing noises. Finally they were treating her as if she had accomplished a major feat. She supposed it was true, it was the one thing Barry could never do, but so what? She herself hadn't achieved anything: it was biological.

On the other hand she did feel a certain pride.

'And did you decide what you're going to name him?' asked Grace.

'Cassius,' said Peyton.

'Cassius!' Grace squeaked. 'I thought it was all decided, either Jason or Jonathan, wasn't it?' She looked at Leonard with an alarmed expression. Leonard beamed, his eyes now more similar than ever to those of Buddha in his fattest portrayal. She wondered how someone who was not particularly fat could have the eyes of a fat man, a generous frog. She smiled up at him.

'You're not really going to call him Cassius, are you?'

'Grace!' Leonard said.

Peyton nodded. Grace's hand went to her mouth. 'You like that, Barry?'

'I'm getting used to it, Ma,' Barry said in a warning tone.

'Well, well, well,' said Leonard. 'Cassius Amberg, I don't think there's ever been a Cassius Amberg *in* the Amberg family before.'

'You are calling him Amberg, aren't you?' said Grace.

'Yes, Ma, he's an Amberg,' said Barry.

'Well, I didn't know, after all, didn't Peyton want to keep her own name when you got married? So I only wondered . . .'

A nurse came in to give instructions in breastfeeding. She saw the eyes of the men – her husband, her father-in-law – flick involuntarily to her breast. What was their obsession about, anyway? Other cultures didn't have it. There were whole tribes of people wandering around, the women topless, lamprey-kids attached to nipple, the men weren't stuck on the sight like children in a toy store, ogling.

She couldn't bring herself to attempt to nurse in front of the three of them, so she sent them away.

The nurse showed her how to get her nipple into the baby's mouth. Nothing was happening, really; the kid wouldn't suckle. What was wrong with him, that he had no desire to be suckled? She knew a woman – a friend of Victoria's – who had nursed her child until he was almost five years old. The mother must have liked the attention, a big lout of a boy at a party (she had witnessed this) clambering onto his mother's lap and almost ripping off her top in order to get at her breast, while the men watched in fascination and the women in horror.

Outside the room she could hear Grace complaining to Barry. 'It's just terrible, Cassius Amberg, was it the name of someone in her family? How's he going to go to school, the other children will –'

'Ma!' Barry's voice was as screechy as his mother's. 'We'll call him Cash for short, Cash is like, you know, a baseball player's name.'

'I've never said anything to you, Barry, about your wife not being Jewish –'

175

'Yes you have, Ma, you've said plenty –'

'Oh, I think not – my main concern is that you are happy – and of course, without the mother being Jewish, the child isn't – but do you think she'll be willing to give him a Jewish education, within reason? She's not planning to have him baptized, is she?'

'Her name's Peyton, Mother! No, we're not going to have him baptized. And I'm sure she won't mind if you bring him to synagogue or Hebrew school on the weekends, but that'll be years away . . .' The voices grew hushed, perhaps they had walked down the hall. At least she could stay in the hospital for forty-eight hours, she couldn't face going back home. Maybe there would be some complications and she would be allowed to stay in this stupid room, a room that resembled a low-to-medium budget room in a hotel, with fake-wood walls and a TV set tucked in an armoire . . . She dozed off and after a bit heard them return; she didn't open her eyes. 'Oh, she looks exhausted, poor thing,' said Grace. 'But she's lucky, a two-day stay! Nowadays they mostly get them in and out, I guess that must have been thanks to you, Barry!'

'We'll see you over the weekend?' This was Leonard. 'Shall we bring some food to you, Friday night Shabbos?'

'I'll have to ask Peyton, Dad, when she wakes up. They'll be arriving home on Friday, she might want some time with just us.' There was a pause and she knew that, looking at his parents, Barry had felt overcome with guilt. 'I tell you what, will Saturday work for you? And that way we'll have one night alone as a new family, and then Cash can get to know his grandparents!'

'Saturday we're taking the train to Philly to see Aunt Felice, Barry,' said Grace. 'Believe me, you'll have the rest of your lives to bond as a family.'

'It'll be *an* early evening,' said Leonard. 'We'll bring Chinese from that place you like and that *way* you don't have to worry *when* you get home from work – you'll be picking them up, it'll be nice not *to* get home to an empty house.'

'And maybe Peyton will appreciate having someone with previous experience get the baby settled that first night, which can be difficult.

Meanwhile, let me get on the phone with the mohel – we'll do the bris on the Island.'

They were going to have to skin the kid's dick because his grand-parents were Jews, she couldn't help but think.

She had told Barry she wanted them to have a first night together, alone; it wasn't so terrible that he hadn't been able to fight them off, go along with her wishes, not theirs. But inside her now-empty belly something ugly, possibly evil, had cemented its sticky tentacles in the slack gap and begun to take root.

The birth of the baby proved to be the highlight of the experience. Her body now was not her own. She could not adjust to her flabby belly, sagging, where for the past few months it had been a taut container; her breasts were sore and tender and she couldn't stand Cash nursing. His eager lips on her nipples were irritating, she was almost consumed with the desire to shove his head away, and his suckling reminded her so much of Barry in the throes of making love. She hadn't minded Barry's suckling so much, it seemed connected to her clitoris, but this infant, even balder than Barry, with his greedy mouth, now felt obscene. She kept waiting for a welling up of maternal feeling but nothing like this occurred.

The way he stared at her, unblinking, all she could think was that his eyes were too close together and his face peeved and worried. She was unable to see him as an infant. He resembled an old man, an incontinent old man. His diapers constantly needed changing and when he wasn't sleeping he was yowling. When she picked him up his hands would latch on to her hair, lock and pull in a fashion that she interpreted as deliberately vicious, and as he got stronger he was not cuddly, just an entity to be constantly protective of and protected from. On more than one occasion she thought he had broken her nose.

After a few months she took him to a 'Mommy and Me' class for mothers and infants at the local gym, and the other new mothers, with their ponytails and bright, concerned faces, so adoring and attentive of their new babies, made her almost physically sick.

The days stretched endlessly before her. She had thought she would not go back to work, that she would be a full-time mother – it wasn't like she had enjoyed her job – but now she was frantic to get out of the house. She had envisioned herself tidying, cleaning, organizing, filing, throwing things out, baking and preparing nice meals while Baby slept, or going to the park, exercising by pushing him in the expensive stroller she had purchased before his birth.

Now all these things were stupefyingly impossible; boring. It was probably post-partum depression but she didn't have the energy to do anything about it. It took all of her strength to get him to the pediatrician. According to the doctor the baby was doing fine, though his nose was constantly running, he was colicky, and on his face he wore an unpleasant sneer. She tried to nurse him but her breasts, though big, had many cysts and small fibroids; she had trouble expressing milk. He didn't mind when she switched him to formula full-time. He was not an easy baby, though Barry was very good as a father and spent hours walking him at night.

He reminded her of those translucent-skinned twins and triplets she saw on the street, pushed in double and triple carriages by older mothers. Products of fertility treatments. In her neighborhood it was easy to spot them. There was something *pinched* about these infants: put on this earth through unnatural means, products of an egg and sperm forced together who had no interest in becoming one. Cash had that quality too.

The rich stinks and poots of childhood; the chortling farts, sour-milk custard belches; the rage of furious infancy by an entity who was simultaneously helpless and demanding – she could not enjoy any of it.

She kept calling her girlfriend, Victoria, calling her, desperate – Victoria was too tired to come to visit, she didn't feel well, she was breaking up with Boyfriend – Peyton thought their friendship was over, finally; that Victoria was too jealous now that she had a baby. Then at last – how long was it, really, almost twelve months – Victoria announced, rather grandly, 'I tell you what, I feel so bad that things have been so busy for me – it's not as if I haven't been trying – but why don't I drop by, on Saturday afternoon?'

Even though she was exhausted she was pleased that Victoria would come by. She did her best to look like one of the rich women she had seen on the Upper East Side. Tailored trousers, fawn-colored high heels, a blond cashmere cardigan, her hair sleeked back in a ponytail, matt gold jewelry. The overall effect didn't quite work . . . she couldn't help but sex things up a bit, wearing a push-up bra, the cardigan half-unbuttoned, the heels so high she was teetering, and wisps of hair flying loose.

Anyway, it was more her style to look this way. She planned to get things in honor of Victoria's visit at the local gourmet supermarket. The place was always crowded, with narrow aisles, but here one could buy pre-cooked meals, eggplant casseroles, fried veal cutlets, smoked fish, various breads and pastries – she would show Victoria her life was simple, elegant, full of luxury. She had come from a flea-infested apartment, with a crazy mother, a criminal brother; now it was Victoria who was unmarried, living with a friend, still trawling for men . . .

The phone rang. It was Victoria.

'Listen,' she said. Peyton could scarcely hear her above the noise of her kid, she had broken out in a sweat. 'I'm not going to be able to make it after all.'

'Well, that's fine,' she said, curtly. 'Everything okay?'

'Yup.'

'Some other time, then.'

If Victoria had had a baby Peyton would have been the first to visit, it was so petty to be jealous, particularly when she at least could have told Victoria, once you do this, your life is over. Nevertheless. She was livid: she had forgotten all these years to make real friends, but now what was she supposed to do about it? Then later, of course, she found out Victoria had been diagnosed HIV-positive that very week, which later, much later, turned out to be full-blown AIDS. But at the time how could she possibly have known, and then the whole sordid business dragged on and on . . .

179

While Cash was napping she loaded him into the stroller and went to the market anyway, throwing jars of caviar and smoked oysters into the basket in a kind of crazed spree, trying to grab as much as she could before he woke up. Then, in the line for the checkout, she jostled him trying to get the basket off the back of the handles; of course he woke up squawling, shrieking, stinking – she had always hated people who went around with screaming babies; and hers really needed a diaper change, the stench was appalling and it was worse that it had happened in a fancy supermarket.

Her purchases – blood oranges, a pale white melon, thin seeded flatbreads, extra-sharp cheddar, tunafish, a pound, pre-made, some big black prunes, fat flies, from a barrel, the caviar, the oysters – were already being rung up by the cashier. It totaled nearly two hundred dollars which she put on her credit card. She knew when the bill arrived Barry would query her about the expense and yell at her saying she could have made tunafish and a salad with ingredients and it would only have come to five or ten bucks at the most . . .

By the time she had signed for the stuff Cash's decibel level was even higher and she was totally distraught. She had trapped herself, built her very own cage, a husband, a two-bedroom apartment that was already too crowded and had only a sliver of a view, a child, and why? Because she was afraid of having to work in a cafeteria like her mother? What had been so dreadful about being single, childless, perhaps her job hadn't paid much but at least she was free, there was nobody questioning her every move; she looked back on the few short years when she was unmarried as a time of supreme freedom, a time in which she hadn't known or understood what freedom was . . .

And then, after all that, she remembered half the things on her list, which she had left at home: they needed milk, there was some kind of cider Barry wanted that you could only buy here, yogurt, butter, and since Cash had by now fallen angrily asleep once again (after all, they had left the store, he didn't have an audience), she went back in –

And she was standing in line to pay for the second time when a man alongside her on the other line said, 'Hi –'

He seemed familiar, he had ebony skin, really the most beautiful blue-black – for a moment she thought she knew him, but from where? And then she suddenly realized, oh, he's that famous performer – I do know him, but how?

Barry appeared next to her and tapped her on the shoulder, and said, 'Hi!' and at the same time the black man – what was his name? – Yussef Jones – also said, or added, 'How are you doing?'

So she said, without really directing it to anyone in particular, 'What are you doing here?' One of her items fell from her hands and on to Cash, who woke up howling with rage. 'Darn it!'

Barry began to say, 'I saw you forgot the list and so I came out to get the juice – I figured you wouldn't remember –' There was a crush of people and the aisles were narrow and he bent over Cash nervously, adjusting him.

The famous comedian or actor was saying 'Didn't I see you – in Las Vegas – yes, I know that I saw you in Las Vegas, I am sure –' He had a melodic foreign accent, more French than anything else.

'Yeah . . . I've been to Las Vegas, but . . . not recently . . .'

'Maybe, perhaps, three years ago?' the man said.

Then it dawned on her, she had seen him in the elevator when she was with Sandy.

'Oh, no,' she said. 'I wasn't in Las Vegas three years ago. Sorry.' She smiled at him nervously. She had in fact been in Las Vegas two years ago but if she said that he might say, you were there with some man or something weren't you, I saw you in the elevator. Of course she remembered seeing him in Las Vegas. In the elevator. When she was with Sandy. She had thought, at that moment, why is it that it's only when you're with one guy that you meet – or at least see – another and he looks at you that way? There was some weird law of physics that made this happen. Now he was still staring at her, didn't he see that this time she was with her husband, her kid, that she had dribble on her? She turned to Barry. 'Barry, since you're here, will you please, please take Cash and the groceries home? I'm just not doing that well with him today, and if you take all this stuff I can get my other errands done, I have to go to the drugstore –'

'You got the cider I wanted?'

She signed the credit-card slip. The groceries, the second batch, were already bagged. 'Yes, yes.'

'Isn't Victoria coming over?'

'She cancelled! Barry, this is Yussef Jones –'

'Hi . . . So what did you get all this for, if you're not entertaining her?'

'Barry, we still need to eat! Please take Cash, I need a break.'

'All right, all right, but don't stay out too long, I have stuff I want to get done. Nice to meet you,' he said to Yussef as he pushed the stroller out of the store.

She knew Barry was irritated that he had to take over child-minding when he hadn't planned to.

'Beg your pardon,' said Yussef.

'Could it have been two years ago?' she said. 'Because . . . I was there two years ago and I remember seeing you . . . How could I forget? Actually, I've always had a major crush on you—'

'I didn't know anyone even knew who I was anymore,' he said.

'Oh, please! You? My God, it's like watching a panther in action.'

'You live in this neighborhood, don't you?' he said. 'I've seen you around.'

'You have?' She was an idiot. 'You know what? I think I'm having a nervous breakdown.'

'Why?'

'I don't know! Just . . . everything. Having a kid. Being married. It all seems . . . overwhelming.'

'You look like you could use a drink.'

'That's for sure! . . .' She wasn't certain if he was asking her. 'Don't you . . . you can just go out shopping like this? Don't you get mobbed on the street?'

'Are you sure you have the right person? My television show was a flop.'

'I didn't even know you had a television show!'

'There you go.'

'I mean, if I had known you had a TV show, I would have watched it, but I didn't know – I guess it wasn't on for long, I just know your comedy stuff – you're so funny –' He had paid for his items and they were standing on the sidewalk while the pedestrians swirled past them on both sides, water hissing around two pebbles at low tide.

'Would you like . . . do you want to go and get a cup of coffee or a drink?'

'A drink. I would love to but . . . I have to be quick, my –'

'Let's go then. Oh, you have errands, don't you? I forgot. Do you really need anything?'

'No,' she said, 'I can get the stuff later. Where can we go, nearby, that's quick?'

'I'm subletting a place just around the corner, do you mind if we stop there first so I can drop off my things?'

'No, that's fine – you don't live in New York?'

'Paris, mostly, but I'm over here performing now, at the City Academy – I'm playing Lucky in –'

'You're everywhere these days! I saw you on the *Sheik Y'abouti Show*, and weren't you just interviewed on the news?'

'Oh, you saw me, did you? Here, come along, it's just here I am staying.'

They had arrived back in his sublet. 'Come in,' he said. He put his bags down on the floor in the kitchenette and she followed him. 'Have you seen this? I do not know what is happening here.' A huge cloud of tiny fruit flies swarmed mindlessly around the light and garbage bin. 'The flies! I have never seen so many flies! I do not know what to do, is this a common occurrence?'

She began to laugh, slightly dementedly. 'No! That's crazy, it seems like something from one of your comedy routines – were there this many flies when you moved in?'

'No! There were no flies when I arrive. But each day, I come in the room and . . . from below, from the apartment beneath, rises up a terrible odor. I have thoughts, my neighbor perhaps keeps a corpse.'

'Did you complain to the super?'

'No. I have no time. Rehearsals, and now, the performances – come.' The living room was all glass, on a high floor but he crossed the room and began pulling shut the curtains. 'What do you think?' he said. 'Will you like to stay here and have a drink? It will be much easier than –'

'Do you have any vodka?'

'But of course!' He went back into the kitchen. 'No, I am afraid I do not. Is there something else I can get you? A whiskey? A gin?'

'What are you having?'

'Me? I am not much of a drinker. Maybe some tea.'

She couldn't stay here and just have a tea. 'Gosh, I don't know. What about . . . just a small whiskey, I guess.'

'With ice?'

'Yes.' The place was hideous, it had to be some kind of commercial rental . . . What was she doing here, anyway? A married lady, though she had lost all the weight since having the baby her stomach was still a bit flabby, she had stretch marks. 'Well, uh, cheers.' He handed her the glass and she guzzled a large swig. 'So, uh –'

'You like to take your clothes off and make love? You are so beautiful, I would love to see you without your clothings.'

She drank the rest of the whiskey. What had she thought would happen, anyway? She must have known, there was a subtext, hadn't she herself appeared receptive? At least a man still found her attractive – and besides, she had never slept with anyone famous before. It might be her last chance. Her only chance. Perhaps if she pretended she was the one in control, it might all be less . . . peculiar. 'I'd like to see you without your clothes on,' she said, and stepping forward began to unbutton his shirt. Then she was sick of herself and she was sick of him, a couple of bad actors in a bad movie and in her head she saw a screenplay, typed out bits –

At first Peyton was delighted to get married, have a baby. But in the past months it has begun to dawn on her that this is no longer the life she wishes to lead. Until now, however, it has not occurred to her how difficult it will be to extricate herself.

She visualized the tremulous-lipped actress, fraught with sensitivity, emotion. What movie had it been, anyway – that actress with the wistful smile that made you want to smack her and a perpetual herpes sore about to blossom on her perpetually bee-stung lips . . . She was pushing this guy, backwards, to where? She knew where she was going, and, sure enough, there was a hall, a bedroom, a pile of things on a chair beside the bed – what was this, a tie? She tied up his wrists while he slithered out of his pants – obviously he liked this, he needn't have gone on if it didn't appeal to him – and then she found another item, a dirty shirt, something, and tied it around his eyes – my God, she should have been getting paid, she was good at this!

She had his little dick out of his pants – there was that stupid myth ruined – she spread his legs wide apart and tied up the testicles and the base of that little cock, pinched his dark nipples and he came all over the place, just shot his load, ugh, all over his stomach and her hands, and she thought, 'You know what? I'm not enjoying this,' and she got up and went down the hall, washed her hands in the fly-filled kitchen and went out the door.

He followed her around for weeks after that, leaving bouquets of flowers and tickets to his show with her doorman and once she bumped into him back at the supermarket and he said, 'Listen, I have to go back to France, my production has ended, I guess you know by now that I have fallen for you in a big way, I am in love with you, if you wish, I will leave my wife, I will seek divorce, if you will come to be with me or let me come here –'

'I just can't,' she said.

'But listen, this is good news, I have now a role in a big movie, it will be filming in Morea, I could send you a ticket to meet me there on the set, a beautiful beach, I will buy you the South Sea pearls, the black ones as big as grapes – may be you are not ready to make up your mind, or a commitment but –'

She couldn't help but feel flattered and she went to his rented apartment for one last drink. She had her period; she would tell him that was why she wasn't going to sleep with him. It was nice to know a movie star. Especially one who wanted to marry her. When she walked in the door he was all over her in seconds and had her pants down. 'I can't,' she said, 'I have my period, I –'

He seemed crazed and forced his dick in around the edge of her panties and even though she had a tampon in there he fucked her anyway, shoving up alongside the cotton wadding tube. Some kind of an aggressive humping rabbit. It didn't really hurt but it didn't feel good. 'Please,' he said. He was almost in tears. 'I'm sorry, I couldn't help myself, please say I will see you again.'

She wished she could feel sorry for him, but she couldn't. She should never have screwed somebody on her own territory, in her own city. Even a dog knew better than to soil its own nest.

16

'You think what I'm wearing isn't appropriate?'

Germano shook his head. 'You are a beautiful young woman, it would be a pleasure for me to choose something for you to wear. Please allow me.' He managed to convey a look at once slightly bored and disdainful: she would be foolish not to let him do so. Other women her age would have thought nothing of it – she knew this for a fact – why did she have to be so Victorian, so prudish? Here was a rich man she had met at the airport, treating her like a daughter. Anyway, none of this need ever get back to Barry.

She shrugged. 'Well . . . okay! I mean, I really didn't bring much with me and I don't want to embarrass you in front of your friends. Unless . . . you don't want me to come along?'

'Nonsense, it is only a small dinner at the home of one of my ex-wives, who is Brazilian.'

'That will be so interesting for me!'

'Come.' He looked at his watch. 'This will have to be fast, I have some phone calls to make and a meeting with a business associate here in the suite. Perhaps you will have tea at the bar or you have something else to do during that time . . . I fear it will be boring for you.'

His breath in the elevator smelled faintly of Scotch, malty, masculine and when he took her arm, saying, 'Watch your step,' as they got out, she was incredibly attracted to him. He was alien: half minotaur or satyr, a mythologic figure. The barrel chest, the politician hair, the pale, honeyed sheen of wealth, French cuffs and testosterone. Money was his aftershave lotion.

The boutique had only a few items of clothing in it and looked so expensive, the sales clerks so haughty, she never would have dared go in on her own. 'What do you like?' he said, gesturing. She began to look through the clothes. She thought she would pick out something inexpensive but there were no price tags and they had labels with unrecognizable names; the racks held nothing but a few wispy items: pale moss-green chiffon, thin drapey cashmere things tipped with chartreuse dyed bits of fur, the palest sequins shimmering, dried fish scales from a dead mermaid.

She took an item from its hanger. It was impossible to imagine how it was to be worn so low-cut in front and back, with a kind of spray, almost of sea foam, as a bustle. On the floor were a few select pairs of shoes which matched. 'Here,' Germano said impatiently, and pulled the green chiffon thing from the rack, 'try this one on.'

'But – it . . . it doesn't even have a price on it, it must be hideously expensive.'

'Come, try it on. It is for me to decide.' He spoke a few words to the salesgirl. Had Peyton been in there on her own the woman would have raised her eyebrows but now – although she was almost a foot taller than her – the woman shrank into something humble, fawning.

In the dressing room she tried to put the dress on over her head but the sales clerk indicated she remove her bra.

It was the most stunning dress she had ever put on and she suddenly understood how some people could spend a lot of money on clothes; it fit her as if she were a movie star. Her breasts were held up by wiring, about to explode, her bottom was high and round, the fabric was shimmering, intricately cut – but it dragged on the ground. The woman tied lacy strings, hooked hooks, did up zippers. It wasn't fussy or old-ladyish, it was sophisticated and looked expensive. 'Oh, but it's . . . too long,' she said. She didn't want to say that it made her breasts look enormous, a joke. 'Anyway, I don't have anything else that would go with it.'

'Let me see,' Germano called.

She came out of the dressing room and he looked at her with such intensity she thought she would faint. No one had ever looked at her this way before, it was more than pure lust: a jaguar sprawled across a branch and she a small gazelle realizing, too late, what lay above. It made her breathless. 'That is the dress,' he said after a pause. Was it legal for someone to look at her that way? This was something she had been missing out on all this time.

'It's too long, I mean it's meant for a taller person.'

He spoke to the sales clerk. Finally he said, 'She says it will be possible to have it hemmed for this evening. Take it off.'

The woman spoke to him again in Portuguese. 'Yes, yes,' he said, just as she had turned to go into the fitting room. 'Your feet – what size shoes are you wearing?'

'Six.'

More discussion ensued and the sales clerk reappeared with a high-heeled pair of shoes in soft kidskin. A whimsical evening bag went with the whole ensemble, a sort of swollen pair of testicles on a string, pimpled with long hairy things, ridiculous, amusing. Germano looked at his watch. 'Good,' he said. 'We are done. Why don't you go to have your hair done, or your nails, whatever women do in such places, there is the beauty salon, which she says is still open around the corner in the lobby; have the bill sent to my room. I must leave you now. I will see you later. You must be prepared to go to dinner at ten o'clock.'

While her nails were drying a man washed and fixed her hair, arranging it in an intricate chignon; someone else put on make-up, different than what she usually did, silvery pink lipstick, almost no mascara, smoky brown around the eyes – even in her dowdy skirt and T-shirt her aura was now that of a rich person. Hours had passed. She went back to collect her shoes and bag and dress. The sales clerk did a double take. She hoped she didn't resemble a dictator's wife pretending to have class, taste, style.

The dress was ready. She decided to change in the shop – that way the woman could help her and she wouldn't spoil her hair even if it was too fussy. Now the woman was much friendlier. 'Mr Germano is your boyfriend?'

'Huh? Oh, no, um . . . he's just a family friend.' My gosh, she was like a mistress already. What if she was his mistress? Was he married? The way he looked at her made her want to undress in front of him, just thinking of him made her nipples feel icy; she could never sleep with someone else, how hurt Barry would be, she would never want to hurt Barry. 'By the way, how much was the dress?'

'In US dollars? Two thousand five hundred. It is a good deal, no, I think? So beautiful. And the color so especial on you.'

This kind of betrayal – what would it be, after all? It had been going on since the world began, did it have to have meaning? Wasn't it the way men had always behaved? The only option for women without money was to be young and phenomenally beautiful, as she, Peyton, had been, which enabled her to marry a dentist. Now she saw, if she had had money, something resembling a good background, she wouldn't have settled for Barry. Meeting Germano might be her chance to upgrade to a fancier model – even if Germano was, maybe, in his mid-fifties.

But that fact might not even be a demerit. If she was the second or third wife of a man in his fifties, a rich man, a handsome one, she would be the wife who reaped the benefits and rewards. She would be the cosseted, pampered, final wife; not the one at home while he worked full-time and was still young enough to want to screw around.

In the mirror was a different person. She was no longer an American bimbo, a middle-class housewife. How stupid was she, to have once thought that Barry, his mother Grace and father Leonard, represented a class and social status she could never achieve? She saw now they were only boorish and slightly vulgar citizens of a country that had abruptly sunk far below her new dreams.

She was stunning. The pale lipstick, the smoky brilliant blue eyes thick with dark lashes, the upswept hair smooth as an eel, the perfect figure shrouded in seaweed. Her breasts might burst out at any moment, break loose from the green seams. The first bloom had not begun to fade, she was at her peak, with each cell in her body a sac of fresh water, ripe and ready to be picked.

She turned from the mirror and smiled at the shop clerk. The woman's skin, she saw now, was not so good, rough, a bit acned. Before her eyes the other woman had begun to shrivel.

The shoes fit her feet perfectly. The heels were so high they caused a certain amount of pain to shoot up through the back of her calves – what was that movie about the mermaid who was allowed to be human and walk on legs? She too was willing to suffer.

She returned through the lobby. Now everyone was staring at her, but it was different: a strange sizzle trailed behind her. She could have sworn a man who had been talking to a couple of other guys got up, totally against his will, and began to follow her. She was right; he got into the elevator behind her and though she looked off absently into space he began nervously asking her something in Portuguese.

The elevator operator, impassive, squat, did nothing but press buttons although the elevator was automatic and his presence was not really required. 'Twenty-four, please,' she said to the operator and then added, to the other man, 'I'm sorry, I don't understand; I don't speak Portuguese.' She gave him her most sincere smile and looked into his eyes. Normally she would have been shy. Someone else now occupied her body.

The man seemed unable to speak. Then, in rapid, flawless English, he began to babble. 'Oh, I'm terribly sorry, I assumed you were Brazilian; I don't know what to say exactly, I do hope I'm not bothering you. Are you by any chance an actress?'

She smiled and kept looking into his eyes while shaking her head.

'My name is Ian Sackfield, I produce videos, I hope you don't mind my introducing myself; I don't know, perhaps you're a singer? Forgive me, I thought I recognized you from somewhere and hoped we might work together – are you working on any projects at the moment?' He was almost incoherent. 'I'm probably making a total fool of myself. Is there any chance – could I make it up to you by inviting you as my guest to dinner? Or for a drink?'

They had reached Germano's floor.

'I'm sorry,' she said. Now she knew what it meant, that strange expression about a cat swallowing the butter. The doors opened and she got out.

'Wait! Do you ever get to London? Let me give you my card!' He was holding the door and thrust his card at her. The elevator operator, too, acted drugged, dazed; surely it was his job to prevent this man from pursuing her. She was amused, the two men in a stupor or trance, while a bell signaled it was time for the doors to shut. 'What about tomorrow? Are you around?' he said.

'Maybe.'

'I'm in room 603. Please don't think I'm an idiot. Maybe I'll see you at the pool? I'll be there in the morning . . .' The elevator operator snapped from his trance and began shouting at Ian Sackfield to release the door.

She turned to wave as she walked down the hall. It had been the most perfect moment she had ever achieved.

She had the key and swept in, about to go and throw herself at Germano with excitement and gratitude over her new outfit, when she saw he was sitting on the sofa opposite another man. Germano got to his feet quickly – too quickly – and said, loudly, 'Ah, here is the friend of my daughter I was telling you about.' The other man got to his feet. His eyes narrowed when he saw her. He was younger than Germano, dark, Latin, slightly scruffy in an expensive suit and T-shirt. 'Allow me to present to you my friend Felix Rodriguez.' The man extended his hand. 'And this is . . .' Germano's face went white – he couldn't remember her name. 'This . . . is . . .' He was staring at her as he began to mutter.

'Peyton,' she said. She reached for Felix's hand but instead of shaking hers he leaned over and kissed it. She blushed. Nobody had ever kissed her hand before, it was totally absurd and yet glamorous. The dress had transformed her into one of those old actresses – she couldn't remember their names, but she had seen the movies: *Gone with the Wind*, *Jezebel*, *Gilda*.

'And how is Jacinta?' said Felix slyly.

'Who?'

The man Felix had very white teeth. 'Germano's daughter?' His smile was that of a laughing dog.

'Would you care for a glass of champagne to take to your room?' Germano said. 'I am afraid we must complete a bit of work and I hope you will excuse us.'

It took her a few seconds to realize this meant she was supposed to leave. He poured her a glass of champagne. 'So nice to meet you.'

It was unfathomable that two men really did, could or would order a bottle of champagne in a hotel suite and sit around drinking it. She picked up her glass and carried it to her room. 'Nice to meet *you*,' she said to Felix before closing her door.

The champagne did not taste very good, dry and almost sour with bubbles that frizzled her nostrils, but she drank it. She was afraid she would spoil her make-up. If she lay down she would mess the perfect hair. The TV was almost all Portuguese channels – a man was picked from a live studio audience to guess which hole a chicken was going to run into on a studio set – but finally she found a news station in English. Some sort of flood had occurred in India. She didn't even know where India was, only the abbreviations of the names of the airports. There had been a shooting in New York, in which fourteen people were killed. She couldn't help but wonder if one of them had been Barry. It would make things easier, in a way.

She wandered around the room in a state of sexual excitement, the tops of her legs rubbing together. The view out the other window faced away from the sea. Far below were tiny shacks built onto a slanted hillside, with corrugated tin roofs, falling-down walls. One false move and her breasts would be out of the top of the dress. Almost as a joke, she pulled the two sides down and apart so that her nipples were exposed. She was a bitch on heat, a baboon in estrus; what was wrong with her? Her dreary life was all she deserved. It grew dark outside almost at once, like a light switched off, and she thought this must be what was meant by a tropical sunset, no twilight period. There was a knock on the door. She didn't turn around.

'I apologize for that,' Germano said. 'I hope you weren't embarrassed –'

She turned around, her dress top still pulled down. He looked at her and for a moment she thought she had misunderstood everything, his earlier look of lust, and that she had now made a total slut fool out of herself and he was going to laugh at her. But he came over almost at once and cupped her breast in his hand and, picking it up, put his mouth on the nipple as though someone had tossed him a bottle of beer; his other hand went up under her dress and pulled her panties to one side, almost roughly but then his fingers were quite gentle and fiddled with her labia; an index finger stroked her anus, which made her nervous, she was didn't want to get a urinary tract infection if he then put the same finger in her vulva. His hand and mouth left her breast and he unzipped his pants; a huge dick, fat and purple, leapt out stiff, veering off to one side and he hoisted up her dress and he was just about to shove it in her.

'Hey, hey, what's your rush?' she said, her voice sounded much tougher than she was. 'Anyway, you've got to wear a condom, where are they?'

'What?' he said.

'A condom.'

'I don't need a condom. I have good control. I will not come in you.'

'No, but what about diseases?'

'I am perfectly healthy and I think you are too.'

'I don't care. I can't do anything if you don't put one on.'

'Do you not trust me? You must believe me. Did I not take care of you at the airport? It will be fine. It is not the sort of thing I carry around. I do not know you but I am not that sort of man. Do you have one with you?'

Almost against her will she put her hand on the purple dick. It was so forceful, so independent, it stood out between the two of them like a third party who had decided to join in. They both looked down at it helplessly. Then he leaned forward and kissed her and the thick tongue that had almost seemed deformed pushed into her mouth and his hands began undoing her hair while the tongue probed; at last she turned away and murmured 'Are you sure it's okay?'

'I am totally clean,' he said and before she knew it her legs were apart and his dick had begun to push its way relentlessly inside her. 'That thing is huge,' she said, 'It'll never fit . . .' It was inexorable, gigantic, she felt she was being split apart.

'I must get something,' he muttered and pulled out of her.

She lay back on the bed her legs still spread and the beautiful dress pulled up to her waist and pulled down below her breasts; the dress was being spoiled, she didn't want it to be ripped, there was no way she could undo the hooks at the back and then she thought, what the hell am I doing and stood up, tugging it back up in front; she hadn't even taken off her high heels; how sexy she must look. The thought of how she looked made her even more aroused.

Then he returned. 'What are you doing?' he said. 'Here, let me help you.' He undid the dress.

'No, no, I don't know.' She panicked, tried to protest. 'I can't do this, I'm married and . . . it was, it's too big, your thing is too big to fit in me, it's not going to fit, it will hurt . . . I can't, go through with this . . .'

'Don't worry . . . don't worry, I will be gentle . . .' He had removed his jacket and shirt in the other room and was standing in boxer shorts, holding a tube of some kind of ointment; the big penis was in his shorts but she could see the outline, though it was no longer hard, as it lay against one leg. 'My God, you make me feel like a young kid again.' He took his penis out of his shorts and began to rub it industriously with the whitish cream that coiled out of the tube.

17

She got off the plane and found Sandy waiting for her at the gate, swanky in black cowboy boots and a white straw cowboy hat; he was taller than she remembered and a bit more weather-beaten. It all was so exotic – a cowboy, Las Vegas – her mouth was dry with excitement and for a moment the ringing of the nearby slot machines seemed to be going off in her own head.

'Well hi there, little lady! It sure is nice to see you here!' He grinned, revealing tiny teeth. Maybe that was why she found him so sexy, those tiny teeth – he had told her, once, when she had first met him – something about getting kicked by a horse when he was young, and never losing his baby teeth.

'Were you waiting long?'

'Maybe an hour. Well, what do you say, we can catch a shuttle service to the hotel, is that all your baggage or did you have something checked?'

'I do have another bag.'

'You needed another bag, just for two days?' Sandy eyed her carry-on, shaking his head with disbelief. 'Looks to me like you could fit a lot in that one.'

'I know . . . but that's just my make-up and stuff and . . . I brought some special dress-up clothing. I never get to dress up and –'

'Sounds intriguing. See, I got everything in this one carry-on bag. Makes life a lot easier, lemme tell you.' Sandy's bag was from one of those travel catalogs: ugly but expensive. She hated her luggage. Barry had bought her a set for her birthday, hideous checked nylon 'so you can recognize it on the conveyor belt', a mucky color, out of style – he didn't know, poor guy – which is why it was on sale. There wasn't any way she could have returned it, especially not without hurting his feelings.

On their way to the baggage claim she passed a pretty blonde, hair tidily pulled back, wearing a T-shirt that said 'I ❤ Porn', and a man who looked like a serial killer, and then a kid, maybe six years old, with dyed blond hair shaved on the sides and long in the center, a fat woman in farmer's overalls, only with short pants, so that the woman looked like a demented Baby Dimples; a woman in a sequinned jacket and bag studded with rhinestones.

It was the Lourdes of America; every dysfunctional had arrived in search of a cure or was departing . . . How Grace would have hated this place and how happy it made her – a whole realm devoted to people with missing parts, the hole in the Swiss cheese . . .

They waited forty minutes for her suitcase. 'Should we just take a taxi? Half the weekend is over already, it feels like.'

'A taxi's going to be thirty-five, forty bucks,' Sandy said. 'The shuttle's six dollars apiece. Runs on the half-hour and hour.'

'Whatever.'

At last they arrived at their hotel and he didn't offer to pay for the room after all, he said she could put it on her credit card and he would give her a check for the other half – my God, it only came to a couple of hundred dollars, all right, three hundred each, but she said, 'You know, my husband goes over the credit card receipts, and I already told him the hotel was half-price, and I didn't think it was going to be as much as this, anyway: that wasn't the rate I booked on the phone –'

'Well, honey, if they told you a different rate, then you shouldn't let them get away with it –'

It was supposed to be exciting, an illicit affair in Las Vegas, with all the crazy lights and the anonymity of it all; the tawdry hotel in downtown – the cheapest place she had been able to find that wasn't actually a highway motel – they, she and Sandy, had agreed to split it, and though she had told Barry it was practically a free trip, the truth was the airfare was expensive, almost six hundred dollars, which he was surely going to throw a fit about, but she hadn't told him it was a free airplane trip, had she, and she got something of a deduction for being in the travel industry –

If they split the hotel it would end up being only fifty bucks a night, so that was almost free – she wished she had her own credit card, so Barry wouldn't be there analyzing what she had spent each month, but she supposed that, since she had failed so miserably and couldn't pay her own bills, he was entitled to have control over her. Now if she spent anything on the joint credit card, even bought a bunch of bras or underpants, there he was, saying, 'How could you have spent this much, just on underpants?'

'They were on sale, Barry, believe me. You have no idea what other women spend, who don't go to the sales but go to Saks and pay full retail – your mother spends twenty times more than me, for the same item.'

'Yeah, but my dad isn't just getting started like I am! He's the head of the whole entire company, and they're not trying to save up and pay off a mortgage and –' He turned back to his game on TV.

The line behind them for check-in had grown longer and she was irritated. She hadn't come all this way to end up with a man who was as penurious as her husband. If he could have been more like Germano, they would have been staying in an upscale place to begin with, one of those amazing casinos, not in downtown but out on the strip, a room at the top of the pyramid, channeling energy, or a suite with its own private pool and marble floors. Finally it was agreed, they would each put half on their credit cards; it turned out not to matter, anyway, all they needed at this moment was an imprint.

Then they couldn't find their way to the elevators – it was a crazed funhouse with the lights and mirrors. Whichever way they went there were more slot machines; and the whole time she was thinking, when we get up to the hotel room I'll say, come on, let's go get something to eat, I'm starving. Because she didn't want it to appear she had flown this far just to have immediate sex, it would be nicer to let some romance build, and in a way it would be punishment for Sandy's lack of . . . gentlemanliness, putting her through all that at the check-in line, while other people were watching and listening . . .

The room was smelly, old smoke, that peculiar dampness that comes from an overworked air-conditioning unit. There were the two double beds with the polyester coverlets, fake brown brocade – once there had been some television study which showed that in hotel rooms there were traces of excrement everywhere, the whole place was riddled with unsanitary things, E. coli, mucus, invisible-to-the-human-eye cum stains, whatever. But that was what she had wanted, wasn't it? To have some sordid experience?

He didn't even come over to her to try anything, anyway. After all that, he said, 'Well, here we are. How you doing? What would you like to do?' *He* wasn't going to make the first move, but if she wanted to . . .

'I'm starving, shall we go and try to find something to eat?'

Darkness was already falling and the neon lights were beginning to come on; the street was closed off to pedestrians but covered with a thousand million lights of every imaginable color, lights everywhere and a man dressed as Elvis Presley was standing in front of another casino, saying, 'Come on and get a free picture with Elvis!' And the lights all did things, neon cowgirls kicking up their legs, crowns and diamonds and aces and bucking horses and names and words – GOLD NUGGET, FOUR JACKS AND A QUEEN, TOPLESS NUDE DANCERS – so jarring and colorful and crazy, she was a kid at an amusement park, it was the most wonderful, terrible land she had ever visited. And off to the right, a darkened entryway and beyond a vast, dark cave full of thousands of machines, all going *ca-chink-a-chink*: a million peeping squalling birds – 'Come on, let's go in here!' she said joyfully. They were holding hands and she pulled his arm. 'Nickel slots,' she said. 'Come on, Sandy, give me all your nickels! This is great!'

'Now I'm not going to give my nickels to one of these machines. If you want, later, I'll find a decent-looking blackjack table, you can watch. I remember, on my honeymoon, wife number three I believe, we went to Reno and I won enough to pay for the whole trip plus a new horse for my bride –'

The fizzy candy air was going out of her. 'Okay, okay, let me just try it, though, I've never played a – what are these, one-armed bandits? – and it's only a nickel.'

He took a dollar out of his billfold and gave it to one of the women clad in a pink Egyptian-style minidress, her hair wrapped with a golden snake, and handed Peyton a few coins.

'What if I win – gosh, that one says you can win sixty thousand dollars! That'll be great!'

He lounged behind her while she put the money into the machine. Next to her a woman was feeding three machines at once; one of the machines began to scream, fire engine shrill, and all kinds of lights went on at the top, twirling and whirring and thousand upon thousand of nickels began spewing out, spewing out in a metallic upchuck; the woman began mechanically shoving the money into a gigantic plastic cup and feeding it back into the machine.

Within minutes Peyton's dollar was gone.

'Come on, let's get out of here, we can try out that $2.99 Steak Special we passed on the way.'

They had to go through a huge casino to get to the restaurant, which turned out to be some dark coffee shop in the back; by now she wasn't even hungry any more, all she wanted was a drink and when the waitress came over she said the only time there was a steak for $2.99 was between the hours of 3:30 and 5:30 A.M. and if they wanted a steak now it was $14.99.

She started drinking Bloody Marys and after the first one she felt better and by the third one she felt kind of good. He was gorgeous, sitting across from her, he had removed his hat and gone to the men's room to comb his hair, and he was drinking bourbon, even across the table she could smell that sweet, smoky smell and she thought, in a while I'll go back to the room with him and fuck him senseless and see what kind of tricks that old dog has up his sleeve. His eyes were green, almost emerald, flecked tiger-yellow, and he winked at her and said, 'Say, did I ever show you where the horse bit me?'

'No.'

He grabbed her knee under the table and gave it a squeeze. 'Ha!

You fell for that one. What can I say, except, you shore are pretty and it shore is good to see you.'

They had hamburgers and French fries. She thought she had never tasted anything so delicious in her entire life, why was that? The soft bun and the onions, the tangy ketchup, the meat in the middle, and the French fries, it all was incredible, salt and fat and meat, with the different textures . . . And by now it was, what, eight, nine o'clock at night, and in their hotel lobby she put some quarters into one machine – she couldn't pass the machines without wanting to feed them – and they decided to go back up to their room, why, though, what was the excuse? She couldn't actually remember. And on the way to the elevators they got lost again, and so they stopped at the bar and had another drink – it was so much fun to watch the people going by, not that the place was particularly crowded, but the light made everyone look so freakish, or perhaps they *were* freakish – anyway, it was impossible to figure out who they were or why they had come here—

The elevator was crowded but he was holding her hand and they were grinning at each other and he lifted her palm to his mouth and kissed it. There was a man across from them, in the other corner, watching them; she couldn't help but notice, he was a black man, in an elevator of white people, in a city that was mostly, maybe 90 percent, white tourists, and she realized he was someone she knew – well, she didn't know him, he was a comedian – Yussef Jones, that was his name, he was French or something – for years she had had a sort of crush on him.

She wondered what he was doing in the elevator in this tired hotel – even if he was performing somewhere in Vegas, didn't the stars have their own elevators? – and he was quite famous, he had been on all the late-night talk shows, and in a few movies. For a second he looked at her intently, with lustrous black eyes, and then someone else in the elevator said, 'Why hey, it's you, that Yussef Jones guy from TV! Would you mind, could I get your autograph, it's not for me but my sister –'

The elevator stopped and the performer got out, followed by the guy who had started talking to him.

'You know, I have a surprise for you, when we get upstairs,' Sandy whispered in her ear.

'What kind of surprise?' She had already forgotten Yussef.

'Oh, you know – for when we . . .' He grinned. She was nervous. What if he was crazy? What was he going to do to her? – but also excited, a dull ache started in her groin, a bird painfully trying to peck its way out.

And then they were back in the room and she said, 'I'm going to call room service for a drink. You want one?'

'Okay, if you're having one – Jack Daniel's – I could have picked up a couple bottles for us at the liquor store, though, it'd be cheaper –'

She went over to him. She hadn't been going to make the first move but now she thought, I can't help it, I can't wait. Her arms, unattached to her, went around his neck and he put his hands on her breasts – at least now he was being more aggressive – and she pulled her panties down. He pushed her back onto the bed, so she was lying on her back, her cunt at the edge, and pulled apart her legs – she was still fully clothed, even the high heels, just the hairy cunt exposed and he grabbed a pillow and shoved it under her, so that it was entirely sticking up in the air, black and hairy and she felt she was going to die; she was so excited it was almost painful –

'Room service!'

'Damn it! Now what am I going to do about this?' He pointed to his doggy-pink dick which was sticking out of his unzipped fly.

She pulled down her skirt. 'I'll get it.'

'Yeah? You sure, honey?'

She staggered over to the door, teetering on her high heels, and the deliveryman carried a tray across the room to the Formica coffee table. 'Here good?'

'Yeah, that's fine.'

'Sign here.' She added a hefty gratuity. Sandy was opening a closet door, facing away. 'Thank you!'

Finally the waiter left and she sat on the brown sofa making sure her skirt was still under her bottom, she didn't want to drip on the furniture, and leaning back took a sip of her Bloody Mary.

'Now where were we, before we were so rudely interrupted?' he said as he sat on the edge of the bed and pulled off his cowboy boots. He slipped off his jeans and crossed the room to where she was sitting on the sofa. 'Oh yes, sorry to keep you waiting. Now if you'd scoot down some and get your feet up into the stirrups, I'll be able to get on with my gynecological examination.' He grabbed her ankles and pulled them roughly, widely open and up.

'Please don't be too rough, doctor,' she said.

But the next time they screwed she had a strange feeling: he was lying on top of her after they had finished and she had this idea, which was probably stupid, that there was some kind of swirling life force hovering just overhead and sure enough when he pulled out of her the condom was still up her twat and it was two weeks until her period was due, which meant she was probably right in the middle of ovulating.

'Fuck!' she said. And she reached inside and with two fingers pulled out the used condom, a hot, shrunken sack.

'Weren't you using any birth control?'

'No – you were.'

'Well, it's not too likely –'

'No, it's not likely that *you* have anything to worry about –' she snarled.

By the afternoon of the next day she was nervous and bored with the casinos and the jangling glitter and she wanted to rent a car so they could drive around. 'I don't know, there's all these shopping malls, outlets, or some kind of state park or something, that might be kind of interesting, don't you think? I'm just getting a bit antsy, it's, like, too much sensory input –'

'Well, let me find out what it'll cost to rent a car –'

He must have been on the phone for two hours trying to find the cheapest place. She just wanted to smack him and say, What is the big deal, it's like fifty or eighty bucks, just book the damn thing and get it over with!

When the car arrived it was already three in the afternoon and it was a stupid car, without much power, but she got in behind the wheel and felt better. The city soon faded, and then there were endless highways stretching in all directions and on every side of the highway was construction. She felt okay, as long as she was driving and had on her sunglasses and he sat next to her without speaking. Just as long as he didn't speak.

She pulled into a liquor store at a strip mall next to a supermarket and told him to get her a pint of vodka and whatever he would be drinking later, if they wanted to have a drink up in the room, and she would run into the supermarket for some snacks.

There were people in the supermarket, ordinary people, shopping, with grocery carts containing boxes of cereal and meat and eggs and canned tomatoes and oranges and cat litter. And they were all just there, shopping, like there was some sense to their lives. As if they weren't a bunch of crumbs on a white tablecloth, waiting to be scraped up and squeezed into a familiar shape resembling a loaf of bread.

That night he put on a porn movie and she thought she should probably act a bit embarrassed. She had never watched any adult films before, Barry curled his lip at them and said how stupid they were, and derogatory toward women, and in fact it was true, she supposed. A rough-looking woman in a tight catsuit and mask was giving one man a blow job in a dark alley while another entered her from behind; the woman had apparently stalked the two men down the alley and then forced them into this?

She couldn't quite make out what was going on, she was already a bit sloshed, they had stopped at a bar for a couple of beers on the road, and a vodka and orange back at the hotel, she hadn't actually eaten much, maybe they would go out later.

But then the movie, which had weirdly, curiously, aroused her, in a way that was unconnected to her brain, merely seeing the act of sex made her think she should do it, too – like seeing a film of people eating would make you think you had to eat? – went off, the whole television turned itself off, and frankly she was relieved. She didn't think, really, that she wanted to watch more of it. Sandy said, 'You know, little lady, you should really make sure your hotel door is locked, almost anybody can get into these rooms –' and he grabbed something, she didn't know what, a bunch of things, so she was blindfolded and her arms were tied, and her ankles, though she was protesting, mildly. And he pretended to rape her. It was wildly exciting; anyway, it was being an actress, in a movie. And she thought, next time is my turn, what will I come up with?

After they were lying in bed and she said, 'Sandy, I'm only fooling around, 'cause I know you get nervous, but I want you to tell me that you're crazy about me and whenever I want I can come and live with you.'

He had been restless, next to her, but now he stopped moving and lay still.

'Believe me, I'm not going to, I just want to hear you say it.'

'Okay,' he said at last. 'Whenever you want, you can come and live with me, and if you want, your husband can come and live with us too, but whatever happens, you can't bring your yappy little dogs. I hate chihuahuas and if I had six of them around, they wouldn't live a week.'

He might as well have put a vacuum hose in her mouth and sucked out so much air that her stomach and windpipe collapsed. It was the ugliest thing he could have said. That she could live with him, and her husband, but not her dogs. Was that what she had asked him to say? All he had to say was, 'Darling, anytime you decide to leave your husband I'll be waiting for you in Texas,' or some such mush, and everything would have been fine. But that he had said, in that prissy tone, you can't bring your dogs – what was it to him? Just a nasty dig, a jab.

In the morning when she woke she knew that he was lying next to her in bed debating whether or not he should lean over and begin sex with her. But that really what he was hoping was that *she* would lean over and aggressively start to come on to him.

That was what they all wanted, basically, wasn't it? When had women had to take over the male role of the pursuer, the seducer? She got up and showered, dressed as quickly as possible. Such pretty things she had, she threw them into her suitcase, a lace teddy with corseted waist, a garter in white with a sheer top and pink ribbons; a tiny red T-shirt studded with rhinestones saying ME, ME, ME; tight cut-off shorts of pink denim – everything she bought, owned, because it had glitter, diamonds, beads, was of plush fabric – crushed velvet, silk chiffon, the wings of pale, dusty moths, lurex, shiny spandex; she was a tiny girl, sensual, greedy for color and touch and attention. A Thumbelina in a toy store window that passers-by assumed was for display purposes only.

'Good morning,' she said, trying not to show that her feelings for him had been – overnight – totally transformed.

'Good morning, Miss Peyton!' he said. 'Gol' dang it, I knew I should have slid over to you and given you some loving while I still had the chance – now you're all dressed and ready to go, already, but I didn't want to disturb your beauty sleep.'

'Oh, that's a shame. So, we should probably get going, Sandy. I don't want to miss my plane and it might take a while to return the rental car at the airport. And also, checking out here at the hotel.'

'Don't you think we've got time for a goodbye breakfast?'

She shook her head. 'I think we should just go to the airport and get our coffee or something to eat there. It'll probably be quicker than getting trapped in one of these casino nightmares.'

'Well, golly. Let me just hop in the shower and collect my things. You seem in kind of a rush this morning.'

'I don't want to miss my plane. Airports – getting to them – makes me nervous. I can call down and see if they can bring us up some coffee and toast or something, if it wouldn't take long.'

'No, I've seen that room service menu. Twenty dollars for a cup of coffee and some toast, that's ridiculous.' He got out of bed, grinning at her. She could see how he had once interested her; a cigarette cowboy in an advertising campaign, it would have been cuter if he had on his boots and hat and had a stalk of hay in his mouth. 'But, if you want, why don't you go ahead, jes' get some coffee and I can be dressed and out of here right quick, then maybe we can find something to eat along the way.'

When they went down to check out in the lobby he said, 'You know, I had a real nice time with you. I know your plane ticket cost a good deal more than mine. So I tell you what – why don't you pay for the incidentals, and I'll pick up the bill for the room?'

She tried to be grateful but she felt irritated. If he hadn't had a nice time with her he wouldn't have offered to pay? Like she was a prostitute who would only be remunerated if full satisfaction was provided. This from a man who told her his dress cowboy boots, crocodile, had been custom-made for him at a cost of one thousand two hundred dollars and who had just bought a gelding, quarter horse, for himself, from some sort of champion bloodline, and a new horse trailer – when she started adding it up, the things he kept mentioning, he didn't sound like a man who was cash poor at all.

She had a feeling he had a lot more money than he was letting on; at least Barry was tight because they were in debt, and he was trying to save so they could have nice things together, and it was the principal of the matter, that they lived in a society that knew how to pry every last penny out of you. This guy was just stingy.

She had forgotten about the drinks they had had sent up the first night, with the guacamole and chips before they went out; and the phone calls, she had called Barry twice and the hotel charged three dollars a minute plus a surcharge; and then there was a fifteen-dollar charge for a movie, and she said, 'But we didn't watch a pay-per-view.'

So that took another ten minutes for the kid to look something up on the computer, and then he said, 'Manager's Sex Special.' The porn movie. How humiliating.

'Yeah, but that film, it came on for five minutes, and then it turned off, we didn't get to see that movie.'

Eventually the kid took it off the bill. There was no way if that appeared on the credit card – and she didn't know how itemized it would be – that Barry wouldn't query her, 'What is this, "Manager's Sex Special"?' She supposed she could have just been honest and said,

'Oh, yes, I decided to watch a sex movie, since you don't want to watch any with me –' but it was nicer not to have to get into it.

'You sure are quiet today,' Sandy said on the way to the airport.

'I'm tired, I guess. And nervous that –'

'We're going to be there in plenty of time. You know, I sure am going to miss you.' He paused, this was a revelation or a present he was at last giving her.

'Oh, that's nice.'

'Are you going to miss me?'

Part of her thought she wouldn't care if she never saw him or spoke to him again. But if she said that, it would be cruel, it wasn't really his fault and more importantly she could envision him, irate, calling her up at home, threatening to tell Barry what they had done, wrecking everything. 'That's partly why I'm so quiet!'

But maybe she was pregnant.

So when she got home she told Barry they should try and make a baby. The whole thing was simply too stupid to contemplate, that she was already pregnant by another man and saying this to her husband. While they were having sex she kept thinking, the baby will be born and it won't look like Barry, it'll look like Sandy, but Barry won't notice, but Grace will and probably start to whisper to Barry that he should have a DNA test. Or, worse, like some boring Hollywood movie, Barry would die unexpectedly and Grace would get the DNA testing done and then announce that since it wasn't Barry's baby they would make sure the baby got nothing –

A few days later she got her period.

'Don't feel bad, sexy princess,' Barry said. 'That was only the first try.'

18

Then, suddenly, unexpectedly, she fell in love with her son. How old was he then, Ten? Twelve? Which would have made her, what thirty-eight, forty, something like that. Year after year, taking him to the doctor, the eye doctor, tennis on the weekends, soccer after school, swimming classes, chess club. She had done it all, alone, not that Barry was a bad father, but he was always working, it never occurred to him, were they running out of milk? Was it time for Cash to go to piano lesson? Did he need new socks or sneakers?

Sometimes Barry was there to help with homework, or watch him in some school play – mostly not, but then, neither were the other fathers. Both of them – she, and Cash – felt lucky there was, after all, a dad, a husband, and he obviously loved his son . . . it was just that, at least from her point of view, even when he was there, part of Barry – most of Barry – was missing. Sometimes, a long time ago, there had been fights – she felt he wasn't giving enough attention or . . . of himself . . . to Cash.

But then, after a while, a few years anyway, when Cash was beyond those first years of infancy, when he didn't need her so much . . . it began to seem that something in Cash wasn't there either. Part or most of him was missing too. She wondered, if she had had a girl, would things have been different? But the women she knew who had daughters – the daughters were basically the same; though the mothers said, over and over, 'Oh, we're so close' the girls were just other . . . people, whiny, bratty, maybe more interested in shopping – or dolls, or make-up – but also interested in soccer. And that was no reason to have another child, hoping it might be a girl and that if it was a girl it would be someone to be connected to.

There were women she knew who kept saying, 'Oh, you should have another kid, it's easier, the two of them play together.' Only all she ever saw was the two siblings fighting. Or, before she had had Cash, women who had recently had babies saying, 'You must have a baby, it's the most wonderful thing that can ever happen to you.'

It wasn't the most wonderful thing; it was just a thing, another human experience. She wouldn't have sent him back, even if it was possible – it was just that . . . it wasn't what they all said.

She wasn't a bad mother – at least, she didn't think so. Once she had been in a cab, with Grace, Cash was . . . maybe nine months old, he was on Grace's lap, and there was a moment – she had to hold him, and she remembered taking him from Grace who was . . . reluctant, but handed him over and she felt such tenderness toward him until . . . she saw Grace was watching her with relief. Grace had seen that tender look and she realized that Grace had been waiting for such a moment, Grace had been studying her and wondering, does my son's wife love the baby? And now Grace could relax. Only it had spoiled the moment for her: she was being studied, weighed, found wanting.

So when it happened it was peculiar; she could still remember the moment, waking up one morning and thinking, 'Where is he?' And for a split second wondering, who? Where am I? Who am I missing? And the realization that it was her own son, and she couldn't go on living without him, only she didn't have to. Did she? If only this had happened years earlier, when he would creep into bed with her in the early mornings and try to cuddle and she would reluctantly force herself to endure his sticky demands.

He was already off at school – he was old enough by then to get himself up in the morning and take the public bus on his own, which probably meant he was eleven or so, a little young to travel by himself but the bus stop was right outside his door, and so the doorman could watch him and a bunch of his classmates were always on the same bus, the 8:10.

She had stopped working by then, at least, there were a few years when it just didn't make any sense, taxes practically took away more than she earned, though a while later she was restless again when

210

Cash decided to go to boarding school for high school, which is when she found a new job.

She spent the day in a sort of lover's anxiety, thinking, I can't wait for him to get home, maybe we'll walk up to the Museum of Natural History, I know how much he loves rocks and there's some kind of special exhibition on precious gems –

And then he got home, a bit after three, she could hear his key turning in the lock and he yelled 'Hi, Mom!'

'Hi!' She came down the hall to find him. 'How was school today, puppy dog?'

'Fine. Is it okay if I go over to Jaime's after I finish my homework?'

She couldn't stand the boy, Cash's friend, with his sullen face, one finger always rooting in a nostril. He never spoke to Cash without letting her son know how stupid he was. Yet Cash never minded. He was already going to be the type who was happy to be inferior, subservient.

'Well . . . I thought, you and me, we could go to see the gem exhibit at the Natural History Museum, would you like that?'

'No. I want to go see his new Sentinelgrip.'

'At least say, 'No thanks, Most Divine Mother'. I tell you what: why don't you do your homework, we go to the museum and eat dinner out at Accursed Planet, and then you can go to Jaime's later.'

'Really? Dinner at Accursed Planet? How come?'

'Just because . . . I know that's your favorite place, and you've been such a great kid . . .' She had bribed him into spending time with her.

They walked up along Riverside Drive. It was one of those perfect fall days, early fall, when some of the trees had turned pink, pale yellow, and the others were still in that state of shocked, heightened green; perhaps accidentally, a few female gingko trees had been planted years ago and were now full of fruit, squishy gall bladders with the stink of old feet – a Chinese man had spread a blanket under one and was flinging a rope over a branch, which he then yanked, releasing a shower of the soft, smelly nuts.

'My goodness, isn't it amazing, that we live in New York City and can just walk to the museum whenever we feel like it. If you could have seen where I grew up – half a house, and it was on a corner so the highway went by right outside – and I never even ate in a restaurant, not until I met Daddy, just about, and even when I was little my sisters had already left so I had to make my own meals, my crazy mother didn't get home until late at night and there was no money – you don't know how lucky you are –' she said. 'The place had absolutely no heat, the landlord was too stingy, and the wind would just whip in off the Charles River and the bay . . .'

He would never understand, how could he? He was busy stepping on the gingko fruits, some of which had rolled or been tossed by other children onto the sidewalk. There was something about a gingko tree – it was the oldest kind of tree in the world, something like that, around when there were dinosaurs – she was going to tell him but she knew he would only say, irritatedly, 'I was the one who told you that.'

'Don't do that, your shoes are going to stink,' she said. She could scarcely bring herself to speak to him in what – only yesterday – would have been a normal tone. Now all she thought was that she didn't dare let him see that she had for no apparent reason fallen into this swoony love-sick state; he would be confused, he would be alarmed, he would only want to take advantage of it.

'Why are you taking me out? Is something wrong? Are you and dad splitting up?'

'What? No, no. I just thought it would be nice to spend some time together.'

'Oh, is that all? I really would rather have gone to Jaime's.' He was almost always polite to her; too polite. The other mothers she knew asked how she did it, he was like a kid home from boarding school on his best behavior, while their own kids were sullen, rude, and fairly polite or reasonable only to the fathers. She hadn't done such a bad job, after all, and it wasn't her fault that she had not been able to feel the passion for him that she was supposed to. He had wanted a big dog, she got him a big dog, even though she had had to fight Barry, who claimed things were bad enough with the endless parade of chihuahuas. Barry said he was allergic to dogs, Barry said they had to keep a bowl of water by the door to wash their feet when they came back from a walk. Barry said a big dog was going to need exercise: he wasn't going to be the one to do it when Cash was too tired. But she got Cash the dog anyway.

She had tried not to smother him, even though out of sheer guilt and nervousness that had been her natural tendency. And now this: this huge, trembling thing, an outpouring of love. She wished she could take him and put him back in her stomach like a kangaroo with an oversized joey protruding from its pouch.

He had blossomed into a good-looking kid. For years she had looked at him and thought only that his skin was sallow, he had an anxious, whiny expression on his face, his eyes were dull. Now, in the past year, his hair had grown in quite differently, it was sleek and black like hers and the dull expression in his eyes had matured into one of introspection; he was no longer a chubby child but was shooting up, reedy, a saluki pup who knew that soon his training in the desert as a hunting animal would begin. 'I wish you wouldn't wear those clothes, Cash.' She couldn't help herself, though she knew it was a mistake; the words had already sprung out, loose, released fish that could not be hauled in. 'I buy you such nice things, why do you have to wear that old ripped stuff, those pants are dragging on the –'

'Me? What about you? Why do you wear those weirdo outfits, Ma? And everybody stares at you –' He sounded similar to Barry, speaking to Grace.

'Me? I thought I looked quite pretty.' She had on fishnet tights, and a short skirt – her pink, ruffled blouse was low-cut – she had never looked good in trousers – how was it that her son even noticed what she had on, was it a sign of homosexuality? 'Do you think you're gay?'

'No, I like girls. And boys.'

'Well, let me put it this way: when you grow up, do you want to marry a girl or a boy?'

'A girl.'

'I wouldn't mind if you were gay – but it will definitely be easier to be straight, in this society. Even if you are gay, it's still one step up from being a woman – at least in New York. If you're young and gay and male, older, successful men will pursue you and then, when you get to be old and successful, you can nab some nubile flesh. If you're a woman, when you get older – even if you are successful – going out with a young guy makes you a joke, and men your own age only want young women. Tell me, does your dad ever talk to you about sex?'

'No . . . but you have.'

'And what did I tell you?'

'Don't remember.'

'The man has a penis. He puts it in the vagina. Sperm comes out and if there's an egg it gets fertilized and the woman has a baby. I admit it sounds peculiar, but I'm not making it up.' She could never understand why people were so odd when it came to talking to kids about sex. At least here was one topic on which she could inform him. It was all scientific fact, it was what animals did, and people, why then was there the nervous giggling, why did people think they should wait until the kid was grown up and had already learned about sex – incorrectly? But the child seemed pensive. 'So tell me about your day at school.'

'I don't know.'

'What was your favorite thing you did?'

'I don't know. Nothing, I guess.'

Now she saw that the only way she could ever get a response out of him was when she made him defensive. 'What about that horrible teacher, who gave you such a bad mark for your essay?'

She was needling him, the way Grace had always needled Barry – and his tone to her was exactly the same as that of her husband to his mother. 'It was a good mark! I got a ninety, what do you want from me?'

She didn't like to be this way, but it was preferable to being addressed as if she was a corpse. 'Remember, we have to get a present for Tosara. It's her bat mitzvah next week. What are we going to do for your bar mitzvah?'

214

'We have, like, more than a year to decide, Mom.'

'Are you sure you even want to have one? You don't have to, you know.'

'I'm going to do it, for Grandpa and Grandma. Can I go stay with them this weekend?'

'We'll see.'

'But they want me to! And I want to. What do we have to wait and see about?'

'How you behave. Say, would you like it if Mommy arranged a trip, for us to go somewhere fun over the Christmas break?' She knew he was an ordinary child, she had always known that but it no longer mattered, she was thrilled with his perfect ordinariness.

'With Dad?'

'I don't know. It'll depend how much work Daddy has.'

'I don't want to go unless Dad can come.'

'It's not a very easy time of year for Daddy to get away. I could see if there's a . . . ski trip, or something like that.'

'Well, I forgot – Jaime wanted to know if I could go with him and his family to Bermuda. Please, Mom?'

'I don't know. We'll see. It's a long time off, anyway. We haven't even figured out our plans for Thanksgiving.' He didn't want to go on a trip with her. She knew that. He was bored with her, there had to be something she could offer him to win his interest; she wanted a drink. There was that moment when the vodka packed the veins, an embalming-fluid chill.

In the museum the echoing halls were filled with the sweet stink of children after school, sour sugars and ferments. Tourists, out-of-towners, fathers who had the children on Wednesdays after school, grim West Indian nannies wheeling puffed infants with popcorn faces, larvae-white.

He was no longer interested in gems, he wanted to look at the dioramas – they had always been her favorite thing in the place – and gaze at the glass cases with their moldering remains of lion, eland, flamingo. She had always thought, what a waste to have a boy, if he had been a girl at least she might have had a friend on this planet – but now although she had no clue what he was thinking she felt incredibly happy, her trip was accompanied by some mysterious stranger who was connected to her forever by a silver chain.

Yet when he turned to her after staring for an eternity at the inhabitants of the African veldt she saw she was mistaken, he had not been thinking, as she had, that if it were possible to go to the airport and get on a plane right that minute the two of them might have taken off to a place where cheetahs ran at top speed after zebras and brought them down with a bite to the jugular, one glorious mouthful of hot, still pulsing blood. All he said was, 'These are really stupid, they should get rid of them and put up something like a virtual reality thing. Can we get out of here now? I'm starving.'

She took him to Accursed Planet where she had a double vodka on the rocks which gave her the sense that the back of her skull – lowdown, well below the fontanel – had been deliberately crushed, a chocolate Easter egg shell filled with fondant. She wished someone would notice her but even her own son didn't know, really, that she existed.

They each had a vampire burger and fries. 'You know, you should be eating a lot more fruits and vegetables,' she said. 'Shall I order you some broccoli?'

'No. I hate broccoli.'

'At least will you have an apple when we get home?'

'No.'

'Why do you think you complain that you're constipated?'

'Mom!'

It wasn't until after they got home and he had dashed upstairs to Jaime's and returned only after his father arrived home, that she realized just how close he and his father were – Cash grabbed Barry by the hand, begging him to come into his room, the two of them were in there for hours, she could hear their laughter, some sort of sport event was on Cash's TV – and there was no way she could enter their private world at all.

And then a few years later he announced he wanted to go to boarding school for high school. He came home at school breaks but during the summer break there was always a camp he wanted to go to with his friends, a sailing camp, a tennis camp – he had been there with her for such a short time, the time it took for some creature to gnaw a few leaves and make a cocoon from which it then hatched, prematurely, wingless, to stagger off with its companions.

That was it, then – he applied for college, thought of being a political science major – she had been right, really, at least a girl would have called home crying, needing advice about boyfriends: Mom why didn't he call me? They could have gone shopping together, had beauty treatments, tried to figure out a life for a girl that might not end up being a repetition of the lives of all women who had come before.

Instead her son, when he spoke at all, talked about baseball games, or cars, or baking bread (he had a brief obsession with cooking, perhaps he was gay but she knew if he had been gay she would have felt more of a connection with him, they would have had more in common) and he belonged, ultimately, to a species of animals that once they had left the nest, were unable to recognize their parents if encountered in the woods.

He went to a small college in Pennsylvania. He had never suffered from homesickness, he got okay grades, came home at Thanksgiving, Christmas, occasionally, or went somewhere to be with his friends. Mexico. Vermont. He drove a used Audi his father had bought from a patient. There were different girlfriends – she was happy, after all, that he wasn't gay, not that she objected to homosexuality, only that it was so much easier to be a conforming member of an existing society. As far as she could tell, she had passed on none of her inner demons to him.

Now she was alone with Barry. If there was no reason to stay together, there was no reason to separate or divorce, either. If she had left, within weeks, she knew, he would have found a replacement for her – someone younger, more successful, attractive, more charming – the whole city was crawling with them. They had reached some stable place together, if it wasn't friendship it wasn't a war, either – and if he had ever had an affair, or affairs, it didn't seem he was having one now. He was successful, wherever he went people made a fuss over him, at Christmas hundreds of patients sent potted plants – African violets, mums – or needlepoint pictures of a dentist. Or bottles of wine, or fruitcakes. He wasn't a very good dentist but he was a man and apparently that – in and of itself – was a major accomplishment.

She emptied out Cash's room to turn it into a study and guest room. In a bag in the back of his closet she found a box of brilliantly hued crayons – violet, lemon yellow, neon blue – and she remembered how disappointing they always were, producing only a wispy pale tint that, however hard one pressed, bore no resemblance to the color within the paper-covered waxy tube.

In all those years Cash had not broken a single one of them. They were lined up, intact and perfect, as if just purchased.

She was about to throw them away but then she thought some other child might want to use them and when she went out to walk the dogs she left the box on top of a garbage pail on the street.

By the time she came back, someone had tipped them out and the sidewalk, the gray cement, was covered with the broken stubs, some still partially labeled: apricot, hot pink, scarlet, cherry, lemon yellow, tangerine, ochre, sepia, flesh.

19

She thought after the fiasco with Sandy she would try and be nice to Barry but he didn't notice the difference and right away she started feeling restless. One night Barry came home in an unusually talkative mood – right outside his office there had been a car accident, a person had been hit, not seriously, but the man had lost his crowns, or caps, literally – they had gone right down the gutter – and so he had just staggered into Barry's office.

The man was English, so nice, so charming – and Barry was not only able to fix the guy's teeth but vastly improve them – and this man, who turned out to be a lord or an earl or a marquis, or one of those English people with a title – was so grateful he wanted to take the two of them out to dinner one evening while he was still in town. 'Oh, God, where?' said Peyton and Barry named a restaurant that was perpetually expensive and fashionable, so she said, 'All right.'

She had never been to this restaurant and she spent the day getting ready for the event: had her hair blown dry, her legs waxed, nails done, trashed her closet, finally settling on a black lace outfit with lace stockings and very sexy high-heeled pumps with straps that went around the ankles. Barry was oblivious – at least, when they were at home – but once they were at the restaurant and Henry, Lord Henry Battan-Bouwery turned out to be his name, was obviously enamored of her, the dress showed a lot of cleavage, then all of a sudden Barry took an interest and put his arm around her and kind of effectively cut her off from any possible flirtation. Not that she was intending to do more than flirt, but none the less it irked her, that he was some guy with a box of baseball cards in his closet to which he was indifferent until he found out the other guys wanted them. 'How perfectly wonderful of you to join me for dinner,' Henry said. 'Do you know, your husband absolutely saved my life. My teeth were in an appalling state, even before the disaster, he's an absolute genius!'

Henry had a long, angular face, a sheaf of thick hair topping the expression of a surprised scarecrow. His hands might have belonged to a great concert pianist and almost involuntarily he tapped his teeth, those playable keys. He wore a dinner jacket which Peyton figured was tailor-made, and resembled one of those British actors, a kind of mating between Leslie Howard and Peter O'Toole and Alec Guinness, or David Niven – a lanky breed not currently in vogue in motion pictures.

But she found him too dry and proper to be sexy although he was attentive to her in a way she could not remember any American man being: curious, polite, a bit flirty – it was odd. American men either paid you full attention because they found you sexually attractive, or they paid you no attention at all, making it clear you were not their type. In either case they weren't interested in conversing.

It was exciting, though, to be in the restaurant whose very name was instantly recognizable; so exciting, in fact, she didn't notice that the other diners were from out of town – Long Island women with their husbands and dressed-up children celebrating a sweet sixteen, an engagement, a bat mitzvah – or were, like Henry, from abroad and out of touch with where the authentically fashionable were dining, this week, in New York.

Henry was in charge of his family's estate, it was a full-time occupation, there were thousands of acres and managed farm lands and it was, according to Henry, terribly boring but there you had it. All his life he had, really, longed to do something 'hands on' perhaps not going so far as being a dentist, but if only he had been a doctor! He would have gone to refugee camps, belonged to Doctors without Borders, operated on children with heart defects or traveled to Peruvian villages to cure people of malaria. Done some genuine good in the world.

220

Things could have been a great deal worse; after all, his younger brother had only recently been handed the position of the Keeper of the Queen's Privy Purse.

Peyton didn't know if that was what Henry had actually said: she could scarcely understand him; either he still had loose teeth or the marble-mouth of an upper crust British accent.

'It sure sounds weird to me!' she said. 'What is it, like your brother has to hold the Queen's pocketbook while she goes to the bathroom?' She was eating a slab of foie gras on a bed of caramelized figs – the foie gras, not she, was on the bed – and while she was speaking she realized the nipple of her left bosom had peeped out, of its own accord, visible to anyone. She quickly stuffed it back in.

'I've had such a lovely time with the two of you,' said Henry. 'I can't thank you enough.'

His family's estate was in Wiltshire. He had a weekend house there, on the property, a small Norman castle he had restored, with a rather magical walled garden. Perhaps she and Barry would like to come down for a weekend, when they came to London?

They rarely went out together any more – had they ever? – now that Cash was at college Barry would often meet up with his friends after work, or attend events on his own. He was on the board of a non-profit avant-garde jazz club, he coached soccer on the weekends, he was a member of a fly-tying club, none of which were her interests. Then to her surprise he mentioned an upcoming benefit, a few weeks away, and wanted to know if she would go with him.

The event was a costume ball, at Halloween – it was to raise money for scholarships to dentistry school. It wasn't something she wanted to attend but he needed or wanted her to go with him and for the sake of being amenable she agreed.

She decided to go as a sick tooth-fairy after she saw a huge pair of pink feathered wings in a toy store. In a dance shop she found a tutu with a lace leotard, constructed some antennae, then draped the whole thing with fake necklaces of teeth and decorated her chest with additional pointy pink nipples that attached to her chest with some sort of latex adhesive. She couldn't remember whether papillae were warts or nipples but it didn't matter.

Gleefully Barry announced he would go as pasta – 'Al Dente, get it?' He constructed a sort of spaghetti box with a plastic front revealing a picture of a plate of noodles where his stomach would have been. Then he put on a wig made of thick white yarn.

He had long since lost his hair. It had begun thinning when he was still quite young; it had never occurred to her, until then, how awful it was for a man when his hair fell out. He had used quantities of some ointment but it didn't help. What would she have done if her own hair had fallen out, it must be a bit like being a leper, body parts abruptly abandoning one. She had a flash of sympathy at the time, *oh Barry, you mustn't worry, I will never leave you* – which of course was ridiculous, he was bereft over the loss only briefly but got over it – after all, bald men were hardly freaks.

It was peculiar, seeing him now with hair – even fake hair. His face had become feminized. She saw how he would have looked, had he been born female and how he would appear as an old woman. He was not that much older than she, but when she looked at herself in the mirror she didn't appear to have changed. At some point time had stopped for her, she thought, though she didn't know how or why.

The party was being held in a fancy hotel restaurant downtown; everyone attending was a dentist or married to one. There was the usual table of crudités, clam dip, chips, also waiters with platters of lumpy hors d'oeuvres, and an open bar. To her surprise she saw that there were at least a half-dozen men all dressed in women's clothes, as dental hygienists with blond wigs, fake breasts, thick make-up. Was this what the world had come to, that so many men, at least in New York, wished that they were buxom blondes? At what point had the condition of being male become so untenable that their fantasy was to be the opposite sex? And for the first time in years she felt a sort of bossy tenderness toward her husband, with whom she had lived for so long trying only to maintain the status quo: her husband, the wet noodle.

The sensation was so oddly unfamiliar, alarming, that she went to

222

the bar to get another drink, knocking three people along the way with her wings, which actually had rather stiff, sharp edges. 'Excuse me,' she kept saying, 'I'm sorry, it's my wings, I can't manage them.'

The costumes were all rather pathetic – a mouse, a male-orderly-bride, a sailor, and a lot of tooth-related attire: a husband-and-wife pair of 'amalgamated braces', a tube of toothpaste, a man in drag ('Sister Cary'), an implant, a tongue accompanied by a tongue depressor – and they were all given numbers for the costume competition to be held later.

She had pushed her mask up onto her forehead and was standing with Barry at the side of the room when a small woman dressed, she supposed, as a geisha, came over to them and said admiringly, 'Oh, your costume is so great!' She had thought at first the woman was talking to Barry and it took her a moment to realize the woman was speaking to her. It was a shock, to get attention. Years had gone by in which she had been Barry's wife: an almost non-existent entity who accompanied the white male the way remora fish accompanied sharks and were tolerated only because they were useful skin-cleaners.

'Thanks,' she said, 'So's yours. I'm Peyton Amberg, this is my husband, Dr Barry Amberg – and – uh, are you a dentist, or –'

'You know,' said the woman, 'I know you from somewhere, and I can't – you know what, I remember seeing you, gosh, it was years and years ago, but I'll never forget it, you were with your girlfriend, at the manicurist, and you were talking about –' the woman looked at Barry coyly, 'oh, I remember – you were talking about having an affair –?' she raised her voice. 'It was something I never forgot, because you were so . . . intense. At Noble Nails!'

'Noble Nails? A nail salon? I don't think so – I go to the one on Thirty-fourth Street – it's not called Noble Nails –' Peyton's fingers were icicles, long cold spikes that could have been broken off and used as weapons. She took a sip of her white wine and pulled her mask back down. 'Oh, look, Barry! I mean, Al Dente! – Isn't that Rachel, your office manager? You didn't tell me she was coming –'

'Oh, it's not Noble Nails, it's Nails of Nobleness, on Seventy-second Street, that's the one I go to –'

Now Barry seemed agitated as well. 'Rachel! I almost didn't recognize you! What are you supposed to be?' They stood off to one side, chatting. Peyton had always thought Rachel was the person Barry should have married instead of her, if people got their lives correct. His office manager was a nice Jewish girl, reddish hair, freckles, a bit frumpy, an aura of the Passover Seder, an invisible schtetl shawl around her shoulders. At least he was distracted now from the geisha who had put her under attack.

'Nails of Nobleness. You're right. Yeah, I must have been there with my girlfriend, Victoria! My poor friend. She's always having some loopy affair with someone in this city. God knows what that one was, if it was years ago – excuse me just a minute.' She turned to Barry. Rachel, in her silly ballerina disguise, had disappeared. 'Come on, let's go get another drink.'

Barry shuffled passively alongside her in shoes he had wrapped with white string similar to that of his wig. He hadn't been listening. Or if he had, he trusted her, believed in her, never would have suspected her of having an affair. Or perhaps he did think she might have had one, but didn't want to know.

It was impossible. Nobody could remember that arbitrary detail, a conversation overheard in a nail parlor in New York City, how long ago, ten years ago? Longer? And then to recognize her, come up to her – though it was true, she supposed, she also overheard or listened to snippets of things all the time. On the subway, two women speaking intimately about the scriptures, it was baffling, really, their low muttered voices, pretending to have a conversation but in fact merely lecturing one another, or bragging: who was able to quote from which passage. A guy, late at night, on an empty car, talking to two friends sitting opposite about his break-up with a woman named Kristy. But she would never have gone up to this guy, years later, at a party, when he was standing with a woman, and started repeating his words, even if she had recognized him.

At around ten-thirty she was taken to one side by a party organizer and told that she was one of the finalists in the contest and would she mind coming up to walk across an area that had been designated an

224

impromptu stage? She couldn't help but be pleased. Perhaps she would even win; the first prize was dinner for two. She knew Barry was a bit disappointed that he hadn't been one of the finalists.

Her fake-teeth necklaces, over the course of the evening had become more and more tangled so that they now one after the next dropped to the ground; wherever she went she left behind a toothy trail. When she got to the microphone and the MC asked what she was supposed to be, she said, 'A sick tooth-fairy.'

After a pause, the winner was declared. 'Number twenty-three, Peyton Amberg!' First place. She almost wanted to cry. She had never won anything before in her whole life – not that the prize was anything so spectacular, though it was nice, but it was just that for once she had been appreciated for something she had actually done.

When they had married it was always, oh, she's so beautiful, no wonder Barry married her. But being beautiful – that wasn't something she had achieved, that was just how it was. And all the time Barry was praised for his brains, for his skill, ability, and she was a lowly travel agent – but even if the situation was reversed, she knew they would still be saying, Barry is so talented, he's going to run a whole travel empire; whereas she would be just another dentist in a not particularly glamorous or sexy field of medicine.

Afterwards Barry looked at her slightly disapprovingly. Her costume was revealing, but she thought, screw him, and didn't put on her cover-up wrap. 'Peyton,' Barry was saying, 'this is my friend, Dr Somi Singh, we were in dental school together – he wanted to meet you.'

'Barry, you old fox, I haven't seen you in years, I didn't know you had such a beautiful wife!' Somi had dark sleepy eyes with bovine lashes, full-lipped, like an Indian pop star, a milky mamma's boy. In a previous incarnation he might have been a concubine in a Persian seraglio; or a larva, spoon-fed on royal jelly.

'Hi . . .' she said. 'So, uh, where are you from?'

'Oh, I am from Rajasthan. I am a Rajput. Do you know what that is?'

'No . . .'

'It's the warrior caste. We had much land and many palaces – in what is now Pakistan, on the border. When Partition came – they took everything away. It is a very good costume you are wearing, by the way.' He smiled sleepily at her, preening his black lashes. One fell glistening onto his cheek like the front leg of a fly. She wet her finger and reached out to remove it.

'It's unfair, a man having eyelashes this long,' she said, staring at her fingertip. Touching him she was energized. No one had looked at her so intently, since . . . what was his name? Germano. She hadn't believed anyone would ever look at her that way again. It was an electric charge. Didn't he realize what he was doing? Omar Sharif in, what was the movie, *Dr Zhivago*, had stared that way at Lara, who was played by Julie Christie. And there was that scene, when they got off the train, stumbled through the forests and the snow and into a palace empty after the Revolution, where snow had blown through the open French doors, piled up in heaps in the corners of the looted ballroom, the servants long since fled . . .

And then, back home, she and Barry were having some of the hottest sex they'd had in years; it didn't make any sense, they had long ago stopped having sex frequently; oh, once in a while, two old elephants scratching one another's backs with tender, slightly bored concern. When they had first been married she knew that during the act Barry was struggling to connect with her – maybe not struggling, but she could feel that he wanted to be connected, spiritually, which drove her nuts, not in a good way, it irritated her.

She simply wanted to have sex, two bodies and a sex act, something slightly dirty, obscene and instead there was this loving oneness. She had never wanted loving oneness, at least, she didn't think so. And then, over the years, slowly, his mental struggle, to connect with her and make her *be there* had gradually faded.

In the beginning he loved her to be adventurous in bed; doctors, dentists, she thought, were often like that, they had to do things to other people all day. So at night they wanted to be the one to be . . .

operated on. While he was watching TV she'd tell him to ignore her, pay her no mind – then tie him up, not seriously, but with scarves, and blow him or toy with him until he was hard and sit on his dick, promising him it would only hurt a bit.

He was such a good boy. He didn't even drink, apart from the occasional glass of wine with a meal. Or a lite beer on a hot summer day. Maybe he had smoked pot a couple of times in high school. If she suggested it, let's get some dope, have a smoke, screw around – he was horrified and would recoil from her overtures. She could have said, what do you say, shall we try some Ecstasy, just once? You want to try a three-way, rent some porn, buy some sex toys? And he would have looked at her with squinted eyes, maybe she had gone crazy. He liked the idea of having a wanton wife – but not the reality.

And perhaps she had never had that much sexual interest in him. If anything she was glad when now, at last, the whole thing diminished. In her heart he was not her husband: her husband, her soulmate, was somewhere else, just around the corner, or in another country.

They were probably a bit drunk, screwing in bed – Barry never would have done it on the couch, or the kitchen, he was too tame and respectable for that – but they were naked and he was rolling her nipples between his fingers, she had her hands on his testicles, it was all a bit blurry but they were going at it – she was on top of him, having one orgasm after the next – cold, blunt, pure sex, without the tender qualities. 'Come on, fuck me harder.' It was the first time she had talked dirty to him, though she could have done it to anybody on the planet, just about. 'Look your balls are so big and swollen, I'm dripping wet for you –' She was thinking, dressing as a sick tooth-fairy was the first time she could remember being praised because she had thought of something, created something by herself. 'Come on, baby, don't you wanna fuck the winner?'

Suddenly he lost it, his erection, and she fiddled around down there for a minute or so, he wanted her to try some more, but she was too bored. She had had an orgasm, she was tired. 'I'll make it up to you, tomorrow,' she said. 'I'll give you a blow job.' She rolled away from him and thought that perhaps by the next day he would have forgotten her promise, or maybe wouldn't be in the mood – it was too weird, having sex with her own husband.

Women met men, fell in love and married. Then they lived with a person to whom they were connected. A soulmate. The husband was a friend; the man and woman had conversations, shared thoughts, feelings, discussed the other guests after a dinner party. They were a kind of team, bonded more closely than parent and child; certainly the relationship was closer than that of, say, two girlfriends. Or was she mistaken? The years had gone by and there was no glue between the two of them to hold them together, the bond had not taken.

She was living with another person with whom she shared a child, an apartment, meals – but if he had left the room and never come back she wasn't sure that she would ever remember that he had existed. Yet that was not enough reason to split up. Other women had 'the love of their life' or at least some did – the duchess's mother, running off with an Argentine polo player, abandoning her aristocratic position, her children, for love.

Of course, there was the distinct possibility that this woman had come to believe she had made a mistake: now she was trapped on a hacienda on the pampas with just another dolt who spent all day buying new horses, who made the same bad-smelling farts at night in bed as the dolt she had left behind in England. On what day had that happened, after pitching everything away in the name of love, to wake up and realize . . . Or had she gone on, year after year, swooning with happiness that she had made the right choice and found this . . . other half?

Peyton didn't believe in another half. There was only herself and a vague awareness that others did exist, but only as flickers of light seen on the periphery. Even if Barry had arrived home at night with bouquets of flowers, or those wretched diamond anniversary presents as shown on TV (he did not, was not that sort of a guy) she knew enough about herself to understand that she would have been more harassed than charmed by him; only a jerk would make such a fuss over her. It was no different than not wanting to go to a party to which you were invited – but feeling irate if you weren't asked.

In the end it seemed the only real love could be between two people who didn't know each other. She was lucky that Barry was so oblivious to her existence he hadn't noticed – or hadn't minded – that she traveled around the world in search of the unobtainable.

It was weeks before she stopped brooding about Somi. His stare, his look – each time she remembered, it made her dreamy. A Rajput cowboy. It was so long since she had experienced anything like it – the marigold heat, the honey-blossom gaze. It was the difference between living in a world in black and white and then one launched in Technicolor, a moment which utterly ruined the previously pleasant black and dull gray of life before.

She caught herself mooning around at odd moments, standing in the supermarket staring at cans of tomatoes for endless minutes without making a move: small fugue states of limerance, a sort of narcolepsy that was unbearable – she was frozen, unable to function – but pleasurable at the same time. She kept replaying those brief minutes in her head and each time felt the same slippery breath-stopping sensation. Gradually, though, as she relived it the intensity grew less and finally, after six months or so, she could not recapture the feeling at all.

One day she went to her internist – the same guy she had been seeing for years, a boyish man with gold wire glasses and an Austrian empire demeanor of Old World formality that made him appear older than he probably was. He might as well having been wearing a starched white shirt front, a waistcoat, a pince-nez; even his office, on the Lower East Side, was in a house unchanged since it was built, with sliding paneled doors, plaster molding darkened by age. A silent place where the only sounds were the dull ticking of clocks, and office equipment that came from the pre-electronic age of medicine. Usually he worked with his wife who was a nurse, a woman who lacked his charm, but was efficient, also Germanic; she might once have been youthful but now was worn – perhaps by the somber doctor, perhaps by her own stern genetic destiny.

Nevertheless, she liked the wife, though the woman, Gisela,

always went out of her way to keep a stilted, business manner with her.

Anyway, she had an appointment to see him – just a check-up, her kidneys were bothering her, probably nothing serious but she kept having to get up in the night to pee – and on that day Gisela wasn't there. His offices were always quiet, there were never any other patients. She was about to make small talk – she knew he had always liked her, looked at her admiringly, and she thought, well, he was nice enough, a nice man, she would ask where his wife was, how their children were – when something made her stop.

And as he looked at her she saw he was a man absolutely ripe and ready to be picked. With the slightest bit of encouragement from her he would have been saying, 'Might I take you out to lunch, one day next week?' and trying to pretend there was no sexual connotation in doing so.

She didn't encourage him and for a few weeks she thought things over; the lunch, the rental of a hotel room – some anonymous mid-town hotel, not a sleek modern place but one that had been around since the New York of the 1940s, with a dark, formal lobby, rooms in which the sheets were cold and there was a wooden armoire, mahogany, and small windows with heavy drapes – and how he would take off his clothes, carefully, and put them on a hanger or fold them neatly, and place his glasses carefully on the bedside table so that the lenses would not get scratched and afterward perhaps shed a few tears, of guilt but also pleasure for the beautiful experience –

It lacked . . . something.

But when six months had gone by and she was once again feeling desperate, restless, bored, and she had gone back to work but that only made things worse – then she made up some excuse to go and see him, a flu shot, a tetanus shot, a blood test – ready to let him know, she found him attractive . . .

It would be worth the dreariness, the plebeian quality, to have someone – anyone – look at her with total admiration and desire, even if, shortly, she would find it necessary to dissuade him and tell him that, though he was such a dear, dear man, she had decided . . . to work on her marriage, or whatever.

So she dressed . . . a bit provocatively, letting some cleavage show, ruffled, lacy blouse, lacy underwear, perfume, mascara and smiled to herself, thinking of his eyes, so soft, generous, with that courtly, wistful glance; and waited in the waiting room (this time it appeared he actually did have other patients) and when she was taken into an examination room (now it appeared he had hired a nurse, his wife wasn't there) she arranged herself prettily, sexily, on the edge of the table – for a flu shot, after all, it wasn't necessary to undress . . .

When finally he came into the room, something about him had changed. He didn't meet her glance, appeared guilty. He was – different, no happier but wilder, had a kind of testosterone aura that had not previously been there. She realized, almost immediately, someone had reached the cherry tree before her. He was plucked.

He had been out in that heavily charted water that was new only to him, where sealife swam – shrimps, or foraminifera, tiny crustaceans that shed myriad shells on the ocean floor. Creatures about whom no one could say, really, if their lives were lived more or less intensely than those of human beings.

20

In London they stayed at a small hotel near Notting Hill Gate, 'Whiteoaks of Jalna', recommended years ago by someone. It was nice, though their room was a third-floor walk up; the walls of the hall and rooms were decorated with framed old textiles, lace, pieces of embroidery, and it was very clean. As soon as they had checked in she went to sleep beneath a heavy feather comforter. The sheets were white and cold. Her eyes ached and her clothes had that strange odor of airplane, the mildewed smell of air, microwaved food, oxidized sweat.

Barry went out to a bookstore, he was collecting old dentistry texts, and old fishing rods made of cane – reed? Whatever, surgical supplies from when a doctor was also a dentist and a barber – and when she woke, hours later, the scent of an unfamiliar brand of coffee and the clinking of forks and knives on china from the restaurant on the first floor made her remember she was not at home, this was England. And she was not with a stranger, even though, for a moment, she had hoped so.

Outside everything was so much older and smaller than New York – a kind of muffled chill that went into her bones – and the central square, behind an iron fence, was a lush, green garden. The streets were full of adorable schoolchildren accompanied by nannies mothers, au pairs, posh kids dressed in prim uniforms, plaid and gray, girls with long coats and pom-pom hats, all blonde with blue eyes, small boys in a sort of disproportioned baseball cap with – despite the cold – short trousers, revealing raw blue knees.

*   *   *

By the time she got back to the room Barry had returned, in a state of great excitement – he had found some old dentistry prints, in an antique store, he wanted her to come and see –

They rented a car – how exotic the place names sounded, Tufnell Park, Ladbroke Grove, Sutton Veny, Devizes (this last haunted her particularly, as they drove in silence, over and over in her head she kept thinking, *they were left to their own Devizes*) – until finally they arrived at Henry's estate. There was a gate and a gatehouse and a drive marked 'Private' that went on for miles, through wooded forests and past shaved green meadows edged with hedgerows. 'This is all . . . Henry's?'

'No, it's his father's, but Henry and his wife live in one of the houses – a castle? – on the estate, his wife restored it, I forget when he said it was from. Can you read me the directions for once we get through the main entrance?'

'His wife – what's she called?'

'Tinkle.'

'Tinkle? What kind of a name is that?'

'It's a nickname, I guess. I don't know what her real name is. But that's what he always calls her, so that's what I call her too.' Barry had met her on some other trip to London on which she hadn't accompanied him.

'Tinkle? I can't call a grown woman Tinkle.'

They made a wrong turn and went through another gatehouse and then they were in a small village and she hopped out and went into a little shop advertising local honey. 'Excuse me,' she said and held up the paper with directions on it. 'I'm looking for . . . Bouwery Castle . . .'

'Oh, you're visiting Lord Henry, are you? You've just missed him, he was in the shop a few minutes ago with Lady Battan-Bouwery, getting supplies – anyway –' The woman finally explained where they had made the wrong turn.

There was something about the way the woman had said 'Lord Henry' that made her uneasy. She didn't doubt for a minute that Lady

233

Tinkle would make her feel loud and vulgar – and who else would be there for the weekend?

At last they found it. The place was the shell of a former Norman castle, with a completely new interior, restored turrets and parapets. The host, the hostess, the guests, were on the croquet lawn. Each of the men came up and shook hands enthusiastically, golden retrievers in human, male form. The women approached more shyly, drooping gazelles with needle horns beneath soft hair – if threatened, they might attack with vicious, sharp butts. 'So nice you could come,' said Lady Battan-Bouwery, 'I'm Tinkle – we're right in the middle of a game, I hope you won't mind finding your own way up to your room, we've put you in the turret over there, right at the top; I thought you might enjoy the view, and anyway, the other rooms were already taken –'

'Oh, that sounds wonderful –'

'Or anyway, perhaps I'll have Desdemona show you up, if she's not busy with the children –' She turned and let out a peacock shriek. 'Dezzie! Dezzie, can you come here for a mo?'

'No, that's fine – we'll find our way okay.'

'Are you quite sure you'll be all right?' said Tinkle firmly and turned back decidedly to the croquet game. It was remarkable, Peyton thought, how clearly one could be put in one's place; how one's social position and status (the bottom rung, not even worthy of being assisted by . . . the nanny, or au pair, or whatever this Dezzie person was) could be established and communicated by these English people, just like in a Merchant-Ivory film. But Barry was chatting happily to Henry so she went to get her overnight bag out of the car and find her way upstairs. The round bedroom at the top of the turret was a steep walk up an endless flight of stairs, with no sign of a bathroom at any stage of the way – certainly there wasn't a toilet at the top. Probably she would have to go to the bathroom during the night, which would mean breaking her neck as she went down in the darkness. She peeped out through one of the slitty windows. There they were, on the greensward below, the women in wrinkled billows, the men in seersucker, straw hats to protect their delicate skin from the occasional wisps of sun. God, she would have given anything to be one of these lanky, long-limbed English people with their musty blond locks who had lived this way for generations, genetically preserved apart from the rare influx of occasional American heiress blood. Instead she was short and dark, big-breasted, a milkmaid from a trailer park.

She took a nap. She was too nervous to talk to the others just yet. When she did go downstairs it was to find everybody – Barry included – still playing croquet. The women were all dressed differently from her, things plucked from an attic chest, items belonging to a grand-mother or great-grandmother; but lovely, bits of lace, green satin silk, everything ripped and torn. In her pink sweater and American jeans she shriveled with dowdiness, ordinariness.

'Come on!' called Henry, 'It's too late for this game, but you can take over for me.' She shook her head.

On a bench against a wall, in front of some kind of tortured flowering plant – no doubt a *quince*, she thought, remembering the gardening lady from some stupid movie, which she had hated at the time but which now at least had some reality, or an *espaliered pear* – was a woman sitting with her arm in a sling and she joined her. 'Hi!' she said, and almost immediately regretted her own voice, loud, American. 'I'm Peyton –'

'Yes, we did meet before you went up, but you probably don't remember all our names. Are you still jet-lagged?' The woman's name was Meg and she pointed out who all the others were – the women were Augusta, Alayne, Pheasant, Adelaide and Tinkle. The men were Rennie, Piers, Finch, Eden, Wakefield and Henry.

According to Meg, they all, apart from Henry – who had to manage the estate or something like that – had professions for people who never had to worry about money, that someone must have subsidized: they made handbags, or had a band (she was the one whose husband owned a recording company); one was a painter, another a landscape designer who, thus far, had only had one commission, from an old family friend who owned a Mexican estate.

One dealt in antiquities, another with a famous last name hosted a television program. She couldn't figure out why Meg was telling her all this stuff, but at least it helped to give her a handle on the situation: she was an intruder in this refined realm. After the game was finished they came over. The women all had pink noses and soft paws that they limply extended. The men looked at her with a sort of jovial curiosity. They were so tall and rich, so assured – yet there was something naïve about them. They were not anti-Semitic so much as anti anybody who didn't come from their world . . . Barry was so removed he was just a pleasant kink in the day. Something temporarily on the property, who at the end of the weekend would go back to the zoo. A curiosity in their midst viewed affectionately, a visiting American celeb, a ball-player. He was relaxed, oblivious. He had grown up with money, even if it wasn't this sort. She was going to be looked upon as a trashy slut, inferior.

She would never make it through the next couple of days.

Hours had gone by. A lifetime of feeling loud, stupid, insignificant. I can't take it one more minute, she thought, being in this house with these deliberately nasty English girls, wiggy rabbits, the tips of their noses permanently pink and wet – did they always have a cold? And these neutered men playing whatever it was, snooker, and drinking lager or shandy or champagne; there were lots of children, petal-cheeked and blond, in some sort of nursery or game room, attended by various nannies and au pairs, playing video games, or swinging from climbing equipment, and strewn everywhere the beautiful remnants of previous generations – the rotten old rocking horse with a mane and tail of real hair, the elderly mohair teddy, a tin wind-up double-decker bus: these families had been sheltered in this way for hundreds of years.

The house was damp and freezing cold; it couldn't be any colder outside, and gazing out of a narrow window she saw that it had begun to rain. It was only a weak drizzle, so she said, 'Barry? I'm gonna go out for a walk.'

'There's a lovely path that leads through the forest,' said Henry. 'It makes a nice loop and will take you back around beside the cow pasture – when you go out the door make a right and down the lane on the left. And you'll find wellies out in the mud room – do borrow a pair, you'll find it rather muddy, I'm afraid.'

So she headed out; it was warmer outside than in, the original owners must not have minded the cold. It was late April and everything was green, green but so cold and in one field she saw sheep, some with lambs, and she passed a barn full of hay – then she turned and went down a wooded path. Henry had said it was, unfortunately, too early for the bluebells, whatever they were, but it was so beautiful, smelling of fir and rot – there was a stand of what she supposed must have been beech trees, gigantic, lonely trunks, each one so massive it could have been six of her torsos tied together, and the ground beneath bare except for leaves as soft as a cake. She kept walking. She thought, I don't care if I get lost, I could just walk and walk and maybe I'll come to the station; if I had brought money I could just get on the next train and end up . . . I don't know, in London or Edinburgh, or from London take a train to Paris, but she hadn't brought any money and if she had used a credit card Barry would have been able to trace her – if he had wanted, or, if not, he could have simply cut off her account . . . Would she be any better off, really, starting someplace entirely new? She saw herself in some tiny apartment, in a city where she knew no one and sitting next to a phone that never rang, in the dark, or eating alone in some bar . . . She couldn't see that this fantasy, in her head, was any improvement over reality. She had to keep reminding herself, I live in Manhattan, I'm married to a successful dentist, we have a car, a co-op, we take trips, I have a lovely figure and lovely clothes . . . None of it had any meaning.

She kept walking and then she saw a man on a horse – she noticed the horse first, it might have been part of a period film shooting in the area, the horse was so perfect, it was a stout horse, with a cropped mane and tail and a huge fat ass, and because as a kid the only books she had ever voluntarily read in her life were those about horses, right away she thought with delight, That horse is a *cob*. The man on the horse was stout and handsome as well, and he was dressed in . . . was

237

it some sort of hunting outfit? . . . Jodhpurs or tight beige trousers, and tall black boots, and a pink jacket, a crop tucked under an arm. Behind them followed a small dog, wiry, short-legged; the dog began to bark and rushed at her in a fury with bared teeth.

'Heathcliff!' the man said. 'Stop that at once! Pay no attention to him, he's perfectly harmless – unless he thinks you're frightened of him.'

'But I am frightened of him!' She saw the man was not young, he might have been in his sixties, with a pinkish face that might have come from drinking claret or a lifetime of owning a particularly fine, extensive, wine cellar and a butler who brought up selected bottles . . . He was so tall, up on the horse, which now snorted and curled his lip at her and yet at the same time there was something peculiar transpiring; the man was obviously the *squire* or the *lord of the manor* or one of those wacky things out of a Harlequin romance, or maybe a movie (there had been all those horse movies, *Black Beauty* and *My Friend Flicka* and on and on) – anyway, they just kept staring at each other, with the dog jumping on her, and she knew that, if he had wanted, he could have leapt off his horse and fucked her, as if she were . . . what? The housemaid? Some local loose woman? Only she wouldn't have screamed and tried to run and fight him off, she would quite happily have gone and done it with him. Maybe they were having some mutual past-life regression; not that she believed in that stuff, only it was a sense of *déjà vu*. But he didn't have the glamour of . . . what's his name . . . in Brazil . . . when she had been so madly in love. And now she knew there was never going to be anyone to take care of her; she would always be alone. And even if there had been someone to look after her, an adoring sugar daddy, it would only be a matter of time before she grew to hate him as much as she despised herself.

'Just give him a kick!' he shouted. 'Heathcliff, I'm going to beat you bloody senseless when we get back to the stable.'

She couldn't help herself; she started to laugh.

'Well I'm glad you find it amusing,' he said. 'Are you one of the Americans staying with my son?' At this, for some reason, the dog began to sniff a rock embarrassedly, what he had intended to do all along. She wished she could have said something; she had the feeling that he thought she was laughing at him; but she couldn't speak and so she simply nodded. 'See you later on then, perhaps,' he said. 'Henry said something about stopping by for a drink.' And, kicking the horse sharply, he said, 'Bucephalus, move on!' and the man and the gray cob – which indeed from behind did have a very large bottom, a head boy who thought of himself as dignified – took off at a stiff trot through the wooded trail, followed by the dog.

And then she had to go back to the house in a kind of paroxysm of lust. Really, it was just crazy, to be in this altered state, when she had thought – hoped, prayed – she was finished with all of that. The women were in the kitchen, 'organizing lunch' and gave her vacant, superior smiles when she offered to help, saying there was nothing, really, she could do, it was all taken care of. And then they all sat down at a long plank country table and drank white wine and ate peculiar things: 'beetroot and goat's cheese pie' and cold sliced ham and salad, followed by 'trifle' and 'summer pudding' – which was bread drenched in berries.

It was someone's birthday, the tall, dyspeptic youth who sat at the far end and blushed bright red while the others sang 'Happy Birthday to You'. A horse race was on TV, so they all went to watch and outside it started to rain, a cold, angry drizzle. It was all too much, that there were people who lived in this gloomy pile: twittering birds, so fragile and nervous that at any minute the entire group might have had to be carted away by keepers in white coats.

'I saw your father!' she announced to Henry. 'Wow, what a character! He was like, all dressed up, on a big horse –'

'Ah yes, you ran across Duncan. I'm afraid he's never quite forgiven me for taking over the estate, you know.'

'Why did you?'

'I have no idea, really. Why did you become a travel agent?'

'I guess because . . . I wanted to travel. And, well, I didn't know any better, at the time.'

'Good answer. I suppose one doesn't, does one?'

'What?'

'Know any better at the time.'

'It was different for Barry. He always wanted to be a doctor, but his grades weren't that good – and in dentistry, not only did he know he probably wasn't going to kill anybody, it had regular hours, I mean, he wasn't going to be called in the middle of the night to deliver a baby.'

'Quite right. Come, shall we go round to my father's house for a drink? He was quite intrigued by you too. I've already spoken to him on the phone.'

The father and his wife, Henry's mother, (whom Henry referred to as the Boa Constrictor, though not in her presence) lived in the stately home that was open to the public on Tuesdays and Thursdays from May to October. Duncan had attempted to make the place profitable but none of his ideas had ever worked. There was a lake that had been built to contain sea lions which had sadly all died due to the lack of salt in the water; there was also a maze, which unfortunately had been mostly blown down in a recent storm. Other attractions on the grounds were the Tudor Rose Garden, a grotto and a two-mile miniature train that ran on coal, with a station where, in summer months, ices and veggie burgers were sold.

The mother wore a necklace of pearls the size of quails' eggs.

The group sat awkwardly drinking champagne. There was conversation of a sort, but she couldn't understand much of it because they all talked like their mouths were full of bullets and the references were to people she didn't know and the living room was full of dogs, one of which had become sexually infatuated with her; there was also a parrot who shrieked uncontrollably. She knew she should consider herself lucky to have a glimpse into this other world. All this time if she had gone somewhere with Barry she had always felt slightly . . . embarrassed, that she was married to a nebbishy Jewish dentist – it wasn't the Jewishness so much as that he was such a specific type, there was nothing exotic about him – but now it was thanks to Barry that they were there, visiting, and he was engrossed in a loud conversation with the mother, what was her name? Aileen? And then suddenly the father announced, 'Now, who can be coerced into coming beagling with me in the morning?'

'I will!' she said. 'What's beagling?' They all laughed.

Nobody else was willing to go.

She rose at six. Outside the house Duncan was waiting with four other men, dressed in special outfits, and a pack of thirty or so big dogs – if they were beagles they were huge – and at that time of day it was freezing, she didn't have the right clothes, but Duncan gave her some coffee from a thermos that was mixed with brandy and after that she didn't care. They walked for hours over mucky fields with the pack of dogs racing ahead. The job of the dogs was apparently to find a hare, which was similar, apparently, to a big rabbit, and kill it; she didn't want to say, this is cruel, because the dogs were so happy and Duncan kept assuring her that the dogs almost never did catch a rabbit.

He waited alongside her until finally they had lost the pack, even though they could hear the beagle master blowing his horn, some distance away, and Duncan said, 'I'm afraid in this cold my sciatica is playing up again, shall we call it quits?'

They were miles from either home but he said the grotto was nearby, would she like to see that?

So they walked around the edge of the lake, which he explained had been planted originally by Capability Brown, though the grotto was a later addition, a spongy cave made entirely of shells and coral a flight or two below ground coffee mixed with brandy and they sat on a damp stone bench and drank more. 'Suppose we should be getting back,' Duncan said. His hands were clasped around his stomach and he looked down. 'I hope you've enjoyed yourself.'

'Oh, yeah.'

'Marvelous. And how long are you planning to stay?'

'I think we're leaving tonight.'

'What a shame. We must arrange for you to come back.'

'That would be great! Do you . . . do you ever get to New York?'

She knew she was being seductive. Why did she have to come on to this big old red plum who probably had a scrotum down to his knees? Couldn't she keep her trap shut, it was a hideous psychic ability, that all she had to do was meet some man and think of him sexually?

'I haven't been, in twenty years. Never really had any need to. I suppose it's time for me to take a trip . . . Tell me my dear, how long have you been married?' said Lord Duncan.

She shrugged. Water dripped from the ceiling of the absurd shell-lined cave. 'I don't know,' she said. 'For ever. My feeling is, things could always be worse. A lot worse.'

'Quite right,' he said approvingly. 'I've always wondered about this American insistence that one should have a happy marriage or else divorce. As soon as someone tells one they're happily married one always feels obliged to begin prodding around in search of a hole to make bigger, like a sweater.'

'I like sex though. I like sex a lot but marriage isn't really the venue to have it in.'

'Ha ha ha! Jolly good! You're a very funny gel as well as a very attractive one. Things certainly have changed since I was young.'

'In what way?'

'Hmmm. Excellent question . . .' He looked pensive for a long time. 'Loo paper.'

'You mean . . . toilet paper?'

'It used to be dreadful. Nasty little rough brown squares.'

'Ah.'

'Oh, a great deal is different; only none of it's coming to mind at the moment, however . . . Drinks used to be different, I remember. Nowadays nobody ever asks for a Gin-and-It or Gin-and-French.' He glanced at her admiringly as if she had coaxed a reluctant confession from him and now he was happily cornered. 'You really have got me thinking. I hope I'll see you again.'

If it wasn't for Barry she wouldn't have been here, she knew that. On the other hand, if it wasn't for Barry she could have had a real adventure, even if it just meant picking up someone in a hotel bar. But maybe this sort of adventure wouldn't have kept happening to her.

She would have sat, day after day, in a dreary hotel room, and toured museums, or whatever real tourists did. 'Well, you don't seem all that old! But you've certainly been . . . fascinating, things must have been so different!'

'Absolutely. There you have it.' He continued to stare at her, a sly expression in his small eyes. Then, as if emerging from a cocoon into daylight, he jumped up. 'My goodness, will you look at the time! It's gone half-past. We'd better be getting back. Listen my dear you seem like a very free-thinking, free-spirited individual, do you ever get back to England or London on your own? I would very much like to see you if you come over.'

By then, though, she was pregnant, and what was she going to do? Fabricate some excuse to fly to London in the hopes of seeing the Earl, old Duncan Battan-Bouwery, with her fat tummy sticking out? With his big stomach and her big stomach they would simply bounce off one another like two rubber balls. He obviously wasn't going to say, this will be simply delightful, I can't live without you and your unborn child by a different man – it was too late.

And after . . . she was so busy, she was in a sort of stoned daze, getting the baby's room ready and just being pregnant, and then giving birth and not getting enough sleep for years and years, and during the day – even though she did have, eventually, a woman who came in for two or three days a week to look after Cash and she went back to work part-time – she could never get caught up; she was always trying to take him to the playground to get some fresh air, or buying diapers, or preparing fresh formula, or taking him the pediatrician – he was sick a lot, with earaches, colds, some kind of eczema that wouldn't go away – and the last thing she was thinking about was having an affair.

She was too flabby and ugly, anyway and too tired and lazy to do sit-ups, so that her belly was a saggy saddlebag around her midriff. And Cash was always crying, colicky, with a runny nose, or diarrhea.

One day she had put him on the floor, on a big blanket, he was just starting to crawl and for no discernible reason he began to have a shrieking fit, he just lay on the floor on his back screaming, his face bright purple, punching himself in the face, his big mouth open revealing those few teeth that stuck through the pink gummy hole, a creature from an another-planet movie and she was so tired that, instead of picking him up, she sat down against the wall and laughed – at the whole total nightmare absurdity of it all. The squalling red face of a furious old man. And it was her own fault for getting herself into this mess – and then Barry came in. Had he been tying fishing flies at his desk in the other room, or back from work?

She couldn't remember, only that he came into the room and looked at the shrieking baby and the mess, the kid was filthy, he had crapped himself and she hadn't changed him yet, and that she was leaning against the wall, laughing – did she have a glass of wine? Probably, it was a hot day and the air conditioner hadn't been working right and she was still waiting for the repair service to come and fix it – instead of picking up their son to comfort him – and she saw whatever love Barry had for her leaving him. She hadn't even known it was there, and now she watched as the last of it fizzled out of his body like air from a helium balloon.

And that was that. He looked at her and shook his head and bent over and picked up their child and took him to the changing table, saying, 'There, there. Poor little Cash, you've got heat stroke, let's take off this nasty old diaper and put you in a cool tubby, shall we? Now why would your mommy put you in all these clothes, on such a hot day?' And he gave her a look and, wrapping the poopy diaper in a tidy ball, left it on the table, and carried the smelly, naked kid out of the room.

21

She couldn't get enough of him. She was soaking wet, covered with sweat and if she didn't have an orgasm she would die but she couldn't get there; her new make-up must have been totally sweated off and her perfect hair was down around her shoulders. Across the room in the mirror on the armoire door she glimpsed herself, a moth sucked into a fan, broken wings and dust.

Maybe it was his smell or maybe it was his skin, an old person's skin, not that he was so ancient, but it was different than her own skin, or Barry's, much drier and almost baggy in places, an elephant was mounting her. Young people had skin that was moist, each cell plump with water, firm. What was his name, anyway? . . . Germano, she would never get used to it, like a germ . . . He might have been fifty, but my God that dick – it wasn't normal to have something that huge inside her almost splitting her in two, making her feel she was being turned inside out.

Once when she was in her teens, after she had started sleeping with Ernie, the Portuguese bartender, she had gone to be fitted for a diaphragm and it was awful, having to get up on the examining table in a stiff gown, with her legs spread wide apart in the stirrups, her butt down at the edge of the table, no underpants, and the nurse said the doctor would be through in a minute only he didn't come and didn't come and she just had to lie there, a turkey waiting to be stuffed.

And when the doctor finally arrived – he had horrible metal glasses, resembling a surgical device, a cold sneer and butcher's hands – there she was, splayed, her boobs slopping to either side. 'Scoot down,' he said. 'More. More.' He pried open her vulva with a stainless steel apparatus like a giant eyelash curler, and said, in a tone of disdain, 'Well, I'm going to have to give you a size seventy-five, you're so big in there.'

He said this with so much . . . disgust, or contempt, as if he had never examined such a huge abscess or pit in his entire life, that forever after she always thought, I must have a really sloppy, huge vaginal canal – the equivalent, she supposed, of some man being informed he had a tiny penis. Only this was even worse.

Germano turned over without pulling out of her so that he was on his back and she was on top of him; her big breasts were in his face and he delicately caught each tip of the nipple in his stumpy thumb and index finger and twisted, which hurt in a sort of beautiful, exquisite way; and he had that big, hard stomach – a third party laughingly involved in the whole enterprise – and she couldn't even have said why she found any of this so wildly exciting except that there was nothing between them, there was no mental connection, no soppy emotion. It was just two bodies fucking, and yet his was expertly handling hers. He might have been driving a race car.

He took her hips in his hands, just a bit below her buttocks and squeezed them together which pushed her over the edge into orgasm, and for a moment she thought with alarm she was urinating as well. She tipped forward so that she was lying on top of him, flat; her face was down at his neck and she drooled a bit, her orgasm wasn't stopping, and then he let out a dull animal yell, a sort of blues shout, and his penis throbbed – she guessed he was having an orgasm too, since he shoved her down on him once more, with force and then stopped.

'That was fabulous,' she said after a pause. They lay glued together, starfish shriveled in the hot sun on a rock. And for a second she thought, I really do love him. It was his smell, alien, masculine, and his great big body, not tall but heavy and dense; he would always protect her or keep his dick in her, filling her up. But after a minute he pulled out of her and moved away.

'Shall we have some more champagne?' he said, picking up the phone.

'Oh, sure!'

He sat on the edge of the bed, draping the sheet over his genitals and ordering from room service in Portuguese. 'Would you like a snack to eat, too?'

She had no idea what one might order from room service for a snack and when he saw her blank look he passed her a room service menu from the drawer. In the Appetizers and Snacks category there was a shrimp cocktail, for $28. Caviar and toast points, $105. Miniature pizza, $23 – it was frighteningly expensive, she didn't want to run up his bill any further than she already had by letting him buy her the dress and the spa treatments. She shook her head.

'Just the champagne then. I have had a very late lunch and am not the least bit hungry; but Susannah will not serve dinner until late and she has the most marvelous cook – I should know, she used to be my cook – and I do not want to spoil my appetite. I always look forward to my Brazilian food when I come here and it has been more than six months, for me, since my last trip. But, I must shower and shave.' He couldn't meet her gaze. He went into his bathroom and returned in a hotel robe, tossing a second one to her. She put it on.

'I can't even move,' she said.

'There is time to have a bath.'

She thought now she would tell him about herself: her husband, her boredom, her life in that stupid house and as a travel agent. She knew he was married, but maybe things weren't going so well for him either. But he had left the room and there was no moment of intimacy.

Wet stuff dripped down the inside of her legs as she got out of the car and she hoped it wasn't staining on the back of her dress. They had been in the car for an hour, and, seated in the back, consumed another bottle of champagne. Now she was slightly nauseous. A matched pair of dogs came bounding toward her, white and brown with slavering square faces; Germano began to shout at them in Portuguese; the dogs obviously knew him and stopped their onslaught to lie on their backs, squirming in pleasure.

The house could have been in a James Bond movie, vast and modern, atop a cliff; the front steps appeared to be cascading with water but as she got closer she saw it was just a clever trick: the tops of the steps weren't wet, the water was trapped at the back. A uniformed servant escorted them in. The living room contained a fountain with pink and blue dolphins, glass, larger than life, spouting through blow-holes. They continued out to the terrace which opened up right from the living room. At the far end where the cliff began, a blue pool seemed to drip off the edge into space.

There were four or five people sitting around outside on massive sofas and swinging chairs. A diminutive blonde, a certain flossy type, perfectly coifed with the sort of hair Peyton knew would be dried grass to the touch, rose to greet them. She made squeaking noises at Germano and, kissing Peyton hello, introduced herself – Susannah – then rattled off a list of names of the others there. Felix waved hello; he had a vaguely impatient, sour expression on his face; he had been so spoiled all his life that the slightest lag in services of one kind or another – entertainment, stimulation – was enough to sink him into a rage of self-pity, despair.

She had never seen such glamorous people – a woman, probably her age, who might have been a fashion model, only more interesting, with a regally pointed nose and slightly protruding teeth, dressed in a cloud of shrouding; Felix, whom she had met at the hotel, and a couple of other men, one American; one was fat, ringed with fat, with the brutal head of a Roman senator. His steel-colored hair should have been crowned with a wreath of gilded leaves. More champagne was thrust at her and the hostess pointed to a chair that had been pulled over where she was supposed to sit.

'May I use your bathroom?' she said timidly.

'Oh yes, I will show you,' Susannah said and led her to a room so large it took her a while to realize this was the bathroom. There was a tub the size of a small swimming pool, a shower stall, several sinks – the toilet she found at last hidden behind a low wall. There were white and pink orchids everywhere, in glass vases, nobody could have so many orchids in their bathroom.

When Peyton emerged, having done her best to try and tidy up the drippings, Susannah was waiting. 'Come, I know you will like to see the house. This is the screening room – and in here, the gymnasium – and here, the rooms of my sons who are now grown and gone –' None of this required any response on Peyton's part although she wondered how the woman could look so young and have children who were adults. It didn't seem possible, until the woman said, 'Tell me, what brings you to Rio? Are you here for the facelift?'

'Me? No.'

'No, no, you are too young, I am sorry, of course. How old are you?'

'Oh . . .' she wanted to sound sophisticated and it wasn't Susannah's business. 'Does it matter?'

'Here in Brazil it does not matter. We tell each other everything. Maybe you are not too young for the facelift?'

'I'm twenty-six.'

'Twenty-six! And you are with Germano? But . . . you do not find him too old?'

'How old is he?'

'What do you think?'

'I don't know . . . fifties? In his sixties?'

'Ha! Funny! He will be insulted. Of course at twenty-six, if that is your age, you are too young for a facelift. You are not even thinking of such things! But . . . you have had your nose done?' Peyton shook her head. 'It is not a secret here, like in New York. You can tell me. I am forty-nine and have had two facelifts. Do not laugh. Any time, when you are ready, you can come and stay. As you know Germano is my ex-husband and we are very good friends, and I am friends with his wife, as well, though she lives in São Paulo and I do not see so much of her these days; I have no need to go there, now that my house is finished and I have met Dylan.'

Peyton thought Dylan must be the other American at the party, not bad-looking in a vapid, surfer-dude-from-California way. They wandered from room to room; what sort of human being could require so much space – there was a restaurant-sized kitchen and a painting gallery displaying the work of Brazilian artists. Susannah knocked at one door and a tiny woman emerged, also in a uniform, and several small white dogs. 'This is my housekeeper, Consuela, she is my mother – well, I call her my mother, she is like a mother to me.'

Peyton didn't like to ask, why do you make your mother wear a uniform?

'It is hard, I have such a big staff, right now I have nine people but here in Brazil you must hire so many people – if you hire one you must hire their husband and brothers and sisters as well, then suddenly they request you hire their children, and their cousins – since you pay them so little, you do not mind, the people must have some work!'

Upstairs the guests were snorting cocaine from the glass coffee table. Vast quantities of meat had been laid out, buffet-style, on a round table and another table nearby under an umbrella was set for dinner. She didn't see how she could get out of snorting the cocaine with the others – Susannah immediately went over and snorted some – the idea of sticking a rolled tube – was it money, or a straw? – up her nose in front of people was humiliating, and she had never snorted cocaine before –

'Like, I've only been here six months and I don't know how long, legally, I can stay without a resident's visa; maybe I'm gonna have to get married to Susannah to get a resident's card!' Dylan was saying. He looked across the blue pool and shrugged. He was probably thirty, thirty-five, no signs of intelligence beyond a few unctuous permanent-house-guest skills. His laugh was a mirthless, chugging, saliva slurp. 'I mean, dude, I wouldn't mind hanging out at this poolside for a few hundred years!'

He didn't even look like he'd be good in bed. No matter how much money a woman had, pickings were slim, apparently globally.

Susannah was vaguely out of it. 'Have I offered you all food? It is ready.' No one showed the slightest inclination to get up. 'Here, will you have some cocaine or do you prefer marijuana?' she asked Peyton, and then announced, 'She is twenty-six years old, she says.

Do you know, Germano, how old she thinks you are? She thinks you must be in your sixties!' Peyton couldn't bring herself to look at him. 'How do you still pull the birds, Germano?' Susannah said. 'That is an English expression, is it not? Do you know how old is Germano?' Peyton shook her head. 'He is in his early fifties! He had his first facelift five years ago, it was my idea, I said, "Germano, men with wrinkles are handsome but your neck is like that of a –" how do you say? – "a vulture!"' She went to the back of the couch and put her hands around Germano's neck to demonstrate how the tissue had been pulled taut. 'The neck of course is the most difficult region.'

While Susannah was turning Germano's head to show that no scars were visible behind his ears, Felix winked at her and gestured toward the cocaine. She supposed if she was going to have to try some it was better to do it now and get it over with; at least no one was paying too much attention, they were all beginning to describe their own operations and show their scars or absence thereof.

The blonde with the pointed nose was saying she was thirty-two, too young, though many people wanted her to get her nose done . . . No, you mustn't!' said the Roman senator. He had an effeminate, high-pitched voice that did not match his appearance. 'You have a nose that can be found in paintings by Fra Angelico, a pure line descended from the Borgias!'

Peyton didn't want anybody to examine her snub nose, boringly American, the tiny rabbit nose that, until now, she had liked. She was incredibly nervous but she didn't want to be naïve, not in her new, glamorous existence.

The cocaine burned, a powdered cleaning solution, though she supposed it was good quality and not some sort of poison – had it been, the others would have been dead by now – but Barry had always warned her how, during his residency, he had been called to the emergency room when a woman had been brought in with her teeth eaten away from having snorted some sort of acid.

Tears came into her eyes. She wanted to go and cry in the bathroom but this would be unsophisticated. Then all of a sudden she felt totally confident – energized. She started talking to everyone, non-stop – she

wasn't a talkative person, she still felt she had nothing to say but
nevertheless she was going to talk . . . a fish, belly-up on dry land,
flopping with a pale green soft-fleshed stomach . . .

She must have gone back to her own bed around three in the morning.
Whether Felix had left before then or after this she didn't know. She
couldn't sleep but lay looking out at the pocked, bloodless moon that
hung over Corcovado until the first morning light began to slop across
the sky. At first she had no feelings at all and then a sullen amusement
came over her; how quickly she had fallen from a nice married girl
living on the Upper West Side with her Jewish dentist husband.

A kind of panic set in. Now she was in love with Germano, she
wanted to spend her life with him, now he would never respect her or
consider her marriageable. He would never beg her to leave her
husband to be with him; he would never set her up somewhere in
a pied-à-terre and call her constantly on the phone, like an obsessed
gangster. She had wrecked everything by going along with the idea
that all three of them should go to bed together, and only a few
glimpses of how it happened came back to her – that they had started
drinking vodka, done more coke, she had sat on Felix's lap and told
him how handsome he was – hoping, she now recollected, to make
Germano jealous – and now her beautiful dress was spoiled.

She would never be able to sleep. Her eyes had been rubbed with
coarse sandpaper. Naked, she paced the room. Her boobs were sore.
She went into the bathroom and tried to throw up but couldn't. Her
stomach was a roiling mess of oily vodka and stale champagne,
topped with a garlicky slick of shredded meat and beans – she had
vague memories of eating something from the dinner. She had to get
the stuff out. Finally she stuck her fingers down her throat, tickling the
uvula until, with a horrible gagging, the chundering stuff spewed up
like a geyser, leaving her stomach a twisted wreckage. Then she
brushed her teeth and ran a bath.

While the water ran she checked on Germano. His room was dark
and the curtains drawn. In the sliver of light that came through a gap
she saw he was asleep, his mouth slightly parted, his big, comforting

belly rising and falling beneath a rumpled sheet. Such a dense block of human fat and muscle could have protected her from anything, a shield of money and royal weight, kingly.

Her bath was full. She dropped the fizzy yellow crystals in the water. There was a hissing sound and the scent of citrus, lemon trees, filled the room. After she bathed she would cream herself and slip back to his bed, fresh, reborn; she would wake curled into his belly, a small cat.

But by the time she got out of the bath the effects of the cocaine had worn off. She lay down on her bed and before she realized it, had fallen asleep in her damp hotel robe. When she next opened her eyes it was late morning; there was no sign of Germano in the suite. On a silver tray was a pot of coffee and she poured some into the second cup and carried it to the window. The sky was clear and she could see Cristo Redemptor, his back to her, arms raised, outstretched, far away on top of Corcovado. The coffee was tepid but she drank it anyway.

22

'Peyton, you're deteriorating. You look like an ordinary, middle-aged housewife.'

It was true her brother was a little drunk, his eyes were two yellow yolks, one with a spot of blood. He had probably stopped for a few beers before meeting up with her. He didn't look pinned so she didn't think he was back on heroin. She had just had a new haircut, very tidy – but even if it wasn't flattering, he didn't have to say that. An ordinary middle-aged housewife, what kind of comment could be worse? It meant her husband was now the only man who could, apparently, get it up for her. She had gone down to Florida to cheer herself up and instead as soon as she saw him, Donny took one look at her and made that remark.

Cash was five years old, kindergarten, and she said you know what, Barry, it's his school break, I can see my sister and my brother and my nieces, and Cash can get to know his cousins a bit, do you . . . want to come? He said he didn't think so, he had too much work – he had to plan his vacations six months in advance, so that his secretary didn't book anybody for that time, and he planned to go on a fishing trip with some buddies in April –

It was better that they mostly took separate vacations, anyway; the ones they took together never worked out quite right. Barry wanted his holidays to be . . . educational, art museums, castles, historical sites. She wasn't interested in that stuff. The only thing she could ever remember having enjoyed, apart from shopping, was when one time they were in Paris for a weekend discount package and they visited the catacombs, five stories below ground, where endless bricked passageways led to rooms filled with bones that had been moved from various cemeteries. Room after room of bones, leg bones, arms, skulls stacked floor to ceiling . . . vaults of teeth. The bones were organized artistically, according to type, no longer owned by people, no longer named.

No one remembered them now but even if they had, the bones were oblivious. They were only calcium stalks, yellowed and crumbling. And even now, among the living, there were billions upon billions of people, each one with thoughts, needs, wishes, wants, desires – did any of it, ultimately, make any difference? It had upset Barry; but she had liked it.

She was secretly relieved that he didn't want to come to Florida. This way she could act slightly indignant and say that, after all, if he had already planned his own vacation, the least he could do was give her the money to stay at a hotel in South Beach, so she and Cash didn't have to cram into her sister's house; her sister was able to get her a discount, one of the hotels was a client at the PR firm where Kathy worked.

Mirabel was fifteen and Anita was twelve; Kathy and Manny were divorced, things were not going well for Kathy, who had their mother living with them now. She was afraid that Mirabel was going to end up pregnant; Manny was constantly late on the child support payments; it was difficult living with Nell, after all those electroshock treatments, since medication hadn't helped her depression. And the PR firm kept replacing staff with younger and younger people – kids, really.

Donny was actually doing okay – he had joined the volunteer fire department and had saved or acquired enough to buy a bar out on Biscayne Bay, which his new wife ran – they were about to have a baby. So in a sense it would be a family reunion, apart from her sister Brenda.

It was only the first evening, though, when she and Cash had arrived – they had spent the afternoon on the beach, across from the hotel. It was actually quite cool and windy, and Cash was afraid of the water, he didn't even want to go in wading at the edge. Peyton was keen to swim and said, 'You don't go in the water but just play in the sand and Mommy will have a dip and be right back.'

But the minute she set foot in the water he started shrieking and screaming bloody murder, 'Mommy, come back! Come back!' and spoiled the whole thing for her. She had envisioned herself in the blue sea, swimming so far out that the land and the strip of sidewalk and the hotels became only a faint, distant blur behind her, but she couldn't leave him screaming there and even if she had just decided to tough it out and ignore him, when she got back it would take him hours to recover from his meltdown.

She would have had a whole different method of child-rearing but Barry was such a diplomat, such a negotiator, that Cash was accustomed to being cajoled, distracted, coaxed if anything was not going his way. A blunt and direct 'No' would never work.

So she gave up and they went back to the room to shower and change. Donny was already waiting downstairs, working on a beer. The place had a tiny bar but it was really cute, decorated with crazy tropical colors, golden fake palm trees, and one of the seats at the tables beside the bar was a sort of swing-seat, so she said to Cash, who was a bit sulky, 'Look, isn't this fun! A swing-seat!'

She ordered Cash a glass of milk and herself a vodka tonic, and Donny tried to talk to Cash – who naturally went very shy and refused to say a word. Donny was rambling on a bit, he had a slurry way of talking even without a drink, kept talking about his new bar and said he'd take them to see it the next day, 'I'm gonna re-name the place, call it "Biscayne Donny's" what do you think, huh, Peyton, isn't it great? You're really gonna like this place, Peyton, I bet you never thought I'd get my shit together, huh?'

'"Biscayne Donny's"? Oh, gee, you're kidding. That's ridiculous. It's not like you're from around here. Why don't you call it "Dorchester Donny's" or, I don't know, "Druggy Donny's"?' She was just teasing but it was then he announced, looking her intently up and down, 'Well, Peyton, you're deteriorating –' and so on.

Why did that devastate her so much? She had vague memories of sex games from when they were kids – he was only a couple of years older than she, after all, though still her big brother. There hadn't been anything wrong at the time that both of them ran around naked or bathed together – her mother was pretty lax about such things, in fact, she had to face it, totally indifferent – and she would fondle his penis, or watch him pee – certainly she had never wanted a penis but it would have been nice to be able to urinate standing up – and for a while he had made her lie down in an empty lot near their house and take off her underpants and he sold glimpses of her weezer, which had sprouted two black hairs, to his friends for ten cents or a quarter – like, big deal.

Anyway, then Donny took them over to Kathy's – but he couldn't stay, he had to get over to the bar, he really was transformed, working almost round the clock at his new place. Kathy actually looked pretty good but her mother, what a disaster – she wasn't even sure if her mother recognized her at first. Kathy had said they were wondering now if it was Alzheimer's – but then her mother would kind of pull herself together only to start in with the same old routine again, 'You know I was raised thinking I would get married and have kids and be a housewife, all I wanted in life was to have children, and then when your father said he wanted a divorce – and he had been screwing around for years – I had finally had enough, his sulking, and then he brought his girlfriend home to live with us, what could I have been thinking? My lawyers said I could have fought and gotten a lot more – somehow he had taken our assets, which were really mine to begin with, and transferred them into an account with his name – and I just thought, well, he's a fair person, I'm sure he's making sure we're all taken care of –'

'Okay, Ma. Let's just try and be happy, on this beautiful afternoon. Barry's not planning to divorce me and if he does, first of all I'll make sure I get a fair settlement, second of all, I can take care of myself, I have a decent job, or at least if I wanted to I could work full-time –'

Mirabel came in. At fifteen she was utterly stunning, with moony eyes and the appearance of peach at the absolute moment of perfection, one more day of tree ripening before being picked, and Peyton felt a pang of jealousy. She saw now by comparison that that thing – whatever it was – was gone for her. But whatever Mirabel had now she would waste; at fifteen who knew how to capitalize on it, or even that she had it? And in this society that was all that was left for women, the one day when an insect gnaws its way from a chrysalis and flies around for a bit before crumbling into too-dry wings.

'How are you, Aunt Peyton?'

'I'm fine. You look gorgeous. Cash is so excited to see you, I think he's out back on your old swing-seat –'

Kathy made them all drinks, some sort of fruit-vodka-club-soda combo and brought the pitcher and glasses to the table. 'Here you go, bottoms up!'

'Cheers. Ma has a birthday coming up, doesn't she?' Peyton didn't really need another drink, but it was such a beautiful day and it wasn't easy, seeing her family, and besides, she was on vacation.

'I know,' Kathy said. 'What do you think we should get her? I was thinking, one of those vibrators –'

'Would she use one?' The two women giggled.

'They're multi-purpose. They sell them over at the drugstore. They come with different attachments, for muscle pain . . . etcetera.'

'It sounds like a good idea. I'll go halves with you.' From the backyard she could hear squeals of pleasure from Cash, who was being chased by Mirabel. 'Where's Anita?'

'God knows. I told her you were coming, but –'

'Mirabel looks great. You, too.'

'Oh, please. If I had a hundred thousand dollars I could start to think about getting new teeth, a facelift, a decent haircut, then maybe I'd have a chance of meeting someone – believe me, Peyton, the last thing you ever want to do is end up divorced. I mean, things were bad, being married, but now I'm doing everything I was doing before and – not that Manny was much use – but at least there were two incomes, and occasional sex, and once in a while he took the kids out for the afternoon –'

She couldn't bear to be around her family any longer. 'So what are the plans?'

'How long are you staying? What do you want to do while you're down here?'

'Well, see all of you, of course. We're here till Monday. You know who I wouldn't mind getting in touch with – Manny's brother, the guy you work with –'

'Luis?'

'Mmm.'

'I'll call him, if you want – the only thing I sort of thought we could do, while you're around, is Donny is dying for you to see his bar, and tomorrow they're going to have a cook-out, so in the early evening we can all go there – it's kind of a fun place – and if you want, I'll see what Luis is up to tomorrow and I can babysit Cash for the day, give you a break.'

He said he was free and would be happy to meet up and if she wanted, they could go to thrift stores and yard sales and the flea markets, and get lunch somewhere.

In the morning Kathy came with Anita and picked up Cash who was quite happy to go off with them and then Luis arrived in a baby-blue Mercedes sports car and they drove around for the day, two giddy teenagers, rummaging in thrift stores and along Lincoln Avenue where he bought her a coral necklace that she spotted for five dollars, so she would have a souvenir of Florida, and they had lunch out – he took her out to lunch, actually, she couldn't remember when a man had done that – she had a huge Cobb salad, it was delicious and the first time she had felt hungry in weeks, very crispy bacon and heaps of blue cheese and egg yolk and chopped romaine lettuce and she didn't know what else, it almost hurt her mouth with the tangy crispiness; she had some wine, very cold, dry, white wine, a Pinot Gris, perfect, with the greenish fragrance of a fresh-cut lawn, which Luis had picked out but he didn't want to drink because he was driving; then he said, what the fuck and he had a glass, too –

And then in one store where all the china was broken or chipped, but the prices on them were exorbitant, they started laughing. In the back was a vast area of really foul-smelling, moldy clothes, rags on hangers. 'Come on, let's look at the clothing,' Peyton said.

'Oh, God, I'm getting out of here!' Luis shrieked. 'Don't go near those clothes, they're totally filthy. I can never look at thrift-store clothing since I lived in New York – you know, when you would get on the subway and some homeless person would come on, that smell? And it was rush hour and you were trapped on the car with them? Ugh!'

'Come on now Luis! You come here right now and don't move!' She was teasing him and it was unlike her she thought, to be so bossy but she didn't feel shy around him any more, it was so nutty and goofy, to be out thrift-store shopping with her former brother-in-law's brother; he was so cute with his bright eyes and half-sickened grin, she thought, My God, I have a total crush on this guy! He's my best friend! What had happened, was some Cupid up there, shooting off arbitrary demonic arrows? But he was looking at her with the same expression, too; they were crazy about each other.

Anyway, then he took her to Kathy's; she asked if he wanted to come with them to the cook-out at Donny's bar, but he was busy. 'I tell you what, though – are you going to be around tomorrow night?'

'Great,' she said. Then he got nervous and said, if she didn't mind maybe just having a drink, around nine o'clock, or a quick bite to eat – he would be taking a break from work and would need to get back, later, to finish some stuff – it would be Sunday night, but he really had to put in the hours, especially now as they were heading toward the deadline for a presentation to try and land a big new client.

After the perfect day Donny's cook-out was something of a disaster – the kids were all sulky, especially Brittney, who had planned to be out with her friends that night, and Anita was obviously a sad case, too; she was always going to be plain compared to her sister. You could see everything that was going to happen in the next ten years already embedded in the eyes of the two girls – the drug problems, the dropping-out from high school, the teen pregnancies – why did they have to bother going through all that when it was so obvious?

The bar was kind of a rough, honky-tonk waterfront place, no screens, a porch out over the waterway; that liquid, chirping Florida night, citrus and salt and boat-gasoline. Palmettos and brown dirt, and guys with ponytails drinking beer and bourbon, ignoring the women dressed in tight T-shirts, denim and ruffles, outfits in styles that they had been wearing since the 1970s but which were currently back in fashion. Fat children up past their bedtime threw pieces of bread and French fries into the oil-slicked, greasy water, poked sticks through the slits in the floor and at one another, the Tiffanys and Heathers and Jasons who would grow up to take their parents' places at the bar.

Under other circumstances she might have been appreciative, might have eyed some mechanic type in a baseball cap who was already drunk, sitting in the back with his rowdy buddies. But the day had been so perfect and all she could think now was that she wished she had been able to go out with Luis that evening, instead of spending time with her family. Her mother kept nodding out, she was on too much medication, or the wrong kind, and she didn't much care for Donny's new girlfriend – wife? – who kept sneering at her, obviously jealous, and Kathy drank too much and started practically making out with some red-neck. Peyton wound up calling a taxi that cost almost forty dollars to get them back to South Beach.

When she and Cash got back to the room and Cash was watching TV while she got ready for bed, there was a knock at the door and she panicked – who could it be? What if it was Luis? She had already taken off her make-up; Cash hid under the bed. 'Who is it?' she said.

'Room service.'

Maybe it was one of those things where some burglar or rapist breaks in, but she didn't know what to do. She opened the door – after all the hotel wasn't that big, someone would surely hear her – and it was room service, a waiter with a Martini, one perfect icy cold Martini, and a note that said, 'Hope you enjoy this! I had the best time with you today! Luis.'

It was so sweet and fabulously romantic and even though she had been just about to brush her teeth and didn't really need or want a drink she lay down on her bed and let the icy stuff trickle into her veins. And that night she had a dream about smoking opium, not that she had ever done this, but she kept thinking, 'I want to chase the dragon.' And in the morning the phone rang and it was Luis and she said, 'Oh, thank you for that Martini, that was so wonderful!' and the first thing he said was, 'You know what? I really wish we could smoke some opium.'

'Yeah!' she said. 'Me too. That's just what I was thinking.'

She and Cash spent the next day on the beach – did she really need to put in any more time with her family? She fed Cash an early dinner; she wasn't the slightest bit hungry. Then she took a long bath, and gave Cash a bath. They were to meet Luis at eight o'clock but he was a half-hour late and she had already had a drink by the time he got there.

He had told her to meet him at the most elegant place, with wide coral steps, a sort of Italianate amphitheater, and she wished more than anything that she and Luis were together and that Cash was their child, the three of them, dark, exotic, elegant – well, Cash wasn't exactly exotic, a bit reddish from the sun, with his wispy taupe-colored hair, but they would have other babies, dark-haired, with the vivid purple-blue eyes that would be a combination of his and hers. And she would live where it was warm and there were palm trees and it was almost always hot and sunny.

She had a double vodka. She hadn't eaten much all day and now it was too late, by the time he arrived she was looped but didn't care and the last thing that interested her was food.

'. . . I used to have a crush on you,' Luis said abruptly.

'You did? You? When?'

'Oh, you know, when you came down to visit Manny and Kathy – when when was that? Five years ago?'

'Six, at least,' she said. 'God, I had no idea . . . but you . . . I mean, you're so fabulous, you don't . . . I thought you only went out with boys.'

'I've had girlfriends, too . . .'

'You have? You slept with girls?'

'Mmmm-hmmm.'

'And you had a girlfriend? What was her name?'

'Um . . . Susan.'

'And you didn't mind . . . sleeping with her?'

'I want to go to the playground! I want to go on the swings!' Cash had noticed the kiddy-park across the street.

'Shall I take him?' Luis said. 'That way you can finish your drink.'

'No, let's both go.'

There were tall palm trees on the sand and a swing-seat and slide and merry-go-round, but the street lamps here gave off an evil blue light and the sand was whipping up quite a bit and it no longer seemed so romantic. She sat on a bench and he pushed Cash on the swing and she knew at any moment Cash was going to have a fit or temper tantrum of one sort or another; she had let him get too tired and in fact when she did say, 'Come on, Cash, let's go,' he started wailing. 'We'll come back in the morning, though, okay?' She pulled him off the swing but Cash kicked, began punching, so she put him down and he lay in the sand thrashing.

'I'll carry him,' Luis said.

'Don't pick him up, he has a vicious kick,' she said. But for whatever reason, Cash flung his arms around Luis's neck, monkey-style, and Luis carried him over to the park bench and put Cash on her lap and within five minutes Cash had fallen utterly asleep. 'He's so adorable!' said Luis. 'He's really smart, too.'

'Are you crazy?' she said. 'What a brat; to me he seems totally spoiled.' She knew he had to get back to his office and with a kid it was impossible anyway but then he said, 'Shall I come up to your room with you?'

'Yeah, sure!' she said. 'That'd be great. We can have a drink in my room.'

'I'll carry him.'

'No, no, if I move him now he might wake up . . .'

He was heavy, a deadweight, but she staggered back down the block, though Luis kept offering . . . In the moony orange light of her lobby she realized she was more sloshed than she thought and when they got up to the room she put Cash down on the double bed on the

263

far side. When she went into the bathroom to pee she saw her lipstick was smeared and she looked Crazy Lady, slightly sunburned, mascara smudged. She did her best to tidy herself up and when she came back out Luis was sprawling on the other bed, opposite the sleeping Cash. 'Let me call room service, you want a drink?'

'Yeah, sure,' he said. He put his arms under his head and turned on the remote control for the TV.

'Sorry, we don't have anybody to deliver the drinks just now,' said the bartender, 'I'm the only one here, if you want I can make you a drink and you can take it back up.'

'They don't have anybody to deliver,' she said. 'I'm going to go down and bring us up a couple of drinks, what do you want?'

'Whatever you're having,' he said languorously.

She came back to the room with the drinks and Luis was still lying in bed and stared at her with half-closed, sleepy eyes, smiling at her seductively as he sat up and reached for his drink. 'What time is it, anyway?'

'I dunno. Maybe ten-thirty – watches never work on me.'

'I don't have to go back to the office for a while.'

'Good.' She sat in the chair next to the bed he was on and put down her drink. She really was looped. 'You know what, this overhead light, it's terrible.'

'I was going to say, isn't there some way you can dim it?'

She went to the door and flicked the switch but now the room was ridiculously dark, only for people about to go to sleep. 'I know!' she said. 'I'll turn on the light in the closet.' The light from the closet with the door three-quarters shut was more flattering and there were a number of small pinholes in the door, oddly, that let the light out like stars that were immensely distant. 'Look at this!' she said. 'This is so nutty – can you tell me why there are these pinholes in the door? I didn't even know they were there until I turned on the closet light and the main light was off!'

He giggled. 'You're right! That is so goofy! Like gloryholes.'

'But they're too small for that. Do you think, like, maybe one person can hide in the closet and watch the other person having sex out here?'

'Ooo.' They were both snickering, nervously. The wicker chair creaked when she sat back down. Luis turned on his side with his head propped on his hand and with the other brushed his hair from his eyes. 'Your kid is so cute. I'd love to have kids, some day. You're really lucky.'

'Poor thing, he's out for the count,' she said.

'Mmmm,' he said. His legs in his tight jeans were parted and he shifted on his back, propping up his head on a couple of pillows while he sipped his drink. 'Oh my gosh, I'm tired – I could just stay here all night.'

'That would be nice . . .' Everything about him had taken on the seductive manner of an actress playing a courtesan in a period film. 'So . . . I can't believe you have trouble, finding a boyfriend, if that's what you really want . . .' she said after a pause. 'You're so gorgeous.'

'I tell you –' He looked at her coyly; she might be shocked. 'The problem for me is, I'm a top. I'm never the bottom – and that's not so easy.'

She was perplexed. She supposed that meant that he was the one who stuck his penis into the other guy's tush. Why would a man prefer only one type of hole, a male anus? What the hell was the big deal? Anyway, if you were a woman you were always the bottom, in that you didn't have a penis to shove, only a receptacle to receive. 'I can't believe they're not lining up around the block?'

There was a sense that something was about to happen. Was she supposed to climb on top of him now and unzip his fly, and get his dick hard and then insert it in her? Surely he would make some indication – reach out a hand to touch her on the knee, gesture for her to lie down next to him – she supposed she could take the aggressive role if he made even a tiny encouraging gesture. But what kind of top just lay there with no indication at all? This must be what men went through, all the time – girls coming back with them to their hotel room and lying around provocatively, the poor guy uncertain if that was a signal to make a move. But she wasn't a guy, was she?

'You know, Cash is sound asleep.' Her voice was husky. It took all of her courage to lean forward and touch his elbow through his shirt. 'Do you have a condom with you? I could make it easy for you.'

'Oh.' He sat up abruptly and almost knocked over his drink. 'No, no. I have to go, I really should be getting back to the office. No, no.'

She was utterly humiliated. 'Oh, gee. Well, it would have been nice,' she said. 'Believe me, there wouldn't have been any repercussions. It just seemed like it would have been a fun thing to do . . .' She was trying, desperately, to cover up. 'Anyway, don't take me all that seriously. We can still be friends, right?'

'I don't know.' He rose and headed for the door. 'Keep in touch! It was great to see you! Thanks for the drinks!'

She went into the bathroom and, kneeling on the tiles, puked violently into the toilet bowl.

23

She had to return from Brazil with some kind of report – evaluation, tips, ideas – for her travel agency. Even if she never saw the resort she should at least have other things to recommend or talk about to clients. But she didn't know what to do. Near the coffee table she found a note from Germano, apologizing for his absence – he had meetings and engagements all day and had to see some old friends for dinner but he hoped she would keep herself occupied and he would telephone her later on.

She was bereft. She didn't want to leave the room in case he called; if he did call she would see if he planned to come back to the room and then she thought she would seduce him; there had to be some way to connect with him. It hadn't been such a good idea to let the other man – Felix – get in that threesome, now she felt pieces of herself were scattered all over, and that the non-verbal glue that had been established between her and Germano had weakened.

She shouldn't sit in the room all day. She told the front desk to take a message if there were any calls for her and she left a note on the table saying where she was. Her bathing suit was only a one-piece, Victorian in a place where even the most obese woman crammed herself into the tiniest bikini that scarcely served to cover nipples and pudenda, but it was all she had. She put on the high heels and the hotel robe and went out.

It got hotter and hotter for the next hour or two but the water in the pool was too cold to swim and there was nobody else there. It was only Tuesday but she would be going home the next day. Probably she should call Barry – what if he had tried to call her at the bungalow resort and they said she had never arrived, he would be in a panic – but it was too unnatural, too unreal, to telephone him; she would have to force herself to do it later on.

After a few hours she was hungry and there hadn't been any calls for her, it was almost one o'clock. She went back upstairs. If Germano was going to come back it would probably be around now, before lunch, or around five or six, to shower and have a nap before going out to dinner. Anyway, she had an idea that this was what would happen. She didn't want to miss him in case he appeared and she thought she looked very nice in her swimsuit and heels, so she didn't change but ordered from room service, apprehensively, a Diet Coke and an expensive grilled chicken Caesar salad.

It wasn't what she really wanted. She would have much preferred the grilled sea bass but that was more than twice as expensive. Throughout the long afternoon he didn't turn up and around four she decided to go out for a walk along the beach and be back in an hour in case he returned. She put on the clothes she had worn on the airplane, hoping that, by wearing something baggy, she wouldn't attract attention, she was nervous that men might bother her.

There were couples sitting at the plastic tables on the sidewalk by the beach drinking beer or sipping from whole huge coconuts and she would have liked a beer but was too frightened to try to order one and then sit there alone sipping it, so she kept walking. After a while the beach was boring and every few feet a man was selling pareos or pants and dresses made from the same fabric, rayon with Thai fake-batik patterns, trying to get her to stop and buy things and kids were following her with boxes of gum or candy bars, also trying to get her to buy, so she headed away from the sea to a shopping street and even there the stores with the elegant clothing were too frightening to enter.

She passed a supermarket. Mustering all her courage she went in and spent a long time studying the food. The cereal boxes looked so exotic in a different language with different cartoon characters from those in the States; there was some Brazilian honey, which she thought might make a nice gift for Grace and Leonard, and then she found some beer, which was sold individually by the can, not tied together in a six-pack by loops of plastic – the beer was also different, the brands were unfamiliar, and that was exciting so she grabbed a couple of cans of that too and after she had paid she felt she had accomplished a major feat: shopping alone in a Brazilian grocery store.

At a stand nearby people were sipping the most amazing fruit drinks at a counter and she went up for a moment but studying the sign couldn't figure out what any of the fruits or vegetables would be in English and it was all so overwhelming she gave up and headed back to the hotel. It was five-thirty but there was no sign of him and no message at the front desk.

She opened the first beer but it was warm and she put the second in the mini-bar. At least she wasn't racking up his room tab. There was no ice in the mini-bar and she didn't know where she could get the ice bucket filled and it was a bit much to ask room service just to deliver up a bucket of ice if she hadn't ordered anything. She kept thinking maybe Germano would call and ask if she was free, after all, to meet him for dinner and so she showered, listening all the time in case the phone rang and she blow-dried her hair until it was a silky black cloth; she carefully put on make-up, violet eyeshadow, plummy lips, not what they had done to her the day before in the spa but, she thought, it looked better.

Now it was almost seven-thirty and probably if he was going to call to find out what she was doing, he would have done so by now. Barry would be getting home from the office but when she called he wasn't there, the answering machine picked up and she left a message saying that the hotel whose number she had left on her itinerary hadn't worked out but she was staying at another, there was no news and he shouldn't bother to call her back, she'd be home tomorrow.

She waited until about nine o'clock and it occurred to her she could go out onto the street and go to a restaurant to eat. But then she thought how fatiguing it would be to go to a place where she wouldn't be able to read the menu. Then she thought she would order room service, but it would be awful for Germano to come back and see how much more money she had spent. Besides, she wasn't that hungry and it would be a good way to lose weight. She would just make an early night of it and start getting ready for bed. Maybe he would want to spend some time with her the next day.

The phone in her bedroom started to ring. She got very nervous and grabbed her second beer, freezer cool, from the mini-bar, and dashed to her room. 'Hello?'

It wasn't too late for her to meet Germano somewhere, he could send his car and driver.

'Peyton?' It was Barry. 'I just got home and got your message. What happened, sexy princess?'

'Oh, gee, I don't know. The place was, um, overbooked, so they put me here instead, it's very nice.'

'How could they do that? Didn't they have your reservation? That's not right!' He was indignant.

'No, no, it's no big deal. Actually I think this is a much nicer place.'

'Well what if I had tried to reach you or something?'

'I'm sure they . . .' Why was she arguing with him? 'Is everything okay?'

'Everything's fine, except the transmission on the car blew up completely, it was a good thing I didn't take you to the airport – it would have blown up on the way there. Anyway, it looks like we're going to have to think about getting a new car; or maybe leasing one.'

'It died while you were driving?'

'On the highway and I was like, waiting for an hour for the service.'

'God, that's awful, you're lucky you weren't in an accident. So how did you get back?' It was trivial, unreal, but at least discussing the car kept the tremor from her voice. What if he had been killed? She didn't want him to die, far from it, but she would have had to start over, from scratch, how strange it would be to tell Germano. Maybe she would even get a small apartment and stay here. Now she felt even worse for having such thoughts, but what was she supposed to do, stop herself from thinking? It wasn't possible, the stupid things that flew into her head. Of course she loved Barry and none of this was real.

'Oh, the service guy drove me. So what are you doing now? Are you having fun? What time is it there?'

'A bit after nine. I was going to go out and get something to eat but I'm kind of whacked, you know, jet lag, so I'm probably just going to go to sleep.'

'No, don't go out. Just order room service. You're in the city, not out at this resort?'

'Yeah, but it's very nice; upscale.'

'Rio is really dangerous. Just be careful. I'll see you tomorrow.'

He loved her. He didn't know anything had happened. He forgave her. He didn't know her at all and it didn't matter to him, he had created an idea of her, an illusion, and with it he was satisfied. She would go out. There had to be someplace around the corner, nearby, that she could deal with; how dumb to be in Brazil for only three days and stay holed up in a hotel.

She didn't move. She put on the TV for company and began to rummage in her bag for her monkey-print pajamas. The phone rang and she was about to say 'Barry? I miss you –' when she realized it was Germano.

'Ciao! I am just calling to say hello and see how you are doing. Did you have a good day?'

'Oh, very. Lots of fun.'

'Good, good.' It was noisy, wherever he was calling from, and she could hear the chink of glasses and roaring laughter and the mellotone sounds of spoken Portuguese. 'And what are you doing this evening?'

'I don't actually have any plans.' She blurted this out thinking he was about to ask her to join him.

'Oh, that is a shame. I am sorry you are not here with me.'

'Me too!'

'You will go out and have dinner alone? There is no one you wish to see?'

'I don't know anybody here.'

'I am thinking if I had known this earlier I might have organized for a lady friend of mine to take you out, to keep you busy.'

'Oh, I'm fine, really.'

'There is a charming restaurant, only a ten-minute taxi ride from the hotel. Do you wish me to make a reservation there for you?'

271

'Honestly, no thanks. I'm actually pretty tired, from jet lag . . . and last night.'

'Yes, that was a lot of fun.'

'I need to get Susannah's address from you, so I can write her a thank-you note. I hope I didn't behave too badly at her house.'

He didn't respond to this last remark. 'Yes, I will give you. Are you free to have lunch with me tomorrow? What time is your flight?'

'Not until eight-thirty at night. Yeah, I'm free for lunch.'

'Very good. And my driver will take you to the airport. So I will see you then? Sweet dreams.'

'You too!'

She hated herself. Obviously he despised her and thought she was nothing more than a total slut who had been fun to screw, once or twice. Now her body wanted his; she wanted only to lie next to him and sniff him, his tawny warm skin as taut as a casing stuffed with sausage. Why hadn't she told him how much she missed him, that he should wake her when he came in? She thought of going to sleep in his bed but it seemed too forward: what if he came back with someone else, or what if when he got back he wanted nothing to do with her and felt furious that she had crept in between his sheets?

She would try to wake up when he got back and at least go to his door to see if he invited her to share his bed. It wasn't late which perhaps was why she couldn't fall asleep; or maybe she was hungry but she lay tossing. The window was partly open, she didn't care for air conditioning, and from below rose the sounds of a loud party, kids playing Jamaican reggae music, songs that had been around for years, the only lyrics of which she knew were '*now that we've found love, what are we going to do with it?*' and '*no woman no cry*'.

The same songs had been playing over and over in the hotel on her honeymoon. But while then they had sounded hokey, for tourists, now these songs were addressed to her, soppy anguish hammered into her bones by the repetition. Now that she had found love, what should she do? She mustn't cry. But basically that was the way all pop songs were, two people breaking up, a man leaving a woman, a woman who had left a man. There wasn't anything else real in life, all the other human emotions were thin and watery, a bland gruel, by comparison with the one true feeling of being dumped.

She fell asleep, leaving the door to her bedroom partly ajar, thinking that he could choose to come to her if he wished. Or perhaps she would hear him and wake. But when she woke it was light outside and he was in tight black bikini trunks, gut protruding above a shining sack of foie gras, partially covered by his robe. 'Hola! Good morning! I am about to go for a swim – will you like to join me?' His manner was brusque, courteously professional.

She rubbed her eyes, embarrassed to be in monkey-print pajamas, without make-up. 'You sure get up early! Gosh, I'm sluggish at this time of day.'

'No? And things were all right for you, yesterday and last night? You did not lose your room key, or passport?'

'I never lost anything! It was stolen.'

'Yes, of course. Well then. I will be back to change quickly, but then I must go to my meetings.'

'So, uh, we're going to meet for lunch?' Her voice was plaintive, almost whiny. She could have slapped herself.

'If that is still good for you. I will meet you back here at, shall we say, two o'clock for lunch, is that okay?'

'Great.' She gave him her most seductive smile. If only he had come forward and begun to kiss her and dragged her off to bed. She might at that moment have stepped forward but what if he pushed her away? She didn't think she could deal with that. As things were he wanted to have lunch with her; if she acted too . . . needy, he might call, later in the day, and say that he had to cancel.

While he was swimming she drank a cup of coffee and ate a piece of leftover toast from his breakfast order, then quickly dressed in her drab skirt and clunky sneakers before she went downstairs. She had to appear busy, she didn't want him to think she was just sitting waiting for him, a slug without an inner life.

The shops were still shut but there was an open-air fruit and vegetable market and the men were vying for her to buy oranges, watermelons, bananas. There were heaps of strange fruits that looked to be miniature apples, only queerly shaped, with a bean-shaped object attached to the top; finally she figured they were cashew-fruits. The alleyway between the stands was narrow and crowded with early morning shoppers and men lugging tin buckets of huge frothy orange flowers, candy-fluff – a sort of mimosa perhaps? She wanted to buy something, fruit for the airplane, but it was frightening. The men were intimidating, they looked ferocious, with huge eyes and shouting voices, grinning sharply.

She tried not to make eye contact. Didn't foreign men pinch and rob women? But there were women shopping here, carrying baskets, joking back. Finally she dug in her bag and found a few small notes; there was a man with a stand of round warty green things and large lemon-like objects in net bags; and she ended up with four of each, the green things and the lemon things. She didn't know if she was being tricked into paying far too much but the total only came to six and a half, which she supposed was around a dollar, so ultimately it didn't matter. She still had a few hundred; if she didn't spend it she supposed she should keep some for the airport, in case of emergency, and give the rest back to Germano.

She left the market and then came across a shop that had all sorts of pretty things, a short skirt with flowers and a matching T-shirt, and each of these was only twenty-nine Brazilian money, so she bought them – at least she wouldn't have to look so dowdy at lunchtime – and then next door was another shop, with strappy platform sandals similar to those that a Japanese geisha would wear, and the shoes were even cheaper, only twenty-three, and so she gestured at her feet and said, in English, 'Size six, US' The boy who worked there went away to find her size. She would change into the new clothes in the room. She would never again pay any attention to what Grace told her to wear. Maybe it was elegant on Long Island, where her mother-in-law lived, but it sure wasn't here.

Then she walked over to the beach – hobbled, actually – and bought two pareos, one for herself and one as a present; it took her twenty minutes to decide which colors to buy, finally she settled on a red and white floral pattern and one in dull shades of melon and jade, about which she was slightly less certain.

Now it was only ten-thirty but she didn't know what to do. She headed back to the room. There were no other guests at the concierge desk and she stopped for a minute to gather up tourist brochures. There were all sorts of things she supposed she might do, but any tour groups or sightseeing trips that were half-day had already departed and she couldn't face trying to get a cab and going on her own to Sugarloaf, the big mountain reached by cable-car; Corcovado wasn't far from the hotel, but she had no interest in seeing the statue of Cristo Redemptor close up.

But it would have been something to say she had done.

'Do you wish me to book you a car?' the concierge said.

'I don't know,' she said. 'I can't decide. How long would it take?'

'For the car? Maybe ten, fifteen minutes, he will be here.'

'Um . . . I'll let you know.'

She had had enough of the pool, even though nobody had bothered her there. She tried on her new things and spent a long time in the bathroom, trying to poop so she wouldn't feel too constipated and bloated at lunch but she hadn't eaten enough vegetables or her system was wacky from the airplane flight and the late night and the cocaine and alcohol and all the salty meats so she took a shower and carefully shaved her legs with a slightly old razor. Afterward her legs looked perfectly smooth but they were still slightly bristly to the touch, which was awful. Then she dressed and carefully packed up her things so that if they ended up together back here after lunch – or skipped lunch all together – she wouldn't be in a panic about getting to the airport in time. She wished she had an expensive suitcase like his and from now on she would always get her nails done: she hadn't known before what a difference it would make; that that was how ladies, real rich ladies, looked, in part, so elegant – they had their nails done.

He didn't get back to the room until almost two-forty. 'I am sorry, there is so much traffic. So, you are hungry?'

'Very.'

'The restaurant here in the hotel is quite good – you have eaten there? No. Or there is a place nearby, perhaps five minutes by car, where I always go whenever I am in Rio, with food that is *typico* Brazilian, of meat – churrasco, feijoada, comida caseira, but also, I think, peixada, some dishes of fish and very good cachaça, if you will like to try, which you must, I think, while you are here. Do you eat meat?'

'Oh . . . yes.' Hadn't he noticed?

'Good, then let us go, it is more nicer, I think, to try something very traditional while you are here, than to stay in the hotel.'

Lunch was not a success. He decided there was too much traffic and he had another appointment later on; he suggested they walk around the corner, to a place he knew; the restaurant there was noisy and not particularly upscale. She couldn't read the menu so she let him order for her.

'Will you have a drink? You must try a caipirinha, I don't think you have sampled our Brazilian drink since you are here.'

'Are you going to have one?'

'No, I must work, and also give my liver a rest. But for you, you have only to sit on the airplane.'

A miniature grill with a tiny, real fire beneath and a platter of meat arrived at their table – sliced steak, and other unidentifiable things – there was more than enough for two and he cooked different bits and put them on her plate and his. She chewed methodically, but apart from salt and garlic there was no flavor at all. She knew she shouldn't but she could not help staring at him with sleepy eyes.

'Well!' he said briskly. 'I have had a very nice time with you and I am glad we met. What a pleasant surprise! I hope our paths will cross again some day.' She couldn't tell if he was sincere.

'Germano,' she began, 'am I ever going to see you again?'

'But of course!' he said. 'I come to New York quite often, you must give me a number where I can reach you.'

'Definitely. When do you think you'll be coming up that way?'

'For the moment, I do not have any plans. But I will be in touch, the minute I know.'

'I've never met anyone like you.'

'You are also very unique. And you . . . were . . . different, than what I expected.'

'What did you expect me to be like?'

'What did I expect? I thought you would be . . . a typical American woman, very prudish. But . . . you have quite a wild streak. And you are – how can I say? Expert at the *popo*.'

She didn't want to say, what's the *popo*? 'Yeah, I know, but believe me, that's not really me at all. If you had met me under other circumstances, you would have thought I was completely different.'

'Then I am very glad I did not. Tell me, did you like the drink?'

'It was delicious!' She had never drunk during the daylight hours before and it had gone completely to her head. The hot sidewalk air, the noise of the passing cars, the great haunches of sizzling meat which were being deposited at tables to their right and left – it was alien and she had the sense that she had to do something, quickly, or lose him forever. 'Did you speak to Felix?'

'Felix? No, we have plans to go golfing over the weekend. Why do you ask? You like him?'

'No, I'm crazy about you. I just thought . . . he might have said something . . .'

'About you?'

'Yeah, something . . . disparaging.'

'But why? We all had an amusing time, did we not? You must not take these things so seriously. Now, I would like to take you and buy you a little something, a remembrance of your pretty ways.'

'Oh gosh, no! You bought me that beautiful dress, and put me up, and gave me cash – I can't even repay you!'

'I insist. It is nothing. A trinket. I like to think of you with your husband wearing something pretty I have purchased for you. Is that very wrong of me? You must permit me, it will give me pleasure. Will you like something else? A coffee? Dessert?' She shook her head. He beckoned the waiter over to settle the bill.

24

A few months after they were married, when all the excitement from the wedding had died down, and the presents had been put away and the thank-you notes written and they had finally settled into their 'married routine' Peyton and Barry went down to Florida to spend a long weekend with Peyton's older sister Kathy. She had never been close to Kathy; Kathy was eleven years older and had lived a childhood so different from Peyton's she might have been raised in a different family. Her husband Manuel did something in computers; she worked for a Miami public relations firm, they had two kids, Mirabel and Anita, aged five and two, whom Peyton had barely met. At least now Peyton could show off her husband, her normalcy – her success in life.

Kathy had never been as pretty as she, she had a strong, bony, waspish face, long in the jaw, dirty blonde hair; but men had always found her very attractive. Her practical, mannish-yet-motherly nature, her lanky, athletic body – she could have been one of those English women the British male aristocracy were so fond of, the tough, no-nonsense type. Manuel had come from some fancy Cuban family, they had left Cuba years ago, without money, but he – and his family, what little she had seen of them – still believed they inhabited some grand Cuban palazzo, when in fact he and Kathy and the kids now lived in a poky house on a dry street at the edge of a canal, some distance from South Beach, just off a highway.

She and Barry rented a car at the airport and got lost when Peyton saw a stray dog running by the side of the highway, limping.

'Barry!' she shouted, 'Pull over, you've got to stop!'

Barry pulled onto the hard shoulder, almost blindly. 'What? What?'

'There's a stray dog, do you see him up there? He looks hurt –'

Before he could say anything she had leapt out of the car and was running over the grass toward the dog. The dog could barely move and had an open wound on its back and his front leg looked broken. Barry slid out the passenger side and followed her. 'My God, you almost got us killed, Peyton, screaming at me all of a sudden like that! I didn't know what was going on!'

'I'm sorry, but I saw the dog and I just – we can't leave him lying here like this, Barry! It's awful.'

'Well, what do you want to do? We can't have a dog. You know I'm allergic.'

'I want to take it to my sister's and then find a vet. Maybe she'll keep it, or, I don't know, she'll know someone who wants a dog.'

'You can't touch that animal. It's going to bite you. Look, it's got mange.'

'Well I'm not leaving it here, Barry!'

'You're going to get bitten. I'm not picking it up.'

'He's not going to bite me,' she said. The dog snarled wearily in the heat. 'Get me a blanket or something to cover him up with.'

'I don't have a blanket.'

'Then get me my sweater from my suitcase.'

She threw it over the dog and carried the animal back to the car. It was hard for Barry to pull back out into oncoming traffic and he was irritated. 'You know, that dog has fleas, they're going to jump off the dog and onto us, if I get bites I swell up – we could call the ASPCA from your sister's and they'll pick it up –'

'Barry, you don't understand. All they'll do is take him to the pound and put him to sleep! I'm not going to rescue him just to kill him! How are you doing back there, poochikins?' The dog had thrown up over the back seat.

It took them almost another hour to find Kathy's house. Barry was furious because Kathy's directions were so poor. By the time they arrived it was after four o'clock. 'Peyton! Come in, come in! I thought you'd be here hours ago!' Kathy was wearing an apron, and her blonde hair was a greenish color, dry, brush-land about to explode at a match. She must have been thirty-five by now, attractive but any sign of youth, whatever that intangible quality was, had disappeared, been transformed into a certain hardness around the eyes. But maybe it was just the light of the Florida sun. 'Let me help you take your stuff in – oh, you brought your dog?'

'No, I found him, on the highway, look, his leg is broken, and so we picked him up and now I have to get him to a vet. Kathy, would you like a dog?'

'No. Absolutely not. Look, let's put him the garage and give him some water and you can get settled and, I just saw in the paper, there's some sort of service that will pick it up, I'll call them –'

'And where are they going to take him?'

'I don't know, we'll figure that out. I think there's a no-kill shelter where you can make a donation –' Peyton carried the dog over to the garage. It was roasting hot inside. 'Kathy, leave the door open, it's too hot for him otherwise!' There was a piece of old carpeting, rolled, against the wall, and she put the dog down and spread out the carpeting and put him on it. 'Do you have any water for him, and some food?'

'Here.' Kathy carried out a bowl of water and some meat on a plate. 'What's that?'

'It's some hamburger. I'm saving the rest for the girls' supper.'

The house smelled of garlic and cigarette smoke and cat urine. Barry wrinkled his nose.

'Sorry I'm such a mess – I was making the kids' supper, I'm going to give them an early dinner because – guess what! – we got a sitter for tonight, and we're all going out! Let me show you guys to your room – you must be Barry, my handsome new brother-in-law –'

They followed her down the hall to a dark room crammed with kids' toys. 'Sorry about all this, I keep meaning to clean it out, it was supposed to be the guest room but we never have any guests and the kids leave all their junk in here. You know, guys, I'm so sorry I didn't make it to the wedding.'

Growing up, Kathy had known their father; he had not yet disappeared, he had been around until just before Peyton was born, and Nell still had some money, enough to send Kathy to a private school, and that was why Kathy had a different accent, not like hers, but as if the back of her jaw had been wired together and she could only speak in a tight, clenched, nasal tone, the voice of a rich Bostonian. She knew this was going to be another thing that would drive Barry crazy, also if somebody smoked, which, she remembered now, Kathy probably did.

'I just couldn't get away, Manny's mother was sick, normally she babysits, I thought of taking the kids, and then I added up the airfares, booking a hotel room – what with everything going on, and Manny thinking about changing his job –'

'Now you can stay with us, if you ever want a weekend in Manhattan,' Peyton said. 'We have a really cute apartment, we're still in the middle of fixing it up, but it –'

'I know, I got your letter. It sounds great.'

'Well, it's not huge. But –'

'Anyway, leave your things here, I hope it'll be okay, here's the bathroom, wash up, whatever, and I'll fix us all a drink – well, it's early but –' Still chattering she disappeared down the hall.

'Open the window,' said Barry. 'Geez, I'm not going to be able to stay here. I can feel my eyes are already starting to –'

'Barry, it's only for two nights and we'll be out most of the time, just try to survive –'

She went down the hall. 'So where are my nieces? I have some things I brought them –'

'Oh, they've been so excited that you're coming! They're over at the neighbors'; they should be back soon –' Kathy took a sip from her glass. 'I'm drinking white wine with soda and ice, do you want some? Or, something else?'

Peyton was shocked: who started drinking this early in the day? 'No thanks, I'm going to wait a while – it'll just put me to sleep. So, have you spoken at all to Mommy?'

'Look, I've tried to call the hospital a dozen times, she can never come to the phone, or when she does she's not making any sense at all – thank God you're not working right now, Peyton, so you can be on top of the situation, because between working full-time and trying to look after the two kids, and the house –'

'I am working, as a temp, and looking for something full-time – it's a little tricky with Barry just starting up a practice. The money from his parents was just a loan –'

'I'm sure they're not expecting you to repay them, are they? They sound like they're loaded, and they won't want the money back, they just say that so you'll be motivated.'

'They're not that rich.'

'I thought in your letter you said the wedding cost ninety grand.'

'It was a hundred.'

'Darling, that's – at least for me – an unbelievable amount of money to spend on a wedding. Did you bring photos?'

'Yeah, I'll get them out later. So, what news of Donny?'

'Donny was down here, oh, I don't know, last month. Six weeks ago. He's back on heroin. He had his daughter with him. I feel really bad for her.'

'How's Brittney doing?'

'You know, actually, it's weird – she's seems perfectly fine, even with an addict dad and Larissa who is just totally materialistic. But he's going to end up in jail or dead, I just know it. I mean, he didn't take anything from here, but I have no idea where he gets his money. He's got to be stealing things, that's the only explanation. Thank God you married into a family with a decent bloodline, a nice Jewish dentist –'

'Larissa seems – she seemed very together. I never thought of her as materialistic – only crazy for marrying Donny. What the hell did she ever see in him?'

'Well, remember, that was back in Larissa's druggy days and Donny is kind of cute, in that rough trade, rock-star way. I mean, he should have been one of those movie stars, you know, with the biceps, and the cut-off sleeveless T-shirt, and the tattoos. Not my type, even if he wasn't my brother, but let's face it, you could be a three-hundred-pound man working at a gas station and you'd have no trouble finding a cute girlfriend.'

Peyton had done very well with Barry, who had a job, a good job, and was attractive, and loyal in a faithful coon-houndy way, even if he did have allergies. 'Anyway, you didn't do so bad, with your handsome Cuban prince –'

'Things aren't exactly perfect around here, but I'm not going to get into that just now –'

Barry came into the kitchen. 'Is there any way to open some windows?'

'Barry's very allergic to smoke. It makes him really sick.'

'Shit, I'm sorry! The air conditioning is on. Don't it work very well? I'll turn it up. It's pretty cool in here, you know. I know I have some air freshener around. Barry, you want a drink?'

'A drink? Um, no thanks, Kathy – I don't drink.'

'That's not true, Barry!' Peyton said. 'You sometimes have a glass of wine with dinner. And in Jamaica –'

'That was our honeymoon. I think I'm allergic to alcohol.'

'No, you got sick because you got sunburned, ate bad chopped liver or something, and stepped on a sea urchin – oh, God, what about the dog? Kathy, did you call the dog taxi or whatever it is? I'm going to go check on him.'

The dog had eaten the food and was gone. 'Barry, we have to go look for him. He can't survive, especially with that leg –'

She spent an hour wandering the streets but there was no sign of him. Each house had a patch of lawn, covered with rusty tricycles, a shriveling palm tree or a driveway with an ugly boat on a trailer. Overhead two brown pelicans, ungainly as pterodactyls, circled for a landing. The wind was impossibly hot. It was the end of the world; and she remembered growing up in Boston, how it was always gray, either with summer heat or wintry clouds and she had thought for most of her life that she would never escape. Her passage down the vaginal canal had only led to a less attractive womb: elementary school smelling of chalk and pencil shavings and a teacher in the front with warts on her eyelid screaming at the kids and denying them recess as punishment. She had bad handwriting and the teacher particularly disliked her – what grade had that been? – and she had spent the year in the back of the class, nibbling white paste from the glue pot and watching Mary-Louise Pitkin pick her perpetually runny nose and wipe her fingers under her desk.

But she had escaped, after all.

Her nieces were back at the house, running around the living room, and they stopped, a bit shy at her unfamiliarity. 'Hi, guys!' she said. 'You guys have grown so much! I wouldn't even have recognized you! I have some presents for you – come on!'

'Gimme!' said the younger, Anita.

'Yippee!' said Mirabel. 'What are they?'

She had brought a tea-set for Mirabel and an outfit with a ruffled denim skirt and top trimmed with pink rick-rack; there was a similar outfit for Anita, only of glittery purple denim, and a large stuffed horse.

'What do you say?' said Kathy.

'Tanks!' said Anita.

'Thank you Aunt Peyton,' said Mirabel.

'Now, are you guys in school yet?' The girls looked at her blankly. 'Is it nursery school or pre-k? I don't know this stuff.' Talking to children was apparently just as difficult as talking to adults. There was no way to connect. Manny, her brother-in-law, had arrived home and was in the kitchen talking to Barry at the table. He got up and kissed her hello. 'How are you? I see marriage has agreed with you, you look gorgeous.' His hair was receding which gave him, she thought, an even more aristocratic look, with his long slim face and dark, thickly fringed eyes; he was wearing a beautiful suit, though he was narrow-shouldered his hips were slim as well and he looked foreign, exotic, a successful global businessman.

She wished Barry would dress that way, dark blue, pinstriped – but his idea of an outfit was cargo pants with pockets below the knees, shirts with epaulet-style detailing. For him it was still 1970. She had tried to dress him, gone out shopping with him: he sneered at everything she picked for him and said he would never wear it.

'You look great too, Manny! How have you been? The girls look so grown up, I can't believe it!'

'Good, good! Kathy's just taking a shower and getting dressed for this evening – we have very big plans for tonight, did she tell you? Are you going to be up for it?'

'I don't know, what are we doing?'

'My brother, who works at the same company as Kathy – he's the one who introduced us – is taking us all out to a new restaurant and I think it will be a lot of fun.'

'I hope it's not going to be smoky.' Barry looked glum. 'So, I was telling you how I got so lucky: I was wandering around the neighborhood, when we were thinking of buying the apartment, and I noticed, there really weren't any dentist's offices. And a few days later, I was reading my alumnae mag, and I happened to see, somebody was retiring and wanted to sell their practice, and it was, like, two blocks away! So –'

'Oh, you should have moved here, if you wanted to buy a practice from someone retiring!' said Manny. 'The dentist I go to, sometimes I think he's already dead! And they're all like that, down here.'

'– as I was saying, the start-up cost was a lot more than I had envisioned. I ended up having to buy so much new –'

He would go on for another half-hour, if she didn't put an end to it. 'So what should I wear tonight? What kind of place is it?'

'Whatever; you can dress up, if you want; Kathy is going to wear a dress –'

'Oh, I want to wear a dress!' she said. 'This is so exciting! This is going to be so much fun! Manny, I think actually I will have a drink now, while I'm getting dressed. Do you have any vodka?'

Barry gave her a dirty look. 'You better go easy, Peyton, you haven't had anything to eat since breakfast.'

'Barry, did you bring anything dressier? A suit? Do you want to borrow something of mine? We are approximately the same size –' said Manny.'

'Why? Do I have to wear a tie or jacket or something? Otherwise, I have clean dress pants and a long-sleeved –'

By 'dress' pants he meant polyester with a permanent crease. She didn't want to say anything. What difference did it make, after all, the clothing he wore, if it made him happy; it was not her job to spoil things.

She showered and changed into a black miniskirt, a tight lace top. Manny's eyes narrowed when she emerged and she could tell, though he didn't comment, that Barry was pleased, too, to be able to show he owned an attractive piece of merchandise that other men saw as desirable.

Kathy had on a navy silk dress, low-cut, but she was quite flat-chested, even after two kids, and with her gold necklace and earrings she looked respectable, an attractive matron.

The kids were in the living room watching TV with the babysitter. 'Okay, Heather, I don't know what time we're going to be back,' Kathy said. 'If it gets too late, though, I left out a blanket; just go to sleep on the couch. We're going to take a taxi, I think, so we can all drink. I don't know who will be able to drive you home.'

'That's all right, Mrs Hernandez, I'll stay over –'

'Well, I'm not drinking, so I can be the designated driver,' said Barry.

'Are you sure, Barry? I mean, you're really not going to drink?'

'At the most, I might have one beer, or a glass of wine – believe me, I'm really not a drinker.'

Manny's brother, Luis, was waiting in front of the club with three others, all men. 'I thought I'd meet you guys out here,' he said. 'This girl was supposed to have our names on the guest list, now she says she can't find them, so I told her to go and get Davide, the owner, who's supposed to meet us here. 'Kathy, *belinda*, you look gorgeous.'

'Luis, this is my sister Peyton and brother-in-law, Barry –'

Luis was handsome, blue eyes, short, curly black hair, out of a tango film. But it was more than that: he had an aura, there was some kind of weird vibration going on, a man under a white spotlight, on stage while all around him everything was dark. He came over and kissed her hello and whatever happened between them in this embrace was so intense that even he took a step backward, looking puzzled, and tried to cover up by saying, 'So, does that mean you're my sister-in-law, too? Let me see, if my brother is your brother-in-law, and your sister is –' He shook Barry's hands and clasped him on the shoulders. 'Welcome to the Hernandez family!'

'Welcome to the Amberg family,' said Barry.

'These are some of our friends – Matt, Chris Roy, Peter –'

'Hi,' she said. 'And you all work in public relations?'

'No, these guys are in advertising at a magazine,' said Luis. 'But we do a lot of work together and I knew them at school! Anyway, I don't know how this place is going to be but we're guests of the owner – if that bitch at the door is actually going to find him – is that your car, guys? You better give your keys to the valet, you can't leave it here.'

'How much is valet parking?' Barry said.

'Here? I don't know. Ten, fifteen bucks.'

'Can't I just park it myself, in a lot, for less?'

'You want to park it yourself?'

'I don't want to give some guy fifteen bucks to park a car!'

'I don't know; there's a garage, but it's like, four blocks away –'

'I'll go park it and come back and meet you inside.'

'Do you want me to come with you, Barry?'

'No, you stay with the others, you're wearing high heels.'

A man came out on the sidewalk. 'Oh, hi, Luis! What are you doing out here?'

'Listen,' Luis took the man to one side and lowered his voice. 'This stupid bitch at the door has such an attitude problem.'

'Come on in, I'm really sorry, Luis – I'll have a word with her – come in, everybody.'

'This is Davide, Davide, this is Kathy, um, Peyton, and her husband will be back in a minute, and Chris, Roy, Matt and Peter –'

Davide led them inside the club. The light was strange, a fish tank at night, or somewhere blurry deep in the sea and the air was very cold; the music was so loud it was a physical presence, a hammering entity of noise. 'What does everyone want to drink?' Davide mouthed. 'Shall we have some champagne?'

They were taken to an enormous round couch, sunken, in the middle of the room, lined with pillows.

'I want to sit next to Peyton!' Luis said.

'Oh, goody!' she said. She was so nervous she drank the champagne quickly; then they had another glass each, and another, and then she moved on to vodka. Somewhere in the middle of all this Barry arrived; she had forgotten him. The girl at the door had refused to let him in, he had been out there arguing for half an hour, finally Luis had got up to look for him and got him in. Then for a minute she thought Luis wasn't going to sit back down next to her but he did.

The waiter brought snacks, raw fishy bits, cold eggplant things; she knew she should eat something but then the waiter looked at Luis with such lust and such a direct message in his eyes she almost burst into laughter. Imagine if she had been born a gay guy! It was so unfair, that gay men could do that, there was no messing around, one guy could just look at another and make things perfectly clear without words. But Luis didn't notice – perhaps she was mistaken about him?

Anyway, by the time anything resembling a meal arrived she was so drunk she couldn't even look at the food and Luis said, 'I can't eat this, either. Let's go dance, or find somewhere where I can actually hear what you're saying.' They climbed out of the sunken sofa.

'Luis is going to dance with me, Barry!' she said. He waved glumly. She whispered in Luis's ear, 'So how come Manny never introduced me to you before? I've been down here –'

'I did meet you, you just don't remember.'

'I don't believe you. I would never forget that Manny had such a gorgeous, smart brother.'

He whirled her around in his arms and picked her up off the ground. 'You are just the cutest, most adorable thing I have ever seen in my entire life! I love you!' he said.

Of course she never would have done anything; she was a newly-wed.

25

A few blocks away was what appeared to be a giant department store. The lobby was crowded with Japanese tourists, men dressed in dark suits, groups of women also in black, elegant, all of them tiny and perfect. They came from a planet of tiny, perfect, elegant people.

They got a pass and were taken by a saleswoman up to the third floor. The room was very fancy with shiny black glass and mirrored walls and there was deep, rich brown wall-to-wall carpeting. Women in uniforms went around with trolleys holding bottles of water and soda and champagne. There were small cubicles and at each cubicle sat two or three people: some appeared to be couples trying on wedding rings, or women out shopping; one table had a loud American man talking to the uniformed woman who sat opposite; at another was a Japanese woman, two children and the salesperson. At their cubicle the salesperson had a nameplate: Purima Srinavasi. She was middle-aged, at least forty, with a bleary complexion; it did not seem possible to Peyton that she would ever get so old; that was never going to happen to her. And the woman looked desperate. Working on commission selling jewelry to rich people had taken its toll, even though she kept smiling eagerly, grimly. Germano chatted to her in Portuguese and then Purima switched to English to address Peyton. 'So, you would like to see some earrings?'

'I don't know, whatever he says.' She had never seen anything like this place. So this was how rich people shopped for jewelry; it was so organized, all these people taken into cubicles to be shown, privately, glittering junk.

'Very good. And your ears are . . . with the holes?'

'Pierced? Yes.'

'And is there any particular color that interests you? Your friend says you would like to see something with semi-precious Brazilian stones; as you know, there are many beautiful stones here in Brazil, in addition to those we are perhaps best known for: the emeralds. It is all completely duty free; Brazil is the only country in the world where you may buy and at Customs to the United States there is no duty.'

She hadn't even known she might have to pay duty. She had never owned any real jewelry, apart from her engagement ring which had belonged to Barry's great-grandmother, a tiny platinum filigree ring with a large aquamarine, and their wedding rings, though they had both decided on simple gold bands. 'Um . . . either green or pink,' she said.

'And you like shiny gold, or matte?'

'I don't know.'

'Then we will look at some of each.'

She signaled to a worker in a different style of uniform who disappeared through doors on one side of the room. Drinks were offered and she was given a cerulean-blue bottle of water, very elegant, and a glass. Finally, after a lengthy wait, a tray was brought to their table containing different sorts of earrings: gold hoops inset with green or pink stones and others with dangling pink or green stones. Some had pavé diamonds on either side of the stones. Even if she had money she wouldn't have bought jewelry of this sort – it was the kind of thing Grace might wear, shiny, costly, from some mall on Long Island. She pointed at a pair with heart-shaped pink stones surrounded by tiny diamonds.

'Oh, you have selected well,' said the woman. 'That is the most expensive. Few people know that here we have pink tourmaline, the rarest in the world, and the richer the color, the more valuable. These would cost two thousand dollars US but you see here, with these stones that are much lighter in color –' and she picked up another pair, equally garish, '– that is only eleven hundred.'

'What about these?'

At least these were simpler, gold hoops inset with green. 'Seven hundred and fifty, US. Would you like to try?'

She put them on. They did look very nice against her small pink ears. 'I like these the best,' she said and smiled lovingly at Germano. 'But are you sure? . . . They're so expensive!'

He waved his hand dismissively. 'What I wish to know – are you sure these are the ones that are your favorite?'

'Oh, they're beautiful!' she said, 'I know I'd get the most use out of these. I can put them on and never take them off. I mean, they can go from day to evening.'

'Good. We will take these.' His duty was over, he was relieved.

'Yes?' said Purima. 'And will that be all today? Will you like to look at something else? Some cufflinks for you perhaps, or a bracelet?'

He spent forty minutes deciding over two bracelets. One, emerald, was eighteen thousand and another was eleven. For a minute she thought he was getting them for her; he asked her which one she preferred and to try them on. They were stunning. There was a difference between something for seven hundred and fifty dollars, more money than she would ever have dreamed of spending in her life, and these genuine precious stones.

Finally he settled on the cheaper of the two, though it had been the emerald ones that she liked and he explained to her, quietly, when Purima had gone for a moment to get some cufflinks for him to look at, that whenever he felt guilty he always returned home with some trinket for his wife. He said this with a wry grin – of course she would understand – but she felt bad. She had lost something she hadn't even known she had. When Purima came back with the cufflinks Germano looked impatient and leapt up, saying they had to get going.

They had to go down two flights to pay and here were souvenirs: stone necklaces for ten or twenty dollars, letter openers, straw baskets, and she picked up a few small gifts. A dappled agate bowl, so thin it was almost translucent – Barry could use that to put paper clips in – a set of stone coasters for Grace; espresso spoons with quartz knobs on the end of the handles for her mother or maybe Victoria; a cloth bag containing Brazilian coffee.

At the cash register her bill came to forty-eight dollars, US, but Germano didn't offer to pay for these. He gave her the box and the receipt so she wouldn't be charged at Customs. 'Oh, thank you so much!' Throwing herself on him, she gave him a hug and a kiss on the cheek before he pulled away.

'It is nothing.' He curled his lip embarrassedly. 'It is only a trifle. It has been wonderful to spend this time with you.'

He accompanied her back to the hotel so she could collect her things and take his chauffeured car to the airport. 'I am sorry I cannot go with you, but Alonso is a very responsible driver and I hope you understand.'

'Of course! I never thought you'd come with me – it's just great you can lend me your car!' She went over to him on the couch and sitting next to him lovingly began to nuzzle him. She slid her hands down his sides and onto his crotch. Somehow she thought if she could seduce him one last time or at least give him a blow job he would have to see her again; he would want to. But he pushed her away, not roughly, but nevertheless – even though she didn't particularly want to have sex, let alone give him a blow job, she couldn't help but feel rejected.

She supposed she could have been more aggressive. Maybe he didn't realize there was no work involved in it for him; all he had to do was lie back and she would take care of everything. But what if she was more aggressive and he still pushed her away? On the other hand how could she thank him – for the jewelry, for the help? Maybe it didn't even work some of the time, and that was why he didn't want to do anything with her now. It would be so awful to have a penis, not just because some of the time it didn't obey and other times it would spring up, awkwardly, in the wrong place and time but also because they were (though probably not to men) so ugly. Who would want one of those turkey-wattle things dangling between one's legs, raw-looking with a hairy meat-sack hanging beneath? The vulva was bad enough but at least that was tidily tucked away.

He shook her arms gently. 'My dear,' he said. 'Let us save that for the next time we meet, which I am very much looking forward to. I don't want you to miss your plane, there will be traffic, and you have to go through security; and I too have appointments – you and your pretty ways will distract me.'

She stood up, embarrassed. 'Oh, I hope I see you soon,' she said.

'Come, let me help you down with your things, you have only this small bag, we do not need a bellman.'

At the curb he shook her hand and kissed her, slightly furtively, on both cheeks, as though he thought someone might be observing them and reporting.

She was hours early for her flight. She had never drunk alone at a bar before and felt too shy to start now but in the duty-free shop a woman was pouring samples of Ukrainian vodka and single-malt Scotch into miniature paper cups and she took a cup of the Scotch and drank it. How was she ever going to be able to live with herself now? All she could think was that she had to put as much physical distance between her and this place as possible. When she went to the toilet she saw her period had started, almost five days early, or else her record-keeping hadn't been correct.

At least she wasn't pregnant. She wouldn't have known whether the father was Barry or Germano or Felix. My God, what would she have done? Instead she had terrible cramps: someone had grabbed her uterus in a giant fist and was pummeling it. Wringing it. Squeezing it.

Usually she didn't bleed a lot right away but by the time the plane was boarding her panties were covered in blood and she had no sanitary napkins or tampons with her. She quickly ran to the lavatory before the flight took off and stuffed massive quantities of paper towels between her legs. The towels were rough as newspaper and scratched the sides of her legs.

The flight was almost empty. She lay down across three seats and put a blanket over her but she could neither relax nor sleep. Her agitation was limitless. What kind of person did the things she had done? She had betrayed not only Barry but herself as well. She was a nothing. She was good for nothing and no one knew or cared whether or not she existed. She was useless. What use was a woman unless she was young and some man wanted to sleep with her?

As soon as women got older they were almost non-existent while someone like Germano could just go bopping around the world, a rich, powerful older man. Her window of excitement had already slammed shut, like a spinster's, or old married ladies (who were actually only forty years old) in a movie set a long time ago. She was now a married matron and she had to get used to it. That had been the last adventure she would ever get to have – the unexpected, the scary, the thrilling feeling of being wanted and in control. And now she had to hate herself because of it.

She had never been in control, she had just put herself out to be used and dumped. She was an idiot. How could Barry not tell what she had done? She supposed it was fortunate she had her period; normally he would want to have sex that night; this way she could say her cramps were too bad, although he would still say that making love might help. He wanted to screw almost every night and each night it was like climbing a skyscraper. There was a glass window between herself and sex that took – at least with Barry – all of her strength to prise open.

She found the effort of rousing oneself from a contented, sleepy, non-sexual state into a marathon race for orgasm depressing. And he knew instinctively when she didn't want to have sex: that was when he wanted it most.

Or maybe it was that she had only wanted to have sex when they weren't married. Then it was a challenge: to find a place to do it, to get together, to make him, by having sex, want it, her, more, to get him in a sense addicted. Now there was no challenge, only getting out of her comfortable flannel pajamas when she would rather keep them on.

Idiotic bits of her time with Felix and Germano kept replaying: herself on all fours, breasts swinging, Felix entering her from behind, Germano's dick in her mouth. Germano at first grabbing her wrists, saying roughly, half-jokingly, 'Do as we say and you won't be hurt.' At that moment it had been a game, or a dream, but now that it was not a dream it had no sexy or positive qualities to it. Watching a porn movie might have aroused her but being in a porn movie would not, could not. And then a fragment, something being said and Felix laughing, loudly, which had been great at the time but now in retrospect the sound of his laugh was that of a bitter, angry person who obviously felt he was superior to her; how could she not have sensed it at the time?

Her life had been a field of landmines that she had accidentally managed to avoid stepping on. She had not even known the landmines were out there. And now she knew they were out there, covering the plains, and if she made one false step, had one minute of not paying attention, she could lose a leg, or her future. One misstep and walls would crumble around her.

There was a little animal, she couldn't remember the name, which at certain times of year got up and followed its friends, stupidly trotting along with the others until it reached a cliff at the edge of the sea and kept going. But how could it know what was going to happen, where it was going until it was already too late?

A flight attendant, a man, came around with a trolley of drinks. He had a toothy, oversexed smile, erect whiskers; he had spent his life rabbiting around the world to nightclubs where men who were strangers to one another stuffed penises into starfish-anuses, and surreal dicks drooped, Dali-esque amoebae, sea-cucumbers, through anonymous holes in the wall. Organisms that spent hours lurking in mildewed environments, waiting to be slipped into yet another orifice. Some creatures, squid, limpets, paramecium or feathery krill, never later berated themselves for what they had done.

When he got to her she said, 'Um, I'm wondering . . . I guess I'd like a Scotch and soda?' Her voice was timorous. But he poured her a plastic cup of soda and handed her a miniature bottle and his eyes did not connect with hers, though they might have had she been a man. She cracked open the Scotch and poured it into the salty fizz. The taste reminded her of Germano: malty, confident, an old man who had spent his life in an elegant velvet robe before a blazing fire. There were people who got through their existence without a single disaster or tragedy. She should have known enough about her own genetic destiny to realize she would manage to fuck things up.

Now she was starving and the tobacco-y taste coated her dirty tongue. There was no sign of the dinner cart being wheeled out, though from the kitchen a hot, dead smell wafted, something bland

and pasty being reheated. She searched wildly through her bag, hoping to find something to eat and then finally came across the four fruits that resembled smooth, oversized lemons in their plastic net sack and she broke open the net and with her fingers crushed open the fruit: it had a heart full of small black seeds surrounded by mushy pulp like frogs' eggs. A bowl of semen blown up under the microscope to preposterous size.

Perhaps it was poisonous, but she put some on her lips. Passion fruit, sour and delicious; she slurped the contents of all four. The sourness puckered her mouth in a way that could have been painful, had she not been so hungry, and the combination of the hard, brittle seeds and the pulp tasted of the tropics, sweet and tangy.

Barry was waiting for her outside Customs and her heart sank. If she could only have had more time, a transition – she had thought she would get a taxi home, take a nap, maybe go in to work that afternoon, though her boss had said she needn't come in until Friday; she was going to work over the weekend to make up the lost time. That way, there would have been a sort of break, a cleansing. His doggy face was sweeter than she had remembered it. 'I told you not to meet me!' she snapped. It wasn't even seven A.M. yet.

'I know, but I missed you,' he said. 'I wanted to see you . . . I canceled my morning appointments.' His voice was higher pitched than she remembered, more Long Island nasal. As she walked around the railing he came forward and kissed her, slipping his tongue into her mouth insolently like a reptile and against her will she flinched. He was so American; he didn't think to offer to take her suitcase as Germano would have done, though it was true it only had to be pulled along on wheels. He was either oblivious or believed that by not offering to assist her it meant he considered her his equal.

'I thought the car blew up? The . . . transmission?'

'They gave me a loaner for the time being.'

He was a few steps ahead of her when she pictured his penis which would now, always, by comparison with Germano's, seem small and pubescent. She understood why women were once upon a time supposed to remain virgins until marriage: that way if the husband had nothing in the way of dark and mysterious rhythms the bride would have no way of knowing that other men out there had hot syrup for blood and a dick that could crawl up inside your belly, tentacled, monstrous.

He kept his hand on her thigh in the car. 'So, how was it? Did you have a great time? How come you had to stay in a different place?'

'Oh, it was great. But I didn't really get any sleep on the plane. I'm kind of woozy.'

'I'm not surprised. Was the flight full?'

'Actually, it was pretty –'

'Anyway, the car is just totally shot. You didn't mention what you think of this one!' It was a beat-up old wreck, so she supposed he was joking. 'It's just a loaner they gave me until I decide what to do. Dad says we should think about a Volvo. They have a great safety record.'

'But those are so expensive! How are we going to pay for that on top of all the other stuff? Are your parents going to chip in?'

'Hey, I told him, I'll look for something used and cheap. But I have a feeling he wants to get us a Volvo for our anniversary.'

'Wow. But Barry, where does he keep getting so much money from? Our wedding cost a fortune, and our apartment, and I know they're planning Belinda's wedding –'

'Beats me. This isn't definite or anything, but my office manager isn't working out. Maybe if I let her go, would you want to come and help me? I'd pay you the same salary, but that way we could be together all –'

She wanted to scream, 'Are you kidding! No!' but she kept her voice even. 'Oh, gosh, that's so, uh, romantic, but first of all, I'm too tired even to think right now and besides, I don't think it would be fair to Rachel until you've given her –'

'Well, you can start thinking about it. I don't need you to decide right now. It's so good to have you home!' He slid his hand between her legs and made a playful, diddling gesture that made her think of someone teasing a clam.

'Barry, please keep your hands on the wheel! The drivers around here are crazy!'

It wasn't just that he drove too fast but his timing was off and for some reason at a red light he would speed up, almost goosing the car ahead, or when there were curves in a road, go into racer-driver mode, never leaving enough time to slow down so that being in the car with him was a serious of constant jolts, nauseating, terrifying; now, though he put both hands on the wheel, he first clasped her hand and put it on his fly. 'Peabo missed you too, why don't you unzip me so he can say hello?'

His words were aluminum foil on her teeth and now she was stricken that it no longer seemed cute or playful that he referred to his penis as Peabo. And if she did unzip his trousers there it would be, pink, winking clownishly, as if he had given birth to a sticky baby; she pulled her hand away.

'What did you do while I was away? Did you masturbate?'

'No. Peabo wanted me to, but I made Peabo wait until you got home.'

'So what else happened? Did you see your folks?'

'I had dinner with them one night at the club. Then another night Chris was in town, so he came over and we watched the game on TV and ate the macaroni-and-cheese you left.'

He pulled into the parking lot they used down on the West Side. Her apartment building was foreign, it was no longer hers. Inside everything was in its place but it now appeared so dreary, so provincial, things selected from a catalog or showroom without thought or passion, tawdry imitations or reproductions made by aliens to give some uniqueness . . .

Three days before she had been proud of her apartment, rooms copied cleverly out of pages from magazines. She had just had tweedy-pink wall-to-wall carpeting installed in the half-bath off the foyer. Now as she went in she saw it should have been tiled, perhaps vaguely Spanish or one of the Moroccan designs the magazines were all showing now. She had thought it would be cozier with carpet, the ancient hiss of the radiator diminished, but already the carpeting was embedded with stray hairs, her own, black. Some of the tiles were about to fall off the walls. A gray mildew was beginning to creep up the glass door of the shower stall.

'Come on, let's go to the bedroom,' Barry called as she flushed the toilet. 'We just have time for a quickie, before I go to work.'

'Oh God, Barry, I just got my period and I've been up all night without a shower and I feel like a sweaty mess.'

'I like it when you're a sweaty mess.'

'It's going to be such a disaster, blood on the sheets and everything –'

'Come on. I'll put down a towel. Where do you keep those old towels that don't matter if they get stained?'

She trudged behind him down the dark hall to their bedroom.

26

If she wasn't over Germano, exactly, it had sunk in that she was never going to hear from him or find him again. The only thought she had to placate herself was that maybe he had lost her business card, in which case how would he ever find her?

There was a man named Sandy Cooper who owned a dude ranch near Big Bend, Texas. He sent a letter to her travel agency, saying that a couple of times a year he ran a horseback-riding pack-trip. He himself was the guide on these expeditions and if anyone from her agency wanted to go he was offering a discount for one or two people for the last week of the summer. 'Do you want to go?' she asked Barry. 'Doesn't it sound like fun? Nobody else from my office with seniority wants to; so the two of us could go.'

'I don't really see how I can take the time off,' said Barry. 'Besides, being around horses . . . my allergies . . . Too bad it's not fly-fishing. You should go, anyway; why don't you ask Victoria or some other friend?'

He was so good to her, so kind, even though she felt irritated at his doggy, blind expression, eyes vacant beneath beetling brown eyebrows as he wrote down stuff on a chart while watching TV – he was in some sort of football league, she couldn't figure out what it was exactly, but he spent hours on the phone every night with his friend while the TV was on, choosing players for some imaginary team – he had to spend money to play this game.

The phone didn't ring at home and it didn't ring at the office, not with a call from Germano or even Felix, whom she wouldn't have minded seeing. She thought of his reedy dick beneath his elegant

Italian suit with some amusement; she remembered the way his eyes had rolled, steer-like, and the tangy metal of his cocaine breath. At least to see Felix would have been a connection, however intangible, with Germano.

'Ciao, bella,' she could imagine him saying, 'Remember me?' And she would have agreed to meet him, for a drink, at some exclusive hotel bar, plush and smoky, and afterward gone up to his room for a quickie and then made it clear she never wanted to see him again.

Her fantasy only served to make her feel more rejected. If she had left it alone, in time her images might have gone away. But she could not stop herself from replaying the events in Brazil over and over in her head, picking at a spot until it turned into a sore that refused to heal.

The name of Germano's company was something like Percebon or Placebon but though she called Information and looked in the telephone directory there was no listing for anything even remotely close. What had happened between them was so intense, however brief, that she couldn't believe he wouldn't contact her. At night she went to bed hoping Barry would fall asleep in front of the table over which he peered while tying flies. Most nights he did.

Around twelve or twelve-thirty she would creep down the hall, mute the sound on the TV, switch off the lights, trying not to disturb him. If the cartoon monster was awakened – not exactly an ogre, but something similar, a caveman – he would want to have sex.

At least one good thing was she lost weight. She was so short that even an extra pound or two tended to collect around her waist. But now she was as skinny as she had ever been and food had neither flavor nor taste. She might as well have been eating a dry sponge, cellulose, or dampened newspaper sliced into strips. Probably she should go see her gynecologist and get tested for any sexually transmitted diseases; if she had caught something she had no idea how she would ever explain it to Barry. But as time went on she had at least no visible symptoms. The night she had the threesome, both men had worn condoms – though it might still have been possible to catch something, it was unlikely.

Most of her waking hours were consumed with wondering what she might have done differently. On the phone she would find herself staring at the computer screen while trying to locate some alternative flight for a client and forgetting what it was she was supposed to be looking for. Was it the ménage à trois that had put him off? Still when she remembered his creamy hands, brutal, peasant-like, dangerous, pampered by a lifetime of emollients and oils, the way they had stroked lines from earlobe to nipple and picked up her breasts – turning her body into a piece of merchandise, fruit being weighed, an animal being inspected – she was aroused.

She thought she would never again be hot for her husband unless she pretended he was Germano. He didn't notice the difference. Out of guilt, perhaps, she tried to make up for this by giving him frequent blow jobs, especially if he was watching TV. By paying attention to the audio portion of the show she could almost pretend it wasn't happening, that she wasn't choking on a sticky penis about to explode in her mouth in a hot stream tasting of bleach and glue.

At the moment, feeling as stunned and shattered as she did, she did not want to get into any fights or bad marital patches. She thought of herself as the sort of girl – woman – who obeyed the rules, who had struggled to pull herself out of a pit – of poverty, lack of options – had lucked into this prime position, only to discover that she was all too ready to toss everything away; that she was a total slut but had never known it. A monkey in the zoo, raised in captivity, could not have gone on a wilder bender on a weekend pass from its cage.

Barry was excited about his new equipment – was it a laser, for instant dental veneering? – that had cost nearly eighty thousand dollars – he hoped this would expand his patient-load dramatically – and was too preoccupied to notice or mind when she said she would go on the Texas trip.

This time Grace was neither alarmed nor perturbed at the thought of Peyton traveling without Barry; it was no longer the terrible situation she had imagined when she had been told Peyton was planning to go to Brazil. Maybe by now she hoped Peyton wouldn't return.

In other eras people must have had much deeper feelings. Her passion for Germano was so intense, how could her feelings for Barry have diminished so drastically? On the other hand, she could not remember ever having felt this sort of passion for Barry in the first place. What would happen to her, if they divorced? After such a short time of marriage she would not get alimony – she had a job, after all; she had always thought of herself as self-sufficient – they would sell the apartment, or he would stay there, since it was he who was paying off the mortgage, with assistance from his parents – she would try to find a job in the city and be one of those lonely girls in a minute, overpriced rental, being friends with – who? Other travel agents? She would become one of those women trawling for men. What else was there for women? They trawled for men, or they had a man. The rest of it – jobs, career, whatever you wanted to call it – was just icing, the cake itself was the man. Whereas for men, it was the other way round.

In any event her situation wouldn't be improved. Besides, she was now afraid to be alone. And she didn't want to hurt Barry's feelings; unless, of course, it could not be helped.

Sandy Cooper called her at work to go over the list of items she needed to bring for the horseback trip. He had a twangy voice and said that on this trip, in addition to herself, there would be a journalist who was writing up the trip for a newspaper; a man who owned a travel agency that specialized in adventure travel; eight to ten people, most of whom were repeats, generally 'older folk'; himself and four staff. The sort of language that he used – 'folks'; 'such-like'; 'city-slickers'; 'jes'dandy' and 'okey-dokey' – made her think he was an older man, probably sixty, with a weak chin and handlebar mustache, the comic relief in a black and white Western. But at least going away for a week might help to block the repetitive imagery from her mind and replace it with a mountain landscape.

It was the custom among young women to get a manicure and pedicure at a beauty shop; these were on every city block, just about, with workers who were almost always Korean women. On a Saturday shortly before she was to leave on the trip, she met up with her friend

Victoria just off Seventy-second Street, a few blocks away from her apartment on the Upper West Side. Some time ago, Victoria had moved to the city from Boston and was working as a nurse in an intensive care unit at a teaching hospital. They had arranged to meet at the small parlor Peyton now went to regularly.

Nails of Nobleness was not fashionable, nor particularly clean but it was fairly inexpensive and crowded with other working-class girls or young married women who had come into the city for the day with the same activities in mind. Women lined the room, seated on leatherette sofas, reading year-old magazines, their covers long since torn.

Peyton decided to get false nails applied – recently 'linen' or 'silk' wraps had become popular. She didn't know that these false nails required constant upkeep and had to be retouched and strengthened often, and that once applied it was impossible to remove them without ruining the nail bed underneath. Thus she was committing to yet more hours each week of a beauty routine – waxing, plucking, dyeing, shaving, powdering, creaming – to which men – her husband – were ultimately oblivious, but which occupied chunks of a woman's life that otherwise might have been used productively. But, if she had been asked, she would have said she was doing it for herself.

She had never paid much attention to the place. Nails of Nobleness was like all the others, more or less. Even if Peyton had been interested, what good would it have done, to know about the lives of the manicure-girls? These women did not get paid, apart from tips; they were working to repay the owner of the shop for their plane tickets from Korea or their housing – many of them lived an hour and a half or more away, in remote sections of Queens or Brooklyn, sleeping six to a room; they spoke little English and spent the days inhaling lacquer fumes and being admonished by fat women who wanted their cuticles clipped more, or less, or to have thick pads of calluses removed with a razor or pumice. The customers used the opportunity to try on the role of imperial, imperious duchess. Perhaps they thought that once upon a time they would have been in charge of a whole staff, housemaid, chambermaid, lady's maid, cook – when, in fact, had they been alive in an era when servants were plentiful, *they* probably would have been the servants. On some level Peyton was vaguely aware, though, and she always tipped well and knew the women by name – the names they had given themselves when they arrived in the US.

Finally her friend Victoria arrived. She was fair, with that reddish-colored hair that always made Peyton think of a newborn mouse, blinking eyes, a bit chinless, but for whatever reason – pheromones, a friendly, accessible smile – men always went wild over her, initially, at least. 'Victoria! How are you?'

'Oh, God! I have the worst PMS. I keep thinking I'm about to get my period and I always get incredibly horny, so last night I did the stupidest thing.'

'What did you do?' The two of them sat on the raised plastic thrones, their naked feet in brine baths of hot pink suds.

'I'm so sore I can't even walk,' Victoria announced. 'I had the most nightmare experience last night. I mean, the sex was actually pretty good –' she chortled, 'the guy turned out to have the biggest dick – but believe me, Peyton, you have no idea how lucky you are to be married.'

'Why? What happened?'

'Oh, God, I don't know. There are no decent men in this city, you've got it made, having a nice apartment and a husband who adores you.'

'Yeah but it's boring. So tell me, what happened?'

'Well, I've been going out with this guy – Calder Smith, maybe I mentioned him to you – but I was being really careful this time, not to sleep with him straightaway, like you told me, and getting to know him, because I thought, at least, we could be friends – but, you know, we had maybe four dates over the past six months – because both of us are busy – so last night, one thing led to another and he came over; and the first thing he said was, "So, where are your sex toys?" I mean, here I am, it's the first time we're sleeping together and that's the first thing he wants to know! And then he said, "Can you call up a girlfriend for a threesome?" And I said, "Calder, right now I'm just interested in getting laid, but let me give you a condom." And he said, "A condom! I never use a condom, it interferes with sensitivity and I don't have any diseases. You must have birth control." And I was shocked, just totally shocked; I said, "Besides being a racist and a sexist you sound really old. Because no young guy would ever think of having sex without a condom, it's the first thing he would do." Peyton, if I don't get my period I'm going to go crazy. I keep bingeing, on salt. Which is weird, because normally I do chocolate.'

Her honking bray carried across the room. She should have been a movie star, tall, pink-blonde with a lot of teeth; apart from her loud voice, nasal, rough Boston, she looked like the heiress to some American trust fund and she didn't discriminate between a fireman and a restaurant owner and a wealthy commodities broker. She slept with girls and boys, she went to church and the first thing she did on meeting a man was to talk about her two-inch-long nipples.

Yet she went for months at a time without a date – though there was always a lecherous doctor ready to plug her in the supply room, they never called for dates after they had screwed.

Things would have been easier for Victoria if it was the forties or fifties and she wouldn't have dared to have sex for fear of pregnancy; but now it was worse to be considered a nice girl than to be a tramp. It was Peyton who was living some antiquated, retro lifestyle, marrying a dentist, keeping a dreary, suburban apartment.

How could it be that she was so easily shocked when all her life she had been exposed to such filth? It was all over everything: magazines for women showing women's breasts, lips, how to sex yourself up – billboard posters, gossip columns, was there nothing else?

'So how did it turn out?'

'He wore the condom but he wasn't very nice about it; I'm telling you, though, his dick was like, from my wrist to my elbow. I didn't think I was gonna get it in and today I can barely walk!'

'Are you going to see him again?'

'He said he had a good time and he's going to call . . .'

'Victoria, I did something terrible.'

'What?'

'You know I went down to Brazil – without Barry – well, I met this guy and I slept with him.'

'You little slut! Good for you!' Victoria shrieked with delight. 'Who was he?'

'I don't know; I mean, he was older and what do you call it – debonair.'

'Ooo. You slept with a debonair guy.'

'You know, he was like, one of those guys wearing cologne; I never did figure out whether he was Italian or Spanish, sort of one of those weird mixtures with an accent. He bought me these earrings.'

'Oh! My! God! You go, girl! Good for you. Are you going to see him again?'

'I feel like I can't go on unless I do see him. But he hasn't called me and I don't know how to reach him. I mean, I swear, I'd leave Barry and throw over the whole thing if I could just see him one more time, I really thought . . . we had connected somehow and now I can't even sleep at night, I feel so desperate . . .'

'Oh, gee.' Victoria spoke harshly to the pedicurist, a meek-looking girl with opalescent skin and intelligent black eyes. 'Watch it, please! Not so hard, you're cutting me.'

'Victoria, what am I supposed to do?'

'Beats me. You're talking to the wrong person. I never hear from these guys again. It's different for you – he'll probably call.'

'I don't think so . . .' But internally Peyton cheered. A long time ago people met and fell in love and even if they died they wandered across the moors howling their beloved's name, like in that old English movie where the actor walked around howling 'Kathy! Kathy!' For fun she used to yell at her sister that way, when she was little.

On the floor near where the woman kneeled to clean beneath her toenails, a large cockroach traipsed across the floor, perhaps poisoned, perhaps just brazen. Insects had feelings, she was certain, and there were some that mated for life; birds, animals, amphibians – the world was full of creatures harboring intense feeling. Only humans, it seemed to her now, were occupied with trivial thoughts and emotions that at best did not last very long.

'Was he any good in bed?'

'It was unbelievable! I mean, Barry's . . . fine, and I know he adores me, but with this guy, it was so much fun!'

'Really? How old was this guy, anyway?'

'I don't know. At least forty. Maybe fifty?'

'You're kidding! That's ancient. Like Ray. I mean, let's face it: their dicks aren't as hard and their skin . . . it's got that dried-out feeling.'

'Yeah, and why is it . . . that old people always look like they've been in a train wreck or some kind of major catastrophe –'

'I know what you mean. All kind of worried and stricken.'

'The old guys . . . it must make them feel youthful or something, if they have a young girl they don't notice their own skin is wrinkly. But . . . this guy, though, I don't know. I can't stop thinking about him. I'm telling you, it was so glamorous.'

'So, maybe you should get a divorce.'

Across the room, Peyton noticed a woman staring at her with a smirky expression. She glared at the woman and lowered her voice. 'If I leave Barry, what's the point? Unless I hear from Germano, and he wants to be with me, I'm not going to be any better off.'

She now knew she was the worst person on the planet. At least Victoria didn't pretend to be anything other than what she was – or if she did, it was only that she pretended not to be desperate. How terrible was that? Whereas she, Peyton, pretended to have values, morals, ethics, but the truth was while she might have advertised herself as having these, her body just went out and did whatever it wanted. And she would have to go on living with this evil creature with whom she could not make peace.

The woman across the room was still staring at her. She was tiny, no taller than Peyton: even looked similar, only older, a bad version of herself, with an inept nose job, frizzy black hair, dumpy figure. The woman wanted to tell her something. She couldn't help it, she gave the woman a look of intense hatred. What right did this person have to eavesdrop so obviously, to look at her with such a gibbous expression, her eyes about to pop out of her head on two stalks, a horrified crab?

'Didn't you hear what I said? The last time you cut too deep! God, you stupid idiot! Do you not speak English?'

They went to a bar nearby. A sporting event was about to take place and the bar, musky with the scent of ripened beer and testosterone, was full of men who were going to watch the game and men about to head home from work on the commuter train. All around the room were teams of women, pairs, angling for male attention – though the men ignored them, obviously too terrified to speak to them, these women who were there for one reason alone, trawling for men as an Olympic sport.

All the women had the same shade of blonde hair. It was peculiar, how exactly the same the color was, unvarying from woman to woman, as strict a code or formula as in the days when it was obligatory for women to wear white gloves, or girdles, or stockings, or skirts with hems two inches below the knees.

Peyton was the only dark-haired woman in the room. If she had been there on her own she would have sat at the bar, not speaking to anyone. Men were afraid of her. Though there was always that one weirdo, a loser, who would tell her to 'Cheer up! Let's see you smile!' as if she was obliged to keep a happy expression on her face simply to placate the male sex. But she had forgotten what it was like to go out with Victoria; it was thanks to Victoria she had met Barry.

'So did I tell you about my friends and the vibrator?' Victoria said in a loud voice. 'Sam bought a present for Megan – a remote-controlled vibrator. You can wear it inside, and then the other person can control the remote control. Anyway, Megan's got it in, but when Sam turns on the remote, the thing is so loud everybody in the room starts staring at where the noise is coming from!'

Almost immediately they were in the center of a group of three guys; two were firemen, off-duty, the other was their friend from childhood, a commodities dealer. 'So I have something kind of unusual about me,' Victoria began. 'I'll bet you five bucks none of you can guess.'

The game went on for some time.

'I'll give you one clue.'

'Is it a physical attribute?'

Finally she announced. 'I have nipples that are two inches long!'

There was a puzzled silence among the group. 'You talking about – the whole thing, the . . . *aureole*, or the center part?' said the commodities dealer in a professional tone. He spoke with the authority of a man who had read a great many Letters to the Editor in sex magazines.

'Yeah,' another joined in eagerly. 'You mean – long? Or around? That's the aureole, right? I mean, which part exactly is the nipple? If it's around, that's not that big a deal.'

'No, I'm talking about the pointy part, in the center. Imagine, like, you know, a pencil eraser –'

'And they're two inches long? How come they're not sticking out now?'

'I'm wearing a bra. I kind of have to roll them up and tuck them down. Plus, you know –' she looked around coyly, 'Something has to happen to kind of make them get . . . *erect*. So let me ask you this –' Now she had the rapt attention of all. 'You guys use condoms?'

'Yeah.' They all three nodded.

'What would you do if you were me. I was going out with a guy – dating – and when we finally went to bed together, the first thing he said was, "So, you got any sex toys?"'

'What kind of sex toys? You mean, a vibrator?'

'A vibrator, a strap-on, a dildo, butt-plug, whatever. So I said, "No, right now I'm just interested in getting to know what you're like, I don't want to bring out the paraphernalia."'

'This was like, your first time sleeping with the dude?'

'Mmm-hmm. So he says, "Well, what about, can you call up a girlfriend, for a threesome?"'

'Wow,' said the married-looking one of the three, 'You do that?'

'Actually, I prefer just to have sex with women. I'm quite open about my sexuality.'

'How 'bout you?' The men finally looked at Peyton for the first time.

'Oh, I'm married. We don't do anything.'

The men laughed appreciatively. One muttered to the other, 'See? What did I tell you?'

'So I said, "Let's just fuck, I'll get you a condom." So he said, "A condom?"'

The men finished their beers and left to catch their trains. 'See?' Victoria said at last. 'I don't know what I do wrong. My grandmother told me, "Victoria, at this point, just find some married man and go for it, you're running out of options." I don't know why men just screw me and I never hear from them again . . .' Her pale furry lashes, Peyton saw with surprise, were fringed with tears. 'You know, I've never actually come just from straight sex.'

Peyton was shocked. 'In that case, why do you bother?'

'I keep thinking, one day I'll find the right dick!'

27

She wanted to spend every second, night and day, with Xian Rong. He felt the same way, too. He said he'd only be in town one more day; his company spent part of each month in Milan.

The sex was so amazing she realized that it was the only time she had felt connected with a person sexually and spiritually. How could she not have known that real sex wasn't just a physical act, that it was possible for connection in another sphere? She started to cry and he said, well, listen, I have some good news for you I can stay one more day and the next day he said, listen, why don't you come with me to Milan . . . I have a ticket for you, meet me in a couple of days, I will get you at the airport . . . and it seemed to her if she didn't grab the time with him she would never get anything like this again. That was it for her, this was the love affair she had never expected to happen . . .

For however long he wanted, for however long it lasted, it was going to be her last chance to find what she was looking for.

Then for no good reason it came back to her, when she was eighteen and she went on some sort of trip – was she with her mother? Some kind of free weekend at a ski resort or timeshare, and . . . maybe it wasn't her mother, it might have been a trip with Victoria . . . and she, Peyton, had drunk so much she had picked up some old guy who was sixty and how he had seemed so old and it was horrible, that wrinkled, dried, old flabby skin and it wasn't that he couldn't get it up but he wasn't sleeping with *her* – he was reliving every sexual experience he had ever had, so that it wasn't actually she who was in bed with him, it was all these other women from his life – and he had even said oh you remind me of the maid who I slept with when I was eighteen with your little pointy nipples . . . she had felt humiliated, was he comparing her to a maid or that they had peculiar breasts . . . ?

When she and Xian Rong got to Milan and she learned she was going to be staying with eight or ten other guys in a filthy two-room apartment, in a place where immigrants, workers, poor people lived, two hours at least from any fashionable area, she panicked – temporarily – and bought an international phonecard to call Barry from the post office.

'Sexy princess? Where are you? Where have you been? I couldn't get hold of you!'

'Is everything all right?'

'Well, yes and no – where are you?'

'I'm in Milan.'

'Milan? What are you doing there?'

There was no way she could explain that she was with a criminal who traveled to different cities to steal things and then fled back to some hideout in China. 'I just . . . you know, I just had to get away for a while. I needed a break.'

'Are you coming home? Does this mean – are you leaving me or something? Do you want a divorce? If this is about that silly thing with Rachel, you know I –'

'A divorce? I . . . no, I don't know, Barry, I just needed some time. I . . . I've only been gone ten days, and I'm having fun.'

'Well then, stay as long as you like, but at least please keep me posted.'

'What else is wrong?'

'I – we – are probably going to have to declare bankruptcy –'

'Why?'

'I don't want to settle this lawsuit out of court! The crazy woman says she'll sue, my lawyers say I should just let my malpractice insurance cover it – but I told her the risks a million times, and as far as I can tell there's absolutely nothing –'

'Bankruptcy? My God, Barry, just settle out of court! Don't be absurd! These things happen all the –' She was taking the wrong tack with him. He was a sailboat that could only be steered by pushing it in the opposite direction. If she told him to settle it would only make him huffier, righteous – she knew this, but her statement had just blurted out.

'Are you okay? You sound so . . . odd. Shall I come over for a weekend and hang out with you?'

Her bald dentist husband. American to the core, in his loafers and khaki pants. She could envision herself shuffling along beside him, visiting that fortress or castle – whatever that was on the outskirts of town – eating dinner in some restaurant at seven o'clock, two tourists, while he bellowed, 'Does the cutlet have any garlic in it? Are you sure? Because I'm allergic.'

'I've got to go, Barry, other people are waiting to use the phone. No, no, don't come over – I'll call you again, in a few days.'

She hung up. How could she ever go back? Once marriage had represented freedom, from poverty – there would always be the two of them – and for a while, her life in New York City. Now both those things seemed worse than a glass cage, a public solitary confinement – but even if she never went back, age – Old Age – was pursuing her and the walls were shutting in.

In Milan she followed Xian Rong around, a wheedling dog with a nasty master. A kick from him, a sneer, was almost as good as a pat. It was no different than needling her own son: any response, a curse, was better than nothing. Half the time he was attentive, adoring – then for no reason would lash out at her. 'You know nothing! You never had to work for anything, or go hungry – now you come around for excitement, not because you care for me! Pay me money, you just want to "get laid".'

'You know it's not like that . . .'

'How could I know? That's the way American women are – I've seen it on TV – just looking for sex, a good time party.'

How could he be so nasty to her in public and so passionate when they were alone? She knew he was a thief, not a political refugee who wrote poetry, as he had first claimed. He was not in the import-export business. He was a criminal and though what he did was contemptible beyond belief she could not bring herself to care. That was the way he was and it was bad and wrong and there was no accepting his justification. He said that these were all rich people who were covered by insurance, who wouldn't pay more than fifty bucks on their credit card charges after he had stolen them. He said that their luggage would be replaced.

It was still just plain wrong. But it still didn't change her feelings.

Opening someone's handbag, photographs of their children in a red leather folding travel-frame. Expensive sunglasses studded with rhinestones; allergy medication; nail file; rippled leather wallets embossed with fancy logos, gilt-edged address book, return plane tickets, tiny silver pen, tins of glucose drops in old-fashioned flavors, horehound, blackcurrant lipsticks in gold metal tubes, miniature cameras. Perfume atomizer, lip balm, toothbrush, floss. Four tampons in a case, spearmint gum.

It was true these things were only things. Invariably she had the sense that the contents of one handbag could be replaced with the contents of another. There was nobody out there. If a million ants were all carrying handbags there would be virtually no difference between any of them.

And even the one or two messy bags: crumpled receipts, scrawled notes, US pennies, half-eaten dried apricot rolls, tissues. An envelope stuffed with photographs of a couple and a note: 'Dear Trisha, Here we are on our honeymoon, in the Chilean Alto Plano – it was fabulous! When are you going to be in New York?' Two pink burnt faces squinting in front of a lunar landscape. The note was signed XOXOX's ❤ ❤ ❤ *Marcy and Dan*. A happy couple, white, middle-class, boring, setting out on their happy course of marriage. If she had wanted to she might have tracked them down, back in New York, befriended Marcy, like some bizarre, creepy stalker.

She supposed the owner's DNA covered every surface, but she suspected within a day, or a week, the owner would have completely forgotten who or what was in their bag and even the sensation of what was in their brain at the moment of discovering their possessions had . . . gone missing.

* * *

They worked in teams of two: one team, dressed in the suits of Hong Kong businessmen, patrolled the airport or another chosen location, the other two were in the van, one driving and one on the telephone. When one man saw, say, a laptop computer or handbag on an unattended airport trolley he signaled the second, who telephoned the guy in the van. The computer or bag would be lifted, slipped to the second, so that no one appeared to be running and if the first man was stopped he had nothing on him; then the second would transfer it to the guy on the passenger side of the van.

Sometimes, the two guys would stop to question someone with a trolley in front of the airport, ask for directions; the passenger of the van would hop out, grab the stuff, start running and leap into the van which had pulled up just beyond or was moving at slow speed. Later in the room they would divide up the stuff; credit cards, passports, IDs were sold to a broker, the cash split four ways, other stuff fenced. They never spent long in any particular city and they never traveled out of Hong Kong on their own passports; they had men working for them in China who were paid to acquire visas to various countries, travel and vacation visas – they would sell them to the gang, along with, temporarily, their passports. Later, back in Hong Kong, one man would travel up to the border and hand them back to the accomplice. At least, this was as much as she was able to piece together. The apartment in Milan was horrific: hours away from the center of town, in a bad area of rough workers, a couple of dingy rooms in a fifth-floor walk-up, just by the path of the train, which rattled through day and night. There were not many Chinese here, the majority was Albanian; then there were a few Bulgarians, Turks, filthy gypsy kids, West Africans, drug addicts – almost all men – from alien parts of the world trying to make a buck to survive or send home. Persians, Arabs, Indians, Peruvians – any emerging nation in the world had a few who were able to escape from their barrio, slum, favela, only to end up somewhere even crueler.

Overpriced Laundromats where machines destroyed clothes, filthy bedsits with shared toilets down the hall – yet only a short train ride away were shops selling suitcases emblazoned with designer logos for thousands of dollars, sunglasses, tubes of cosmetics, ostrich shoes purchased by people who would have thought they had been carried off to a different world had they been brought here.

And in the apartment there were at least eight men who came and went at various times, she could never figure out who was who or what scam they were participating in.

She had never particularly noticed Asian men before; it was, she supposed, not dissimilar to men who never noticed blondes, or small-breasted women – she had nothing against them, it was just that Asian guys had never registered on her sexual radar screen. She had assumed, for some reason, their hairlessness, whatever, they were asexual. It occurred to her as strange that a sizable portion of the global population had not, previously, existed for her. All that had changed now, and she thought they were the most attractive men on the planet, feral as cats, lurking in unexpected places.

. . . and so she went first, she had a fur coat, a mink, that he had given her, as flashy as you could be in a totally understated way, with the fur on the inside and the actual skin on the outside. He had made her get her hair cut at some place where rich ladies got their hair done, it was shaggy, tousled yet impeccable; a frosted lipstick, beigey pink. Nails done, beige high-heeled boots – not beige so much as camel, a neutral color for rich people – beige trousers, cashmere sweater: she was the same as a million other rich women on the planet, those rich women who occupied two streets in each city, and on each two streets were the exact same shops. London, Madrid, Rome, the Upper East Side of Manhattan, Paris. Louis Vuitton, Hermès, Gucci, Prada, Fendi. Once the names would have been House of Worth, Poiret, Cunard Lines or . . . what? Who would or could remember the status symbols of an earlier time, unless it was something that had been around forever, a brand name almost extinct and then cleverly revitalized, revamped – Balenciaga or Chanel, or who cared, the names were symbols, shorthand, slang, for only one thing: money. The streets had names and the shops had names and in each city the women had the same names, or at least looked the same, wearing

Chopard wristwatches and gold chains around their impossibly thin necks.

It was amazing how easy it was to disguise herself as one of them. Not on the inside, of course, but on the outside – and after Xian Rong had taken her to all the places where these women became who they were (the manicurist, the hair colorist, the dermatologist – how had he known all these things?) and somehow, somewhere gotten her this fur coat (swiped from a restaurant? stolen from a shop? she didn't want to know) and the hideous pigskin handbag, with only a few flecks of tobacco in the bottom to remind her she was a total fake, he had looked at her for the first time with something akin to love. It was worth it, in the end, becoming someone else's creation if the payoff was to be a sculpture caressed by the sculptor.

Of course it was not so easy getting this look together in that bleak walk-up apartment, five flights up, with rattling old pipes, peeling paint, caked with fats and oily walls. Wherever she glanced there was this kind of black grease, soot, ash, dust, composed of who knew what; where there were angles, or joints, or junctures, the apartment was growing its own leprous skin. Even when she tried to clean it, with some spray cleaner and towels she bought at the cheap African store around the corner, the stuff did not come off. The kitchen was inches deep in grease. These men liked to fry food; or they would whip up a Chinese meal, washing off plates and pots and knives that were permanently encrusted in the sarcophagus of the sink filled with emptied cigarette ashes.

And the men all over the place, five, eight, ten, reeking of garlic and cigarette smoke, who stayed up all night playing some betting game with cards, hunters around a campfire.

They were noisy at night and the light was a bare bulb hanging from the ceiling; if he felt like it he came in when she was asleep and threw whoever else was trying to sleep out into the hall while he had sex with her. It was serious sex. There was no playing around, it wasn't the same as with Sandy, making him pretend to be a gynecologist, or that she was a child and he a sick Lolita molester; that had been fun, plain and goofy fun.

This was brutal, without preparation, he treated her the way he might have handled an expensive car, a car he had stolen but about which he nevertheless felt proprietorial. He didn't notice whether she was ready, or interested, it was far more as if he had the keys and was now turning on the engine. It didn't matter.

He had only to get within a foot or two of her, even when she was asleep (though she was never fully asleep in that place, could never really get what she felt was rest, it was far closer to the state in which a young Zen monk in training is kept awake for days on end, made to rise at five A.M., four A.M., three A.M., to be in a state of constant fatigue, until finally accepting Zen is the easiest thing of all because there is no choice) and she would find herself gasping, at his presence, at his touch. Just being near him pushed her over the edge so that by the time his dick pushed its way in her she was screaming for it.

There must be certain animals who lived in this other realm of pure sexual excitement and energy – stingrays in mating season, or jelly-fish, or sea anemones – it had to be that they had some feeling along these lines; since they had no real brains or thoughts it would be their God-given compensation.

But mostly if she thought at all now, it was simply with expectation – when would he come to her? – and on those nights when he did not come she thought she was going to die. There was no longer anything else she wanted or could bother living for and she was at his mercy. So when he said, 'Tonight we're going to do a practice run at the airport, we'll see how you work out, here's your cellphone,' and he stared at her coldly, she didn't care what he wanted her to do as long as she could get back the other expression in his eyes.

She only had the one outfit but he gave her a new white silk chiffon shirt, sheer as tissue, with French cuffs, still on an expensive hanger from an expensive store and told her to put it on without a bra.

In the greenish light of the bathroom she put on her make-up. No matter how often she cleaned up in here the men always left drops of urine on the toilet seat and the floor and the sink was encrusted with scum, the enamel long since worn off. Finally she was ready and came out, feeling horrid at being so exposed without a bra under the sheer shirt. 'Okay, put the coat around your shoulders,' he said and led her into the other room where three of the men were sitting drinking beer. Their eyes focused only on her nipples.

Xian Rong spoke to them in Chinese and they all burst into laughter. Now she felt even more self-conscious. 'You're perfectly safe,' he said. 'I tell them, no one's ever going to remember your face, it's a perfect disguise, they all be busy looking elsewhere.' He gave one of her nipples an affectionate tweak and she thought for a minute she would get out now while she could so she need never look at the other men again. But for all this time, even in these cramped quarters, she had been fond of these guys and sat up all night drinking Mai Tais and beer, playing cards, joking around – often while Xian Rong and some others were out. One of the guys would cook them all a meal and she had picked up a few words of Cantonese, they all got along. Only now . . . something had changed.

What was wrong with her? She had done something, something to make him change. Now he was treating her with contempt. Was she too old? It was true she was older than he; if it could have been reversed, perhaps he would have loved her.

But none of it seemed real, she was only playing at this life; there was no reason she couldn't walk away at any time. She would walk away. She would never allow herself to be treated with contempt. Only . . . she couldn't.

He gave her a pair of sunglasses, tawny tortoiseshell, and she felt better once she had put them on.

They got into the car. It was crowded. Two men were taken to the bus station in the city center. It would be another hour and a half's ride out to the airport. She sat in the back. The smell of cigarette smoke was making her nauseous. She hadn't eaten since the morning. Xian Rong had said afterwards they would go someplace for a meal. She wondered if everyone was going to go or if finally they might get to spend some time alone.

She didn't ask because if she did then he would definitely make sure some of the others came along. Finally she asked in a low voice if someone could unroll the window, but once they did she was freezing cold and bundled the fur coat around her more tightly. 'When you get out, you will walk around the airport. I'm going to follow you to help you tonight. You must telephone Wei Hao Jiang.' That was the guy sitting next to her; she liked Wei Hao, he was sympathetic. 'And give the location and explain what you have seen.'

'I don't really understand.'

'Never mind. You figure it out when we get there.'

There was a woman – one of those consumptive Englishwomen, blonde, maybe fifty years old, with the flared nostrils, the look of great self-importance – pushing a trolley in front of the airport, on her way to check-in – the trolley was laden with alligator valises, old things that were so chic they had to have been inherited, with ancient Cunard stickers, and newer labels that exuded an aura of having been acquired on trips to exotic locales – Sardinia, Namibia, Lama Island – and she was talking into a minute cellphone. Perched on top of the trolley was a handbag, expensive, and below it what appeared to be a personal computer, a leather computer case, so she punched into her pager 'blonde doorway 61', which would let them – James and Lo Lao Tse (they called him 'Teacher Lo' because of his specs, circa 1930, that and the fact that he knew everything) – know where to go and she darted inside to watch; out of the corner of her eye she saw Shieuw Ng approach the woman and begin to ask her some question – the woman stopped – Shieuw Ng always did look kind, trustworthy.

There was something familiar about the woman . . . it seemed to Peyton she had seen her somewhere before . . . and then with a jolt she realized it was . . . what was her name? Tinkle, the wife of Henry Battan-Bouwery, they had stayed once at their castle in England . . . Barry had fixed Henry's teeth – but it just couldn't be the same woman, could it? She was about to say something, try out the name, saying 'Tinkle?' to see if she responded but it was too late.

From the other direction Lo Lao Tse came up and grabbed the handbag and tried to make a grab for the computer in the case, which slipped onto the walkway; the woman turned around, mouth opening and shutting, a hooked fish – then Lo Lao Tse ran ahead just as James pulled up to the curb in front and Lo Lao Tse hopped in with her bag . . .

Shieuw Ng made himself disappear. The woman began shouting for assistance on the curb and scrambling to retrieve her computer case. Her face was white and her mouth was open in a squawl, a baby's squawl, like the big mouth of Peyton's son when he was an infant and Peyton had felt nothing for him – only now her eyes filled with tears and she would have done anything to undo not just this, but everything. If she could have only gone back to pick up her son, when he was bawling. If she could have put the entire video on 'rewind'. Even if it meant never meeting Xian Rong.

There was no way she could sink lower than having contributed to this.

She was supposed to meet Xian Rong at ten-thirty back at the restaurant, Paper Moon, but he had been so pissy and irritable lately . . . She thought she would take her own time about it; maybe even have a drink at the airport lounge, watch the people go by, she was not too anxious to slog back into town on a bus which took two hours, or the train, but he hadn't given her enough money for a cab . . . She was watching a rather handsome, elderly man walk across the crowded airport lobby when he began to look at her with a rather puzzled expression and then came over and said, 'Peyton?'

'. . . yes . . .' She stared at him coldly, unable to identify this old guy.

'Do you remember me? Germano? This is amazing: I have just written to you with the dates I will be in New York, I don't know if you received it – what are you doing here? My God, you haven't changed a bit, you are more beautiful than ever –'

'Oh my gosh, yes, I did just get your letter! This is amazing! How are you?' She never would have recognized him; and yet the fact that he was so easily able to identify her, she was pleased, obviously she hadn't changed all that much . . .

'What are you doing? Do you want a lift into Milan?'

'Oh, great –'

'So. I still retain my old powers, that you are appearing before me. You are arriving from where?' They walked together to meet his driver. 'You look exactly the same! How is it possible? But tell me, where is your luggage?'

'I don't have any . . .'

'Oh no, you are not in trouble again, are you? Were your things stolen? I have never forgotten, how I met you in Rio, with your money and credit card missing. How did it happen your passport was not stolen as well?'

'I –'

They were getting into his car.

'But you know, I have never stopped worrying that I behaved quite badly on that occasion. I hope you did not feel that you had been taken advantage of –'

'No, no – I was a willing participant. I only felt bad when I never heard from you –'

'Ha, I thought about you always but I felt . . . you know, for many years I was in a very . . . difficult situation and now . . . my wife has recently passed away –'

'Oh, gee, I'm so sorry –'

'Well, yes, it was all very sad. But I did not want to contact you before now, as I did not feel it would be right. What about you, you are still married?'

'Yes, but –'

'But you travel alone,' he chortled. 'I understand. And where do you stay?'

'I have some friends in –' She named the district.

'But that is miles away, far on the other side of the city! Can you not call your friends and tell them you are busy, and I will arrange a room for you in my hotel –'

Maybe she wouldn't even call Xian Rong, let him sweat it out for the night, wondering what had happened to her, where she had gone. Or maybe she would call him and just say, honey, I won't be back tonight, which would be . . . polite, respectful in that she was letting him know, but disrespectful in that she so obviously had the upper hand.

'Anyway, you will decide. Are you hungry?'

'Starving.'

'Good. So. Let me drop my things and we will go to dinner. I will see if I can get a table at the best restaurant in Milano. Normally, they are booked one year in advance, but I know the owner –' He began, officiously, to dial his phone and then spoke in rapid Italian. 'Good. It is organized.'

'How many languages do you speak?'

'Oh, well. Spanish, German, Portuguese, French, Italian, English and Arabic, a little, not so good.'

'Seven languages! That's unbelievable.'

At the restaurant she got totally looped. She was afraid to call Xian Rong but why should she? And then Germano said, 'So my dear what do you wish to do?'

He had dismissed his driver – the restaurant was not far from the hotel – and she was too drunk to take public transportation and she couldn't face begging money off Germano to take a taxi back to the apartment. The meal must have cost him around five hundred dollars, the bottle of wine alone was a couple hundred bucks – she had taken a quick peek at the wine list – and she would probably throw up in a taxi anyway. It wasn't, at that moment, such a big deal, at least she would get a decent hot shower and be able to wash her hair properly and clean towels, clean sheets, it would smarten Xian Rong up in a big hurry, to spend time away from him, so she said, 'I want to come back with you –'

'Good, good –'

He had a big room with a king-sized bed and there was no mention now of getting her a separate room and he poured them each a cognac and she went and took a shower. It was all so clean and wonderful after the filth of the stupid crowded apartment with all those men reeking of sesame oil and cigarettes and the grimy bathroom where the water was turned off for repairs to the plumbing almost every day and when it did work there was never any hot water. And when she came out wrapped in a robe – there was even a hairdryer in the bathroom, how divine, things that once would have been so . . . ordinary – he was under the sheets, his big paunch rising up in the middle and she slipped off the robe and got in next to him. He smelled so clean, of expensive cologne and crisp money; she was totally sloshed and played a bit with his dick but it stayed soft and he said, 'I am nervous around you and I do not wish to lose you again.'

She wanted to say, 'Are you kidding? You're about twenty years too late –' but she saw he was old now and even though he still had a big gut, the mound of gold, his arms were thin and his legs had shriveled and his skin was dry and a bit baggy and he was on the verge of becoming a scared old man. And that he saw her still in her twenties, in his mind she hadn't aged. So she said, 'That's all right, baby.'

At least she was remaining faithful to Xian Rong.

All she could think of was Xian Rong and how she hated him for having power over her and how distant and mean he had been lately and this meant he was losing interest.

And in the morning Germano smiled at her and said I am so happy to see you are still with me and he began to pull her on top; apparently he was able to get an erection in the morning. So she climbed on top and fucked him. She didn't come, though. She kept thinking about Xian Rong and that what she was doing made her sick but at least by doing it some power or hold he had over her would be broken; she would revert to being the one in charge.

They had some breakfast in the room and then he said he had meetings all day and she said she had to go back to her friends' apartment for her things –

'But will I see you later on? Do you have the number of my mobile phone?'

'I'll call you –' she said, knowing she wouldn't but she felt bad. She was admiring some things through the window in one of the stores in the lobby, an expensive valise of pale brown cowhide with gold fittings and it reminded her of the pieces of luggage owned by Tinkle at the airport the night before. And Germano said, 'Oh, you like that suitcase, yes it is very nice, would you like me to get it for you?'

And she said, 'God, I bet it costs a fortune –'

And he said, 'Come, let us find out –' and she followed him into the shop and he bought her the suitcase.

Then he kissed her goodbye on the sidewalk in front of the hotel and said that he would tell them at the front desk that she was staying with him so when she came back she could pick up the key and meet him in the room if he wasn't there. And it was obvious that he felt strongly enough about her that he wanted it to be a public event; he didn't need to keep her a secret.

28

She was going to take a bus and a trolley back to the district in which the apartment was located. It would take a long time but it was the least expensive way and the only one she had enough money for. She started to walk to her bus stop. The suitcase was very heavy. But after she had gone one block somebody grabbed her hair from behind and pulled, very hard, and it was Xian Rong and he took the suitcase from her hands and grabbed her wrist to pull her along, which hurt. And they got on the bus and then the trolley and it took hours to get home and he wouldn't speak to her even though she said, 'Listen, nothing happened, I bumped into an old friend, that's all, and was too tired to go home and I wanted for once to have clean sheets and a decent shower!'

But he still didn't speak.

When they got back to the apartment she walked past all the men who were sitting around the wobbly table, playing cards or Mah Jong, smoking those endless filthy cigarettes, and went into the bedroom and he followed and he began to curse at her in Chinese and, with the other men outside – she could hear them laughing – he punched her in the stomach.

For a long time she couldn't breathe, and then he hit her again, so ferociously she thought for a minute he might have smashed her kidney; he ripped off her clothes and he shoved her legs apart – and from any touch of his she was always, instantly wet – but now he began to push his dick up her ass, the pain was blinding. No, she said, no no no, but he didn't stop; he was ripping the edges of her rectum like someone lacerating the petals of a flower, No, she said, no, please stop I love you I love you I'm sorry. He had not used lubrication, each motion from his penis was a tear in her anus then she felt the hot white stuff go in her, burning, angry acid, and he rolled off her and the room smelled of fear and shit and he said you don't know what is love and he spat before he kicked her a couple of times.

She turned over to throw up and she could see in the dim light his lips curled with disgust. He wiped his penis on the sheet the way a sparrow wipes its dirty beak on a branch and he threw some money on the bed and said, There you go, that's your share. All this time I was distracted thinking how I am going to stop being a criminal and get job so I can support you and we can be together always. No need now to worry! You go home now, goodbye.

No wait, she said, please don't go. She had never felt so repulsive, she had made him physically sick, someone she cared about so much and would have done anything for, but still she prayed he would hold her now, apologize. All she kept saying was, I'm sorry, thinking he would say the same thing too but instead he grabbed a bunch of stuff from the room, threw it into a bag, and calling out to the other men something she couldn't understand – she would never understand – without saying a word to her, he walked down the hall and she could hear the door slam.

She thought she was alone in that place. Then the door opened again and she let out a whimper and it was Xian Rong and he said from the doorway, In my heart I was married to you. I'm a gangster, what did you think?

She tried to wipe herself off with the dirty sheet and lay on the mattress with her legs still parted and did not cry. She passed out, or slept, off and on for most of the day and by the time she had collected her things and tried to tidy herself she found there was no hot water. As usual, the Albanian kids had been huffing spray-paint or glue in the stairwell and the smell made her nauseous. It was dark by the time she was marginally functional. *Germano*, she thought. He would help her. He would protect her. He would take care of her. He would look at her as if she was still twenty-six years old and she would never have

328

to stay in one place any more, he would bring her with him around the world and the hotel rooms would always be clean and the showers hot and the room service prompt.

It was dark by the time she got to his hotel. It had taken her ages, staggering on public transportation, off and on three different buses, with her heavy suitcase. She was about to go to the house-phone to call his room when a security guard stopped her and asked her a question in Italian.

'I'm sorry, I only speak English,' she said, and scratched her head. Her hair was tangled and she was filthy and she hurt all over. One of her eyes, her right eye, was puffed shut, what had happened to it? She didn't remember Xian Rong hitting her in the face but maybe she had banged into something without knowing it – or he had slammed her – and she was going to have a black eye. The security guard picked up her suitcase. 'Hey, what are you doing?' she said. He took her by the elbow and for a minute she thought he was pulling her out to the street but he led her to the concierge desk.

'Yes?' said the concierge in English. 'May I help you?'

'Oh, um, yeah, I was trying to call my friend, he's staying here –'

'Oh? And may I ask his name?'

He was looking at her like she was a prostitute. What kind of prostitute, she wanted to say, would come into such a fancy hotel all beat up and carrying a suitcase? 'My friend is named Germano Schmitt, um, something like Germano Schmitt-something.' She tried to sound grand but of course it didn't come out that way, when she couldn't even remember his whole name and there was blood in her mouth, one of her teeth wiggled – what the fuck had he done to her?

'Just a minute, I will look in the registry,' the concierge said, typing into his computer.

'I was about to call him on the house-phone –'

'No, there is no one registered here by that name.'

'He's got to be here! I was with him last night –'

'Perhaps he checked out?' The concierge typed furiously on the keyboard. What was he doing, writing a novel? 'Ah, yes,' he said at last. 'He checked out this morning.'

'And do you happen . . . do you know . . . did he happen to leave a message for me?'

'No, there are no messages.'

'A forwarding address, or where he's going next?'

'No. There is nothing like that. Madame, will you like the doorman to assist in getting you a taxi?'

The man ahead of her in the line was buying a ticket for Antwerp, the next train leaving the Milan station. When it was her turn she said 'Antwerp, please, one way,' and handed over the money. She wasn't scared any more, even though she had never been there.

Her compartment was overheated and smelled of a sweet blue syrupy disinfectant. Background notes of dead mice, long since desiccated, in a dirty corner. Old vomit. Splashes of urine on the toilet floor. Orange peel, carbon monoxide, stale heated air, food heated in a distant microwave. She couldn't open the window. She had two seats but it wasn't enough space to get comfortable and she spent the night scratching, her head itched, she couldn't stand it. Her hair was filthy, all she wanted to do was get someplace and wash her hair and take a hot, long bath – she was bruised and every part of her body hurt. She knew when she took off her clothes she would already be greenish and yellow-blue with bruises. Her clothes reeked of cigarette smoke, smoke was embedded in her hair, her clothes, her skin, there was a bad taste in her mouth.

The last stop was Central Station and she got out.

There were a few hotels near Central Station, but the first one she went to was more than three hundred dollars a night. She could no longer afford it. Her credit card had long since passed its limit. She wished she had not chosen Antwerp. The only place worse might have been Stockholm, full of forthright, good people, without nonsense. Earnest, sincere souls, kindly, but not about to be taken advantage of. People who had never spent time in a cesspool or treacle well. If this city contained only the stalwart, the industrious, the wholesome, she wouldn't last a day. She had crossed an invisible line. With a jolt she understood she had become the sort of person who looked likely to skip out without paying.

There was enough money left from Xian Rong to last a few weeks, maybe longer if she was careful. To one side of the entrance was a zoo and in front was a large, square plaza. Buildings lined all four sides. It was a bit after seven in the morning. The air had a zippy morning smell, clean, damp – the smell of *possibilities* – and people's faces were fresh and awake. The faces belonged to people who had had gone to bed at a reasonable hour, woke to fix hot coffee and bowls of muesli, the faces of people who had showered and were dressed in clean, respectable clothes. They owned alarm clocks; hiked in the country. Good people, ready to begin the day in a universe of white rooms and bottles of antiseptic. They inhabited a different planet than the one she was on.

A couple of blocks away she found a drugstore and she grabbed a bag of Kotex-type product, but she couldn't find lice medicine anywhere and she felt too weak and wretched to try and ask the salesgirl, especially since the store was crowded and these shop girls didn't appear to speak English, what was she going to do, start shouting, Lice! Bugs!? Demonstrate by scratching her head? It was all too tawdry to bear.

When she got out of the shop she knew she wasn't even going to make it back to the hotel unless she found a place to sit down and a toilet to put on one of the sanitary napkins. There was a hole-in-the-wall kind of dive, the name was something African, or West African; several men were sitting around rough tables, waiting, and, a bit glassy, she stumbled in and sat, waiting.

The proprietor was a gorgeous-looking man, Senegalese? Tall, ebony skin, liquid eyes, and he came over to where she was sitting and she tried to smile, weakly. But when he got closer all he said was, in English, 'Lady, you can't stay here.'

'Oh, I'm sorry, I didn't feel well and thought I should sit down for a minute, should I order something?' She tried to smile her sweetest smile although she felt utterly blanched and strangely cold.

'No, no,' he said. 'You can't order anything in here you have to leave. Now.'

She saw there was blood all over the floor and it had dripped down her legs. Why the hell should she be hemorrhaging so much? If he had been nicer she would have been horrified, embarrassed, and would have gone for some paper towels and cleaned up, but he was so rude, didn't he realize there was something wrong with her? Did he think she had been shot, or stabbed – but then why throw her out? She shrugged huffily and tried to get up with her heavy suitcase but her heel got caught in the chair and she tripped and almost went down but caught herself in time. 'Nice place,' she said sarcastically, 'Stupid asshole.'

Twenty-five years of marriage. Once such a huge stretch of time would not have seemed possible. Getting to be thirty years old, impossible. Forty, then fifty. How could this have happened? She did not know what she had expected, only that life would at some point begin and while she was waiting for it to start she would get married. Some parts – some months, some years – had been worse, some better.

With real-estate prices escalating so fast they never did get it together to buy a bigger place and once Cash was gone they didn't need one. When Cash was about ten Barry expanded his office, hired a partner and announced he wanted to get more into Judaism. This was right after the wretched business with the malpractice suit, the first time – fortunately then there had been enough insurance cover-age, but who knew what would happen this time around? He should never have gone into medicine, even in dentistry, which was hardly neurosurgery, he had shown himself . . . not very competent, to say the least, even though she knew that all doctors sooner or later got hit by malpractice . . .

. . . Barry ordered a second refrigerator and a second set of dishes (though according to the others at reform temple it was good enough to put the meat dishes in the dishwasher before re-using them as milshik), asked her to shop at a kosher butcher, stopped eating shrimp. She had tried, over the years, to be a good wife and had gone to synagogue with Cash and Barry on Yom Kippur, dressed in a suit, head covered as befit a married woman. But the Day of Atonement had no significance for her – she couldn't help but feel that, after all, every day was for her a day of atonement, but without forgiveness.

If there was a God he was not for her; he was not her god. And for her every day was a fast day, in a sense: it was the same for any woman trying to keep her weight down, one extra crumb and her belly bugged out in a balloon. The endless prayers, the davening of the men in talliths, the sermon of the pompous rabbi, the hammy tones of the stout cantor, served only to irritate her. By two o'clock, or three, she excused herself and went out to stretch her legs in stockings and high heels and the weather, somehow, was always too warm for the tweed she had on. Nevertheless when she returned, almost against her will, a certain – transcendence – would come as the afternoon light streamed through the tacky stained-glass windows and the sour breath around her rose in clouds and she forgot her legs ached from standing, forgot she was the worst thing on the planet and became . . . one with the beehive, the swarm of 'A-men' vibrating through the air.

Then, suddenly, it was over, you were supposed to embrace your neighbor, she kissed her husband, her son, almost giddy with relief that she had stuck it out – 'Did you fast well?' 'Good Shabbos.'

The white faces, returning in the evening, the men in suits, yarmulkes, the women in skirts and blouses – a street full of Jews! – and the peaceable illusion of strolling home with her family.

The fast was broken with pasty crumbly biscuits – pugach – that Grace had baked and sent over some time before. And they would eat, slowly, the barley soup, the pieces of gefilte fish with horseradish-and-beets, a slice of plum tart, in the darkening dining room that faced the airshaft and for that time she was allowed to be, could see herself as, the other person she might have been.

. . . looking back she supposed it was all a business thing, certainly by being members of the local synagogue he was able to advertise, so to speak, his services as a dentist.

There had been a few years when Barry acted particularly aloof, sulky, in retrospect she thought he might have had a girlfriend a long time ago . . . Then, something had put an end to this . . . either he had grown tired of the girlfriend, or she had grown tired of him – or he had never had one. Peyton used to tell him, when she knew she was irritating him, 'Just remember, if you get rid of me and get a new wife, pretty soon she's going to bug you exactly the way I am, so what's the point?' Like she had once asked Belinda, 'So, what did you learn? From all this I mean.' Wondering what it was like to be around all those celebrities.

'That people can be replaced,' Belinda said. 'And there's nothing on the planet more desperate than someone who finds this out, apart from an aging movie actress.'

But it wasn't true. People couldn't be replaced. They couldn't even be forgotten. A casual acquaintance, a casual fuck – you had to live with them in your head forever. Even if they didn't call you, or contact you, or remember you, they were with you always, a permanent one-sided mental wedding. Her son, whom she loved. She loved him so much it was painful if she thought of him. Too late. There was nothing she could do. Maybe it wouldn't have turned out differently anyway.

He was a boy, male, he could not connect with her any more than her own husband was able to; men were a different species, it was something she had never understood. She might as well have spent her life berating her dogs for not talking: they were two different species, that was all.

Still, it was her own fault. And there was nothing to be said.

A platter of dead oysters, iced, crumpled shells cradling cold, pearly uvulas, glittered in the window of a restaurant. At what point, what age, did you just stop having these feelings, or make sure you stopped showing them because you were now laughably old, out of the spawning run? Men never had to call it quits. Some eighty-year-old guy could still score – if he still wanted. Only men had the option to decide: you were their type, or you weren't. That was all there was to it – for men. While as a female you were thrilled that a man – any man – paid you attention.

It was too late now. All the men she had missed: the boiled firemen sweating in vulcanized sacks; brilliantined stockbrokers; seedy used-car salesmen in Florsheim shoes; the nebbishy computer boys – carb-faced, hung like donkeys. Joey, Ralph, Marcel, Assam and Sven. Tibetan men greasy with yak butter, narrow-eyed, slurping tea by a smoky yurt fire. Nump-headed Icelanders, shaggy blonds with eye-brows that drooped above their heavy orbital crests.

An image: a dismembered hand near her face. On a subway? The hand was huge, a man's hand, fat and white, the nails manicured and the back covered with sparse black hairs; a gold and diamond ring cut into the curd of the third finger. A voice – her own? – wondering what it would be like to sleep with that hand, the most obscene hand she had ever seen, spoiled but powerful; it might have been the hand of a chief eunuch in the Imperial palace, or a Turkish pasha with an insatiable appetite . . .

Never to lie on the deck of a felucca on the Nile, with a turbaned Sudanese descended from slaves, blue-black skin, ivory and gold teeth, curving scimitar, while the stars of the Southern Hemisphere drifted overhead. No glittering minarets of India, the elephants painted blue and saffron, the languorous seduction of a boy mahar-ajah draped in pearls . . .

She would never get to have any of them now.

At least she had experiences that Barry could not, would not; he would never be so daring. She got to learn about a world that he would always be too frightened to peruse. But he could do things, fix things, build things. Befriend people. People complimented him, gushed over him. And he made it clear that once he had slept with her, married her, she was just another of his accomplishments – a hole in one, a fish he had caught.

He might still escape. But she was going to have to cohabit with herself, every single second of every hour and day, from the moment she got up until she fell asleep. And even then she would be there, in her dreams, unable to fly more than a few feet off the ground, trapped in overhead wires.

* * *

335

Across the street, at a distance, was a bar with smoky, dirt-encrusted windows of a style so old the warped glass was pocked with bubbles. A cheery, old-fashioned neon sign advertised Stella Artois Lager, only the Artois was broken. Over and over again flashed just the *Stella Stella Stella*. **STELLA STELLA STELLA.**

But the place looked friendly. Nobody would mind if she sat there and drank a beer or something stronger. Anyway she couldn't go much further.

She saw now her existence had been one long low-rent fuck trip. Perhaps she had been a man in another, earlier era. A lifetime dining on cellulose fiber, without a clue that wasn't how food was supposed to taste. So much time – minutes, hours, days, years – eked out in a state of fear, trying not to slide off a steep roof, hanging on with her bare nails, palms dripping with sweat. Maybe there had never been any need to try and hang on in the first place. She picked up her suitcase. The sides and the handle were smeared with blood, it was a shame, she wondered how she could clean cowhide.

When had it begun, that women had taken over the man's part?

He looked her up and down before he made the bullish sound of a man inhaling his own snot. Spitting out a lump of phlegm, he adjusted his knapsack straps and gave her a dismissive stare. 'You must be as old as my mother.' Ambling off into the gray Antwerp afternoon he glanced back with a sneering grin from a half-block away. 'You are older than my mother,' he called, one hand shifting his cock in his trousers. 'Lady, you must be fifty!'

Her punishment was no redemption.

ACKNOWLEDGEMENTS

Special thanks and appreciation to: Diane Higgins / Luc and Marianne Courevits / Saint Amour Festival / Ellen Salpeter / Gerard and Nelita LeClery / Phyllis Janowitz / Paige Powell / Tom Bell / Rosemary Davidson / Dr Fred Brandt / Erin Hosier / Yuri Avvakumov and Alyona Kirsova / Nic and Crista Ilijne / Anya Rosenberg / Jocasta Brownlee / Don Weintraub / Sally Richardson / John Murphy / Victoria Millar / Gregg Sullivan / the kind generosity of the Mandarin Hotel in Hong Kong, which is the best hotel in the world and also clean, not like in the book / Nichole Agyres / Dr Larry Rosenthal, D.D.S. / and my fabulous husband Tim Hunt who has encouraged and supported me in every way possible.

A NOTE ON THE AUTHOR

Tama Janowitz is the author of a book of essays, eight works of fiction, one book of non-fiction and a book for children. Her writing has appeared in *Vogue, New York Times Sunday Magazine* and elsewhere. She lives in Brooklyn, NY, with her husband and child.

A NOTE ON THE TYPE

The text of this book is set in Linotype Sabon, named after the
type founder, Jacques Sabon. It was designed by Jan
Tschichold and jointly developed by Linotype, Monotype and
Stempel, in response to a need for a typeface to be available
in identical form for mechanical hot metal composition
and hand composition using foundry type.

Tschichold based his design for Sabon roman on a fount
engraved by Garamond, and Sabon italic on a fount by
Granjon. It was first used in 1966 and has proved an
enduring modern classic.